ALSO AVAILABLE FROM TITAN BOOKS

EDITED BY
**MAXIM
JAKUBOWSKI**

DAGGERS
DRAWN

19 AWARD-WINNING STORIES FROM

**IAN RANKIN
JEFFERY DEAVER
JOHN CONNOLLY
DENISE MINA
JOHN HARVEY**
AND MANY MORE!

TITAN BOOKS

Daggers Drawn
Hardback edition ISBN: 9781789097986
E-book edition ISBN: 9781789097993

Published by Titan Books
A division of Titan Publishing Group Ltd.
144 Southwark Street, London SE1 0UP
www.titanbooks.com

First Titan edition September 2021
10 9 8 7 6 5 4 3 2 1

A C[...] [...] available
[...] from the British Library.

Printed and [...]und by CPI Group (UK) Ltd, Croydon CR0 4YY

TABLE OF CONTENTS

INTRODUCTION

MAXIM JAKUBOWSKI

The Crime Writers' Association was founded in 1953 by prolific author John Creasey and very rapidly attracted to its midst the majority of the British crime, thriller and mystery writers of the day. Three years later, the organisation created its annual awards, the Daggers, which have been given yearly ever since in a variety of categories, and are recognised as one of the more prestigious literary awards in the calendar.

Current categories include the Diamond Dagger for life achievement, the Gold Dagger for best novel of the year, the Ian Fleming Steel Dagger for best thriller of the year, the John Creasey New Blood Dagger for best first novel, the ALCS Non-Fiction Dagger awarded for best true crime or critical book of the year, the Sapere Books Historical Dagger for best historical mystery title, the Crime Fiction in Translation Dagger, the Dagger in the Library awarded by librarians for a body of work, the Short Story Dagger, the Debut Dagger for a previously unpublished first novel, and a recently-created Publisher's Dagger rewarding the publishing house who has best contributed to the genre in a given year. Alongside these is the Red Herrings Award for contribution to the CWA's efforts and activities, which I was honoured to win in 2019.

The Daggers' past roll of honour includes some of the biggest names in the genre, both from the UK, the United States and also from non-English language countries as a result of the International Dagger (now Crime Fiction in Translation Dagger) being inaugurated in 2006.

I have been a member for 35 years, was elected to the board two decades later and have since been Vice Chair, Honorary Vice Chair and, as of April 2021, am the current Chair.

The Short Story Dagger was launched in 1982. In its early incarnation, it was not strictly speaking a best of the year story selected by a panel of independent judges (as all current Dagger decisions and choices are reached today) but was launched as a CWA short story competition sponsored by the Telegraph Sunday Magazine and Veuve Clicquot Champagne. The winner received a cheque for £350, which was then a not-to-be-sniffed-at amount, and a dozen bottles of 'La Grande Dame', Veuve Clicquot's finest champagne. The distinguished and much-missed author and critic H.R.F. Keating was the chief judge. Every year the stories submitted to the competition had to include certain ingredients. The first winner of the competition was Madeleine Duke, to be followed by Stanley Cohen, Reginald Hill and in 1985, gothic romance author Madeleine Brent, who was of course a pen name for Modesty Blaise creator Peter O'Donnell. Peter's obligatory ingredients that year were a bottle of champagne, a cryptic message on a micro computer screen (ah, those were the days!), a beautiful blonde Hungarian pianist and Victoria Station! All of which of course cleverly appear in his story 'Swift 98' which opens this volume. Shortly after Peter's triumph, the rules changed and the award was given to what was judged to be just the best crime short story of the year.

The Short Story Dagger is now 38 years old and the present collection gathers some of the best winners to have emerged during that period. Several writers have won it twice: Reginald Hill, Jerry Sykes, Peter Lovesey, Danuta Reah, Stella Duffy, Denise Mina and Ian Rankin. They all appear here with their own choice of winning story, apart from Reginald Hill, where the rights to reissue the stories proved unavailable.

Some of the great names in crime writing have featured on the CWA Short Story Dagger shortlists over the decades. Aside from the winners, the list includes Celia Dale, Betty Rowlands, Marion Arnott, Simon Avery, Susanna Gregory, Sean Doolittle, Ann Cleeves, Kate Ellis, Judith Cutler, Don Winslow, Val McDermid, Mat Coward, Mark Billingham, Peter Robinson, Martyn Waites, Stuart Pawson, PD James, Ken Bruen, Robert Barnard (whose winning story was also not available to collect here), Kevin Wignall, James Siegel, J.A. Konrath, Laura Lippmann, Michael Connelly, Chris Simms, Lawrence Block, Sean Chercover, Simon Wood, Zoe Sharp, Ridley Pearson, Robert Ferrigno, Michael Palmer, John Lawton, Mickey Spillane & Max Allan Collins, William Kent Krueger, Claire Seeber, Bernie Crosthwaite, Carlo Lucarelli, Neil Gaiman, Simon Brett, Andrea Camilleri, George Pelecanos, Stuart Neville, Dashiell Hammett (for a lost story rediscovered in 2015), Dennis Lehane, Conrad Williams, Christopher Fowler, Ovidia Yu, James Sallis, Michael Ridpath, Leye Adenle, Christine Poulson, Lee Child, Erin Kelly, Christopher Brookmyre, Teresa Solana, Lavie Tidhar, Syd Moore and many more. Several anthologies could be collected from shortlisted stories alone!

But my enviable task here was to assemble some of the outstanding winning stories to demonstrate to the reader the art of mystery short story writing at its best. Every story a winner!

Savour in the dark…

MJ

SWIFTWING 98

PETER O'DONNELL

"And we're not television policemen," said Inspector Lestrade to his new Detective Sergeant, "so make sure you never call me 'Guv'. Right?"

The D.S. nodded. He was a middlesized, strongly built man of' twenty-eight, with a thick neck, placid temperament, and gingery moustache. "Right, sir," he said, watching his superior with mild curiosity as the Inspector glanced back and forth from papers in an open file to the screen of the microcomputer on his desk, wiry fingers dancing expertly over the keys.

Lestrade paused, then touched a single key.

SWIFTWING 98 appeared in green characters. Taking the papers from the file, he stood up and fed them into a shredding machine. The sergeant noticed that a dozen or more similar files, all empty, lay on the nearby table. The desk was clear now except for the telephone, the microcomputer, and a photograph of a smiling woman with blonde hair; a beautiful woman, thought the sergeant, craning his neck to see her better.

Lestrade rested a hand on the shredder. "My personal property," he said, and moved to touch the computer. "Likewise. Not for common use, Sergeant. Right?"

"Right, sir."

The Inspector resumed his seat with a brooding air. He was in his middle forties, with dark hair, dark bitter eyes, and a thin sallow face. "I come from a long line of policemen," he said, "and they'd spin in their graves if we behaved like these actors do on television, so watch yourself. I'm not a friendly policeman. I bear grudges. I *enjoy* letting the sun go down on my wrath. I never let bygones be bygones, even unto the third and fourth generation. Any questions?"

The sergeant smiled engagingly. "Only to ask what you'd like me to start on today, sir."

Lestrade stared hard at him for a moment, then slid the photograph along the desk. "You can start by making sure nobody murders this woman."

The sergeant picked up the print and studied it briefly. "It's Eva Kossuth, the Hungarian concert pianist," he said. "She defected in Paris last week and she's coming to live in England."

"You're an improvement on my last D.S.," Lestrade said grudgingly. "He stopped at the sports pages."

"Why do you think somebody might try to murder her, sir?"

Lestrade nodded at the computer, where *SWIFTWING 98* still showed on the screen. "I feed information in, and I get back probabilities. The information comes from snouts, our central computer, SIS and MI5 liaison, overseas contacts, and any other available source. It's part of my remit to keep an eye on dissident refugees, so-called governments in exile, defectors, and any groups at odds with the governments of their countries." Again he indicated the machine. My little friend says there's a ninety-eight percent probability that Eva Kossuth will be liquidated because her country's intelligence services now believe she's been spying for the West for several years."

The sergeant said, "But who's Swiftwing, sir?"

"That's the code-name I gave Eva Kossuth when I started the programme." Lestrade switched off the computer and looked at his watch. "She's arriving by train at Victoria Station today. A bunch of Free Hungarians will be there to welcome her. You get along to Victoria now. She's not due till one thirty-five, but you can sniff around and see if anything smells funny. I'll be there myself, under cover, when Eva Kossuth arrives. Off you go."

"Right, sir."

For two hours the D.S. prowled the concourse, antennae tuned for any hint of impending danger. Shortly before the train was due, some nine or ten men with instruments and a banner entered the concourse. The banner declared: *Musicians of Free Hungary Welcome Eva Kossuth.* For a moment the D.S. felt a tremor of suspicion, then it was gone, and he struggled to hide astonishment as he saw that the man carrying a clarionet was dark haired with a thin sallow face and dark bitter eyes. Evidently Inspector Lestrade had secured permission for the band to be there.

At Victoria Station few events are sufficiently bizarre to attract attention, and the musicians were virtually ignored. Once, glancing up from the newspaper he was pretending to read, the sergeant caught Lestrade's eye and received a minute nod.

The train came in five minutes late, and when most of the passengers had passed through the gate the sergeant saw Eva Kossuth, tall and slim, blonde head bare, wearing a camel coat. A porter at her side wheeled a trolley with a trunk on it. The band struck up the old Hungarian national anthem, *Himnusz*, and Eva Kossuth stopped short as she came through the gate, smiling and surprised.

The sergeant looked quickly about him, but still nobody was taking much interest. The anthem ended. The grey-haired leader of the group passed his trumpet to a colleague and made a short speech of welcome in his own tongue. Eva Kossuth replied briefly but warmly. The musicians applauded. Passers-by watched idly. The spokesman produced a bottle of champagne and a glass from a basket at his side. The bottle was opened, champagne foamed into the glass. Eva Kossuth raised it high, spoke a few stirring words, then drank.

Again the sergeant glanced around him. Still no hint of trouble. He heard the glass smash, and as his head snapped round he saw Eva Kossuth slump to the ground among the fragments. For a moment there was unbelieving silence, then Lestrade called sharply to the grey-haired leader, "Mr. Schulek! Tell your people to remain quite still!" There was little need for the command. The grey-haired man dragged his eyes from the limp figure sprawled on the ground to look in horror at the bottle he held, while the rest of the musicians gazed in stupefied fashion.

The sergeant moved very quickly for a man of such stocky build. Within seconds he was kneeling beside Eva Kossuth, fingers resting on her neck, feeling the erratic flicker of her pulse as it dwindled to stillness. He looked up, shocked, into Lestrade's angry face and said, "I think she's gone, sir."

The Inspector's hands clenched on the clarionet he still held, then he said in a tightly controlled voice, "I want a call put out over the Tannoy asking if there's a doctor on the concourse. I want an ambulance and the nearest patrol car. I want railway staff to cordon of this area right away. See to it, Sergeant." He turned to the grey-haired man. "Now, Mr. Schulek, I'll take charge of' that bottle, and as soon as some help arrives I shall want to question you and all your colleagues."

It was late that evening when the D.S. tapped on the door of the Inspector's office and entered. Lestrade sat hunched in his chair, feet on the desk. The room was heavy with shadows, a single lamp shining on the small computer.

"Good evening, sir," said the sergeant. "I wondered if you had any news about the Kossuth murder."

"Murder?" Lestrade said acidly. "Don't make unwarranted assumptions, Sergeant. None of the exiled Hungarians had a motive, and Forensic reports the champagne and glass fragments yield no sign of poison. That Hungarian pianist wouldn't be the first victim of heart failure at a moment of high emotion, so it's possible that Nature forestalled the lady's enemies – unless the autopsy reveals anything significant."

"I don't suppose it will, sir," said the sergeant. "I expect you used a shellfish toxin. Very fast, and indetectable."

After a few seconds Lestrade took his feet from the desk and said, "What?"

The sergeant placed a half open matchbox on the desk. In it was a tiny piece of glass, hollow and pointed. "I got to the lady first, sir," he said apologetically, "and this was sticking out of her neck. Part of a glass dart containing the toxin. You must have intended to remove it yourself, but then thought it had come out when she fell. It really was a very good way of injecting a much greater quantity than by just a smear on a normal blowpipe dart. I also think it was a very good idea, sir, to arrange that you'd be among the welcoming party as a fake musician. Your dummy clarionet made a first-rate blowpipe, and you were able to use it at point blank range." He nodded towards the cupboard in the corner. "I was in here earlier, sir, and I've had a look at it."

Lestrade sighed. "You've covered means and opportunity," he said. "What about motive?"

"Well, that puzzled me at first, sir, as did the fact that you gave Eva Kossuth the code-name of a loathsome mythical creature. I failed my degree in Hellenic Studies, sir, but I know that *Swiftwing* was the name of a harpy."

"So you're no longer puzzled?"

"No, sir. Because I happen to be a hacker."

"A what?"

"An expert at getting into computers, sir. I got into yours while you were out this afternoon, so now we both know what happened between 1891 and 1894 to the best known of all detectives. The Great Hiatus scholars call it, as you know, sir, when Sherlock Holmes was believed to have died at the Reichenbach Falls, but then returned after three years and never revealed how he had spent that period of his life."

"You sound like a Baker Street Irregular," said the Inspector grimly.

The sergeant shook his head. "Oh no, sir. I'm congratulating you. After years of patiently amassing information, you uncovered the truth when your computer gave you a probability of ninety-eight percent – a virtual certainty, really – that Sherlock Holmes, inveterate bachelor, fathered a son in Hungary during the Great

Hiatus; that Eva Kossuth was the granddaughter of that son, and also the last and only descendant of Sherlock Holmes."

The sergeant smiled. "So your motive was clear, sir, for it's well-known that you are the great-grandson of that Inspector Lestrade who featured in so many of the Baker Street detective's cases – and was treated by him like a halfwit."

"True," said the Inspector in a quiet, almost dreamy voice. "You know, I was weaned on undying hatred for that sneering, supercilious, fiddle-playing bastard Holmes, like my father and grandfather before me."

"Even unto the third and fourth generation, sir?"

"Yes. He was a cocksure, copper-knocking, condescending, cocaine-injecting big-head, and I'm delighted to have wiped out the last of his seed. She can accompany him on his fiddle in hell, if they have a piano there." Lestrade shrugged. "It's your move, Sergeant."

The D.S. smiled again. "I've read the casebooks many times, sir," he said, "and I agree with you about Holmes. His arrogance was utterly unbearable, and he treated my own great grandfather as a buffoon. I can't imagine why the poor chap put up with being put down through all those years of living with Holmes, *and* even wrote up his cases. But in memory of the good Dr. Watson I've decided to forget what I know about Eva Kossuth's death."

Lestrade stared. "Sergeant Harry... Watson," he said slowly. "Well, it's a common enough name, so I'm not surprised it didn't register with me." He stood up. "Fancy a drink, Harry?"

"I'd enjoy that, sir. Thank you."

"Good. And Harry... I've settled the score now, so I don't care if my constabulary ancestors do spin in their graves. Just call me Guv."

SOME SUNNY DAY

JULIAN RATHBONE

O n more than one occasion Baz has abused her great reputation as a criminal investigator for very dubious ends. The 'murder' of Don Hicks was a case in point. On our return from Las Palomas we quarrelled quite bitterly on the subject. Then, as she has also done on subsequent occasions, she produced a line of reasoning, which, were it not put into practice with remarkable results, I would find endearingly old-fashioned – a naïve amalgam of Hobbes and Nietzsche with a few other 'philosophers' like de Sade filling in the harmonies.

Standing with her back to the forty-eight-inch TV screen which plays continuously but always silently in her living-room, and which serves the social purpose of an open fire, she rocked back and in her Tibetan snow leopard slippers came on like a pompous don.

"My dear Julia," she said, full of smug self-satisfaction because things had gone so well, in spite of my efforts to put them right, "there wis only one personal morality that deserves more than a moment's consideration. Follow your own individual star, the promptings of your innermost soul – be true to that and nothing else—"

I interrupted as mockingly as I could: "Do it my way?"

Baz went on, unruffled.

"The morality you appeal to, the communally shared sense of what is right and wrong, is a fiction, a tissue of lies invented by man in his short aspect to allow society to function, to regulate the transactions we make one with another in our social lives." She sipped ice-cold Russian vodka – neat with a scatter of freshly ground black pepper. "My dear Julia, you are not ill-educated, and you are trained in the social sciences – you are therefore perfectly well aware that all societies hold their own moralities to be the only good ones, yet all societies swiftly and hypocritically change their moralities as soon as their survival is threatened it they do not..."

I attempted an interruption: "I cannot recall a society which condoned or encouraged wholesale robbery on the scale perpetrated by your friend Hicks."

She froze, then gave me that long cold stare which she knows I hate because of its element of Olympian scorn for the foolishness of a mere mortal.

"You forget Ruskin's truism that the wealth of Victorian England was built on the loot of empires."

"And you forget", said I, pleased to find a rejoinder on the spot and not half-way down the stairs, "that he also said you cannot put an unearned sovereign in your own pocket without taking it from someone else's."

Well, enough of that, I leave the reader to judge between us.

I am well aware that Hicks's demise was well-aired in the media at the time, and that a couple of hacks have since cobbled together books about the whole affair, but I am also aware that such sensations are less than seven-day wonders and the more intelligent readers of these memoirs will have quite rightly by now forgotten all but a hazy outline of the sordid business. If however you have that sort of mind that does retain in detail the trivia of what passes for news, then I suggest you skip the next page.

In 1970 a gang of three evil hoodlums carried out the Grosswort and Spinks bullion robbery. In the process they killed a security guard but got clean away with thirty million pounds' worth of gold bars which were never recovered. Their getaway van had been stolen for them by a petty London car thief called Don Hicks, who also drove it in the second stage of the robbery. He was arrested for the car theft and later accused of being an accessory – but the prosecution on the major charge was later dropped and he went down for only two years. The three hoodlums were arrested almost certainly on evidence supplied by Hicks, and they got twenty years each.

When Hicks came out he sold up his south London assets, a garage and a terrace house in Tooting Bec, and opened a small car workshop in Marbella, where he claimed to be providing an essential service a Spaniard could not supply – talking English to the English residents who needed their cars fixed.

Six months later he met and married María Pilar Ordoñéz, who was working as a hotel maid and cleaner. Two months after the wedding they moved into a luxury pad in Las Palomas, the smartest little bay between Marbella and Gibraltar. They had won the big one, the fat one the Spaniards call it, the Christmas lottery – six million in sterling at the then rate of exchange. No one believed them, nobody doubted that the money was the Grosswort and Spinks bullion, but no one could prove it, least of all Detective Inspector (as he was then) Stride, who had been in charge of the case. He was furious at this outcome – that Hicks should get off lightly for turning Queen's evidence was one thing, that he should end up seriously wealthy was quite another.

Sixteen years well-heeled contentment followed, but then Hicks's paradisaical life took two nasty knocks. First, his first wife, Sandra, went to Stride and said she was prepared to tell him all about Hicks's part in the Grosswort and Spinks robbery, including how he had masterminded the whole thing, but most important of all, where what was left of the bullion was, and so on. Second, the three hooligans he had shopped were let out. No one had any doubt at all they would head straight for Las Palomas – in the dock eighteen years before they had promised Hicks, in song, that don't know where, don't know when, we'll meet again some sunny day. The only question was: would Strike get there first?

It turned out not to be a coincidence at all that Holmes and I were also on our way, club BA Gatwick to Málaga. I passed her the plastic ham from my plastic tray and she gave me her orange.

I asked her, "Why?"

"Because," she said, smoothing her immaculately glossy, sleek black hair behind her small perfect ear, "Don is a very old friend. A very good friend."

"You made a friend out of a robber?"

"He has wit, charm, and he is very, very clever."

"But I thought you occupied yourself with putting criminals behind bars."

"I occupy myself solving human problems whose ironic intricacies appeal to the intellectual side of my personality."

And she terminated the conversation by turning her head slightly away from me so the bony profile of her remarkable nose was silhouetted against the flawless empyrean of space at thirty thousand feet.

We were met at Málaga airport by an urchin in an acid house T-shirt which also carried the slogan Don't Worry, Be Happy. He wore jeans and trainers and locked every inch a Spanish street Arab until you saw his eyes which, beneath his mop of black hair worn fashionably stepped, were deepset and blue. He shook hands very politely with me, but to my surprise was awarded a kiss on both cheeks from Baz.

"¡*Madrina*!" he cried, "¿*Cómo estás*?"

"Madrina?" I asked, as he picked up our bags.

"Godmother," Baz replied.

I was stunned. I was even more stunned when Juan Hicks ('Heeks') Ordoñéz led us out to the car-park, threw our bags into the trunk of a large silver-grey, open-top Merc, and himself settled, with keys, into the driver's seat. I made rapid calculations.

"Baz," I said, "this lad cannot be more than sixteen."

"Sixteen next September."

"But he's driving. Isn't that illegal?"

"Yes. No doubt it would become an issue if he were involved in an accident. He bears this in mind and drives very well."

You could have fooled me. I was sitting directly behind him, with Baz on the other side. For most of the way Juan steered with his left hand, lay back into the corner between door and front seat with his right hand draped over the back of it. That way he was able to keep up a lengthy and animated conversation with Baz shouted over the roar of the horn-blasting diesel lorries he successively passed.

Baz's Spanish is fluent and perfect – she spent three years of her adolescence there studying guitar with Segovia amongst others – while mine hardly goes beyond the '*Un tubo de cerveza, por favor*' level, but I picked up some of it, and pieced together the rest from subsequent events – enough to offer the reader an approximate and much truncated transcription.

"How's Dad, Juan?"

"Not good. Very upset indeed. He's left the house and gone on the boat. He's there on his own, refuses to have anyone with him. He says the moment he sees Stride or McClintock, Allison or Clough coming out after him, he'll start the engine and make for the open sea."

"What good will that do him?"

"None at all. But the boat's very fast. And very manoeuvrable too. He reckons he can get through the straits and out into the Atlantic before anyone catches him – unless they are prepared to rocket or shell him."

"What then?"

Juan shrugged, head forward on his neck, left hand twisted palm up.

"That's it. Adíos Papa."

Baz thought, then said, "A bad scene, Juan."

"Very bad."

"What does your mother think of it all? And the rest of the household?"

"The household shifts from catatonic trance to histrionic hysterics. Especially the girls, and all my cousins. The servants too. But Mama is doing the full dignified matriarch bit. Clytemnestra when she hears about Iphigenia, you know? But if he goes she'll probably throw herself off the quay. Anyway she'll try to but I shall be on hand to stop her."

"You won't be strong enough."

He shrugged. "Maybe you fat friend should be there too to help me."

After about twenty miles we swung off the *autovía* and into the hills between it and the sea. The hills were covered with urbanization – small villas in lots of a hundred or more, all in each group exactly identical to its neighbours. They all had rosebushes and bougainvillea and tiny swimming pools, all were painted white, had red-tiled roofs which clashed with the bougainvillea, and heavy wrought-iron gates, multi-padlocked.

The radio phone bleeped and Juan picked up the handset without slowing down. Indeed after the briefest exchange he was accelerating with the thing still in his hand.

"Yes?" asked Baz.

"Stride's arrived. We have a friend in the Guardia Civil Cuartel and he says they're planning to move on the stroke of midday, in ten minutes' time. We might well be late."

The next five minutes were a hell of screeching tyres and a blaring klaxon. I was thrown from side to side, and when I held on to the fairing of the rear passenger door I lost the straw hat I had bought in Liberty the day before. It had a board paisley-pattern silk band and streamers and cost thirty-nine ninety-nine, and that was the sale price.

Presently the view opened up and improved enormously. A small unspoilt fishing village huddled round a little harbour, set within a wider cover. There was a small marina beside the harbour, and about fifteen larger boats at anchor in the bay. The hillsides round the bay were dotted quite sparsely with large houses in varying styles of architecture, though 1970s Moorish predominated. The whole area was fenced but very discreetly; only as you approached the red and white striped barrier with its big notice proclaiming *Zona Particular y Privada* etc. did you see the ribbon of twelve-foot fencing snaking over the hillside amongst the olives An armed security man heard us coming, he would have had to be deaf not to, and had the barrier up just in time. I have no doubt Juan would have crashed it if he had not.

Juan had to slow a bit – the streets were narrow and crowded, the car rumbled over cobbles and occasionally clanged against sharp corners. Then the bay opened up, we zipped along a short promenade of palm trees, oleanders and cafés, and out on to the mole that separated the harbour from the marina.

There was quite a crowd at the end. Three green Guardia Civil jeeps with the officers dressed in full fig for the occasion – black patent hats, yellow lanyards, black belts and gun holsters, the men in combat gear with automatic weapons. There was a black unmarked Renault 21 and Chief Inspector Stride was leaning against it. There were two television crews and about twenty journalists with cameras and cassette recorders. Above all there was the household. All the adults were dressed in black, but magnificently, especially three dolly-birds, no other word will do, in flouncy tops, fanny pelmets, and sheer black stockings. Eight children, uneasily aware of crisis but bored too, played listlessly while nannies and servants clucked over them if they went too near the water's edge. But above all was Mother – Señora María Pilar Ordoñéz, a veritable pillar of a woman indeed – tall, pale, handsome with an aquiline nose, heavy eyebrows beneath her fine black mantilla. It was impossible to believe she had ever been a chambermaid.

All eyes were fixed on a large but powerful-looking cabin cruiser at anchor in the roads between the headlands. One could discern the Spanish flag on the forearm, the Blue Peter at the yard, and the red duster of the British mercantile marine over the stern. A little putter of sound came across the nacreous water that just rose and fell with a small swell not strong enough to break the surface, and blueish-white smoke swirling behind the exhaust outlets. Hicks had the engine running, was ready to slip his anchor.

When Stride, a big man in a suit he'd grown too fat for, big pursy lips above turkey jowls, saw us, he lifted his hat and big, arched, bushy eyebrows. He's head of the City of London Police Serious Fraud Squad now and has often clashed with Baz, knows her well. He had been given the job of arresting Hicks, dead against all rules and precedents, solely because he was the last officer still operational who had actually worked on the Grosswort and Spinks bullion robbery back in 1970.

I expect he was about to say something too boringly obvious to be worth recording when the village church clock struck twelve, the notes bleeding across the air above the water. A Guardia Civil colonel, no less, touched his elbow and he and a party of Guardias began a slow descent down stone steps to a smart little cutter that was waiting for them. As they got to the bottom the village clock began to strike twelve again.

"In case you didn't count it the first time," Holmes murmured.

"Aren't you going to do anything for your fine friend?" I asked.

She shrugged with unusual stoicism, and sighed.

"I fear this time for once, my dear Watson, we are too late."

As the last note bled away into silence the cutter edged out from the quay and began to pick up speed. At the same time a figure appeared on the bow of the cabin cruiser and we saw him fling the anchor rope into the sea. He disappeared into the glassed-in cockpit, the cabin cruiser began to move, accelerated, began a wide turn throwing up a brilliant gash of bow-water against the black-blue of the sea and then… blew up. Blew up really well, into lots of little pieces that went soaring into the immaculate sky only to rain down again within a circle fifty metres across. The bang reverberated between the cliffs and sea-birds swooped up and away in a big soaring arc. It was not impossible to believe the soul of Don Hicks was amongst them.

Doña María Pilar at least thought so. With her hand to her throat she stifled back a cry of grief and oved with determination towards the unfenced edge of the quay. Her purpose was clear. I launched myself across the intervening space and grasped her round the waist at the last moment, causing her, and myself, to fall heavily on a cast-iron bollard and cobbles.

Naturally, she was the first to be helped to her feet. She looked down at me and said, in Spanish which Holmes was good enough to translate for me later:

"Who the fuck is this great fat scrotum, and what the fuck does he think he's doing?"

"We know," she said, two hours or so later, "who did it. What Señora Basilia has to do is prove it. If," and she waved a fork from which long strands of spaghetti still hung, "you can prove it so well that the police here will lock up McClintock, Clough, and Allison for ten years or more, then I shall pay you twenty million pesetas."

Well, at that time, just before the British economy went into what will probably turn out to be terminal decline, that was one hundred thousand pounds.

We were all, and I mean all, about fifteen of us, in the big dining-room in Casa Hicks. This was a splendid room, the central feature of which was a big, heavy, well-polished Castilian oak table with matching chairs, up to twenty could be found, for the Hicks family entertained often and lavishly, in the old style. The ceiling was coffered cedar. Three walls were done out with tiles to waist height, the patterns reproduced from Alhambra. Above thee were alcoves filled with arum and Madonna lilies. Persian carpets hung between the niches, except on the wall opposite Doña María Pilar, at the far end of the long table, where the carpet space was filled with a full-length painting of Don Hicks done eight years earlier in the style of Patrick Proctor, possibly by Patrick himself. It portrayed him full length in a wet suit, with a harpoon gun in his right hand, while his left held a three-foot shark just above the tail so its nose rested on the floor. Hicks, done thus, was a striking figure, a very handsome, broad, tanned face set off by a leonine mop of silver hair, the suit concealing the no doubt well-padded shoulders, the swelling tum, and the varicose veins.

The remaining wall was glass on to a verandah with a view of the harbour, but on this occasion rattan blinds were drawn on the outside and looped over the wrought-iron balcony, probably to cut out the mid-afternoon sun and heat while allowing air to circulate, possibly also because none of those assembled were prepared to look down on the spot of oily water, still with some debris floating, where their lord and master had suffered his demise.

"I have already determined to do so," said Baz, "and only required your permission before initiating my inquiries."

There was a murmur of appreciation from all those round the table who were silently or not so silently weeping. It was not a household in which one could readily grasp the relationships unless or until one accepted the unacceptably obvious. María Pilar ruled a harem, or more properly I should say a seraglio. There were her own three children – Juan who had driven us from the airport, his younger brother Luis and Luis's twin sister Encarnación. Then there were three, well, I'm sorry, but there's only one word for it, concubines: Dolores (or Lola), Carmen, and Purificación (or Puri). Lola and Puri were curvaceous and very, very feminine, Lola with deep red hair, Puri's black and gypsyish, both worn long. Carmen was tall, athletic, with natural dark-honey blonde hair worn short above green eyes. Between them all they had, I later gathered, six more children whose ages ranged from one to thirteen, though only the older three or four were with us from lunch.

What was even more scandalous was that Baz herself was apparently to some extent responsible for these arrangements. María Pilar had approached her fourteen years earlier with a problem: after the birth of her twins the doctors had told her more children would kill her. Since she was deeply Catholic this posed a problem: Don Hicks had not risked a lifetime in prison in order to end up a celibate on the outside. María Pilar's pride was such that she could not accept his having clandestine affairs, nor would she tolerate the gossip and innuendoes that would arise if he did. Baz proposed the solution: concubines. María would remain in control and in charge, the locals would have nothing to be sly about because it would be all in the open, and so on. It had been difficult to begin with but once Lola's first child arrived and Carmen moved in, it had worked beautifully – María Pilar finding great fulfilment in playing the role of super-mum to the whole household. As a sociologist I have to say I approve – since it works. As a strongly anti-Catholic feminist I'm not so sure...

"As soon as the shops reopen," Baz continued, "I shall be grateful if Juan will be good enough to take me to the nearest reliable shop selling underwater equipment, I imagine the one his father used to use is reliable, and tomorrow, weather and the police permitting, I shall examine what is left of the wreck."

"You will charge the expenses to Don's account."

Baz inclined her head in acceptance of this offer.

"Meanwhile," she asked, "I need to know when McClintock, Clough, and Allison arrived here."

Luis, an attractive lad, fairer than Juan, chipped in. "They were first seen only yesterday morning. But they went straight to one of the smaller villas on the other side of the bay. It had been booked and prepared for them in advance, so it is likely they have confederates already working in the area."

"In any case," said Baz, "twenty-four hours would have been ample (she pronounces the word 'Ah-mpull', an irritating affectation) for them to have put a bomb in place, or more probably a mine. What very few people are aware of is that Brian McClintock is a member of the IRA and no doubt learnt the technology that blew up your father from those who did much the same to poor dear Louis."

The meal over, I declined a second opportunity to enjoy Juan's driving skills and pronounced myself eager, as eager as one appropriately could be in a house suddenly plunged into mourning, for a siesta. I was shown to a room at the back of the house, which yet had good views of the distant sierra above the alive and almond groves, and which shared a bathroom with the room on the other side, which had been allocated to Baz. My luggage was there ahead of me, and unpacked – a service I always find mildly impertinent on the rare occasions it happens to me.

However, sleep did not come easily, the excitements of the day had been too intense, and presently I pulled on my Bermuda shorts with the passion flowers and plainer but comfortably loose orange top, and set off for a quiet and, I hoped, discreet exploration of the property. In truth I was hungry too. No doubt out of consideration for both the dead and bereaved, María Pilar had allowed lunch to consist only of the spaghetti, which normally would have been the first course merely, and fruit, and the so-called breakfast on the plane had been so relentlessly aimed at carnivores that I had not been able to take on board as much as I like to at the beginning of the day.

I padded down the corridors and stairs I had already climbed, into the spacious circular hall with a glass dome. For the most part the house was silent – the ghastly tragedy that had occurred may have stifled appetites for food, but not apparently for sleep. Though I was surprised at one point to hear two girls giggling behind a door, and then again *sevillanas* played quite loudly on Radio Málaga with castanets added in real. Servants, I supposed, less moved by their master's death than they appeared to be in front of his family.

In the hall, also tiled and with alcoves filled with roses this time, there was no mistaking the door to the kitchens and similar offices: it was slightly ajar, lined with green baize, and the stone steps led down. I now entered a quiet and blissfully cool world of larders and pantries lit only by small grills near the ceilings. It was all very clean and neat too – one could imagine María Pilar's influence was as strong in these partially subterranean halls as everywhere else. Presently I was in the kitchen – hung with whole sets of copper pans, with assorted knives in racks, and, precisely what I had hoped to find, a row of blackish-brown sheep cheeses, one of which had already been cut. The cheese was almost pure white, a sort of creamy marble, and crumbly – in short *à point*, or as the Spanish have it, *al punto*. It was with me the work of a moment to cut myself enough to fill half a *barra*. I wondered where the wine was kept. Such good cheese deserved a fruity red.

At that moment I heard a totally indescribable noise. Nevertheless I shall do my best. It was a sort of rhythmical combination of squelching and slapping, each beat ending with a brisk noise somewhere between a squeak and the noise of torn cloth. It happened about twelve times, then stopped.

Of course I was petrified. Fat people, and I am very fat, live in constant dread of the ridicule which is provoked by the situation I was then in. Nevertheless curiosity, and a loyal feeling too that Holmes should be aware of anything untoward that was going on in the house, prompted me presently to move in the direction from which the sounds had come. I passed through an open but bead-curtained doorway into a short narrow defile between white walls from which the sun's glare was instantly blinding. I waited until I could see – of course I had not brought my shades with me – and followed it into a wide sort of patio. It was clearly used by the gardener as a marshalling yard for potted plants – there were rows and rows of them, mostly perlagoniums in all their wonderful variety ranging from the brilliant simple vermilion people call geranium red, to wonderful concoctions in purples and mauves that to all but the most over-educated tastes rival orchids for exotic beauty.

The floor was of polished terrazzo chips. Pools of water lay round the bases of the flower pots, which, in spite of the adjustable rattan roofing which shielded the plants from direct sunlight, steamed gently in the heat. So too did the strangely shaped splodges of water which tracked, arrow-shaped, pointing away from the door of what was obviously a potting shed, across the yard, and out on to a gravel walk, and finally a steep slope of dried grasses and immortelles that dropped beneath olives to the sea – and I mean the sea, not the bay, for the house was set on the headland between the two. Unable to make anything of this, I returned to my room and ate my *bocadillo*, little mouthful. A little duty-free Scotch with water helped it down *faux du vin*, and soon I felt able after all to have a zizz.

"I hope, Julia, you have brought your long spoon with you."

"We are then, my dear Holmes, invited to sup with the Devil?"

"Precisely so. You know I do not readily indulge in hyperbole or other forms of linguistic excess: so you will heed me when I tell you the invitation came from one of the most evil men I have ever had to deal with."

Generally speaking, Baz's opinion of the male sex is low. We were then to dine with the lowest of the low. I was relived, however, to learn that dining was at least on the agenda.

"The Devil has a name?"

"Brian McClintock. And I imagine Frank Allison and Malcolm Clough will be in attendance."

The bad news was that, Spanish style, dinner would not be served till ten. We were invited for drinks at half-nine.

I asked Baz if her shopping trip to Málaga had been successful.

"Indeed yes. And apart from the underwater equipment I bought one or two other odds and ends which will help us in our endeavours." From her silk and wool shoulder bag, woven in Samarkand, she pulled a small black plastic bag. It was sealed with black plastic tape.

"This," she said, "is a radio transmitter, part of an eavesdropping device of exceptional accuracy and power. While we are dining I shall attach the microphone and micro-transmitter to the underside of the dining-table. Later you will go to the ground-floor toilet which is in a vestibule off the main hall and close to the dining-room. I know all this, my dear Watson, because I also went to the agent who manages the villa our evil trip has rented. All I ask of you this evening is that you simply place this package in the cistern. The micro-transmitter will send its signal to the RT in the cistern, which will then relay whatever it picks up to the Guardia Civil Cuartel in Las Palomas."

"What if they frisk us on the way in?"

"I don't think they will. But if they offer to we shall plead our sex and go home. Not much will be lost, this is simply a back-up to my main strategy."

"I think they will. In their position I would."

"Ah, but what you do not understand is that they believe we are on their side. In fact they have already paid me a retainer."

"My dear Holmes, this is too much!"

"Isn't it just? But it will work out, you'll see."

The evil trio's villa, on the other side of the bay, was perhaps one of the nastiest buildings I have ever been to. Built some ten years earlier, probably on the cheap, it was already showing marked signs of wear. The outside wall by the front door was streaked with orange stains, and the stucco rendering was coming away off the corners to expose ill-laid cheap brick. The door itself was made of pine stimulating oak, studded with nail-heads and with a cast-iron grill simulating a convent gate. The varnish was lifting. Fortunately we could not see much of the garden as the dusk was already upon us, but there was the inevitable bougainvillea clashing with a profuse variety of nicotiana.

We were welcomed into a hall, where black mould grew up the outside wall, by Frank Allison, a tall dark man once handsome and strong, now a ruin of himself. He offered us what must once have been a conman's charm and was now the wheedling flattery of a conniving ex-con. The only good argument for the death penalty, and not one I would discount until the situation is reformed, is what long prison terms in our appealing prisons do to the inmates. I write as one who has been a Prison Visitor.

The interior he took us into had been furnished to appeal to the lowest common factor in taste and had sunk below even that. There were stained-glass lanterns over the lights, others were lacquered brass fittings from which the lacquer had peeled. The upholstered furniture was covered in grubby, ill-fitting loose covers of a wishy-washy design. The upright chairs were made from turned pine with stick-on mouldings, painted black. Cracked leatherette simulated leather. On a wall table a large bowl of opalescent glass in the shape of a stylised swan held English lilac which was no longer factory fresh. Worst of all was a painting of a gypsy girl, pretending to sell sardines but really it was her boobs that were on offer, heavily framed in a bright, shiny gilt above a false fireplace that the occupants had been using as an ashtray.

"Lovely, isn't she?" said Brian McClintock, coming in behind us. He was a short, compact, tough-looking man, with a pale pock-marked face, and eyes the colour of year-old ice. He ran his fingers over the gypsy girl's boobs. "Original, see? You can feel the impasto. Glad you could make it, Holmes. And your friend. I don't think I've had the pleasure."

I took the grey claw he proffered and repressed a shudder at its chill. No shudder though for the chill of the strong g-and-t, well-iced, that came after it, accompanied by canapés of anchovy on Ritz biscuits, cream cheese with tiny pearl onions. Really, one might as well have been in Balham, though I doubt the drinks there would have been served so strong.

Incidentally all what he called 'the doings' were handed round (and probably had been prepared) by the third of the evil trio – Malcolm Clough. He was fat and bald but with forearms and fists still solid and strong, the skin not gone loose, supported by muscle as well as fat. He affected a slightly camp style that went with the apron he was wearing. I got the impression that he supplied the muscle, Allison the mean, low cunning, but that McClintock was the leader – in terms of pure nastiness he had the edge on the others.

After that one drink, taken with the five of us standing and remarking on the continuing brightness of the weather and the possibility of thunder by the end of the week, Malcolm declared his paella would be sticking and would we be so kind as to go through. He showed us to places round an oval table with cracked veneer, dressed with plastic mats and Innox cutlery. Before he 'dashed', he used a Zippo lighter on the single red candle set in a tiny tin chamber-pot bearing the legend 'A Present from Bognor Regis'. The place settings were already filled with bowls of gazpacho – which, I have to say, I found perfectly acceptable. Allison filled wine glasses with a semi-sweet, which was not. McClintock lifted his to Holmes.

"Cheers. Well, Baz. How's it going?"

"Early days yet, Bri, early days. I'm still not quite sure how it was done, but tomorrow I shall find out. Or the next day."

"We saw you was in Málaga," commented Allison, "and bought the under-water gear. Have much trouble explaining why you wanted it?"

"None at all," replied Baz. "You will recall that the other side has retained me to fit you up as Hicks's assassins. In order to do that they expect me to recover faked evidence from the ocean floor. Little do they realize that I shall in fact use the opportunity to discover how Hicks got away from the boat in the second or so between when he was seen on the deck and the moment of the explosion. The evidence has to be there somewhere."

"But we retained you to locate the bastard. Not figure out how it was done."

"Of course, Bri. But since I am sure he has not returned to Casa Hicks, figuring out how it was done will provide essential clues as to how far he has got. And in what direction. So it is important that I should work out just how he did get away. From that we should be able to deduce how far he was able to get in whatever he was using as a getaway vehicle. I already feel fairly sure that it was a heavily armoured midget submarine of Russian design. We know some of your bullion turned up on world markets via the Eastern bloc. If I am right, and there will be cleats on the hull of his cruiser and a hatch to link the two, and these are what I shall be looking for tomorrow, then I think we can safely say he got no further than Tangier, or the coast near by. In fact I already have people working for me there, scouring the souks and bazaars, the pubs and above all the male brothels. Did you know Hicks was that way inclined?"

"I'd believe any filth of a creepy cunt like Hicks," said Allison.

"Come, come," said Clough, returning to serve the paella, "nothing wrong with a bit of bum every now and then."

After the paella there was whisky-soaked bought-in ice-cream gâteau, and as it was served I felt the pressure of Baz's foot on my own. From that I understood that the microphone stroke micro-transmitter was in place, and that the ball was in my court as regards the more powerful transmitter. In fact this was a great relief since the cold of the ice-cream hitting the oily glutinous mass of rice, mussels and prawns had provoked a reaction that brooked no delay. It had become a problem – for if I went the once, how would I explain a second 'visit' so soon after?

"Scuse I," I said, and pushed back my chair. Fortunately a glance at Baz's stony face brought me to my senses just in time, and I managed the obvious question I had been about to omit out of foreknowledge. "Where is it?"

"The ladies' room? Upstairs, second on the right," said Malcolm Clough.

I looked a question at Baz and received a tiny shrug which seemed to say go ahead anyway.

Up there, I popped the bag in the cistern – it was a high-level one but I was able to manage just by lifting the lid – unclipped my braces, negotiated the satin-edged cover on the seat, and then thought again, I did not fancy that the Civil Guard headquarters in Las Palomas should hear the first effects of tarta al whisky on paella. I rehosted the nether garments and stood on the seat – necessary now because the bag had sunk to the bottom of the cistern. The seat, thin pink plastic, shattered. I retrieved the bag, pushed it outside the door, and contrived, with some haste now, and in spite of the shards of broken plastic, to answer one of Nature's more peremptory calls, perched on the cold porcelain pedestal. Then I retrieved the bag from the landing. But, I thought, when they discover the broken seat they may guess I stood on it and for why. I placed it instead in another pink plastic receptacle instructing ladies in terms so coy I cannot recall them to deposit tampons and sanitary towels in here and not down the loo. On my way back down I pondered some of what had happened, and had been said, and came to the conclusion that Baz was playing a pretty fishy game.

"Baz," I said, on the way home, "you're playing a pretty fishy game."

"So it may seem to you, dear Julia, so it may seem to you."

"And that bag you gave me, it's in the upstairs loo. Does that matter?"

"I think not."

We were wending our way down the short drive to the electronically controlled gate. The garden of the evil trio's rented villa was of course untended, and branches of hibiscus and plumbago brushed my face.

"It would be fairer for me, and render me more likely to play my part properly, if you told me the truth."

"Julia, so far you have performed magnificently – and as for the truth, remember, he who tells it is sure to be found out – but, as they say, hist!"

Her sudden movement banished from my lips my riposte to her second-hand epigram and she pulled from I know not where, for she was wearing a single-piece, pocketless garment cut like a boiler suit but made out of yellow wild silk, a small but powerful pencil torch. Its beam, as if laser-guided, fell instantly on the head of a woman standing pressed up against a cypress tree. As the light fell on her she flung up an arm to cover her face, but not before we had both recognized the tall, athletic and sullenly beautiful Carmen – the second of Hicks's concubines.

"We shall ignore her," said Baz, extinguishing the torch, and taking my arm. "She has served her purpose. I imagine too she has the means of opening the gate we are approaching and hopefully has left it open for us."

This turned out to be the case.

Baz was never an early riser, her preferred hours of alertness and work being from midday until two, then from ten at night to five in the morning. She therefore engaged to be on the Hicks's second cruiser, with her underwater gear, no earlier than half-eleven – an arrangement which the Hicks family, being Spanish by birth or habit, found perfectly acceptable.

I, on the other hand, wake at seven and have to be up and doing by eight at the very latest, and that was the hour that found me next morning again padding about an almost perfectly silent house, bored and hungry. This time I felt no compunction about going straight to the kitchen: a hostess who cannot provide breakfast for her guests at a reasonable time must not be surprised if they fend for themselves. I found coffee in a filter jug, which I reheated, milk in a big fridge and a pack of four croissants in a cupboard. I found the means of heating them through, and I speedily got outside the lot. The moment then arrived which I dread – it is precisely as I pour my second cup of coffee that I most feel a dreadful urge to smoke again. I gave up five years ago, but still the only way to keep myself from a mad scramble for the nearest fag is to resort to displacement activity.

I recalled the extraordinarily handsome perlagoniums in the garden's patio outside and resolved to pinch a few cuttings while no one was about. I supplied myself with several sheets of kitchen roll soaked in water and a pair of kitchen scissors, and stepped out into the already hot sunlight. I took my time selecting them, for I felt it would be impractical to take more than eight.

I had just snipped the fourth when I heard noises from the kitchen, much the same sort of noises as I had made a half hour earlier. What to do? Some people can be surprisedly shirty when they catch you taking cuttings, especially if they are of hybrids they have themselves created, as well might have been the case in this instance. I decided to hide in an alcove where there was a stone sink and a coiled hose, and wait until whoever was in the kitchen had gone. I gathered up my impedimenta, and did just that, turned to face outwards and found I was looking across the patio at the man who had to be the gardener himself. He was tall but old, with short white hair and a big white moustache, and a big white beard, both stained yellow. He was dressed in an orange mono splashed with mud and perhaps cement, wore heavy-duty gardening boots.

"¡*Hola!*" I offered. "¡*Buenas días!*"

He said nothing, which is unusual for a Spaniard when offered the time of day, but unbuttoned his breast pocket, took out a pack of Ducados, shook one out and lit it. The smell recalled painfully just why I had been caught so obviously *in flagrante delicto*. Then as he expelled the first puff, sandalled feet tick-tocked out of the kitchen and there was Lola, in a short and transparent nightie as well as gold sandals, carrying a tray with a bowl of coffee and a large chocolatina.

She didn't see me, but put the tray down on a large upturned flower-pot, perched on to her toes and gave the gardener a big kiss.

"¡*Hola, Papa, croissants, no quedan. No sé por qué…!*"

So. The gardener was Lola's father – not an unlikely arrangement. I put down my stolen cuttings and sidled away muttering apologies in mixed Spanish and English which they ignored.

———

At midday then we were all out in the bay on the Hicks's second major craft, an elegant reproduction of a Victorian steam yacht, but with modern engines, radar and so on, and just over the spot where his more conventionally modern cruiser had been blown up. Presently Holmes and Juan appeared from below, clad in wet suits. On the deck they hoisted oxygen cylinders on to their backs, fixed masks, all that scene – one has seen it a thousand times on TV – and finally to the manner born toppled backwards over the taffrail.

When I say 'all' I mean all – not only María Pilar and her children, the concubines including the strange and at the moment clearly agitated Carmen, and their older children, but also Stride, and the Colonel of the Civil Guards – again in full fig, black hat, black moustache, Sam Browne and the rest. Twenty minutes or so went by during which we all watched the rise and plop of bubbles through the oily water. After a time a brown scum crept by on which floated panty-pads and used contraceptives. I was amused that the efforts of the *ayuntamiento* de Las Palomas to cast a cordon sanitaire round their unspoilt haven were visited by the sea – the flotsam of the Costa del Sol, recently named Costa del Mierda, could not be so easily kept at bay. During all this Holmes apparently kept up a laconic conversation with the Colonel by phone.

Suddenly a big break of bubbles through the heaving scum heralded a shout of triumph. The Colonel stood up and explained, in Spanish of course but the gist was clear: "She's got it."

An underling in round, peaked cap strode across to the small funnel that rose in front of the staterooms, and yanked on a small lever. A shiny copper or brass horn near the top of the funnel emitted two short blasts and a long one that echoed across the bay. Our attention was drawn to the villa the evil trio had rented and its purlieus. It was nearer the water and nearer our boat than I had expected. What one saw was a platoon of Guardias, in full combat gear, snaking up over the terraces towards the house. A PA system boomed incomprehensibly, presumably calling upon the occupants to surrender. It was answered by the crackle of small arms, and tiny puffs of blue smoke drifted across the frontage. The Guardias replied and most of the villa's windows, shutters and all, disintegrated in the firestorm. Five seconds and a white flag was waved. Clough and Allison appeared on the terrace, their hands on their heads.

At this moment Carmen uttered a cry expressing horror and despair and jumped from the taffrail. Undeterred by my effort the previous day, I again launched myself at her, but she was too quick for me and I fell on my boobs and face on the spot where she had been standing. She was last seen doing a powerful crawl through the filth of the bay and out to sea. No one, apart from me, seemed bothered to stop her.

A familiar voice behind me: "Well, you could have got us up a bit smarter than that. We've missed all the fun." And Holmes, followed by Juan, both holding black plastic bags, squelched and smacked past me towards the companionway. I looked at the frog-footprints they left, arrow-shaped but pointing back to the rail they had climbed over, and all fell into place.

Lunch on board was, I have to say, magnificent though served as a finger buffet – a system that I normally find unsatisfactory: besides various hams and chicken and so on that I can't take there were giant prawns, calamares romana, Canary potatoes in hot cumin sauce, Russian salad, six other salads, and a huge cold sea bass. There was French champagne and the best in Spanish brandy. Oh yes, I almost forgot, there was cream Catalan, Pyjama ice-cream, water melon, peaches, loquats, and so on. And unlimited coffee.

When it was over we were all called into the main stateroom. A table had been set across one end beneath a second portrait of Hicks, this time one of him steering the boat we were on. Behind the table sat Holmes, Stride and the Colonel of the Civil Guards. The rest of us sat if we could, or stood in a crowd at the back. The Colonel opened the proceedings and Juan, whose English could be as good as his father's, whispered what he said in my ear.

The gist was simple. Condolences to the bereaved family delivered somewhat perfunctorily. Then congratulations to Holmes for so speedily sorting out and proving by whom and how the dreadful deed had been done. Three criminals with an unjustified grudge against Hicks had mined his boat and detonated their explosives by a remote control device, blowing him to bite-size pieces. They had been assisted by Carmen, a close friend of Hicks, but who had also developed a grudge against him. She had been caught on the other side of the headland and confessed all. Meanwhile Holmes had recovered evidence of how the mine was detonated from the sea-bed and the device used to transmit the signal would shortly be discovered in the villa. The Guardias under his command had attempted a peaceful arrest of the three murderers but they had resisted. One of them, Brian McClintock, had been shot dead.

Applause.

Stride took the floor. He was, he said, very grateful indeed to his colleague of the Spanish Guardia Civil, so long a force for law and order respected all over Europe and the world, for this magnificent achievement. Speaking on behalf of the English equivalents, his senior officers in Scotland Yard and in the Special Branch, he would like to say how pleased he was that these three nasties had been wrapped up for good, especially McClintock who was known to have had a hand in the assassination of Lord Mountbatten, even though he had been in prison at the time. No doubt the lefties back home would bleat as they usually did, as they had after the Gibraltar affair, at summary justice executed against known terrorists, but he was confident that Spain's handling of the whole business would be unequivocally endorsed by HMG.

He paused, sipped water, dropped his voice by an octave. He was, he said, saddened by the death of Don Hicks. He had always had a sneaking admiration for the man and had regretted quite deeply the duty that had brought him to these shores – namely to arrest him for a crime nearly twenty years old. So in a way it was a relief not to have to do this, and a great relief to be able to write once and for all finis to the Grosswort and Spinks bullion case. He had no reservations at all about adding his condolences to the Colonel's and offering them to the bereaved family.

Applause.

"Hang on," I said. My voice squeaked but I was determined. "This won't do, you know. Don Hicks is alive and well and living in his garden shed—"

"Julia!" Holmes's voice was like frozen prussic acid, but I ploughed on.

"Those three men were villains, I know, but this time they have been fitted up—"

"Watson!"

"I saw Hicks this morning. Lola, Delores, over there, she brought him his breakfast. In the garden shed. Yesterday I saw his frogman-footprints—"

María Pilar intervened this time: "If no one else will silence that fat scrotum, I shall." And she came for me with a knife.

I don't know why she calls me that. I know I wear mannish clothes, but she can't really believe I'm a man…

On the way back to the airport, Juan driving, my remonstrations with Holmes were again interrupted by a bleep on the radio phone. Juan passed the handset to Holmes.

"It's for you."

Holmes listened, then said, "I'll ask her."

She turned to me and her eyes, deep violet, dilated by the drugs she often uses at the successful outcome of a case, seemed to penetrate the inner recesses of my soul.

"Julia, the police cannot find the radio transmitter that detonated the bomb, and which you hid for me in the cistern of the upstairs toilet of the villa. Please tell me where it is."

Defeated, I told her.

A shadow of a smile crossed her lips though not her eyes.

"I imagine that being men they preferred not to look for it there."

One last footnote. When I got back home I found eight perlagoniums, fully grown, of real magnificence, delivered by a florist who is on the Designer Living Card list, of which more anon in a later tale. The card read 'Gratefully yours, DH'. They are very lovely and I cherish them. But plants bought ready grown never give the same pleasure as those one has reared from stolen cuttings – do they?

FUNNY STORY

LARRY BEINHART

My father is visiting for the holidays. He's an old man now. I'm not exactly young either. At least not the way they used to measure men. Pushing fifty. Pushing it quite hard actually.

My son is six, pushing seven. At that age you can't push hard enough. Time flows like treacle, black, sweet, slow, thick and sticky. You can't move it fast enough. If you charge into it you just get tangled up and slowed down, then you end up having to take a bath.

At my age, when you would give whatever there is to give to slow the metronome down, it seems an enviable state. But try telling that to a kid racing to be a race driver, fireman, policeman, wrestler, Power Ranger, space scientist, karate fighter. Generation upon generation tries to tell their kids that, and each aging parent sounds like a jerk when he does. Even my father did. I don't mention that however.

David, my son, spills his juice on the rug. His mother, my wife, starts scolding and I go to get paper towels to sop it up. "I told you to be careful of the rug," she says. "It's a valuable, very valuable piece. How many times have I told you never to bring drinks on that rug."

"It's an old rug," David says. Which is true.

My father, looks at me with something less than a wink. Possibly a twinkle. As if to say, listen to this, this is how mothers and sons talk, for all time, what a pleasure to hear this.

"The rug was a gift from your grandfather. It's from the old country, and it's a very valuable piece." What a curious expression, the old country. It makes it sound as if we came from one of those rustic peasanty nations that Mercantilism and the Industrial Revolution had more or less bypassed, someplace like Rumania, Albania, Ireland or the Ukraine.

"Is it as old as Grandpop?" David says, awe in his voice, that lets us know that Grandpop is about as old a thing, let alone as old a person, as he can imagine. Grandpop is pretty old, and he looks old, with wrinkles and liver spots and wisps of hair to highlight the baldness of his liver spotted, wrinkly dome. Big veins stand out on his hands and his fingers move stiffly and painfully, arthritic, as well as just old.

"Older," Grandpop says.

"Did you get it new?" David asks.

It's a big old rug, 12' × 18', a Persian. Handmade, hand knotted, with an intricate pattern. I've been told how many knots per square inch, but I've forgotten and experts, when they look at it, instantly exclaim things about the pattern and the clan and, most of all, about its probable price. I can't. I just know it's the second most valuable thing we own. It's worth less than the house, but more than the car, a five-year-old Lexus. But, like the good old Persian it is, in a house with a son and a daughter and a dog and a cat and, from time to time, rabbits, gerbils and wounded birds, it looks old and faded and worn and as comfortable as a home.

"No, not really," Grandpop says.

"Did you get it at like a garage sale, or an auction?" David asks. He's been to lots and lots of both. We've furnished the house, except for the rug and one or two other bits, from garage sales and auctions. This is not to say that it looks like Levittown leftovers. My wife is a woman of terrific taste which she combines with immense ferocity in her search for true value. For her, anything short of getting a $1400 chair for $225 is a furnishing defeat.

"Would you like me to tell you a story about that rug?" Grandpop says.

David looks doubtful. Furniture acquisition stories don't thrill him. He's really had his fill of them. When my wife does make a furnishing score she not only brings the item home, she brings the tale of its purchase with it: the days, weeks, months of searching; the revelatory moment of finding; the strategy and tactics of the negotiation and a blow by blow of the bargaining.

"You'll like it, it's a funny story," his grandfather says.

David is not convinced. Then I, like a schmuck, which means jewel in German but means schmuck in English, say, "That's not a good story for him."

"Tell me, Grandpop," David says.

"Pop," I say. Why I imagine I can still head this off, I don't know. Maybe I don't really expect to stop him and I just think it is the responsible, parental thing to try.

"What? The boy shouldn't know?"

Maybe he shouldn't. "He's a little young."

"Maybe I won't be here next year to tell him."

Try to argue with that. But, nonetheless, I did. "You will. I say he's not ready. If, God forbid, you're not here, I'll tell him. When the time comes."

"Tell me," David says. Of course. "I want to know."

"What's this God forbid stuff," my father asks me.

"It's a turn of phrase."

"It's superstition," he says, more fiercely than seems called for.

"OK, it's superstition. I'm superstitious, I would like you to come back next year and for many years to come."

"How did you get the rug, Grandpop?"

His grandfather gets out of his chair with creaks and groans and sighs. Not the furniture, the man. And gets down on his knees on the floor. He rolls back a corner of the rug. "Look at this," he says. "This is fine, fine wool. Strong wool. It wears like iron. Woven by hand, the threads are tied by hand. The dyes they use in this, they'll last hundreds of years. Today they make millions of everything, carpets, cars, toys, pens, books, chairs, glasses, silverware, they make it fast, they make it cheap. I'm not saying that's bad, or that the stuff they make is bad. I'm not an old curmudgeon, can't move with the times, stuck in the past, can't appreciate progress. I like progress, I like to see everybody, every working man, and woman, with washers and dryers and summer clothes and sports clothes and ski clothes and running shoes, walking shoes, aerobic shoes, tennis shoes, dress shoes, shoes with winking red lights in the heel. Them I like especially.

"But, you should understand, boy, that once upon a time, not everything came out of a plastic extruder by the twenty millions. Once things were made by hand. One at a time. And there weren't so many, many, many things. There were just a few things. Even for

46

rich people, there weren't so very many things. So each thing became more important. Can you imagine going to the pawn shop … does he know what a pawn shop is?"

"Ask him, not me," I say.

"What's a pawn shop, David?"

"I don't know."

"It's a place where you leave something valuable and they loan you money."

"Dad just uses his card at the bank."

'Right," Grandpop says, "I understand. Me too. But once, they didn't do that. When you borrowed money, you had to leave something tangible behind. Something that the person who loaned you the money could hold onto, even sell, if you didn't pay back. In the old days, you could leave a coat and borrow money."

"A coat?" David says, incredulous. As well he might in these days of cheap, and truth to be told, disposable clothing.

"Right, exactly. Material things, they had value. Not just big things like cars, but watches and jackets, even hats. And rugs."

"How did you get the rug, Grandpop?"

I just sighed and shook my head.

"I stole it," he says.

I throw up my hands, make the sound of exasperation, drop my hands and shake my head.

"You stole it?"

"Pop, do you have to do this?"

"Yes, I stole it," David's grandfather says without a trace of shame. Even embarrassment. Without a thought of discretion.

"What kind of role model, what kind of ideas are you putting in my son's head?"

"Just truth," he says.

"It's not funny," I say.

"There's funny and there's funny," he says.

"My dad says not to steal things. He makes me give things back when I steal them," my wonderful son says.

"Your father is absolutely right," the subversive old man says without a hint of sincerity.

"Did you steal a lot of things?" my son asks.

"You bet," his grandfather says.

"Great, just great," I say.

"Really, Grandpop," David says, as wide eyed and fascinated as you would expect.

"Really, David," Grandpop says. "I was a thief."

I suspect that damage is being done here that will take me years to undo. A rogue, an absolute rogue.

"I was more than a thief. I was about the best thief in Munich. Which was a very great place to be a thief because it was then, as it is now, a very rich city. With many rich people who loved expensive things. As they do now. Even though then there was a depression and what is called hyper-inflation. Do you know what hyper-inflation is?"

"He's six, for God's sake," I point out.

"Like in Brazil," my son says. What does he know about Brazil. The kid hardly knows how to buy a candy bar and get correct change.

"It means that every day the money is worth less. Yesterday a candy bar is fifty cents, tomorrow it costs a dollar. A week later, you need two dollars. Than five dollars. In two, three weeks, a candy bar costs ten dollars. Then twenty. That's hyper-inflation.

So it was better to have things than to have money. I never stole money. You understand why?"

"Stealing money is bad?" my son offers as a reason not to steal money. That's the reason he learned at home.

"Because when you have hyperinflation money is worthless. It's junk. It's garbage."

My wife, listening to this begins to gesture at me frantically. This is a conversation I'm not looking forward to. I'm a fairly weak-willed fellow, or, if you wish to be polite, easy-going, and I tend to go whichever way the wind blows. What it is, I'm actually pretty resilient and self-satisfied, so a lot of things just don't matter to me because there is something at the center that stays fairly pleased with itself even when the weather changes. And they are both, my father and my wife, very strong-willed people. I have never been able to silence either one of them or stop either one of them from saying what they thought needed saying, however little it actually needed saying.

"I'll make some tea," I said. Why? Why not say, Pop, I'm going into the kitchen so my wife can tell me to tell you to shut up because this is most emphatically not a story for a six-year old boy. Theft is just the beginning. There's violence and despair and murder.

"He's six years old, for God's sake," my wife says. Severely.

"No shit," I say.

"Well, aren't you going to stop him?"

"Why don't you stop him?" I say.

"He's your grandfather," she says. This is marital tennis. Not a match game by any means, really just a warm-up, stroking matters back and forth.

"He knows David is six. So maybe he has some reason for telling it now."

49

"Don't be ridiculous, what reason could there be for telling a six-year old his grandfather was a thief, a professional thief."

"He was, to hear him tell it, the prince of thieves. He was a cat burglar. Actually, he rather relishes himself as Cary Grant in *To Catch a Thief.*"

"That doesn't make it better," my wife says.

I say, "Achievement is always to be admired."

She is not amused. She says so. She is frequently not amused. I frequently dream about being away from news of non-amusement.

"Maybe he wants to tell David to always be the best you can be, no, the best there is, no matter what your field of endeavor. And do it with style and panache. I mean my father was no worse, or not much worse, than D'Artagnan." David and I are reading *The Three Musketeers* together. What a revelation to rediscover them. Athos, Porthos, Aramis, and D'Artagnan were appalling by contemporary standards. They're all common brawlers who go around drinking in bars, then refusing to pay, then getting into knife fights and stabbing people, sometimes to death. Alright, the knives are really big and they call them swords, but I can't see the difference. On the moral plane at any rate. Porthos and Aramis both live off of women. D'Artagnan claims to be in love with one woman, makes love to another, without a moment's hesitation, then jumps all over the second woman's maid, not even out of lust, but so he can use her. I am more than faintly envious. Athos, the most noble and sensitive and aristocratic of the bunch, murders his wife. Twice. Why? Because he discovered that she had once been convicted of a crime, had been branded, as in having a brand burnt into her flesh with a hot iron just like they do to cows in cowboy movies. The only remotely moral message implicit in these events seems to be get it right the first time.

"Tell him to stop," she says.

"No."

"Tell him," she commands. Demands. Requires.

"Why don't you tell him?" I suggest, sensibly, thoughtfully, fairly.

"He's your father," she says.

I resist the temptation to say, I knew that. I say, "Exactly."

"So? You have to stand up for your family, and this is your family, your wife and your child ..." This is just the wind-up, a prepositional phrase, as it were, for a lengthy and major statement which will be delivered with such fervor and eloquence that, right or wrong, I will certainly feel that her position is unassailable and not to be denied.

There is only one chance and that is to head her off at the pass, fire off a few shots, spook the lead animal and turn the stampede in a different direction.

"It's because he's my father that you should tell him," I said. "My emotional involvement, and his, the roles, father and son, parent and child, are permanent you know. They never go away. You can't unravel them with your parents – in spite of four years of therapy. I'm not criticizing you," I hasten to add. Though I probably am. Though I couldn't say what I need to say without saying it. So what do you do with that? It is a huge amount of work to have a conversation with my wife. I'm tired of it. "I'm just saying that if I say it we get involved in a whole to do about the parent-child relationship and lots of emotional shit. If you tell him, you can tell him adult to adult, in fact you will probably assume the dominant role as parent, which you are to David, and since my father is really playing a boy to boy thing with David, that puts you in a superior position."

"It's your responsibility," she says.

"Morally, that's true. I agree with you a hundred percent." That's one of my best tactics with her. It's very important to her to be right and morally correct. "However, pragmatically, if we want him to stop, he's more likely to listen to you."

Her mouth opens. She wants more to come out.

"You're absolutely correct," I tell her, before more comes out. "It is my responsibility. But, if I do it, it won't work. If you do it, it will."

"Alright," she says. Disdainful of my ineffectuality – but not unbearably so, this time – she goes back into the living room.

As we go back in we hear David ask, "Why did you steal? Was it because you were hungry and your children were starving?" He has heard that some people steal because they must. This is the legacy of liberalism in our immediate culture and in our house: criminality comes from deprivation. When, and if, it is ever true, I suppose it imparts more than an excuse, a certain legitimacy, even nobility, to theft. 'I would steal before I would let my family starve.' Don Corleone morality. However, it is rarely true. The starving tend to just go on and starve and to the degree they steal it is to snatch the bread off the plates of those starving beside them, not by launching daring raids on the manor house on the hill.

"I stole because I wanted to," my grandfather tells my son.

"Isidore," my wife says, commandingly.

"One minute," Izzy says. "You see, I came from a fine family. My grandfather – you see, I had a father and he had a father, I know that you know that but to think about it and see it in your mind, that's something else. My grandfather was a Rabbi. And he had three sons and one daughter.

"His youngest son was a doctor ..."

My wife doesn't interrupt, even though her command has gone unheeded. Perhaps because this part is alright, this is sort of noble family history, roots, capable of generating lots of sentiment, and she likes that sort of thing.

"That doctor was my father. He was very scientific, very secular and very assimilated. Do you know what assimilated means?"

"Or secular for that matter," I put in.

"No," my son says.

"Do you know what a Rabbi is?" my grandfather asks.

"Yes," my son says. "He's like a priest. For Jewish people. And I'm part Jewish."

"Right," my wife says. She's the one who's brought him to temple, though she's not Jewish at all. I'm totally secular. As was my father. Totally. Even adamantly.

"And assimilated, it means that we became, as much as we could, just like the other people around us. You are completely American. We were as German as Germans could be. We loved Bach and Wagner and read Goethe and respected learning and orderliness. Except …"

"Except what?"

"Except for me," Grandpop says. "My father had three sons. One became a medical doctor, as he was. One became a professor of chemistry, and the third, became the black sheep of the family."

"And that was you!" David cries with delight.

"Isidore, would you come into the kitchen. Now." My wife says.

"What for?"

"I don't know how you like your tea."

"A little bit of cream, two sugars," he says. "Cubes, if you have them. I like sugar cubes."

53

"Because I want to talk to you," she says.

"Alright," he says, getting up off the floor with even more creaks and sighs than he required to get down there. "There was so much goodness and orderliness around," he says. "And I had so much sap in me, I just couldn't stand it."

"Now, please," my wife says.

"Is mom going to let Grandpop finish his story?" David asks me as they disappear into the kitchen-conference room.

"I wouldn't like to bet on it either way," I say. I'm curious myself, who's going to win this little to-do.

"Dad, can we go to the video store," he says.

"Sure."

"I want to get a movie called *To Catch a Thief*," he says. "Have you ever seen it?"

"Yes."

"Will I like it?"

"Well, if I remember, it's got a lot of love stuff in it …"

"Yuchey."

"… but aside from that you should like it."

They return from the kitchen. My son and I look toward them, searching their faces for clues as to what will ensue. It's real clear. My father has a slight smile on his face. If you're in a bad mood it can look like a sneer. I remember it well from growing up. And how it used to infuriate me. My wife, on the other hand, looks pale and chastened. I wonder what he could possibly have said to her. I've never achieved that effect. I guess I still have something to learn from the old man.

Isidore lowers himself slowly down to the floor. More creaks, groans, sighs. My wife goes back into the kitchen, hastening, it turns out, to bring him his tea, as he likes it, though not with sugar cubes. We've never had them around. I suspect we are about to start stocking them. She also brings a plate of some not very sweet, adult sort of cookies for Grandpop to share with David.

From where I sit the Christmas tree more or less frames them. Strings of light, little wooden sleds and Santas and elves all made cheaply in China hanging from the branches, along with glass balls and an eclectic assortment of thisment and thatment of ornaments assembled over the years. Presents in patterned paper and glittery ribbons are spread out on the floor behind them.

"Christmas was our best season," Grandpop says. "I had a partner. A young man named Jurgen. This was a very strange time. Germany had its Jew laws, these were laws that were separating out the Jews from the German people. For us, this was very confusing because we saw ourselves as Germans, as Jews hardly at all. But Jurgen and I had become friends before all that and we stayed friends, chasing girls together, you're too young for that, yes?"

"I like girls," David says.

"But not like that," I explain. Though it should not need explanation. "He means he hasn't reached the age where he won't play with girls, not that he's reached the age, which comes after that, where all he wants to do is play with girls."

"Of course," Grandpop says. "We liked, what kids nowadays call life in the fast lane. Cash, clothes, cars." As if suddenly remembering who is in his audience, he adds, with an admonishing finger, a gesture he has surely copied from somewhere because I know it is not innate to him, when he wanted to make a point, a hit, though openhanded and mild, was more his style, "Of course, I would be very unhappy if you were to be that way. You should be more like my brothers. Students. Men of learning. Respected. You understand?"

"Sure," David says, tuning right into his grandfather's conspiracy to commit hypocrisy. In his short life, the only things he has ever expressed a desire to be when he grows up are things that are defined as testosterone-driven activities, things with fighting, fires, vehicles, guns. From today we can add stealing.

"Jurgen was the outside man. I was the inside man. He had a way with serving girls that you would not believe. They loved him. They had but to meet him and their eyes would get big and round like cows' eyes and they would look up at him like this." He rolls his head around with a motion quite definitely evokes mooing and cud chewing. "And they would tell him everything. What the family they worked for was buying as presents, when they were going visiting, when the houses would be empty. I was helping Jewish families sell their jewelry so I knew a lot of the jewelers. I would get information from them about people buying expensive jewelry. Also there were several that were not so honest who would buy the jewelry we stole from us.

"Finally there were a few who worked with us. When they sold expensive pieces, they would tell us. Then we would steal it and we would sell it back to them."

"Cool," David said.

"Isidore," my wife said, very sternly. It is a tone of voice I have come to loathe.

"Sorry," Grandpop said, sounding just like I do when I'm making a meaningless pro forma acknowledgement. My wife glared at me. Of course.

"Anyway, Christmas would come, and we would have our houses picked out. We would know what was inside, or enough to know it was worthwhile, taking the risk. And how to get in and when the house would be empty. The maid's rooms in big houses were usually way up on top and sometimes a window would be left open for us.

"I was the cat," he says, leaning forward, smiling and immensely pleased with himself. "I could climb, I could get my fingertips into the smallest crack, I could stand on the narrowest ledge. And I could jump from one hold to the next. To do this you have to be two things: fearless and skinny. I was both.

"Other times I would pick the lock …" he looks down at his cramped old hands and sighs for the dexterity that they once had and the youth that it represented and all that went with that youth. "Or cut the glass. There were many ways. None of which a well-brought-up young man like yourself should know," he adds. No need to mention that he had been as well brought up as David. Better in fact. Isidore was the son of a doctor, grandson of a Rabbi. David was the son of a composer of advertising jingles, grandson of a thief.

"Anyway, we had costumes. Jurgen would dress as Father Christmas, Santa Claus. I would dress in very dark, dark green. Almost black so that I would be invisible in the dark, and smear dark green make-up on my face so even the white of my face would not catch the light, but, but, if a policeman were to stop us, I would say that I was one of the elves from the Black Forest, one of Father Christmas's helpers. Most of the things we stole would still be wrapped, you see, so we would say we were going to a party and bringing the gifts."

"Did that actually work?" I blurt out, incredulous.

"Only once was it put to the test," he says.

"Why are you filling our son's head with this, this, terrible nonsense?" my wife says.

"It's the story of the rug," he says. Innocently. "It's a funny story."

"Is this true?" she asks.

"As God is my witness," my father says. And who knows what that means. To whatever degree he believes in God, he is very, very angry with Him. And finds His deeds unforgiveable. At least that's what he's told me.

"Can we at least not wallow in the details," my wife says.

"Of course, Moira," he says. "Not an unnecessary word. I will cut to the chase."

"Thank you," she says.

"So, on this particular Christmas, we are doing pretty well. We get into this big mansion that is close to the Englischer Gardens, which is a big park in Munich, like Central Park in New York or Golden Gate Park in San Francisco. What I'm there for is a diamond bracelet, I forget now the details of carats and number of diamonds, but this was worth, today, $50,000, $60,000. Lots of diamonds, lots of glitter, a real show piece. Also there was hidden away, a lessor piece, worth maybe fifteen, twenty thousand. One was for the wife, one was for the mistress. Plus there were many other things, the silver, small art pieces, whatever was small and valuable. Plus they had children. Close to the ages of my children then, who were, one was younger than you and one the girl, was exactly your age. Very pretty she was, and like you she had blond hair. So did I, when I was young and I had hair. Not these white wisps…"

The phone rang. I went to answer it. I knew the next bit. My father saw the rug there. He recognized it. It had belonged to a very rich Jewish banker in Munich, someone very well-known at the time, but whose name meant nothing to me and would mean nothing to David. My father recognized it because he had robbed the previous owner some years earlier. He had admired it then. It was, he said, the best Persian he had ever seen. Now he could not resist it.

The phone call was from one of our neighbors, a sweet young woman named Elaine. She's a widow, but reasonably well off, very attractive, with dark eyes, black hair and a full figure. Our daughter is visiting her daughter and Elaine is calling to find out if I will be coming over to pick Susan up or if she should deliver her. I say I'll come over, which I know is what she wants to hear. It's easier for her and means that we might be able to spend a few adult minutes together. I tell her it will be an hour or so. Elaine says to come whenever I can, when I can will be all alright.

When I hang up the phone Moira is standing there. She has that I-have-things-to-say look in her eye. Actually, it is a look that is rarely absent, even when she is saying the things.

"What," I ask her, pre-emptively, "did my father say to you? To blackmail you into letting him finish telling this tale of the Yiddisher-Deutcher Robin Hood?"

"He said that he had been to the doctor and that he doubted he would be here another year and that he wanted David to know his story, from his lips."

"Can't argue with that," I say, somewhat surprised. He hasn't said anything to me about exceptionally imminent death. He looks pretty damn good. For his age. And, of course, he is prone to dramatization and exaggeration. Especially when he wants to get his way.

"No," she says.

"I have to confess," my father says as we walk back into the room, "that although I had a very lovely wife, who was incidentally a perfect mother to my two children ..."

"Is that my grandmother?" David asks.

"No. That was my first wife," my father says. "The banker, who originally owned the rug, had a very beautiful daughter. Like a princess in a fairy tale. She had spurned me, and I thought it would impress her for me to have the rug."

"Do we have to go into that?" my wife asks.

"It's the story of the rug," my father says as if the rug has its own life, its own fervent history, crying out to be told, a tale that it needs to pass on to posterity. "I'm just trying to be fully honest here."

"Don't," I say. "Don't overdo it."

"Okay," he says. "I can see that it is time to make a long story short. I will not thrill you, little David, with how I slipped out the back door, crept through the bushes and trees on the ground, carrying not just my usual swag, but this huge rug on my back. And how Jurgen, my partner swore at me as a madman when I brought it to the car. How I was adamant that we take it. Why? I don't know why. We all need a little mystery in what we do. Isn't that correct?

"This was Christmas Eve. Jurgen and I we split up our take, which was considerable. Very considerable. It was late and he took me home. I had the rug of course.

"I went upstairs with all my things. My wife, Sarah, was waiting. My children, David and Judith, were sleeping. I kissed my wife and then went, right away, just as your father does with you, to see my sleeping children. There is something about coming home and finding your children safe and sound, healthy, asleep in their beds, blankets tucked around them, that is better, I think than almost anything else in the world. Ask your father if this is not true?"

David looks at me. Moira likes this part. She beams. "Yes," I say, "it's true." It's true, and yet there are fathers, and mothers, who give it up. Or who give up a lot of it – except for alternate weekends, a week in the summer, and practically never on Christmas – because baser emotions like lust and anger are stronger than the sentimentalities of our higher feelings.

"I kissed them on their foreheads," my grandfather says. "Then I added their extra gifts, those I had picked up from rich people's homes in the course of the night, to the ones we already had. I put them under the tree, just like you have here. Then I sat with my wife and we counted our blessings. Our children being the chief ones.

"Not long after we went to bed there was a commotion in the street. Noise downstairs. Then at the door. It sounded like someone was kicking the door down."

"Was it the cops?" David asks.

"I thought so. But I was ready for that. I was prepared, I had a plan, I had an escape route.

"We lived on the top floor. I always kept the stolen stuff, the valuable stolen stuff, if it was in the house at all, in one bag. I could get out to the roof from the window. Once I was on the roof, I was free and clear. Remember, I was the cat. I went from our roof to the next building, then the next, and down the drainpipes into the alley. From the alley I could get into the basement of the apartment building across the way. And soon I would disappear.

"So I turned to Sarah and I said, 'Don't worry, it's me they want. You just tell them I'm not home. You haven't seen me.' I looked at the rug. I wondered if it would give me away. The thing about Persian rugs is, for the most part you have to know something about them to know if it's a good one or a bad one or real one or a fake one. So, quickly, even as we heard the footsteps on the stairs, we spread it across the floor. It was a little bit too big so we just folded the end under. I was certain that no one would recognize its value or recognize it as stolen.

"Then, just as the knock on the door came, I went out the window, with my bag of swag, and took off across the roof tops."

"Did you get away?" David asks.

"Yes," my grandfather says. "I got away."

"Is that the end of the story?" my wife asks.

"It can't be," David says. "What about the rug?"

My father smiles. Or rather his mouth twitches toward a smile and the smile, that smirk that used to so infuriate me, dies, still born. As well it should.

"I went back in the morning."

"Christmas," my wife says.

"Yes. Christmas. Sarah, and David and Judith were gone."

"Where? Where did they go?" my son asks.

"The knock on the door. That wasn't the police looking for a thief. It was the brownshirts, the Nazis, looking for Jews. And they found some. Two of them sleeping, waiting to wake in the morning to see what gifts Father Christmas had brought them in the night. Two of them and their mother. They took them away."

"What happened to them?" David asks.

"Immediately? I don't know," my father says. "In the end, the camps. The ovens. I don't know. Disappeared. Never to be seen again."

My son looks at me. He's not following this. He doesn't have enough information to know what the camps and the ovens mean. To him camp is a place to go and play. Summer camp, arts and crafts, learning to swim, dodge ball. Ovens are where cakes are made and bread is baked. So now I have to tell him.

Which I try to do as simply as possible. "Not very long ago," I say, "When your grandfather was a young man, the people of Germany decided they wanted to get rid of all the Jews. To kill all the Jews. They did this very methodically. As if they were building cars. It was a very terrible thing."

"Why?" my son asks.

"People do terrible things," I say. "Very terrible things. This was one of the worst. But there are others." It is one of those things, of course, for which my father will never forgive God. I tend to agree with him.

"Was that your mommy?" David asks.

"No," I say. "Grandpa married another woman later."

"They took the children's toys, all the Christmas gifts. They left our little tree. And the rug."

Now what's odd is that my father finishes the story there. He hasn't really told the story of the rug. And there is a story of the rug and it's quite a tale. Like many other Jews, especially assimilated Jews who thought of themselves as more German than most of the Germans they knew, he thought that this anti-Semitism was just a bulge in the political hieroglyphics of history and that, like many other excesses, it would reach a high tide and recede. At that point he suddenly understood that things were much, much worse and much more permanent than that.

He, and his friend Jurgen, who adamantly did not want to be drafted, decided to escape Germany for Switzerland. It was not so easy then as it is now to cross a border. Also neither of them wanted to arrive in a new country totally broke. They wanted to get away with their loot. Jurgen had at one point worked for an industrialist who had a vacation chateau on Lake Lucerne. Then they thought of the rug. They could put their loot – and Isidore – in the rug, the rug in a truck and claim they were delivering it to the Chateau.

This they proceeded to do.

I've heard my father tell this tale more than once. Sometimes there is a policeman in it. A German cop who catches them at a roadside inn just at the moment when Jurgen is bringing food out to the truck and Isidore is crawling out of the rug.

They kill the cop.

They are afraid that the corpse will be found and that they will be caught in the ensuing hue and cry. So they drive off with the corpse, looking for a place to dispose of it.

Somehow, when you're looking to do something like that, there never seems to be a right moment at the right place. At every right place there are people present. Whenever you're alone there's no place. The nightmare continued, hour after hour as they approached the Swiss border. Finally they were out of time and out of possible places to dump the dead. They wrapped the cop in the rug – along with Izzy – and crossed into Switzerland, the dead German lying snug beside the running Jew.

That is the story of the rug. Usually.

But my father doesn't say any of that. He ends it there and says, "A funny story, no?"

"No," Moira says. "I don't see anything funny about it at all."

"Well, it's a Jewish story," Grandpop says. He shrugs. "Some people don't get them." But that's because he has not laid the punch line on us yet.

He gets up from his sitting position, to his knees, on the rug, and puts his big, old, veined and spotted hands on my son, touching his shoulders and the fine, soft hairs on his head, which still, sometimes, even now, on the odd and special day, have the sweet smell of puppy fur. "I was a very wild young man," he says. "I did many, many things that were bad. Things that you should never do. If only because I don't think … I don't think the rewards are worth the risk.

"Still, I don't regret them.

"I regret only one thing. That I abandoned my wife and my children. I pretend to excuse it in that I couldn't know what would happen. But really, you see, the statement should go the other way. If you are a man, a real man, you should never leave your wife and children alone, exactly because you do not know what will happen.

"In this," he tells David, "you are very lucky. Because your father is a better man than I am. He will never abandon you. He will never leave you alone. This I know."

My father is a wily old man. As well as having been a wicked one. But how has he divined that that is exactly what I want most to do in the world? Is his telling the tale this way, with this moral, some random event that I am, in my guilt, very attuned to? Is he a messenger, sent by fate, not knowing what he is really saying, sent to warn me of the consequences of my action? Or is this David's grandfather, quite conscious of what he is doing, wily and manipulative, cleverly herding David's father back into line.

I had gathered my strength, my strength for coping, once again, just to make it through the holidays, planning my escape for the cold clarity that I anticipate for January. There's a sweeter woman who flushes with warmth when she sees me and welcomes me in, into her arms, into her heart, into her body. Dark eyes that seem to swallow me whole and flood me with endorphins or whatever chemicals the chemistry of love consists of, so that I feel free of pain and fear. Away from the spats and the sniping and the sword that lies down the middle of the bed where my heart and Moira's used to lie entwined.

My father, who brought this rug to America – where he gave up his thieving ways, he says, and opened a jewelry store – and gave it to me as a wedding gift, has come about the other gifts he has given me.

Among those other gifts that he has given me are loyalty, love of family, and the cherishing of children. I didn't know that those gifts came with an enforcer. Who would show up at the crucial moment with a warning parable. He has put a kinehara on me. I suddenly feel that if I leave them, the evil that men do will come and steal them away and kill them, leaving the weight of their fate on my soul, a curse for which I can never forgive God.

I look at Moira and wonder if there is any way, any way whatsoever back to the garden?

I look at my father, expecting that infuriating smile to be on his lips and see, instead, only pleading eyes and I know that I will stay at home. With my family and the god damn rug.

HERBERT IN MOTION

IAN RANKIN

My choices that day were twofold: kill myself before or *after* the Prime Minister's cocktail party? And if after, should I wear my Armani to the party, or the more sober YSL with the chalk stripe?

The invitation was gilt-edged, too big for the inside pocket of my workaday suit. Drinks and canapes, six p.m. till seven. A minion had telephoned to confirm my attendance, and to brief me on protocol. That had been two days ago. He'd explained that among the guests would be an American visiting London, a certain Joseph Hefferwhite. While not quite spelling it out – they never do, do they? – the minion was explaining why I'd been invited, and what my role on the night might be.

"Joe Hefferwhite," I managed to say, clutching the receiver like it was so much straw.

"I believe you share an interest in modern art," the minion continued.

"We share an interest."

He misunderstood my tone and laughed. "Sorry, 'share an interest' was a bit weak, wasn't it? My apologies."

He was apologising because art is no mere interest of mine. Art was – is – my whole life. During the rest of our short and one-sided conversation, I stared ahead as though at some startling new design, trying to understand and explain, to make it all right with myself, attempting to wring out each nuance and stroke, each variant and chosen shape or length of line. And in the end there was… nothing. No substance, no revelation; just the bland reality of my situation and the simple framing device of suicide.

And the damnation was, it had been the perfect crime.

A dinner party ten years before. It was in Chelsea, deep in the heart of Margaret Thatcher's vision of England. There were dissenters at the table – only a couple, and they could afford their little grumble: it wasn't going to make Margaret Hilda disappear, and their own trappings were safe: the warehouse conversion in Docklands, the BMW, the Cristal champagne and black truffles.

Trappings: the word seems so much more resonant now.

So there we were. The wine had relaxed us, we were all smiling with inner and self-satisfied contentment (and wasn't that the dream, after all?), and I felt just as at home as any of them. I knew I was there as the Delegate of Culture. Among the merchant bankers and media figures, political jobsworths and 'somethings' (and dear God, there was an estate agent there too, if memory serves – *that* fad didn't last long), I was there to reassure them that they were composed of something more lasting and nourishing than mere money, that they had some meaning in the wider scheme. I was there as curator to their sensibilities.

In truth, I was and am a Senior Curator at the Tate Gallery, with special interest in twentieth-century North American art (by which I mean paintings: I'm no great enthusiast of modern sculpture, yet less of more radical sideshows – performance art, video art, all that). The guests at the table that evening made the usual noises about artists whose names they couldn't recall but who did 'green things' or 'you know, that horse and the shadow and everything'. One foolhardy soul (was it the estate agent?) digressed on his fondness for certain wildlife paintings, and trumpeted the news that his wife had once bought a print from Christie's Contemporary Art.

When another guest begged me to allow that my job was 'on the cushy side', I placed knife and fork slowly on plate and did my spiel. I had it down to a fine art – allow the pun, please – and talked fluently about the difficulties my position posed, about the appraisal of trends and talents, the search for major new works and their acquisition.

"Imagine," I said, "that you are about to spend half a million pounds on a painting. In so doing, you will elevate the status of the artist, turn him or her into a rich and sought-after talent. They may disappoint you thereafter and fail to paint anything else of interest, in which case the resale value of the work will be negligible, and your own reputation will have been tarnished – perhaps even more than tarnished. Every day, every time you are asked for your opinion, your reputation is on the line. Meanwhile, you must propose exhibitions, must plan them – which often means transporting works from all around the world – and must spend your budget wisely."

"You mean like, do I buy four paintings at half a mil each, or push the pedal to the floor with one big buy at two mil?"

I allowed my questioner a smile. "In crude economic terms, yes."

"Do you get to take pictures home?" our hostess asked.

"Some works – a few – are loaned out," I conceded. "But not to staff."

"Then to whom?"

"People in prominence, benefactors, that sort of person."

"All that money," the Docklands woman said, shaking her head, "for a bit of paint and canvas. It almost seems like a crime when there are homeless on the streets."

"Disgraceful," someone else said. "Can't walk along the Embankment without stumbling over them."

At which point our hostess stumbled into the silence to reveal that she had a surprise. "We'll take coffee and brandy in the morning room, during which you'll be invited to take part in a murder."

She didn't mean it, of course, though more than one pair of eyes strayed to the Docklanders, more in hope than expectation. What she meant was that we'd be participating in a parlour game. There had been a murder (her unsmiling husband the cajoled corpse, miraculously revivified whenever another snifter of brandy was offered), and we were to look for clues in the room. We duly searched, somewhat in the manner of children who wish to please their elders. With half a dozen clues gathered, the Docklands woman surprised us all by deducing that our hostess had committed the crime – as indeed she had.

We collapsed thankfully on to the sofas and had our glasses refilled, after which the conversation came around to crime – real and imagined. It was now that the host became animated for the first time that night. He was a collector of whodunnits and fancied himself an expert.

"The perfect crime," he told us, "as everyone knows, is one where no crime has been committed."

"But then there *is* no crime," his wife declared.

"Precisely," he said. "No crime... and yet a crime. If the body's never found, damned hard to convict anyone. Or if something's stolen, but never noticed. See what I'm getting at?"

I did, of course, and perhaps you do, too.

The Tate, like every other gallery I can think of, has considerably less wall-space than it has works in its collection. These days, we do not like to cram our paintings together (though when well done, the effect can be breathtaking). One large canvas may have a whole wall to itself, and praise be that Bacon's triptychs did not start a revolution, or there'd be precious little work on display in our galleries of modern art. For every display of gigantism, it is blessed relief, is it not, to turn to a miniaturist? Not that there are many miniatures in the Tate's storerooms. I was there with an acquaintance of mine, the dealer Gregory Jance.

Jance worked out of Zurich for years, for no other reason, according to interviews, than that 'they couldn't touch me there'. There had always been rumours about him, rumours which started to make sense when one attempted to balance his few premier-league sales (and therefore commissions) against his lavish lifestyle. These days, he had homes in Belgravia, Manhattan's Upper East Side, and Moscow, as well as a sprawling compound on the outskirts of Zurich. The Moscow home seemed curious until one recalled stories of ikons smuggled out of the old Soviet Union and of art treasures taken from the Nazis, treasures which had ended up in the hands of Politburo chiefs desperate for such things as hard dollars and new passports.

Yes, if even half the tales were true, then Gregory Jance had sailed pretty close to the wind. I was counting on it.

"What a waste," he said, as I gave him a short tour of the store rooms. The place was cool and hushed, except for the occasional click of the machines which monitored air temperature, light and humidity. On the walls of the Tate proper, paintings such as those we passed now would be pored over, passed by with reverence. Here, they were stacked one against the other, most shrouded in white sheeting like corpses or Hamlet's ghost in some shoddy student production. Identifier tags hung from the sheets like so many items in a lost property office.

"Such a waste," Jance sighed, with just a touch of melodrama. His dress sense did not lack drama either: crumpled cream linen suit, white brogues, screaming red shirt and white silk cravat. He shuffled along like an old man, running the rim of his panama hat through his fingers. It was a nice performance, but if I knew my man, then beneath it he was like bronze.

Our meeting – *en princi pe* – was to discuss his latest crop of 'world-renowned artists'. Like most other gallery owners – those who act as agents for certain artists – Jance was keen to sell to the Tate, or to any other 'national' gallery. He wanted the price hike that came with it, along with the kudos. But mostly the price hike.

He had polaroids and slides with him. In my office, I placed the slides on a lightbox and took my magnifier to them. A pitiful array of semi-talent dulled my eyes and my senses. Huge graffiti-style whorls which had been 'in' the previous summer in New York (mainly, in my view, because the practitioners tended to die young). Some neo-cubist stuff by a Swiss artist whose previous work was familiar to me. He had been growing in stature, but this present direction seemed to me an alley with a brick wall at the end, and I told Jance as much. At least he had a nice sense of colour and juxtaposition. But there was worse to come: combine paintings which Rauschenberg could have constructed in kindergarten; some not very clever geometric paintings, too clearly based on Stella's 'Protractor' series; and 'found' sculptures which looked like Nam June Paik on a very bad day.

Throughout, Jance was giving me his pitch, though without much enthusiasm. Where did he collect these people? (The unkind said he sought out the least popular exhibits at art school graduation shows.) More to the point, where did he sell them? I hadn't heard of him making any impact at all as an agent. What money he made, he seemed to make by other means.

Finally, he lifted a handful of polaroids from his pocket. "My latest find," he confided. "Scottish. Great future."

I looked through them. "How old?"

He shrugged. "Twenty-six, twenty-seven."

I deducted five or six years and handed the photos back. "Gregory," I said, "she's still at college. These are derivative – evidence she's learning from those who have gone before – and stylised, such as students often produce. She has talent, and I like the humour, even if that too is borrowed from other Scottish artists."

He seemed to be looking in vain for the humour in the photos.

"Bruce McLean," I said helpfully, "Paolozzi, John Bellany's fish. Look closely and you'll see." I paused. "Bring her back in five or ten years, *if* she's kept hard at it, *if* she's matured, and *if* she has that nose for the difference between genius and sham…"

He pocketed the photos and gathered up his slides, his eyes glinting as though there might be some moisture there.

"You're a hard man," he told me.

"But a fair one, I hope. And to prove it, let me buy you a drink."

I didn't put my proposition to him quite then, of course, not over coffee and sticky cakes in the Tate cafeteria. We met a few weeks later – casually as it were. We dined at a small place in a part of town neither of us frequented. I asked him about his young coterie of artists. They seemed, I said, quite skilled in impersonation.

"Impersonation?"

"They have studied the greats," I explained, "and can reproduce them with a fair degree of skill."

"Reproduce them," he echoed quietly.

"Reproduce them," I said. "I mean, the influences are there." I paused. "I'm not saying they *copy*."

"No, not that." Jance looked up from his untouched food. "Are you coming to some point?"

I smiled. "A lot of paintings in the storerooms, Gregory. They so seldom see the light of day."

"Yes, pity, that. Such a waste."

"When people could be savouring them."

He nodded, poured some wine for both of us. "I think I begin to see," he said. "I think I begin to see."

That was the start of our little enterprise. You know what it was, of course. You have a keen mind. You are shrewd and discerning. Perhaps you pride yourself on these things, on always being one step ahead, on knowing things before those around you have perceived them. Perhaps you, too, think yourself capable of the perfect crime, a crime where there is no crime.

There was no crime, because nothing was missing from the quarterly inventory. First, I would photograph the work. Indeed, on a couple of occasions, I even took one of Jance's young artists down to the storeroom and showed her the painting she'd be copying. She'd been chosen because she had studied the minimalists, and this was to be a minimalist commission.

Minimalism, interestingly, proved the most difficult style to reproduce faithfully. In a busy picture, there's so much to look at that one can miss a wrong shade or the fingers of a hand which have failed to curl to the right degree. But with a couple of black lines and some pink waves… well, fakes were easier to spot. So it was that Jance's artist saw the work she was to replicate face to face. Then we did the measurements, took the polaroids, and she drew some preliminary sketches. Jance was in charge of finding the right quality of canvas, the correct frame. My job was to remove the real canvas, smuggle it from the gallery, and replace it with the copy, reframing the finished work afterwards.

We were judicious, Jance and I. We chose our works with care. One or two a year – we never got greedy. The choice would depend on a combination of factors. We didn't want artists who were *too* well known, but we wanted them dead if possible. (I had a fear of an artist coming to inspect his work at the Tate and finding a copy instead.) There had to be a buyer – a private collector, who would *keep* the work private. We couldn't have a painting being loaned to some collection or exhibition when it was supposed to be safely tucked away in the vaults of the Tate. Thankfully, as I'd expected, Jance seemed to know his market. We never had any problems on that score. But there was another factor. Every now and then, there would be requests from exhibitions for the loan of a painting – one we'd copied. But as curator, I would find reasons why the work in question had to remain at the Tate, and might offer, by way of consolation, some other work instead.

Then there was the matter of rotation. Now and again – as had to be the case, or suspicion might grow – one of the copies would have to grace the walls of the gallery proper. Those were worrying times, and I was careful to position the works in the least flattering, most shadowy locations, usually with a much more interesting picture nearby, to lure the spectator away. I would watch the browsers. Once or twice, an art student would come along and sketch the copied work. No one ever showed a moment's doubt, and my confidence grew.

But then... then...

We had loaned works out before, of course – I'd told the dinner party as much. This or that cabinet minister might want something for the office, something to impress visitors. There would be discussions about a suitable work. It was the same with particular benefactors. They could be loaned a painting for weeks or even months. But I was always careful to steer prospective borrowers away from the twenty or so copies. It wasn't as though there was any lack of choice: for each copy, there were fifty other paintings they could have. The odds, as Jance had assured me more than once, were distinctly in our favour.

Until the day the Prime Minister came to call.

This is a man who knows as much about art as I do about home brewing. There is almost a glee about his studious ignorance – and not merely of art. But he was walking around the Tate, for all the world like a dowager around a department store, and not seeing what he wanted.

"Voore," he said at last. I thought I'd misheard him. "Ronny Voore. I thought you had a couple."

My eyes took in his entourage, not one of whom would know a Ronny Voore if it blackballed them at the Garrick. But my superior was there, nodding slightly, so I nodded with him.

"They're not out at the moment," I told the PM.

"You mean they're in?" He smiled, provoking a few fawning laughs.

"In storage," I explained, trying out my own smile.

"I'd like one for Number Ten."

I tried to form some argument – they were being cleaned, restored, loaned to Philadelphia – but my superior was nodding again. And after all, what did the PM know about art? Besides, only one of our Voores was a fake.

"Certainly, Prime Minister. I'll arrange for it to be sent over."

"Which one?"

I licked my lips. "Did you have one in mind?"

He considered, lips puckered. "Maybe I should just have a little look…"

Normally, there were no visitors to the storerooms. But that morning, there were a dozen of us posed in front of *Shrew Reclining* and *Herbert in Motion*. Voore was very good with titles. I'll swear, if you look at them long enough, you really can see – beyond the gobbets of oil, the pasted-on photographs and cinema stubs, the splash of emulsion and explosion of colour – the figures of a large murine creature and a man running.

The Prime Minister gazed at them in something short of thrall. "Is it 'shrew' as in Shakespeare?"

"No, sir, I think it's the rodent."

He thought about this. "Vibrant colours," he decided.

"Extraordinary," my superior agreed.

"One can't help feeling the influence of pop art," one of the minions drawled. I managed not to choke: it was like saying one could see in Beryl Cook the influence of Picasso.

The PM turned to the senior minion. "I don't know, Charles. What do you think?"

"The shrew, I think."

My heart leapt. The Prime Minister nodded, then pointed to *Herbert in Motion*. "That one, I think."

Charles looked put out, while those around him tried to hide smiles. It was a calculated put-down, a piece of politics on the PM's part. Politics had decided.

A fake Ronny Voore would grace the walls of Number 10 Downing Street.

I supervised the packing and transportation. It was a busy week for me: I was negotiating the loan of several Rothkos for an exhibition of early works. Faxes and insurance appraisals were flying. American institutions were *very* touchy about lending stuff. I'd had to promise a Braque to one museum – and for three months at that – in exchange for one of Rothko's less inspired creations. Anyway, despite headaches, when the Voore went to its new home, I went with it.

I'd discussed the loan with Jance. He'd told me to switch the copy for some other painting, persisting that 'no one would know'.

"He'll know," I'd said. "He wanted a Voore. He knew what he wanted."

"But why?"

Good question, and I'd yet to find the answer. I'd hoped for a first-floor landing or some nook or cranny out of the general view, but the staff seemed to know exactly where the painting was to hang – something else had been removed so that it could take pride of place in the dining-room. (Or one of the dining-rooms, I couldn't be sure how many there were. I'd thought I'd be entering a house, but Number 10 was a warren, a veritable Tardis, with more passageways and offices than I could count.)

I was asked if I wanted a tour of the premises, so as to view the other works of art, but by that time my head really did ache, and I decided to walk back to the Tate, making it as far as Millbank before I had to rest beside the river, staring down at its sludgy flow. The question had yet to be answered: why did the PM want a Ronny Voore? Who in their right mind wanted a Ronny Voore these days?

The answer, of course, came with the telephone call.

Joe Hefferwhite was an important man. He had been a senator at one time. He was now regarded as a 'senior statesman', and the American President sent him on the occasional high-profile, high publicity spot of troubleshooting and conscience-salving. At one point in his life, he'd been mooted for president himself, but of course his personal history had counted against him. In younger days, Hefferwhite had been a bohemian. He'd spent time in Paris, trying to be a poet. He'd walked a railway line with Jack Kerouac and Neal Cassady. Then he'd come into enough money to buy his way into politics, and had prospered there.

I knew a bit about him from some background reading I'd done in the recent past. Not that I'd been interested in Joseph Hefferwhite... but I'd been *very* interested in Ronny Voore.

The two men had met at Stanford initially, then later on had met again in Paris. They'd kept in touch thereafter, drifting apart only after 'Heff' had decided on a political career. There had been arguments about the hippie culture, dropping out, Vietnam, radical chic – the usual sixties US issues. Then in 1974 Ronny Voore had laid down on a fresh white canvas, stuck a gun in his mouth, and gifted the world his final work. His reputation, which had vacillated in life, had been given a boost by the manner of his suicide. I wondered if I could make the same dramatic exit. But no, I was not the dramatic type. I foresaw sleeping pills and a bottle of decent brandy.

After the party.

I was wearing my green Armani, hoping it would disguise the condemned look in my eyes. Joe Hefferwhite had *known* Voore, had seen his style and working practice at first hand. That was why the PM had wanted a Voore: to impress the American. Or perhaps to honour his presence in some way. A political move, as far from aesthetics as one could wander. The situation was not without irony: a man with no artistic sensibility, a man who couldn't tell his Warhol from his Whistler… this man was to be my downfall.

I hadn't dared tell Jance. Let him find out for himself afterwards, once I'd made my exit. I'd left a letter. It was sealed, marked *Personal*, and addressed to my superior. I didn't owe Gregory Jance anything, but hadn't mentioned him in the letter. I hadn't even listed the copied works – let them set other experts on them. It would be interesting to see if any *other* fakes had found their way into the permanent collection.

Only of course I wouldn't be around for that.

Number 10 sparkled. Every surface was gleaming, and the place seemed nicely undersized for the scale of the event. The PM moved amongst his guests, dispensing a word here and there, guided by the man he'd called Charles. Charles would whisper a brief to the PM as they approached a group, so the PM would know who was who and how to treat them. I was way down the list apparently, standing on my own (though a minion had attempted to engage me in conversation: it seemed a rule that no guest was to be allowed solitude), pretending to examine a work by someone eighteenth-century and Flemish – not my sort of thing at all.

The PM shook my hand. "I've someone I'd like you to meet," he said, looking back over his shoulder to where Joe Hefferwhite was standing, rocking back on his heels as he told some apparently hilarious story to two grinning civil servants who had doubtless been given their doting orders.

"Joseph Hefferwhite," the PM said.

As if I didn't know; as if I hadn't been avoiding the man for the past twenty-eight minutes. I knew I couldn't leave – would be reminded of that should I try – until the PM had said hello. It was a question of protocol. This was all that had kept me from going. But now I was determined to escape. The PM, however, had other plans. He waved to Joe Hefferwhite like they were old friends, and Hefferwhite broke short his story – not noticing the relief on his listeners' faces – and swaggered towards us. The PM was leading me by the shoulder – gently, though it seemed to me that his grip burned – over towards where the Voore hung. A table separated us from it, but it was an occasional table, and we weren't too far from the canvas. Serving staff moved around with salvers of canapes and bottles of fizz, and I took a refill as Hefferwhite approached.

"Joe, this is our man from the Tate."

"Pleased to meet you," Hefferwhite said, pumping my free hand. He winked at the PM. "Don't think I hadn't noticed the painting. It's a nice touch."

"We have to make our guests feel welcome. The Tate has another Voore, you know."

"Is that so?"

Charles was whispering in the PM's ear. "Sorry, have to go," the PM said. "I'll leave you two to it then." And with a smile he was gone, drifting towards his next encounter.

Joe Hefferwhite smiled at me. He was in his seventies, but extraordinarily well preserved, with thick dark hair that could have been a weave or a transplant. I wondered if anyone had ever mentioned to him his resemblance to Blake Carrington...

He leaned towards me. "This place bugged?"

I blinked, decided I'd heard him correctly, and said I wouldn't know.

"Well, hell, doesn't matter to me if it is. Listen," he nodded towards the painting, "that is some kind of sick joke, don't you think?"

I swallowed. "I'm not sure I follow."

Hefferwhite took my arm and led me around the table, so we were directly in front of the painting. "Ronny was my friend. He blew his brains out. Your Prime Minister thinks I want to be *reminded* of that? I think this is supposed to tell me something."

"What?"

"I'm not sure. It'll take some thinking. You British are devious bastards."

"I feel I should object to that."

Hefferwhite ignored me. "Ronny painted the first version of *Herbert* in Paris, 'forty-nine or 'fifty." He frowned. "Must've been 'fifty. Know who Herbert was?" He was studying the painting now. At first, his eyes flicked over it. Then he stared a little harder, picking out that section and this, concentrating.

"Who?" The champagne flute shook in my hand. Death, I thought, would come as some relief. And not a moment too soon.

"Some guy we shared rooms with, never knew his second name. He said second names were shackles. Not like Malcolm X and all that, Herbert was white, nicely brought-up. Wanted to study Sartre, wanted to write plays and films and I don't know what. Jesus, I've often wondered what happened to him. I know Ronny did, too." He sniffed, lifted a canape from a passing tray and shoved it into his mouth. "Anyway," he said through the crumbs, "Herbert – he didn't like us calling him Herb – he used to go out running. Healthy body, healthy mind, that was his creed. He'd go out before dawn, usually just as we were going to bed. Always wanted us to go with him, said we'd see the world differently after a run." He smiled at the memory, looked at the painting again. "That's him running along the Seine, only the river's filled with philosophers and their books, all drowning."

He kept looking at the painting, and I could feel the memories welling in him. I let him look. I wanted him to look. It was more his painting than anyone's. I could see that now. I knew I should say something… like, 'that's very interesting', or 'that explains so much'. But I didn't. I stared at the painting, too, and it was as though we were alone in that crowded, noisy room. We might have been on a desert island, or in a time machine. I saw Herbert running, saw his hunger. I saw his passion for questions and the seeking out of answers. I saw why philosophers always failed, and why they went on trying despite the fact. I saw the whole bloody story. And the colours: they were elemental, but they were of the city, too. They *were* Paris, not long after the war, the recuperating city. Blood and sweat and the simple, feral need to go on living.

To go on living.

My eyes were: filling with water. I was about to say something crass, something like 'thank you', but Hefferwhite beat me to it, leaned towards me so his voice could drop to a whisper.

"It's a hell of a fake."

And with that, and a pat on my shoulder, he drifted back into the party.

"I could have died," I told Jance. It was straight afterwards. I was still wearing the Armani, pacing the floor of my flat. It's not much – third floor, two bedrooms, Maida Vale – but I was happy to see it. I could hardly get the tears out of my eyes. The telephone was in my hand... I just had to tell somebody, and who could I tell but Jance?

"Well," he said, "you've never asked about the client."

"I didn't want to know. Jance, I swear to God, I nearly died."

He chuckled, not really understanding. He was in Zurich, sounded further away still. "I knew Joe already had a couple of Voores," he said. "He's got some other stuff too – but he doesn't broadcast the fact. That's why he was perfect for *Herbert in Motion*."

"But he was talking about not wanting to be reminded of the suicide."

"He was talking about *why* the painting was there."

"He thought it must be a message."

Jance sighed. "Politics. Who understands politics?"

I sighed with him. "I can't do this any more."

"Don't blame you. I never understood why you started in the first place."

"Let's say I lost faith."

"Me, I never had much to start with. Listen, you haven't told anyone else?"

"Who would I tell?" My mouth dropped open. "But I left a note."

"A note?"

"For my boss."

"Might I suggest you go retrieve it?"

Beginning to tremble all over again, I went out in search of a taxi.

The night security people knew who I was, and let me into the building. I'd worked there before at night – it was the only time I could strip and replace the canvases.

"Busy tonight, eh?" the guard said.

"I'm sorry?"

"Busy tonight," he repeated. "Your boss is already in."

"When did he arrive?"

"Not five minutes ago. He was running."

"Running?"

"Said he needed a pee."

I ran too, ran as fast as I could through the galleries and towards the offices, the paintings a blur either side of me. Running like Herbert, I thought. There was a light in my superior's office, and the door was ajar. But the room itself was empty. I walked to the desk and saw my note there, still in its sealed envelope. I picked it up and stuffed it into my jacket, just as my superior came into the room.

"Oh, good man," he said, rubbing his hands to dry them. "You got the message."

"Yes," I said, trying to still my breathing. Message: I hadn't checked my machine.

"Thought if we did a couple of evenings it would sort out the Rothko."

"Absolutely."

"No need to be so formal though."

I stared at him.

"The suit," he said.

"Drinks at Number Ten,' I explained.

"How did it go?"

"Fine."

"PM happy with his Voore?"

"Oh yes."

"You know he only wanted it to impress some American? One of his aides told me."

"Joseph Hefferwhite," I said.

"And was he impressed?"

"I think so."

"Well, it keeps us sweet with the PM, and we all know who holds the purse-strings." My superior made himself comfortable in his chair and looked at his desk. "Where's that envelope?"

"What?"

"There was an envelope here." He looked down at the floor. I swallowed, dry-mouthed. "I've got it," I said. He looked startled, but I managed a smile. "It was from me, proposing we spend an evening or two on Rothko."

My superior beamed. "Great minds, eh?"

"Absolutely."

"Sit down then, let's get started." I pulled over a chair. "Can I let you into a secret? I detest Rothko."

I smiled again. "I'm not too keen myself."

"Sometimes I think a student could do his stuff just as well, maybe even better."

"But then it wouldn't be *his*, would it?"

"Ah, there's the rub."

But I thought of the Voore fake, and Joe Hefferwhite's story, and my own reactions to the painting – to what was, when all's said and done, a copy – and I began to wonder…

ROOTS

JERRY SYKES

For over twenty years the house had been a part of the dark dreamscape of my life, but as I crested the hill it rose anew out of the mist, a burning red ember fanned by the wind of change that blew in my heart.

A pale sun hung low over the hills and the cool mist rolled down the valley, chasing a river that ran sepia from the iron ore in the soil. I could smell wet bracken and new grass through the open window.

I turned off the engine and let the car roll down the hill, tyres crunching on gravel the only sound in the still morning. I pulled up under a huge oak that buckled the road at its roots and watched the house through the rearview.

All the homes in the valley were made of stone, cottages built at the turn of the century for mill workers and their families.

Except the red brick house in my mirror.

The house had been built during the Second World War by a man named Thad Irwin, a foreman at the brickworks a mile further up the valley. Rumour was that he had stolen the bricks a wheelbarrow at a time right from under the owner's nose, the owner turning a blind eye due to the fact that Thad was the only regular worker left, all the others off fighting for their country. Any vengeful thoughts on the part of the owner were laid to rest when his heart exploded a month before VE Day, spraying the inside of his eyes a deep red.

Thad eventually completed his task, but there were still piles of hot bricks in the yard thirty years later when I was a regular visitor of his grandson, Rob.

The yard may have held our attention on cold evenings, but it was the old quarry that lay beyond the brickworks that demanded our presence throughout the summer.

A gaping wound in the green hills that rippled through the valley, the quarry had been abandoned for as long as I could remember. With a huge pond of stagnant water that could only be navigated by rafts built from strapping twisted planks across oil drums, a dirt track worn smooth by daredevil circuitry, a junked Mini complete with four tyres, flowers of rust blooming on the cracked paintwork, the place was considered a death-trap by anyone over the age of thirty, but to us it was the surface of the moon, Monument Valley, and Wembley Stadium all rolled into one.

But the one truth of childhood was that our parents knew best.

Perspiration slicked my hair and ran down my neck, spooking a shiver that snaked along my spine. I climbed on, hands pushing down on my thighs, my ankles tearing through the tangled undergrowth. My lungs felt scorched and tiny black stars exploded before my eyes. I could see the stone wall that rode the hills above me and promised myself a cigarette on reaching it.

A few minutes later I placed my hands on the wall and rested my forehead on my arms. I couldn't breathe deeply enough and I felt nauseous.

Eventually I turned to look out over the valley.

A deep haze shimmered before my eyes, turning the view into a faded water colour. At the foot of the hill I could just make out the abandoned buildings of the old brickworks, the corrugated iron sheets covering the doors and windows booming in the wind like thunder. To the north of the brickworks I could see the old cemetery, the gravestones like broken teeth scattered on the ground, the spire of the church reaching upwards like a skeletal finger to scratch at the sky. To the south, armies of trees ran down the valley and circled the village.

I turned my attention to the sweep of hill before me. Where the quarry had once been there was now only a sunken crater filled with scraggly brown grass, the dead land all that remained of the landfill site. Green grass crept up to the crater's edge and waved at its dead kin.

I wiped the rain from my eyes, felt the sting of tears.

An invisible sun was burning in a clear blue sky as we snaked along the path that circled the brickworks and down towards the quarry. Beads of sweat bubbled on my forehead and I could feel my T-shirt sticking to my back. Rob walked a few paces ahead of me, kicking a football, red dust swirling around his ankles and sticking to his calves.

At the front of the building a group of men were standing on the loading dock. They were stripped to the waist and their torsos glowed red in the light from the kiln. Steam clouded above their shoulders and trousers heavy with sweat hung low on their hips. They looked like the newly dead at the gates of Hell.

As we reached the dirt track that led to the quarry itself, we saw Tom Dillon down by the water's edge. I couldn't see what he was doing, but he looked to be watching something in the water. Rob held his finger to his lips and gestured for me to follow him.

Tom Dillon was a weak child and consequently natural prey to anyone with muscles to flex. He was also well-off, and to someone like Rob, who never had anything of his own, well, that was like taking money out of Rob's own pocket. And Rob wasn't too subtle about hiding that resentment. One winter he had severed Tom's earlobe with a piece of shale hidden in a snowball, drops of blood bursting on the ground like brilliant red flowers. And the previous spring he had chased Tom through the cemetery with a fresh oak sapling torn from the ground, flicking it at his back until welts rose in the skin that looked like worms buried in his flesh.

I scrambled after Rob as he climbed the side of the quarry and into the thick bracken that grew along its edge. We crawled further up the hill until we had a good view of Tom. I looked at the water, slick with oil; ripples carried rainbows to the shore. The raft that Rob and I had built the previous summer had been dragged onto the far bank, the dry warped planks the bleached bones of a giant skeleton.

"What's he doing?" said Rob.

Tom was sitting on his haunches and fiddling with something on the floor in front of him. He had his back to us. The ground by his feet was wet and there were footprints leading to the pond, as if he had been in the water.

"I don't know." I shrugged. "I can't see anything."

"What is it?"

I shook my head.

Just then Tom shifted to the right and I caught sight of the object in his hands.

"Looks like a boat," I said. "A speedboat."

"A what?" Rob looked at me with quizzical eyes.

"You know. Remote control." I mimed the joystick.

"Hey," he said slowly, "let's go take a look."

Rob climbed over the edge of the quarry and ran down the slope, digging his heels into the shale to keep from tumbling over. At the bottom he paused briefly, wiping his palms on the seat of his jeans, before crossing towards Tom. His shoulders were held artificially high and I sensed something nasty was about to happen.

I ran down the slope, fitting my footsteps to the grooves left by Rob, and walked towards them. But something held me back, an intruder in their private drama, and I pulled up short. I shielded my eyes against the sun.

Tom was explaining how the boat worked. It sounded simple enough – two-speed gearbox, forward/reverse switch, joystick – and Rob appeared to be listening. But after a moment I saw a change in the light in his eyes, the way a candle will flicker and then right itself when someone leaves the room, and I wanted to shout at Tom, tell him to run.

Lesson over, Tom took the boat over to the pond and carefully placed it in the water. Rob followed, eager to see the boat in action. I stayed put, a reluctant spectator, my heart thumping in my chest, the sound of blood swirling in my ears.

The boat kicked out a few bubbles and started to move away from the shore, but after a moment its movements didn't tie in with the way Tom was rattling the controls, his fingers knuckled white in frustration.

"It's jammed," he said. His eyes flicked between the boat and the controls.

Rob reached out a hand. "Here, let me," he said.

Tom whipped the controls away and turned his back on Rob. "No!" he snapped. "It's mine." He continued to work the controls frantically, his eyes off the boat.

"C'mon, it's going to crash," shouted Rob, pointing towards the boat.

Then, without warning, he snatched at the remote and knocked it to the ground. The boat responded to the violent command by cutting its engine. Within seconds it came to a halt.

Tom immediately picked up the remote and wiped it clean with the palm of his hand. He gave it a gentle shake. A muted rattle told us something was broken.

The boat drifted in a slow arc thirty feet from the shore.

Tom looked at the boat and then back at Rob. "What did you do that for?" he said. His words sounded as if they were being squeezed out of his throat and tears welled up in his eyes. "You've broken it… I only got it on Saturday."

A sneer appeared on Rob's face. "It's not broken you little fuckin' cry baby. Here, give it to me." He held out his hand for the remote. "Let me have a go."

Tom put his hands behind his back.

Rob looked at his face, at the tears streaking the dusty cheeks. "C'mon…" he said, trying to reach around Tom for the remote.

I couldn't watch it any more. I walked to the edge of the pond and picked up a couple of chunks of shale, thick plates about the size of my hand. I took a step forward and hefted one into the water. It landed with a slap about ten feet from the boat. Ripples shot out but the boat didn't move any closer.

"What are you doing?" squealed Tom. He ran over to me and slapped the other piece of shale out of my hand.

"Hey, we're trying to get your boat back, all right?" I said, holding up my hands.

"You'll break it."

I dropped to my haunches and reached for another piece of shale. "The waves'll push it to shore," I explained.

Just then a loud splash echoed around the quarry. A drop of oily water hit me on the forehead. I saw Tom touch the back of his head and then quickly turn around, his eyes scanning the water.

Small waves lapped at the shore, the shale hissing as the water pulled back. Towards the centre, tiny bubbles broke on the surface.

"Where's my boat?" screamed Tom. He ran to the pool, the toes of his baseball boots in the water. "Where's the fuckin' boat?" He turned to Rob. "What've you done? Where is it?"

"It was only a fuckin' boat." Rob was holding a piece of shale in his hands. He turned to walk away. "No big deal. I'm sure Daddy'll buy you another."

Tom grabbed his arm, pulled him back. "You're mad. Fuckin' mad. Just because you never have anything..." He stopped abruptly, took a step closer. He struggled to keep his voice under control as he focused all his anger into his next words. "Man, you even *live* in a stolen house!"

I saw Rob's eyes flare with a demonic iridescence. He lifted his arm to the side of his head, and then with a force that came from deep within, he brought his hand and the chunk of shale down on the side of Tom's head.

I walked back down the hill, my boots dragging through the grass. The morning dew had yet to burn off and my feet felt damp and heavy. I reached the car and sat for a long while just staring out of the window, thinking of the cheap life I had lived, afraid to enter my imagination for fear of what I might find.

I put the car in gear and headed into the village. It had begun to cloud over and I could taste rain in the air.

I pulled into the gravel car park of the Beaumont Arms and went into the public bar. I climbed onto a stool and ordered a large scotch. There was one other customer in the place, some kid in dirty green overalls playing the fruit machine. A bottle of lager was on the table nearby, a cigarette feathering in the ashtray.

I looked at my watch. It was still not yet twelve. I rattled my empty glass on the wooden bar.

I helped Rob drag the body along the edge of the quarry. I held the right arm, my fingers sinking into the cold flesh, and watched Tom's baseball boots lay down a trail of broken plants and ragged grooves.

Rob had hold of the other arm. It was his idea that we throw Tom from the top of the quarry. The shoreline below was littered with large slabs of shale and other debris and the 'fall' would explain the wound above Tom's ear.

When we reached the spot where we had earlier spied on Tom, I let go of his arm. But instead of flopping to the ground, the arm moved slowly and for one mad moment I thought Tom might still be alive.

I looked over the edge, at the pool of dark blood that had formed around Tom's head as we had watched life drain out of his body. We would have to go back and bury it later.

I looked at Rob. "We can't just throw him over the edge," I said. "It's Tom."

He looked at me with hard eyes. "He's dead, man. He ain't going feel nothing."

I looked at the stranger before me – even his voice had taken on a different texture – and for the first time I felt scared. "We should go back, tell someone." Then, "It was an accident…"

"No," said Rob calmly. "Everyone knows that I never liked the spoilt fucker. Picked on him. They'll just think I took it too far this time." He sounded like he had always known that he would kill him one day.

"But it was an accident." I had to believe that, for it to have been anything else was beyond my comprehension.

I looked at Tom lying in the undergrowth. Most of the colour had drained from his body but I could see where I had held his skinny arms, the impressions of my fingers deep bruises in his flesh.

Rob grabbed Tom by the ankles and nodded at me. "C'mon, get a hold of his arms." I took hold. Rob counted to three and we hefted the body off the ground. He moved his arms to the left and grunted at me. I realised he meant for us to swing the body out over the edge. He started counting again, his voice a painful echo in my heart. "One… two… three…"

The body seemed to hang in the air for ever. I didn't hear it hit the ground.

Tom's body was found later that evening as the sun fell behind the hills above the quarry and turned the clouds a deep purple so that they looked like bruises floating in the sky. His father had got worried when he had not returned at dusk and, knowing that he had taken off with his new boat, had made straight for the quarry, assuming that Tom had just forgotten the time.

As he walked down the dirt track towards the pond, the spokes of the dying sun picking out the acid shapes that whorled around the breaks in the surface, he realised with mounting horror that the small figure lying in the shale, a twisted arm outstretched to the water in grotesque imitation of a dying man reaching an oasis, was the broken body of his only son. It was a realisation that was to tear his heart from his chest, again and again.

When I returned to the quarry later that evening it seemed like the whole of the village was there, etched into the landscape by a string of brilliant white arc lights that hovered in the darkness like giant fireflies. The sounds of whispered conversations drifted in the air and half-raised arms pointed to the spot where Tom's body had fallen.

I looked up at the edge of the quarry and saw disembodied faces staring back at me from the bracken. I wondered if the tracks made by Rob and I as we had dragged the body up the hill had been scrambled by these ghouls.

I looked over the faces of the people that were nearest the pond. Their eyes burned with a religious intensity, as if they were waiting for a spiritual cleansing in the murky waters before them.

On the far side of the pond I could see Rob standing next to Tom's father, tears burning on his cheeks like diamonds embedded in the skin.

The following morning both Rob and I were questioned by the police. I don't think that they ever really suspected us of having anything to do with Tom's death, but as we'd been the last ones to have seen him alive, we'd made sure that our stories were in sync just in case. In the event, the police didn't appear to be interested in finding out what had happened and were happy to absorb the tragic accident explanation that had passed silently through the crowd the previous night.

But far from being relieved at the turn of events, the wall of silence that had been erected around Tom's death served only to cast a dark shadow in my heart. Although I had not dealt the blow that had killed him, I was as guilty of his murder as Rob, and that guilt pumped through my veins with an intensity that would burst me awake at night in a cold sweat feeling that my head was about to explode.

Rob and I did not speak about the events of that day again, but when I saw him in school, his face open and bright, I immediately understood that it was me who would have to bear the burden of guilt for both of us.

The following November an opportunity for atonement presented itself in the shape of a school science project – a time capsule.

The idea was simple: between us the class would collect a selection of items that best represented the year – a newspaper, magazine, records, pages from a diary, photos – that would then be buried in a specially built chest in the school garden, to be exhumed in the year 2000 when a reunion party would be held.

My mind immediately locked into the possibilities and I volunteered to provide some photographs. On the way home that night I talked Rob into helping me out.

Following Tom's death the council had finally caved in to pressure from the parents in the village and decided to do something about the quarry, earmarking it as a landfill site. Work was due to start in the New Year. It was my idea to take photos of the area for inclusion in the time capsule. One of my ideas, anyway – Rob would have to wait to hear the other. I arranged to meet him at eight the following Sunday morning.

As we walked down the dirt track the smell of stagnant water assaulted my nostrils. I turned to tell Rob that I had never noticed the smell before and caught him staring at the spot where he had felled Tom. His eyes seemed to be locked inside his head and his face was bleached of colour. I turned and followed his stare to the edge of the pond. I swore I could see the impression that Tom's body had left.

I swung my rucksack from my back and sat on the shale. I took out the cassette recorder and slotted in a fresh tape.

"What's that? I thought we were going take some photos," said Rob. He had stopped several feet from the water's edge.

"Later," I said. "We've got something else to do first." I pushed the jack of the microphone into the socket. I cleared my throat, but as I tried to speak my words seemed to spin in the air like dust and vanish before reaching the microphone.

I rewound the tape and started again.

"This is a confession," I began. "On the twenty-fifth of August, 1976, I, George Lowell, and Robert Irwin murdered Tom Willis…"

"What the fuck!"

I turned off the cassette recorder.

"Rob, we've got to do something. I'm a nervous fuckin' wreck."

"Shit. You didn't do anything."

"I was there," I said, the calmness of my voice betraying the drumroll of my heart. "I'm as guilty as you are. Rob, we threw him from the top of the fucking quarry!"

Rob looked away, to the spot from where we had thrown the body.

After a moment he sat on the ground, leaning back on his hands. He stared into the water for a long time. "No one's ever going to hear this, right?"

"Not until the year 2000."

"Yeah right. Give me the mike." He flapped his hand at me and I leaned over and handed him the recorder.

Rob lit a cigarette and then spoke into the microphone. "This is the confession of Rob Irwin. In August 1976 I killed Tom Willis. We got into an argument and I hit him on the head with a chunk of shale. Me and George here then dragged him up the side of the quarry and threw him over the edge…" He pulled on his cigarette. "By the time you hear this I will be dead. Suicide. I can live with the guilt of Tom's murder, but I could not go to prison. So, by the time you get to hear this…" His voice broke and he hung his head.

My whole body felt cold, chips of ice floated in my veins.

I ordered another drink and thought of that final day in the quarry. In many ways it haunted me far more than the day of the actual murder. My young heart, already cramped with guilt, was twisted beyond all recognition as we delivered our suicide notes on that day by the dead water of the pond.

As I grew older I began to feel more comfortable with myself, the twin demons of alcohol and guilt becoming the thuggish guardians of my soul, exuberant bouncers that kept the public at arm's length.

My life had been an endless series of temporary postings to increasingly desperate locations, the only constant an expiry date handed to me one day in an abandoned quarry.

Rob had a different story to tell: he had escaped the past and made full use of his time on the planet. As well as successfully riding the software wave, he had been married for over fifteen years and had two healthy children. I had not seen much of him over the years as he had moved to London immediately after leaving college, but we had always met up for a beer on his increasingly infrequent trips back home. It was over five years now since I had last seen him.

It was almost noon. The sun slanted through the dirty window to my left and lit the polished wood of the bar with a grainy light. The drink in my hand burned liquid gold. I looked at my reflection in the mirror behind the bar, at the eyes that were like dead candle wicks behind green glass, dead from lack of air. I thought about the murder and how both Rob and I had handled it, about how Rob had somehow transferred the whole stinking burden onto me. For a long time it had filled me with physical pain, a pain so deep that I could only communicate it through drunken threats and violence. But there was always something inside me that not even physical violence could release, the simple need for revenge.

The call came on a bright morning in December.

I was sitting at my kitchen table watching the neighbours' cat chewing on a bird, my fingers knotted around a mug of coffee, when the phone started to ring. I was carrying a whisky hangover and thought about leaving it to ring and going back to bed, but there was urgency in the tone, as if it may be bad news. I picked up on the fifth ring.

"Hello?" A woman's voice, familiar. I felt my heart step up a beat.

"Yes?" Hesitant. I reached across the table for a cigarette.

"Is that George? George Lowell?"

"Yeah, that's me," I said with a note of finality in my voice, as if by guessing my name the caller had discovered my secret.

"I'm sorry. Have I called at a bad time?" She sounded hurt.

"No, no. Now's fine. I'm just a little…" I waved my cigarette in the air.

"All right, well…" She gave a nervous laugh. "I'll start again, shall I?" Another laugh. "I don't know if you remember me… Claire Wish?"

My mind rewound furiously. Half remembered scenes.

"Sorry, I shouldn't have expected you…"

I sensed the faint echo of a missed heartbeat.

"Red hair and skinny legs?" I said.

I heard her laugh again, a gentle, innocent sound this time. "Well, not so skinny now… but, yeah, the hair's still red."

I walked over to the cooker and lit the cigarette from the gas ring. "What can I do for you?" I said. I looked out of the window and saw that the cat had gone, leaving the torn carcass of the bird in the middle of the lawn.

Suddenly I was gripped by panic.

"Well, do you remember the time capsule we buried…"

My blood ran cold.

"…in the fourth year? At school," she added helpfully.

I couldn't speak. I nodded and hoped she could see me.

"They can't dig it up."

Kaleidoscopic images of the murder flashed before my eyes, moving in and out of focus. Into focus: an iron fist breaking a face of stone.

"They…" I began to feel dizzy.

"You remember they planted it near that row of cherry trees?"

"Go on," I managed. My voice was hoarse. I pulled out a chair and sat down, took a sip of coffee.

"Well, they buried it too near. Too near the trees. The roots have grown over the box."

"They can't dig it up? They can't dig up the tree?"

"No, that's right… Well, they reckon nobody's going to remember what was in the capsule anyway. Or the exact spot where it was buried…"

I felt my heart start to beat again. I struggled to bring everything under control. "So they're not going to dig it up, that's what you're saying? The whole thing's off?"

"Yes and no."

"I don't understand."

"We're going to bury another capsule."

"And dig that one up instead?"

"Brilliant, isn't it?"

"And where do I come in?" I felt a smile break on my face.

"Well, I've been given the job of recreating the whole thing. I've had a new capsule made up, so now I'm just asking a few people – discreetly, mind you – if they've got anything I can use."

"I don't know. I'd have to have a look around. Can I get back to you?"

"Sure."

I took her number and promised to call back later.

My mind was reeling. Was this a sick joke? Had they already dug up the capsule and found the tape? I headed for the loft.

I spent the next couple of days choking on clouds of dust, cold sweat beading my face, until eventually I hauled a cardboard box down into the kitchen and hefted it onto the table. I had stuck things in the box as I came across them, but now I looked at them more closely.

There were items from before and after the murder: a copy of the *Mirfield Reporter* with a picture of the school cross country team on the front page, silver medalists in the Yorkshire Schools; a ticket stub from a Be Bop Deluxe concert at St George's Hall in Bradford; my old school tie; a few singles, now scratched, covers torn, from punk bands long forgotten; a couple of music magazines, including a local fanzine.

I felt a great weight lift off my chest as I realised that these innocent items were going to erase over twenty years of fear.

But as I began to put the things back in the box, I was filled with a deep sense of dread. Something drew my attention to the window. The wind was blowing the apple tree in the back garden around so that its branches seemed to be pointing at me, jabbing accusing fingers. A strong gust threw a branch against the window and as it scratched across the glass I heard the ghost of Tom Willis whisper to me.

The bar was now full. A cloud of voices hung in the air, voices that spoke of emotions I had denied myself for so long. I heard laughter as if it was my native tongue and not the language of my neighbours.

The door opened and in the mirror I saw a man in a black leather car coat enter the bar. He moved his head as if looking around, but his eyes had the dark impenetrability of sunglasses. A spider web of burst veins was tattooed across his face and his belly pushed at his shirt.

I looked at the man for a couple of minutes before I realised it was Rob.

I leaned back on my stool and held up my arm. Rob weaved through the crowd and pushed into the bar beside me. "Large scotch when you're ready," he called to the barman.

Rob turned to face me and I saw nothing but darkness, dead eyes. He stepped back from the bar and pulled aside his jacket. Stuffed into the waistband of his jeans was a large black pistol.

"You remember that confession?" he asked, the words spilling out of his mouth.

I nodded slowly, unsure of what was happening.

"I meant every word of it." His face looked as cold as marble, as if rigor had set in. He swirled the whisky around in his glass. "Every single word."

I looked at him closely. "You remember Claire Wish?" I said, hesitant.

"Right after this drink..." He threw back the scotch and slammed the glass on the bar, wiped his mouth with the back of his hand. He pushed himself away from the bar and made to leave. "Claire Wish? Sure I remember her. What about her?"

I heard my heart beat deep inside my chest, once, twice...

"Oh nothing," I said. "It doesn't matter."

MARTHA GRACE

STELLA DUFFY

Martha Grace is what in the old days would have been termed a 'fine figure of a woman'. Martha Grace is big-boned and strong. Martha Grace could cross a city, climb a mountain range, swim an ocean – and still not break into a sweat. She has wide thighs and heavy breasts and child-bearing hips, though in her fifty-eight years there has been no call for labour-easing width. Martha Grace has a low-slung belly, gently downed, soft as clean brushed cotton. Martha Grace lives alone and grows herbs and flowers and strange foreign vegetables in her marked-out garden. She plants by the light of the full moon. When she walks down the street people move out of her way, children giggle behind nervous hands, adults cast sidelong glances and wonder. When she leaves a room, people whisper 'dyke' and 'witch', though Martha Grace is neither. Martha Grace loves alone, pleasuring her own sweetly rolling flesh, clean oiled skin soft beneath her wide mouth. Martha Grace could do with getting out more.

Tim Culver is sixteen. He is big for his age and loved. Football star, athlete, and clever too. Tim Culver could have his pick of any girl in the class. And several of their mothers. One or two of their older brothers. If he was that way inclined. Which he isn't. Certainly not. Tim Culver isn't that kind of boy. Tim Culver is just too clean. And good. And right. And ripe. Good enough for girls, too clean for boys. Tim Culver, for a bet, turns up at Martha Grace's house on a quiet Saturday afternoon, friends giggling round the corner, wide smirk on his handsome not-yet-grown face. He offers himself as an odd-job man. And then comes back to her house almost every weekend for the next three years. He says it is to help her out. She's a single woman, she's not that bad, a bit strange maybe, but no worse than his Grandma in the years before she died. And she's not that old really. Or that fat. Just big. Different to the women he's used to. She talks to him differently. And anyway, Martha Grace pays well. In two hours at her house he can earn twice what he'd make mowing the lawn for his father, painting houses with his big brother. She doesn't know he's using her, thinks she's paying him the going rate. God knows she never talks to anyone to compare it. It's fine, he knows what he's doing, Tim Culver is in charge, takes no jokes at his own expense. And after a few false starts, failed attempts at schoolboy mockery, the laughing stops, the other kids wish they'd thought to try the mad old bitch for some cash. Tim Culver earns more than any of them, in half the time. But then, he always has been the golden boy.

For Tim, this was meant to be just a one-off. Visit the crazy fat lady, prove his courage to his friends, and then leave, laughing in her face. He does leave laughing. And comes back hungry the next day, wanting more. It takes no time at all to become routine. The knock at the door, the boy standing there, insolent smile and ready cock, hands held out to offer, "Got any jobs that need doing?"

And Martha did find him work. That first day. No matter how greedy his grin, how firm his young flesh, what else she could see waiting on her doorstep that young Tim Culver couldn't even guess at. Mow the lawn. Clean out the pond. Mend the broken fence. Then maybe she thought he should come inside, clean up, rest a while, as she fixed him a drink, found her purse, offered a fresh clean note. And herself.

At first, Tim Culver wasn't sure he understood her correctly.

"So Tim, have you had sex yet?"

Why would the fat woman be asking him that? What did she know about sex? And did she mean ever as in today, or ever as in ever? Tim Culver blustered, he didn't know how to answer her, of course he'd had sex. The first in his class, and – so the girls said – the best. Tim Culver was not just a shag-merchant like the rest of them. He might fuck a different girl from one Saturday to the next, but he prides himself on knowing a bit about what he's doing. Every girl remembered Tim Culver. Martha Grace remembered Tim Culver. She'd been watching him. That was the thing about being the mad lady, fat lady, crazy old woman. They watched her all the time, laughed at her. They didn't notice that she was also watching them.

Tim Culver says yes, he has had sex. Of course he's had sex. What does she think he is? Does she think he's a poof? Mad old dyke, what the fuck does she think he is?

Martha Grace explains that she doesn't yet know what he is. That's why he's here. That's why she asked him into her house. So she could find out. Tim Culver knows a challenge when it's thrown his way.

When Tim Culver and Martha Grace fuck, it is like no other time with any other woman. Tim Culver has fucked other women, other girls, plenty of them. He is a local hero after all. Not for him all talk and no action. When Tim Culver says he has been there, done that, you know he really means it. But with Martha Grace it is different. For a start there is not fucker and fuckee. And she does talk to him, encourages him, welcomes him, incites him. Martha Grace makes Tim Culver more of the man he would have himself be. Laid out against her undulating flesh, Tim Culver's young toned body is hero-strong, he is capable of any feat of daring, the gentlest acts of kindness. Tim Culver and Martha Grace are making love. Tim Culver drops deep into her soft skin and wide body and is more than happy to lose himself there, give himself away.

Before he leaves, she feeds him. Fresh bread she baked that morning, kneading the dough beneath her fat hands as she kneaded his flesh just minutes ago. She spreads thick yellow butter on the soft bread and layers creamy honey on top, sweet from her hands to his mouth. Then back to her mouth as they kiss and she wipes the crumbs from his shirt front. She is tidier than he is, does not like to see him make a mess. Would not normally bear the thought of breadcrumbs on her pristine floor. But that Tim Culver is delicious, and the moisture in her mouth at the sight of him drives away thoughts of sweeping and scrubbing and cleaning. At least until he is gone, at least until she is alone again. For now, Martha Grace is all abandon. Fresh and warm in a sluttish kitchen. After another half hour in the heat by the stove, Tim Culver has to go. His friends will wonder what has happened to him. His mother will be expecting him in for dinner. He has to shower, get dressed again, go out. He has young people to meet and a pretty redhead to pick up at eight thirty. Tim Culver leaves with a crisp twenty in his pocket and fingers the note, volunteering to come back next Saturday. Martha Grace thinks, stares at the boy, half smiles with a slow incline of her head, she imagines there will be some task for him to do. Two p.m. Sharp. Don't be late. Tim Culver nods, he doesn't usually take orders. But then, this feels more like an offer. One his aching body won't let him refuse.

She watches him walk away, turns back to look at the mess of her kitchen. Martha Grace spends the next three hours cleaning up. Scrubbing down the floor, the table. Changing the sheets, wiping surfaces, picking up after herself. When she sits down to her own supper she thinks about the boy out for the night, spending her money on the little blonde. She sighs, he could buy the girl a perfectly adequate meal with that money. If such a girl would ever eat a whole meal anyway. Poor little painfully thin babies that they are. Living shiny magazine half lives of self-denial and want. Martha Grace chooses neither. Before she goes to sleep, Martha notes down the visit and the payment in her accounts book. She has not paid the boy for sex. That would have been wrong. She paid him for the work he'd done. The lawn, the fence, the pond. The sex was simply an extra.

Extra-regular. On Saturday afternoons, after winter football practice, after summer runs, late from long holiday mornings sleeping off the after-effects of teenage Friday night, Tim Culver walks to the crazy lady's house. Pushes open the gate he oiled last weekend, walks past the rosemary and comfrey and yarrow he pruned in early spring, takes out the fresh-cut key she has given him, lets himself into the dark hallway he will paint next holiday, and walks upstairs. Martha Grace is waiting for him. She has work for Tim Culver to do.

Martha Grace waits in her high, soft bed. She is naked. Her long grey hair falls around her shoulders, usually it is pulled back tight so that even Martha's cheekbones protrude from the flesh of her round cheeks, now the hair covers the upper half of her voluminous breasts, deep red and wide, the nipples raised beneath the scratch of her grey hair. Tim Culver nods at Martha Grace, almost smiles, walks past the end of her bed to the bathroom. The door is left open so Martha Grace can watch him from her bed. He takes off his sweaty clothes, peels them from skin still hot and damp, then lowers himself into the bath she has ready for him. Dried rose petals float on the surface of the water, rosemary, camomile and other herbs he doesn't recognise. Tim Culver sinks beneath the water and rises up again, all clean and ready for bed.

In bed. Tim Culver sinks into her body. Sighs in relief and pleasure. He has been a regular visitor to her home and her flesh for almost three years now. The place where he lays with Martha Grace's soft, fat body is as much home to him as his mother's table or the room he shares with an old friend now that he has moved away. Tim Culver has graduated from high school fucks to almost-romance with college girls. Pretty, thin, clever, bright and shiny college girls. Lots of them. Tim Culver is a good-looking boy and clearly well worth the bodies these girls are offering. This is the time of post-feminism. They want to fuck him because he is good looking and charming and will make a great story tomorrow in the lunch-time canteen. And Tim is perfectly happy for this to be the case. The girls may revel in the glories of their fiercely free sexuality, Tim just wants to get laid every night. Everyone's happy. And the girls are definitely happy. It's not just that Tim Culver is good looking and clever and fit. He also, really really, knows what he's doing. Which is more than can be said for most of the football team. Tim Culver is a young man of depth and experience. And of course it is good for Tim too, to be seen to be fucking at this rate. To be this much the all-round popular guy. But as he lies awake next to another fine, thin, lithe, little body he recognises a yearning in his skin. He is tired of fucking girls who ache in every bone of their arched-back body to be told they are the best. Tired of screwing young women who constantly demand that he praise their emaciated ribs, their skeletal cheekbones, their tight and wiry arms. Weary of the nearly-relationships with would-be poet girls who want to torment him with their deep insights into pain and suffering and sex and music. Tim Culver is exhausted by the college girls he fucks.

They are not soft, these young women at college, and they need so much attention. Even when they don't say so out loud, they need so much attention. Tim learnt this in his first week away from home. Half asleep and his back turned to the blonde of the evening, her soft sobs drew him from the rest he so needed. No there was nothing wrong, yes it had been fine, he'd been great, she'd come, of course it was all ok. She wasn't crying, not really, it was just … and this in a small voice, not the voice she'd come with, or the voice she'd picked him up with, or the voice she'd use to re-tell the best parts of the story tomorrow, but … was she all right? Did he like her? Was she pretty enough? Thin enough? Good enough? Only this one had dared to speak aloud, but he felt it seeping out of all the others. Every single one of them, eighteen, nineteen-year-old girls, each one oozing please-praise-me from their emaciated, emancipated pores. But not Martha Grace.

With Martha Grace Tim can rest. Maybe Martha Grace needs him, Tim cannot tell for certain. She likes him, he knows that.

Certainly she wants him, hungers for him. As he now knows he hungers for her. But if she needs him, it is only Tim that she needs. His body, his presence, his cock. She does not need his approval, his blessing, his constant, unending hymn of there-there. And maybe that is because he has none to give. She is fat. And old. And weird. What could he approve of? What is there to approve of? Nothing at all. They both know that. And so it is, that when Tim comes home to Martha, there is rest along with exertion. There is ease in the fucking. Martha Grace knows who she is, what she is. She demands nothing extra of him, what sanctions of beauty or thin-ness, or perfection could he give her anyway? She has none of those and so, as Tim acknowledges to himself in surprise and pleasure, she is easier to be with than the bone-stabbing stick figure girls at school. And softer. And wider. And more comfortable. It is better in that house, that bed, against that heavy body. Martha Grace is not eighteen, and a part of Tim Culver sits up shocked and amused – he realises he loves her for it. The rest of Tim Culver falls asleep, his heavy head on her fat breast. Martha Grace smells the other women in his hair.

One day Tim Culver brings Martha Grace a new treat. He knows of her appetite for food and drink and him, he understands her cravings and her ever-hungry mouth. He loves her ever-hungry mouth. He brings gifts from the big city, delicatessen offerings, imported chocolates and preserves. Wines and liquors. He has the money. He is not a poor student. Martha Grace sees to that. This time the home-from-college boy brings her a new gift. Martha Grace had tried marijuana years ago, it didn't suit her, she liked to feel in control, didn't understand the desire to take a drug that made one lose control, the opposite of her wanting. She has told Tim this, explained about her past experiences, how she came to be the woman she is today. Has shared with Tim each and every little step that took her from the wide open world to wide woman in a closed house. And he has nodded and understood. Or appeared to do so. At the very least he has listened, and that is new and precious to Martha. So she is willing to trust him. Scared but willing. And this time, Tim brings home cocaine. Martha is shocked and secretly delighted. But she is the older woman, he still just a student, she must maintain some degree of adult composure. She tells him to put it away, take it back to school, throw it out. Tells him off, delivers a sharp rebuke, a reprimand and then sends him to bed. Her bed. Tim walks upstairs smiling. He leaves the thin wrap on the hall table. Martha Grace watches him walk away, feels the smirk from the back of his head, threatens a slap which she knows he wants anyway. Her hand reaches out for the wrap. Such a small thing and so much fuss. She pictures the naked boy upstairs. Man. Young man. In her bed. Hears again the fuss she knows it would cause. Hears again as he calls her, taunting from the room above. She is hungry and wanting. Her soft hand closes around the narrow strip of folded paper and she follows his trail of clothes upstairs, clucking like a disparaging mother hen at the lack of tidiness, folding, putting away. Getting into bed, putting to rights.

Tim Culver lays out a long thin line on Martha Grace's heavy stomach. It wobbles as she breathes in, breathes out, the small ridge of cocaine mountain sited on her skin, creamy white avalanche grains tumbling with her sigh. He inhales cocaine and the clean, fleshy smell of Martha. And both are inspirations for him. Now her turn. She rolls the boy over on to his stomach, lays out an uncertain line from his low waist to the soft hairs at the curve of his arse. She is slow and deliberate, new to this, does not want to get it wrong. Tim is finding it hard to stay face down, wants to burrow himself into the flesh of Martha Grace, not the unyielding mattress. She lays her considerable weight out along his legs, hers dangling off the end of the bed, breasts to buttocks and inhales coke and boy and, not for the first time in her life, the thick iron smell of bloody desire. Then she reaches up to stretch herself out against him full length, all of her pressing down into all of him. The weight of her flesh against his back and legs has Tim Culver reaching for breath. He wonders if this is what it is like for the little girls he fucks at college. He a tall, strong young man and they small, brittle beneath him. At some point in the sex he always likes to lie on top. To feel himself above the young women, all of him stretched out against the twisted paper and bones of the young girl skin, narrow baby-woman hips jutting sharp into his abdomen, reminding him of what he has back at home, Martha waiting for the weekend return. He likes it when, breath forced from the thin lungs beneath him, they whisper the fuck in half-caught breaths. Tim has always been told it feels good, the heaviness, the warmth, the strong body laid out and crushing down, lip to lip, cock to cunt, tip to toe. He hopes it is like this for the narrow young women he lays on top of. Tim Culver likes this. He is surprised by the feeling, wonders if it is just the coke or the addition of physical pressure, Martha's wide weight gravity-heavy against his back, pushing his body down, spreading him out. Is wondering still when she slides her hand in between his legs and up to his cock. Is wondering no longer when he comes five minutes later, Martha still on his back, mouth to his neck, teeth to his tanned skin. Her strength, her weight, like no other female body he has felt. He thinks then for a brief moment about the gay boys he knows (barely, acquaintances), wonders if this is what it is like for them too. But wonders only briefly; momentary sex-sense identification with the thin young women is a far enough stretch for a nineteen-year-old small town boy.

They did not take cocaine together again. Martha liked it, but Martha would rather be truly in control than amphetamine-convinced by the semblance of control. Besides that, she had, as usual, prepared a post-sex snack for that afternoon. Glass of sweet dessert wine and rich cherry cake, the cherries individually pitted by her own fair, fat hands the evening before, left to soak in sloe gin all night, waiting for Tim's mouth to taste them, just as she was. But after the drugs and the sex and then some more of the bitter powder, neither had an appetite for food. They had each other and cocaine and then Tim left. Martha didn't eat until the evening, and alone, and cold. Coke headache dulling the tip of her left temple. She could cope with abandon. She could certainly enjoy a longer fuck, a seemingly more insatiable desire from the young man of her fantasies come true. She could, on certain and specified occasions, even put up with a ceding of power. But she would not again willingly submit to self-inflicted loss of appetite. That was just foolish.

It went on. Three months more, then six, another three. Seasons back to where they started. Tim Culver and Martha Grace. The mask of garden chores and DIY tasks, then the fucking and the feeding and the financial recompense. Then even, one late afternoon in winter, dark enough outside for both to kid themselves they had finally spent a night together, an admission of love. It comes first from Tim. Surprising himself. He's held it in all this time, found it hard to believe it was true, but knows the miracle fact as it falls from his gratified mouth:

"Martha, I love you."

Martha Grace smiles and nods.

"Tim, I love you."

Not 'back'. Or 'too'. Just love.

A month more. Tim Culver and Martha Grace loving. In love. Weekend adoration and perfect.

And then Martha thinks she will maybe pay him a visit. Tim always comes to her. She will go to his college. Surprise him. Take a picnic, all his favourite foods and her. Martha Grace's love in a basket. She packs a pie – tender beef and slow-cooked sweet onion, the chunky beef slightly bloody in the middle, just the way Tim likes it. New bread pitted with dark green olives, Tim's favourite. Fresh shortbread and strawberry tarts with imported out-of-season berries. A thermos of mulled wine, the herbs and spices her own blend from the dark cupboard beneath her stairs. She dresses carefully and wears lipstick, culled from the back of a drawer and an intentionally forgotten time of made-up past. Walks into town, camomile-washed hair flowing about her shoulders, head held high, best coat, pretty shoes – party shoes. Travels on the curious bus, catches a cab to the college.

And all the time Martha Grace knows better. Feels at the lowest slung centre of her belly the terror of what is to come. Doesn't know how she can do this even as she does it. Wants to turn back with every step, every mile. Knows in her head it can not be, in her stomach it will not work. But her stupid fat heart sends her stumbling forwards anyway. She climbs down from the bus and walks to the coffee shop he has mentioned. Where he sits with his friends, passing long slow afternoons of caffeine and chocolate and drawled confidences. He is not there and Martha Grace sits

alone at a corner table for an hour. Another. And then Tim Culver
arrives. With a gaggle of laughing others. He is brash and young.
Sits backwards across the saddle of his chair. Makes loud noises,
jokes, creates a rippling guffaw of youthful enjoyment all around
him. He does not notice Martha Grace sat alone in the corner, a
pale crumble of dried cappuccino froth at the corner of her mouth.
But eventually, one of his friends does. Points her out quietly to
another. There are sniggers, sideways glances. Martha Grace could
not be more aware of her prominence. But still she sits, knowing
better and hoping for more. Then Tim sees her, his attention
finally drawn from the wonder of himself to the absurdity of the fat
woman in the corner. And Tim looks up, directly at Martha Grace,
right into her pale grey eyes and he stands and he walks towards
her and his friends are staring after him, whooping and hollering,
catcalls and cheers, and then he has stopped by her table and he
sits beside Martha Grace and reaches towards her and touches
the line of her lips, moves in, licks away the dried milk crust. He
stands again, bows a serious little bow, and walks back to his table
of friends. Who stand and cheer and push forward the young girls
to kiss, pretty girls, thin girls. Tim Culver has kissed Martha Grace
in public and it has made him a hero. And made the fool of Martha
Grace. She tries to leave the café, tries to walk out unnoticed but
her bulk is stuck in the corner arrangement of too-small chairs and
shin-splitting low table, her feet clatter against a leaning tray, her
heavy arms and shaking hands cannot hold the hamper properly,
it falls to her feet and the food rolls out. Pie breaks open, chunks of
bloody meat spill across the floor, strawberries that were cool and
fresh are now hot and sweating, squashed beneath her painfully
pretty shoes as she runs from the room, every action a humiliation,

every second another pain. Eventually Martha Grace turns her great bulk at the coffee shop door and walks away down the street, biting the absurd lipstick from her stupid, stupid lips as she goes, desperate to break into a lumbering run, forcing her idiotic self to move slowly and deliberately through the pain. And all the way down the long street, surrounded by strangers and tourists and scrabbling children underfoot, she feels Tim's eyes boring into the searing blush on the back of her neck.

Neither mention the visit. The next weekend comes and goes. Martha is a little cool, somewhat distant. Tim hesitant, uncertain. Wondering whether to feel shame or guilt and then determining on neither when he sees Martha's fear that he might mention what has occurred. Both skirt around their usual routine, there are no jobs to be done, no passion to linger over, the sex is quick and not easy. Tim dresses in a hurry, Martha stays cat-curled in bed, face half-hidden beneath her pillow, she points to the notes on her dresser, Tim takes only half the cash. Pride hurt, vanity exposed, Martha promises herself she will get over it. Pick herself up, get on. Tim need never know how hurt she felt. How stupid she knows herself to have been. The weekend after will be better, she'll prepare a surprise for him, make a real treat, an offering to get things back to where they had been before. Then Martha Grace will be herself again.

Saturday morning and Martha Grace is preparing a special dish for Tim. She knows his taste. He likes berry fruits, loves chocolate like any young boy, though unlike most, Martha Grace has taught him the joy of real chocolate, dark and shocking. She will make him a deep tart of black berries and melted chunks of bitter chocolate, imported from France, ninety percent cocoa solids. She starts early in the day. Purest white flour mixed in the air as she sifts it with organic cocoa. Rich butter, light sugar, cool hands, extra egg to bind the mix. She leaves it in the fridge to chill, the ratio of flour to cocoa so perfect that her pastry is almost black. Then the fruit – blackberries, boysenberries, loganberries, blackcurrants – just simmered with fruit sugar and pure water over the lowest of heat for almost two hours until they are thick syrup and pulp. She skims the scum from the surface, at the very end throws in another handful. This fruit she does not name. These are the other berries she was taught to pick by her mother, in the fresh morning before sunlight has bruised the delicate skin. She leaves the thick fruit mix to cool. Melts the chocolate. Glistening rich black in the shallow pan. When it is viscous and runs slow from the back of her walnut spoon, she drops in warmed essences – almond, vanilla, and a third distilled flavour, stored still, a leftover from her grandmother's days, just in case, for a time of who-knows-and-maybe, hidden at the back of the dark cupboard beneath her stairs. She leaves the pan over hot water, bubbling softly in the cool of her morning kitchen. Lays the pastry out on the marble slab. Rolls it to paper fine. Folds it in on itself and starts again. Seven times more. Then she fits it to the baking dish, fluted edges, heavy base. She bakes the pastry blind and removes from the oven a crisp, dark shell. Pours in warm thick-liquid chocolate, sprinkles over a handful of flaked and toasted almonds, watches them sink into the quicksand black. Her mouth is watering with the heady rich aroma. She knows better than to lick her fingers. Tim Culver likes to lick her fingers. When the chocolate is almost cool, she beats three egg yolks and more sugar into the fruit mixture, pours it slowly over the chocolate, lifts the tart dish and ever so gently places it in the heated oven. She sits for ten minutes, twenty, thirty. She does not wash the dishes while she waits, or wipe flour from her hands, chocolate from her apron. She sits and waits and watches the clock. She cries, one slow fat tear every fifteen seconds. When there are one hundred and sixty tears the tart is done. She takes it from the oven and leaves it to cool. She goes to bed, folds into her own flesh and rocks herself to sleep.

When she wakes Martha checks the tart. It is cool and dark, lifts easily from the case, she sets it on a wide white plate and places it in the refrigerator beside a jug of thick cream. Then she begins to clean. The kitchen, the utensils, the shelves, the oven, the workbench, the floor. Takes herself to the bathroom, strips and places the clothes in a rubbish bag. Scrubs her body under a cold running shower, sand soap and nail brush. Every inch, every fold of flesh and skin. Martha Grace is red-raw clean. The clothes are burnt early that afternoon along with a pile of liquid maple leaves at the bottom of her garden, black skirt, red shirt and the garden matter in seasonal orange rush. Later she rakes over the hot embers, places her hand close to the centre, draws it back just too late, a blister already forming in the centre of her palm. It will do for a reminder. Martha Grace always draws back just too late.

Tim Culver knocks on her door at precisely three forty-five. She has spent a further hour preparing her body for his arrival, oiling and brushing and stroking. She is dressed in a soft black silk that flows over her curves and bulges, hiding some, accentuating others. She has let down her coarse grey hair, reddened her full lips, and has the faintest line of shadow around her pale grey eyes. Tim Culver smiles. Martha Grace is beautiful. He walks into the hall, hands her the thirty red roses he carried behind his back all the way down the street in case she was looking. She was looking. She laughs in delight at the gift, he kisses her and apologies and explanations spill from his mouth. They stumble up the stairs, carrying each other quickly to bed, words unimportant, truth and embarrassment and shame and guilt all gone, just the skin and the fucking and the wide fat flesh. They are so in love and Tim cries out, whimpering with delight at the touch of her yielding skin on his mouth, his chest, his cock. And Martha Grace shuts out all thoughts of past and present, crying only for the now.

When they are done, she takes Tim downstairs. Martha Grace in a light red robe, Tim Culver wrapped in a blanket against the seasonal chill. The curtains are drawn, blinds pulled, lights lowered. She sits the boy at her kitchen table and pours him a glass of wine. And another. She ask him about drugs and Tim is shocked and delighted, yes he does happen to have a wrap in the back pocket of his jeans. Don't worry, stay there, drink another glass. Martha will fetch the wrap. She brings it back to him, lays out the lines, takes in just one half to his every two. He does not question this, is simply pleased she wants to join him in this excess. There is more wine and wanting, cocaine and kissing, fucking on the kitchen table, falling to the just-scrubbed floor. Even with cocaine, the wine and the sex have made him hungry. Martha has a treat. A special tart she baked herself this morning. Pastry and everything. She reaches into the cool refrigerator and brings out her offering. His eyes grow wider at the sight of the plate, pupils dilate still further with spreading saliva in his hungry mouth. She cuts Tim a generous slice, spoons thick cream over it and reaches for a fork. The boy holds out his hand but she pushes it away. She wants to feed him. He wants to be fed.

Tim Culver takes it in. The richness, the darkness, the bitter chocolate and the tart fruit and the sweet syrup and the crisp pastry shell and the cool cream. Tim Culver takes it in and opens his mouth for more. Eyes closed to better savour the texture, the flavours, the glory of this woman spending all morning cooking for him, after what has happened, after how he has behaved. She must love him so much. She must love him as much as he loves her. He opens his eyes to kiss Martha Grace and sees her smiling across at him, another forkful offered, tears spilling down her fat cheeks. He pushes aside the fork and kisses the cheeks, sucks up her tears, promises adoration and apology and forever. Tim Culver is right about forever.

She feeds him half the black tart. He drinks another glass. Leaves a slurred message on a friend's telephone to say he is out with a girl, a babe, a doll. He is having too good a time. He probably won't make it tonight. He expects to stay over tonight. He says this looking at Martha, waiting to see her happiness at the thought that he will stay in her bed, will sleep beside her tonight. Martha Grace smiles an appropriate gratitude and Tim turns his phone off. Martha Grace did not want him to use hers. She said it would not do for his friend to call back on her number. Tim is touched she is thinking of his reputation even now.

She pours more wine. Tim does not see that he is drinking the whole bottle, Martha not at all. He inhales more coke. They fuck again. This time it is less simple. He cannot come. He cuts himself another slice of the tart, eats half, puts it down, gulps a mouthful of wine, licks his finger to wipe sticky crumbs of white powder from the wooden table. Tim Culver is confused. He is tired but wide awake. He is hungry but full. He is slowing-down drunk but wired too. He is in love with Martha Grace but despises both of them for it. He is alive, but only just.

Tim Culver dies of a heart attack. His young healthy heart cannot stand the strain of wine and drugs and fucking – and the special treat Martha had prepared. She pulls his jeans and shirt back on him, moves his body while it is still warm and pliable, lays him on a sheet of spread-out rubbish bags by her back door. She carries him out down the path by her back garden. He is big, but she is bigger, and necessity has made her strong. It is dark. There is no-one to see her stumble through the gate, down the alleyway. No one to see her leave the half-dressed body in the dark street. No one to see her gloved hands place the emptied wine bottles by his feet. By the time Martha Grace kisses his lips they are already cold. He smells of chocolate and wine and sex.

She goes home and for the second time that day, scrubs her kitchen clean. Then she sleeps alone, she will wash in the morning. For now the scent of Tim Culver in her sheets, her hair, her heavy flesh will be enough to keep her warm through the night.

Tim Culver was found the next morning. Cocaine and so much alcohol in his blood. His heart run to a standstill by the excess of youth. There was no point looking for anyone else to blame. No-one saw him stumble into the street. No-one noticed Martha Grace lumber away. His friends confirmed he'd been with a girl that night. The state of his semen-stained clothes confirmed he'd been with a girl that night. At least the police said girl to his parents, whispered whore among themselves. Just another small town boy turned bad by the lights and the nights of the bright city. Maybe further education isn't all it's cracked up to be.

No-one would ever think that Tim Culver's healthy, spent, virile young body could ever have had anything to do with an old witch like Martha Grace. As the whole town knows, the fat bitch is a dyke anyway.

A season or two later and Martha Grace is herself again. Back to where she was before Tim Culver. Back to who she was before Tim Culver. Lives alone, speaks rarely to strangers, pleases only herself. Pleasures only herself. And lives happily enough most of the time. Remembering to cry only when she recalls a time that once reached beyond enough.

THE WEEKENDER

JEFFERY DEAVER

The night went bad fast.

I looked in the rearview mirror and didn't see any lights but I knew they were after us and it was only a matter of time till I'd see the flashers.

Toth started to talk but I told him to shut up and got the Buick up to eighty. The road was empty, nothing but pine trees for miles around.

"Oh, brother," Toth muttered. I felt his eyes on me but I didn't even want to look at him, I was so mad.

They were never easy, drugstores.

Because, just watch sometime, when cops make their rounds they cruise drugstores more often than anyplace else. Because of the perco and Valium and the other drugs. You know.

You'd think they'd stake out convenience stores. But those're a joke and with the closed-circuit TV you're going to get your picture took, you just are. So nobody who knows the business, I mean really *knows* it, hits them. And banks, forget banks. Even ATMs.

I mean, how much can you clear? Three, four hundred tops? And around here the "Fast Cash" button gives you twenty only. Which tells you something. So why even bother?

No. We wanted cash and that meant a drugstore, even though they can be tricky. Ardmore Drugs. Which is a big store in a little town. Liggett Falls. Sixty miles from Albany and a hundred or so from where Toth and me lived, farther west into the mountains. Liggett Falls's a poor place. You'd think it wouldn't make sense to hit a store there. But that's exactly why—because like everywhere else, people there need medicine and hair spray and makeup, only they don't have credit cards. Except maybe a Sears or Penney's. So they pay cash.

"Oh, brother," Toth whispered again. "Look."

And he made me even madder, him saying that. I wanted to shout look at what, you son of a bitch? But then I could see what he was talking about and I didn't say anything. Up ahead. It was like just before dawn, light on the horizon. Only this was red and the light wasn't steady. It was like it was pulsing and I knew that they'd got the roadblock up already. This was the only road to the interstate from Liggett Falls. So I should've guessed.

"I got an idea," Toth said. Which I didn't want to hear but I also wasn't going to go through another shootout. Surely not at a roadblock, where they was ready for us.

"What?" I snapped.

"There's a town over there. See those lights? I know a road'll take us there."

Toth's a big guy and he looks calm. Only he isn't really. He gets shook easy and he now kept turning around, skittish, looking in the backseat. I wanted to slap him and tell him to chill.

"Where's it?" I asked. "This town?"

"About four, five miles. The turnoff, it ain't marked. But I know it."

This was that lousy upstate area where everything's green. But dirty green, you know. And all the buildings're gray. These gross little shacks, pickups on blocks. Little towns without even a 7-Eleven. And full of hills they call mountains but aren't.

Toth cranked down the window and let this cold air in and looked up at the sky. "They can find us with those, you know, satellite things."

"What're you talking about?"

"You know, they can see you from miles up. I saw it in a movie."

"You think the state cops do that? Are you nuts?"

This guy, I don't know why I work with him. And after what happened at the drugstore, I won't again.

He pointed out where to turn and I did. He said the town was at the base of the Lookout. Well, I remembered passing that on the way to Liggett Falls this afternoon. It was this huge rock a couple hundred feet high. Which if you looked at it right looked like a man's head, like a profile, squinting. It'd been some kind of big deal to the Indians around here. Blah, blah, blah. He told me but I didn't pay no attention. It was spooky, that weird face, and I looked once and kept on driving. I didn't like it. I'm not really superstitious but sometimes I am.

"Winchester," he said now, meaning what the name of the town was. Five, six thousand people. We could find an empty house, stash the car in a garage and just wait out the search. Wait till tomorrow afternoon—Sunday—when all the weekenders were driving back to Boston and New York and we'd be lost in the crowd.

I could see the Lookout up ahead, not really a shape, mostly this blackness where the stars weren't. And then the guy on the floor in the back started to moan all of a sudden and just about give me a heart attack.

"You. Shut up back there." I slapped the seat and the guy in the back went quiet.

What a night…

We'd got to the drugstore fifteen minutes before it closed. Like you ought to do. 'Cause mosta the customers're gone and a lot've the clerks've left and people're tired and when you push a Glock or Smitty into their faces they'll do just about anything you ask.

Except tonight.

We had our masks down and walked in slow, Toth getting the manager out of his little office, a fat guy who started crying and that made me mad, a grown man doing that. Toth kept a gun on the customers and the clerks and I was telling the cashier, this kid, to open the tills and, Jesus, he had an attitude. Like he'd seen all of those Steven Seagal movies or something. A little kiss on the cheek with the Smitty and he changed his mind and started moving. Cussing me out but he was moving. I was counting the bucks as we were going along from one till to the next and sure enough we were up to about three thousand when I heard this noise and turned around and, what it was, Toth was knocking over a rack of chips. I mean, Jesus. He's getting Doritos!

I look away from the kid for just a second and what's he do? He pitches this bottle. Only not at me. Out the window. Bang, it breaks. There's no alarm I can hear but half of them are silent anyway and I'm really pissed. I could've killed him. Right there.

Only I didn't. Toth did.

He shoots the kid, bang, bang… Shit. And everybody else is scattering and he turns around and shoots another one of the clerks and a customer, just blam, not thinking or nothing. Just for no reason. Hit this girl clerk in the leg but this guy, this customer, well, he was dead. You could see. And I'm going, "What're you doing, what're you doing?" And he's going, "Shut up, shut up, shut up…" And we're like we're swearing at each other when we figured out we hadta get outa there.

So we left. Only what happens is, there's a cop outside. That's why the kid threw the bottle, to get his attention. And he's outa his car. So we grab another customer, this guy by the door, and we use him like a shield and get outside. And there's the cop, he's holding his gun up, looking at the customer we've got, and the cop, he's saying, It's okay, it's okay, just take it easy.

And I couldn't believe it, Toth shot him too. I don't know whether he killed him but there was blood so he wasn't wearing a vest, it didn't look like, and I could've killed Toth there on the spot. Because why'd he do that? He didn't have to.

We threw the guy, the customer, into the backseat and tied him up with tape. I kicked out the taillights and burned rubber outa there. We made it out of Liggett Falls.

That was all just a half hour ago but it seemed like weeks. And now we were driving down this highway through a million pine trees. Heading right for the Lookout.

Winchester was dark.

I don't get why weekenders come to places like this. I mean, my old man took me hunting a long time ago. A couple times and I liked it. But coming to places like this just to look at leaves and buy furniture they call antiques but's really just busted-up crap… I don't know.

We found a house a block off Main Street with a bunch of newspapers in front and I pulled into the drive and put the Buick behind the place just in time. Two state police cars went shooting by. They'd been behind us not more than a half mile, without the lightbars going. Only they hadn't seen us 'causa the broke taillights and they went by in a flash and were gone, going to downtown.

Toth got into the house and he wasn't very clean about it, breaking a window in the back. It was a vacation place, pretty empty, and the refrigerator was shut off and the phone too, which was a good sign— there wasn't anybody coming back soon. Also, it smelled pretty musty and had stacks of old books and magazines from the summer.

We brought the guy inside and Toth started to take the hood off this guy's head and I said, "What the hell're you doing?"

"He hasn't said anything. Maybe he can't breathe."

This was a man talking who'd just laid a cap on three people back there and he was worried about this guy *breathing*? Man. I just laughed. Disgusted laughing, I mean. "Like maybe we don't want him to *see* us?" I said. "You think of that?" See, we weren't wearing our ski masks anymore.

It's scary when you have to remind people of stuff like that. I was thinking Toth knew better. But you never know.

I went to the window and saw another squad car go past. They were going slower now. They do that. After like the first shock, after the rush, they get smart and start cruising slow, really looking for what's funny—what's *different*, you know? That's why I didn't take the papers up from the front yard. Which would've been different than how the yard looked that morning. Cops really do that Colombo stuff. I could write a book about cops.

"Why'd you do it?"

It was the guy we took.

"Why?" he whispered again.

The customer. He had a low voice and it sounded pretty calm, I mean considering. I'll tell you, the first time I was in a shootout I was totally freaked for a day afterwards. And I had a gun.

I looked him over. He was wearing a plaid shirt and jeans. But he wasn't a local. I could tell because of the shoes. They were rich-boy shoes, the kind you see all the Yuppies wear. I couldn't see his face because of the mask but I pretty much remembered it. He wasn't young. Maybe in his forties. Kind of wrinkled skin. And he was skinny too. Skinnier'n me and I'm one of those people can eat what I want and I don't get fat. I don't know why. It just works that way.

"Quiet," I said. There was another car going by.

He laughed. Soft. Like he was saying, What? You think they can hear me all the way outside?

Kind of laughing *at* me, you know? I didn't like that at all.

And, sure, I guess you *couldn't* hear anything out there but I didn't like him giving me any crap so I said, "Just shut up. I don't want to hear your voice."

He did for a minute and just sat back in the chair where Toth put him. But then he said again, "Why'd you shoot them? You didn't have to."

"Quiet!"

"Just tell me why."

I took out my knife and snapped that sucker open then threw it down so it stuck in a tabletop. Sort of a *thunk* sound. "You hear that? That was a eight-inch Buck knife. Carbon-tempered. With a locking blade. It'd cut clean through a metal bolt. So you be quiet. Or I'll use it on you."

And he gave this laugh again. Maybe. Or it was just a snort of air. But I was thinking it was a laugh. I wanted to ask him what he meant by it but I didn't.

"You got any money on you?" Toth asked and pulled the wallet out of the guy's back pocket. "Lookit." He pulled out what must've been five or six hundred. Man.

Another squad car went past, moving slow. It had a spotlight and the cop turned it on the driveway but he just kept going. I heard a siren across town. And another one too. It was a weird feeling, knowing those people were out there looking for us.

I took the wallet from Toth and looked through it.

Randall C. Weller, Jr. He lived in Connecticut. A weekender. Just like I thought. He had a bunch of business cards that said he was vice president of this big computer company. One that was in the news, trying to take over IBM or something. All of a sudden I had this thought. We could hold him for ransom. I mean, why not? Make a half million. Maybe more.

"My wife and kids'll be sick, worrying," Weller said. It spooked me, hearing that. 'Cause there I was, looking right at a picture in his wallet. And what was it of? His wife and kids.

"I ain't letting you go. Now, just shut up. I may need you."

"Like a hostage, you mean? That's only in the movies. They'll shoot you when you walk out and they'll shoot me too if they have to. That's the way the cops do it in real life. Just give yourself up. At least you'll save your life."

"Shut up!" I shouted.

"Let me go and I'll tell them you treated me fine. That the shooting was a mistake. It wasn't your fault."

I leaned forward and pushed the knife against his throat, not the blade 'cause that's real sharp but the blunt edge, and I told him to be quiet.

Another car went past, no light this time but it was going slower, and all of a sudden I got to thinking what if they do a door-to-door search?

"Why did he do it? Why'd he kill them?"

And funny, the way he said *he* made me feel a little better 'cause it was like he didn't blame me for it. I mean, it *was* Toth's fault. Not mine.

Weller kept going. "I don't get it. That man by the counter? The tall one. He was just standing there. He didn't do anything. He just shot him down."

But neither of us said nothing. Probably Toth, because he didn't know why he'd shot them. And me, because I didn't owe this guy any answers. I had him in my hand. Completely, and I had to let him know that. I didn't *have* to talk to him.

But the guy, Weller, he didn't say anything else. And I got this weird feeling. Like this pressure building up. You know, because nobody was answering his damn, stupid question. I felt this urge to say something. Anything. And that was the last thing I wanted to do. So I said, "I'm gonna move the car into the garage." And I went outside to do it.

I looked around the garage to see if there was anything worth taking and there wasn't except a Snapper lawn mower but how do you fence one of those? So I drove the Buick inside and closed the door. And went back into the house.

And then I couldn't believe what happened. I mean, Jesus. When I walked into the living room the first thing I heard was Toth saying, "No way, man. I'm not snitching on Jack Prescot."

I just stood there. And you should've seen the look on his face. He knew he'd blown it big.

Now this Weller guy knew my name.

I didn't say anything. I didn't have to. Toth started talking real fast and nervous. "He said he'd pay me some big bucks to let him go." Trying to turn it around, make it Weller's fault. "I mean I wasn't going to. I wasn't even thinking 'bout it, man. I told him forget it."

"But what's with tellin' him my name?"

"I don't know, man. He confused me. I wasn't thinking." I'll say he wasn't. He hadn't been thinking all night.

I sighed to let him know I wasn't happy but I just clapped him on the shoulder. "Okay," I said. "S'been a long night. These things happen."

"I'm sorry, man. Really."

"Yeah. Maybe you better go spend the night in the garage or something. Or upstairs. I don't want to see you around for a while."

"Sure."

And the funny thing was, just then, Weller gave this little snicker or something. Like he knew what was coming. How'd he know that? I wondered.

Toth went to pick up a couple magazines and the knapsack with his gun in it and extra rounds.

Normally, killing somebody with a knife is a hard thing to do. I say *normally* even though I've only done it one other time. But I remember it and it was messy and hard work. But tonight, I don't know, I was all filled up with this... *feeling* from the drugstore. Mad. I mean, really. Crazy too a little. And as soon as Toth turned his back I got him around the neck and went to work and it wasn't three minutes later it was over. I drug his body behind the couch and then—why not—pulled Weller's hood off. He already knew my name. He might as well see my face.

He was a dead man. We both knew it.

"You were thinking of holding me for ransom, right?"

I stood at the window and looked out. Another cop car went past and there were more flashing lights bouncing off the low clouds and off the face of the Lookout, right over our heads.

Weller had a thin face and short hair, cut real neat. He looked like every ass-kissing businessman I ever met. His eyes were dark and calm like his voice and it made me even madder he wasn't shook up looking at that big bloodstain on the rug and floor.

"No," I told him.

He looked at the pile of all the stuff I'd taken from his wallet and kept going like I hadn't said anything. "It won't work. A kidnapping. I don't have a lot of money and if you saw my business card and're thinking I'm an executive at the company, they have about five hundred vice presidents. They won't pay diddly for me. And you see those kids in the picture? It was taken twelve years ago. They're both in college now. I'm paying major tuition."

"Where," I asked, sneering. "Harvard?"

"One's at Harvard," he said, like he was snapping at me. "And one's at Northwestern. So the house's mortgaged to the hilt. Besides, kidnapping somebody by yourself? No, you couldn't bring that off."

He saw the way I looked at him and he said, "I don't mean you personally, Jack. I mean somebody by himself. You'd need partners."

And I figured he was right.

That silence again. Nobody saying nothing and it was like the room was filling up with cold water. I walked to the window and the floors creaked under my feet and that only made things worse. I remember one time my dad said that a house had a voice of its own and some houses were laughing houses and some were forlorn. Well, this was a forlorn house. Yeah, it was modern and clean and the *National Geographics* were all in order but it was still forlorn.

Just when I felt like shouting because of the tension Weller said, "I don't want you to kill me."

"Who said I was going to kill you?"

He gave me his funny little smile. "I've been a salesman for twenty-five years. I've sold pets and Cadillacs and typesetters and lately I've been selling mainframe computers. I know when I'm being handed a line. You're going to kill me. It was the first thing you thought of when you heard him"—nodding toward Toth— "say your name."

I just laughed at him. "Well, that's a damn handy thing to be, sorta a walking lie detector," I said and I was being sarcastic.

But he just said, "Damn handy," like he was agreeing with me.

"I don't want to kill you."

"Oh, I know you don't *want* to. You didn't want your friend to kill anybody back there at the drugstore either. I could see that. But people *got* killed and that ups the stakes. Right?"

And those eyes of his, they just dug into me and I couldn't say anything.

"But," he said, "I'm going to talk you out of it."

He sounded real certain and that made me feel better. 'Cause I'd rather kill a cocky son of a bitch than a pathetic one. And so I laughed. "Talk me out of it?"

"I'm going to try."

"Yeah? How you gonna do that?"

Weller cleared his throat a little. "First, let's get everything on the table. I've seen your face and I know your name. Jack Prescot. Right? You're, what? About five-nine, a hundred fifty pounds, black hair. So you've got to assume I can identify you. I'm not going to play any games and say I didn't see you clearly or hear who you were. Or anything like that. We all squared away on that, Jack?"

I nodded, rolling my eyes like this was all a load of crap. But I gotta admit I was kinda curious what he had to say.

"My promise," he said, "is that I won't turn you in. Not under any circumstances. The police'll never learn your name from me. Or your description. I'll never testify against you."

Sounding honest as a priest. Real slick delivery. Well, he *was* a salesman and I wasn't going to buy it. But he didn't know I was on to him. Let him give me his pitch, let him think I was going along. When it came down to it, after we'd got away and were somewhere in the woods upstate, I'd want him relaxed. No screaming, no hassles. Just a couple fast cuts or shots and that'd be it.

"You understand what I'm saying?"

I tried to look serious and said, "Sure. You're thinking you can talk me out of killing you. You've got reasons why I shouldn't?"

"Oh, I've got reasons, you bet. One in particular. One that you can't argue with."

"Yeah? What's that?"

"I'll get to it in a minute. Let me tell you some of the practical reasons you should let me go. First, you think you've got to kill me because I know who you are, right? Well, how long you think your identity's going to be a secret? Your buddy shot a cop back there. I don't know police stuff except what I see in the movies. But they're going to be looking at tire tracks and witnesses who saw plates and makes of cars and gas stations you might've stopped at on the way here."

He was just blowing smoke. The Buick was stolen. I mean, I'm not stupid.

But he went on, looking at me real coy. "Even if your car was stolen they're going to check down every lead. Every shoe print around where you or your friend stole it, talk to everybody in the area around the time it vanished."

I kept smiling like it was nuts what he was saying. But this was true, the shooting-the-cop part. You do that and you're in big trouble. Trouble that sticks with you. They don't stop looking till they find you.

"And when they identify your buddy," he nodded toward the couch where Toth's body was lying, "they're going to make some connection to you."

"I don't know him that good. We just hung around together the past few months."

Weller jumped on this. "Where? A bar? A restaurant? Anybody *ever* see you in public?"

I got mad and I shouted, "So? What're you saying? They gonna bust me anyway then I'll just take you out with me. How's *that* for an argument?"

Calm as could be he said, "I'm simply telling you that one of the reasons you want to kill me doesn't make sense. And think about this—the shooting at the drugstore? It wasn't premeditated. It was, what do they call it? Heat of passion. But you kill me, that'll be first-degree. You'll get the death penalty when they find you."

When they find you. Right, I laughed to myself. Oh, what he said made sense but the fact is, killing isn't a making-sense kind of thing. Hell, it *never* makes sense but sometimes you just have to do it. But I was kind of having fun now. I wanted to argue back. "Yeah, well, I killed Toth. That wasn't heat of passion. I'm going to get the needle anyway for that."

"But nobody gives a damn about him," he came right back. "They don't care if he killed *himself* or got hit by a car. You can take that piece of garbage out of the equation altogether. They care if you kill *me*. I'm the 'Innocent Bystander' in the headlines. I'm the 'Father of Two.' You kill me you're as good as dead."

I started to say something but he kept going.

"Now here's another reason I'm not going to say anything about you. Because you know my name and you know where I live. You know I have a family and you know how important they are to me. If I turn you in you could come after us. I'd never jeopardize my family that way. Now, let me ask you something. What's the worst thing that could happen to you?"

"Keep listening to you spout on and on."

Weller laughed at that. I could see he was surprised I had a sense of humor. After a minute he said, "Seriously. The worst thing."

"I don't know. I never thought about it."

"Lose a leg? Go deaf? Lose all your money? Go blind?… Hey, that looked like it hit a nerve. Going blind?"

"Yeah, I guess. That'd be the worst thing I could think of."

That *was* a pretty damn scary thing and I'd thought on it before. 'Cause that was what happened to my old man. And it wasn't not seeing anymore that got to me. No, it was that I'd have to depend on somebody else for… Christ, for everything, I guess.

"Okay, think about this," he said. "The way you feel about going blind's the way my family'd feel if they lost me. It'd be that bad for them. You don't want to cause them that kind of pain, do you?"

I didn't want to, no. But I knew I *had* to. I didn't want to think about it anymore. I asked him, "So what's this last reason you're telling me about?"

"The last reason," he said, kind of whispering. But he didn't go on. He looked around the room, you know, like his mind was someplace else.

"Yeah?" I asked. I was pretty curious. "Tell me."

But he just asked, "You think these people, they have a bar?"

And I'd just been thinking I could use a drink too. I went into the kitchen and of course they didn't have any beer in the fridge on account of the house being all closed up and the power off. But they did have scotch and that'd be my first choice anyway.

I got a couple glasses and took the bottle back to the living room. Thinking this was a good idea. When it came time to do it it'd be easier for him and for me both if we were kinda tanked. I shoved my Smitty into his neck and cut the tape his hands were tied with then taped them in front of him. I sat back and kept my knife near, ready to go, in case he tried something. But it didn't look like he was going to do anything. He read over the scotch bottle, kind of disappointed it was cheap. And I agreed with him there. One thing I learned a long time ago, you going to rob, rob rich.

I sat back where I could keep an eye on him.

"The last reason. Okay, I'll tell you. I'm going to *prove* to you that you should let me go."

"You are?"

"All those other reasons—the practical ones, the humanitarian ones… I'll concede you don't care much about those—you don't look very convinced. All right? Then let's look at the one reason you should let me go."

I figured this was going to be more crap. But what he said was something I never would've expected.

"You should let me go for your own sake."

"For me? What're you talking about?"

"See, Jack, I don't think you're lost."

"Whatta you mean, lost?"

"I don't think your soul's beyond redemption."

I laughed at this, laughed out loud, because I just *had* to. I expected a hell of a lot better from a hotshot vice-president salesman like him. "Soul? You think I got a soul?"

"Well, everybody has a soul," he said, and what was crazy was he said it like he was surprised that I didn't think so. It was like I'd said wait a minute, you mean the earth ain't flat? Or something.

"Well, if I got a soul it's taken the fast lane to hell." Which was this line I heard in this movie and I tried to laugh but it sounded flat. Like Weller was saying something deep and I was just kidding around. It made me feel cheap. I stopped smiling and looked down at Toth, lying there in the corner, those dead eyes of his just staring, staring, and I wanted to stab him again I was so mad.

"We're talking about your soul."

I snickered and sipped the liquor. "Oh, yeah, I'll bet you're the sort that reads those angel books they got all over the place now."

"I go to church but, no, I'm not talking about all that silly crap. I don't mean magic. I mean your conscience. What Jack Prescot's all about."

I could tell him about social workers and youth counselors and all those guys who don't know nothing about the way life works. They think they do. But it's the words they use. You can tell they don't know a thing. Some counselors or somebody'll talk to me and they say, Oh, you're maladjusted, you're denying your anger, things like that. When I hear that, I know they don't know nothing about souls or spirits.

"Not the afterlife," Weller was going on. "Not morality. I'm talking about life here on earth that's important. Oh, sure, you look skeptical. But listen to me . I really believe if you have a connection with somebody, if you trust them, if you have faith in them, then there's hope for you."

"Hope? What's that mean? Hope for what?"

"That you'll become a real human being. Lead a real life."

Real… I didn't know what he meant but he said it like what he was saying was so clear that I'd have to be an idiot to miss it. So I didn't say nothing.

He kept going. "Oh, there're reasons to steal and there're reasons to kill. But on the whole, don't you really think it's better not to? Just think about it: Why do we put people in jail if it's all right for them to murder? Not just us but all societies."

"So, what? Ooooo, I'm gonna give up my evil ways?"

And he just lifted his eyebrow and said, "Maybe. Tell me, Jack, how'd you feel when your buddy—what's his name?"

"Joe Roy Toth."

"Toth. When he shot that customer by the counter? How'd you feel?"

"I don't know."

"He just turned around and shot him. For no reason. You knew that wasn't right, didn't you?" And I started to say something. But he said, "No, don't answer me. You'd be inclined to lie. And that's all right. It's an instinct in your line of work. But I don't want you *believing* any lies you tell me. Okay? I want you to look into your heart and tell me if you didn't think something was real wrong about what Toth did. Think about that, Jack. You knew something wasn't right."

All right, I did. But who wouldn't? Toth screwed everything up. Everything went sour. And it was all his fault.

"It dug at you, right, Jack? You wished he hadn't done it."

I didn't say nothing but just drank some more scotch and looked out the window and watched the flashing lights around the town. Sometimes they seemed close and sometimes they seemed far away.

"If I let you go you'll tell 'em about me."

Like everybody else. They all betrayed me. My father—even after he went blind, the son of a bitch turned me in. My first PO, the judges. Sandra. My boss, the one I knifed.

"No, I won't," Weller said. "We're talking about an agreement. I don't break deals. I promised I won't tell a soul about you, Jack. Not even my wife." He leaned forward, cupping the booze between his hands. "You let me go, it'll mean all the difference in the world to *you*. It'll mean that you're not hopeless. I guarantee your life'll be different. That one act—letting me go—it'll change you forever. Oh, maybe not this year. Or for five years. But you'll come around. You'll give up all this, everything that happened back there in Liggett Falls. All the crime, the killing. You'll come around. I know you will."

"You just expect me to believe you won't tell anybody?"

"Ah," Weller said and lifted his bound-up hands to drink more scotch. "Now we get down to the big issue."

Again, that silence and finally I said, "And what's that?"

"Faith."

There was this burst of siren outside, real near, and I told him to shut up and pushed the gun against his head. His hands were shaking but he didn't do anything stupid and a few minutes later, after I sat back, he started talking again. "Faith. That's what I'm talking about. A man who has faith is somebody who can be saved."

"Well, I don't have any goddamn faith," I told him.

But he kept right on talking. "If you believe in another human being you have faith."

"Why the hell do you care whether I'm saved or not?"

"Because life's hard and people're cruel. I told you I'm a churchgoer. A lot of the Bible's crazy. But some of it I believe. And one of the things I believe is that sometimes we're put in these situations to make a difference. I think that's what happened tonight. That's why you and I both happened to be at the drugstore at the same time. You've felt that, haven't you? Like an omen? Like something happens and is telling you you ought to do this or shouldn't do that."

Which was weird 'cause the whole time we were driving up to Liggett Falls, I kept thinking something funny's going on. I don't know what it is but this job's gonna be different.

"What if," he said, "everything tonight happened for a purpose? My wife had a cold so I went to buy NyQuil. I went to that drugstore instead of 7-Eleven to save a buck or two. You happened to hit that store at just that time. You happened to have your buddy"—he nodded toward Toth's body "with you. The cop car just happened by at that particular moment. And the clerk behind the counter just happened to see him. That's a lot of coincidences. Don't you think?"

And then—this sent a damn chill right down my spine—he said, "Here we are in the shadow of that big rock, that face."

Which is one hundred percent what I was thinking. *Exactly* the same—about the Lookout, I mean. I don't know why I was. But I happened to be looking out the window and thinking about it at that exact same instant. I tossed back the scotch and had another and, oh, man, I was pretty freaked out.

"Like he's looking at us, waiting for you to make a decision. Oh, don't think it was just you, though. Maybe the purpose was to affect everybody's life there. That customer at the counter your friend shot? Maybe it was just his time to go—fast, you know, before he got cancer or had a stroke. Maybe that girl, the clerk, had to get shot in the leg so she'd get her life together, maybe get off drugs or give up drinking."

"And you? What about you?"

"Well, I'll tell you about me. Maybe you're the good deed in *my* life. I've spent years thinking only about making money. Take a look at my wallet. There. In the back."

I pulled it open. There were a half dozen of these little cards, like certificates. *Randall Weller—Salesman of the Year. Exceeded Target Two Years Straight. Best Salesman of 1992.*

Weller kept going. "There are plenty of others back in my office. And trophies too. And in order for me to win those I've had to neglect people. My family and friends. People who could maybe use my help. And that's not right. Maybe you kidnapping me, it's one of those signs to make me turn my life around."

The funny thing was, this made sense. Oh, it was hard to imagine not doing heists. And I couldn't see myself, if it came down to a fight, not going for my Buck or my Smitty to take the other guy out. That turning the other cheek stuff, that's only for losers. But maybe I *could* see a day when my life'd be just straight time. Living with some woman, maybe a wife, and not treating her the way I'd treated Sandra, living in a house. Doing what my father and mother, whatever she was like, never did.

"If I was to let you go," I said, "you'd have to tell 'em something."

He shrugged. "I'll say you locked me in the trunk and then tossed me out somewhere near here. I wandered around, looking for a house or something, and got lost. It could take me a day to find somebody. That's believable."

"Or you could flag down a car in an hour."

"I could. But I won't."

"You keep saying that. But how do I *know*?"

"That's the faith part. You don't know. No guarantees."

"Well, I guess I don't have any faith."

"Then *I'm* dead. And *your* life's never gonna change. End of story." He sat back and shrugged.

That silence again but it was like it was really this roar all around us. "You just want… What do you want?"

He drank more scotch. "Here's a proposal. Let me walk outside."

"Oh, right. Just let you stroll out for some fresh air or something?"

"Let me walk outside and I promise you I'll walk right back in again."

"Like a test?"

He thought about this for a second. "Yeah. A test."

"Where's this faith you're talking about? You walk outside, you try to run and I'd shoot you in the back."

"No, what you do is you put the gun someplace in the house. The kitchen or someplace. Somewhere you couldn't get it if I ran.

You stand at the window, where we can see each other. And I'll tell you up front I can run like the wind. I was lettered track and field in college and I still jog every day of the year."

"You know if you run and bring the cops back it's all gonna get bloody. I'll kill the first five troopers come through that door. Nothing'll stop me and that blood'll be on your hands."

"Of course I know that," he said. "But if this's going to work you can't think that way. You've got to assume the worst is going to happen. That if I run I'll tell the cops everything. Where you are and that there're no hostages here and that you've only got one or two guns. And they're going to come in and blow you to hell. And you're not going to take a single one down with you. You're going to die and die painfully 'cause of a few lousy bucks. But, but, but…" He held up his hands and stopped me from saying anything. "You gotta understand, faith means risk."

"That's stupid."

"I think it's just the opposite. It'd be the smartest thing you'd ever do in your life."

I tossed back another scotch and had to think about this.

Weller said, "I can see it there already. Some of that faith. It's there. Not a lot. But some."

And yeah, maybe there was a little. 'Cause I was thinking about how mad I got at Toth and the way he ruined everything. I didn't want anybody to get killed tonight. I *was* sick of it. Sick of the way my life had gone. Sometimes it was good, being alone and all. Not answering to anybody. But sometimes it was real bad. And this guy Weller, it was like he was showing me something different.

"So," I said. "You just want me to put the gun down?"

149

He looked around. "Put it in the kitchen. You stand in the doorway or window. All I'm gonna do is walk down to the street and walk back."

I looked out the window. It was maybe fifty feet down the driveway. There were these bushes on either side of it. He could just take off and I'd never find him.

All through the sky I could see police-car lights flickering.

"Naw, I ain't gonna. You're nuts."

I expected begging or something. Or him getting pissed off more likely—which is what happens to me when people don't do what I tell them. Or don't do it fast enough. But, naw, he just nodded. "Okay, Jack. You thought about it. That's a good thing. You're not ready yet. I respect that." He sipped a little more scotch, looking at the glass. And that was the end of it.

Then all of a sudden these searchlights started up. They was some ways away but I still got spooked and backed away from the window. Pulled my gun out. Only then I saw that it wasn't nothing to do with the robbery. It was just a couple big spotlights shining on the Lookout. They must've gone on every night, this time.

I looked up at it. From here it didn't look like a face at all. It was just a rock. Gray and brown and these funny pine trees growing sideways out of cracks.

Watching it for a minute or two. Looking out over the town. And something that guy was saying went into my head. Not the words, really. Just the *thought*. And I was thinking about everybody in that town. Leading normal lives. There was a church steeple and the roofs of small houses. A lot of little yellow lights in town. You could just make out the hills in the distance. And I wished for a minute I was in one of them houses. Sitting there. Watching TV with a wife next to me.

I turned back from the window and I said, "You'd just walk down to the road and back? That's it?"

"That's all. I won't run off, you don't go get your gun. We trust each other. What could be simpler?"

Listening to the wind. Not strong but a steady hiss that was comforting in a funny way even though any other time I'da thought it sounded cold and raw. It was like I heard a voice. I don't know. Something in me said I oughta do this.

I didn't say nothing else 'cause I was right on the edge and I was afraid he'd say something that'd make me change my mind. I just took the Smith & Wesson and looked at it for a minute then went and put it on the kitchen table. I came back with the Buck and cut his feet free. Then I figured if I was going to do it I oughta go all the way. So I cut his hands free too. Weller seemed surprised I did that. But he smiled like he knew I was playing the game. I pulled him to his feet and held the blade to his neck and took him to the door.

"You're doing a good thing," he said.

I was thinking: Oh, man. I can't believe this. It's crazy. Part of me said, Cut him now, cut his throat. Do it!

But I didn't. I opened the door and smelled cold fall air and wood smoke and pine and I heard the wind in the rocks and trees above our head.

"Go on," I told him.

Weller started off and he didn't look back to check on me, see if I went to get the gun… faith, I guess. He kept walking real slow down toward the road.

I felt funny, I'll tell you, and a couple times when he went past some real shadowy places in the driveway and could disappear I was like, Oh, man, this is all messed up. I'm crazy.

I almost panicked a few times and bolted for the Smitty but I didn't. When Weller got down near the sidewalk I was actually holding my breath. I expected him to go, I really did. I was looking for that moment—when people tense up, when they're gonna swing or draw down on you or bolt. It's like their bodies're shouting what they're going to be doing before they do it. Only Weller wasn't doing none of that. He walked down to the sidewalk real casual. And he turned and looked up at the face of the Lookout, like he was just another weekender.

Then he turned around. He nodded at me.

Which is when the cop car came by.

It was a state trooper. Those're the dark ones and he didn't have the light bar going. So he was almost here before I knew it. I guess I was looking at Weller so hard I didn't see nothing else.

There it was, two doors away, and Weller saw it the same time I did.

And I thought: That's it. Oh, hell.

But when I was turning to get the gun I saw this motion down by the road. And I stopped cold.

Could you believe it? Weller'd dropped onto the ground and rolled underneath a tree. I closed the door real fast and watched from the window. The trooper stopped and turned his light on the driveway. The beam—it was real bright—it moved up and down and hit all the bushes and the front of the house then back to the road. But it was like Weller was digging down into the pine needles to keep from being seen. I mean, he was *hiding* from those sons of bitches. Doing whatever he could to stay out of the way of the light.

Then the car moved on and I saw the lights checking out the house next door and then it was gone. I kept my eyes on Weller the whole time and he didn't do nothing stupid. I seen him climb out from under the trees and dust himself off. Then he came walking back to the house. Easy, like he was walking to a bar to meet some buddies.

He came inside. Gave this little sigh, like relief. And laughed. Then he held his hands out. I didn't even ask him to. I taped 'em up again and he sat down in the chair, picked up his scotch and sipped it.

And, damn, I'll tell you something. The God's truth. I felt good. Naw, naw, it wasn't like I'd seen the light or anything like that crap. But I was thinking that of all the people in my life—my dad or my ex or Toth or anybody else, I never did really trust them. I'd never let myself go all the way. And here, tonight, I did. With a stranger and somebody who had the power to do me some harm. It was a pretty scary feeling but it was also a good feeling.

A little thing, real little. But maybe that's where stuff like this starts. I realized then that I'd been wrong. I could let him go. Oh, I'd keep him tied up here. Gagged. It'd be a day or so before he'd get out. But he'd agree to that. I knew he would. And I'd write his name and address down, let him know I knew where him and his family lived. But that was only part of why I'd let him go. I wasn't sure what the rest of it was. But it was something about what'd just happened, something between me and him.

"How you feel?" he asked.

I wasn't going to give too much away. No, sir. But I couldn't help saying, "That car coming by? I thought I was gone then. But you did right by me."

"And you did right too, Jack." And then he said, "Pour us another round."

I filled the glasses to the top. We tapped 'em.

"Here's to you, Jack. And to faith."

"To faith."

I tossed back the whisky and when I lowered my head, sniffing air through my nose to clear my head, well, that was when he got me. Right in the face.

He was good, that son of a bitch. Tossed the glass low so that even when I ducked, which of course I did, the booze caught me in the eyes, and, man, that stung like nobody's business. I couldn't believe it. I was howling in pain and going for the knife. But it was too late. He had it all planned out, exactly what I was going to do. How I was gonna move. He brought his knee up into my chin and knocked a couple teeth out and I went over onto my back before I could get the knife outa my pocket. Then he dropped down on my belly with his knee—I remembered I'd never bothered to tape his feet up again—and he knocked the wind out, and I was lying there like I was paralyzed, trying to breathe and all. Only I couldn't. And the pain was incredible but what was worse was the feeling that he didn't trust me.

I was whispering, "No, no, no! I was going to do it, man. You don't understand! I was going to let you go."

I couldn't see nothing and couldn't really hear nothing either, my ears were roaring so much. I was gasping, "You don't understand, you don't understand."

Man, the pain was so bad. So bad...

Weller must've got the tape off his hands, chewed through it, I guess, 'cause he was rolling me over. I felt him tape my hands together then grab me and drag me over to a chair, tape my feet to the legs. He got some water and threw it in my face to wash the whisky out of my eyes.

He sat down in a chair in front of me. And he just stared at me for a long time while I caught my breath. He picked up his glass, poured more scotch. I shied away, thinking he was going to throw it in my face again but he just sat there, sipping it and staring at me.

"You… I was going to let you go. I *was*."

"I know," he said. Still calm.

"You know?"

"I could see it in your face. I've been a salesman for years, remember? I know when I've closed a deal."

I'm a pretty strong guy, 'specially when I'm mad, and I tried real hard to break through that tape but there was no doing it. "Goddamn you!" I shouted. "You said you weren't going to turn me in. You, all your goddamn talk about faith—"

"Shhhh," Weller whispered. And he sat back, crossed his legs. Easy as could be. Looking me up and down. "That fellow your friend shot and killed back at the drugstore? The customer at the counter?"

I nodded slowly.

"He was my friend. It's his place my wife and I're staying at this weekend. With all our kids."

I just stared at him. His friend? What was he saying? "I didn't—"

"Be quiet," he said, real soft. "I've known him for years. Gerry was one of my best friends."

"I didn't want nobody to die. I—"

"But somebody *did* die. And it was your fault."

"Toth…"

He whispered, "It was your fault."

"All right, you tricked me. Call the cops. Get it over with, you goddamn liar."

"You really don't understand, do you?" Weller shook his head. Why was he so calm? His hands weren't shaking. He wasn't looking around, nervous and all. Nothing like that. He said, "If I'd wanted to turn you in I would just've flagged down that squad car a few minutes ago. But I said I wouldn't do that. And I won't. I gave you my word I wouldn't tell the cops a thing about you. And I won't. Turning you in is the last thing I want to do."

Then what *do* you want?" I shouted. "Tell me!" Trying to bust through that tape. And as he unfolded my Buck knife with a click, I was thinking of something I told him.

Oh, man, no… Oh, no.

Yeah, being blind, I guess. That'd be the worst thing I could think of.

"What're you going to do?" I whispered.

"What'm I going to do, Jack?" Weller said, feeling the blade of the Buck with his thumb and looking me in the eye. "Well, I'll tell you. I spent a good deal of time tonight proving to you that you shouldn't kill me. And now…"

"What, man? *What?*"

"Now I'm going to spend a good deal of time proving to you that you should've."

Then, real slow, Weller finished his scotch and stood up. And he walked toward me, that weird little smile on his face.

NEEDLE MATCH

PETER LOVESEY

Murder was done on Court Eleven on the third day of Wimbledon, 1981. Fortunately for the All England Club, it wasn't anything obvious like a strangling or a shooting, but the result was the same for the victim, except that he suffered longer. It took three days for him to die. I can tell you exactly how it happened, because I was one of the ball boys for the match.

When I was thirteen I was taught to be invisible. But before you decide this isn't your kind of story let me promise you it isn't about magic. There's nothing spooky about me. And there was nothing spooky about my instructor, Brigadier Romilly. He was flesh and blood all right and so were the terrified kids who sat at his feet.

"You'll be invisible, every one of you before I've finished with you," he said in his parade-ground voice, and we believed him, we third-years from Merton Comprehensive.

A purple scar like a sabre-cut stretched downwards from the edge of the Brigadier's left eye, over his mouth to the point of his chin. He'd grown a bristly ginger moustache over part of it, but we could easily see where the two ends joined. Rumour had it that his face had been slashed by a Mau Mau warrior's machete in the Kenyan terrorist war of the fifties. We didn't know anything about the Mau Mau, except that the terrorist must have been crazy to tangle with the Brigadier – who grabbed him by the throat and strangled him.

"Don't ever get the idea that you're doing this to be seen. You'll be there, on court with Mr McEnroe and Mr Borg – if I think you're good enough – and no one will notice you, no one. When the game is in play you'll be as still as the net-post, and as uninteresting. For Rule Two of the Laws of Tennis states that the court has certain permanent fixtures like the net and the net posts and the umpire's chair. And the list of permanent fixtures includes you, the ball boys, in your respective places. So you can tell your mothers and fathers and your favourite aunties not to bother to watch. If you're doing your job they won't even notice you."

To think we'd volunteered for this. By a happy accident of geography ours was one of the schools chosen to provide the ball boys and ball girls for the Championships "It's a huge honour," our headmaster had told us. "You do it for the prestige of the school. You're on television. You meet the stars, hand them their towels, supply them with the balls, pour their drinks. You can be proud."

The Brigadier disabused us of all that. "If any of you are looking for glory, leave at once. Go back to your stuffy classrooms. I don't want your sort in my squad. The people I want are functionaries, not glory-seekers. Do you understand? You will do your job, brilliantly, the way I show you. It's all about timing, self-control and, above all, being invisible."

The victim was poisoned. Once the poison was in his system there was no antidote. Death was inevitable, and lingering.

So in the next three months we learned to be invisible. And it was damned hard work, I can tell you. I had no idea what it would lead to. You're thinking we murdered the Brigadier? No, he's a survivor. So far as I know, he's still alive and terrifying the staff in a retirement home.

I'm going to tell it as it happened, and we start on the November afternoon in nineteen-eighty when my best friend Eddie Pringle and I were on an hour's detention for writing something obscene on Blind Pugh's blackboard. Mr Pugh, poor soul, was our chemistry master. He wasn't really blind, but his sight wasn't the best. He wore thick glasses with prism lenses, and we little monsters took full advantage. Sometimes Nemesis arrived, in the shape of our headmaster, Mr Neames, breezing into the lab, supposedly for a word with Blind Pugh, but in reality to catch us red-handed playing poker behind bits of apparatus or rolling mercury along the bench-tops. Those who escaped with a detention were the lucky ones.

"I've had enough of this crap," Eddie told me in the detention room. "I'm up for a job as ball boy."

"What do you mean – Wimbledon?" I said. "That's not till next June."

"They train you. It's every afternoon off school for six months – and legal. No more detentions. All you do is trot around the court picking up balls and chucking them to the players and you get to meet McEnroe and Connors and all those guys. Want to join me?"

It seemed the ideal escape plan, but of course we had to get permission from Nemesis to do it. Eddie and I turned ourselves into model pupils for the rest of term. No messing about. No detentions. Every homework task completed.

"In view of this improvement," Nemesis informed us, "I have decided to let you go on the training course."

But when we met the Brigadier we found we'd tunneled out of one prison into another. He terrified us. The regime was pitiless, the orders unrelenting.

"First you must learn how to be a permanent fixture. Stand straight, chest out, shoulders back, thumbs linked behind your back. Now hold it for five minutes. If anyone moves, I put the stopwatch back to zero again."

Suddenly he threw a ball hard at Eddie and of course he ducked.

"Right," the Brigadier announced, "Pringle moved. The hand goes back to zero. You have to learn to be still, Pringle. Last year one of my boys was hit on the ear by a serve from Roscoe Tanner, over a hundred miles per hour, and he didn't flinch."

We had a full week learning to be permanent fixtures, first standing at the rear of the court and then crouching like petrified sprinters at the sideline, easy targets for the Brigadier to shy at. A couple of the kids dropped out. We all had bruises.

"This is worse than school," I told Eddie. "We've got no freedom at all."

"Right, he's a tyrant. Don't let him grind you down," Eddie said.

In the second and third weeks we practised retrieving the balls, scampering back to the sidelines and rolling them along the ground to our colleagues or throwing them with one bounce to the Brigadier.

This was to be one of the great years of Wimbledon, with Borg, Connors and McEnroe at the peaks of their careers, challenging for the title. The rivalry would produce one match, a semi-final, that will be remembered for as long as tennis is played. And on an outside court, another, fiercer rivalry would be played out, with a fatal result. The players were not well known, but their backgrounds ensured a clash of ideologies. Jozsef Stanski, from Poland, was to meet Igor Voronin, a Soviet Russian, on Court Eleven, on the third day of the Championships.

Being an ignorant schoolboy at the time, I didn't appreciate how volatile it was, this match between two players from Eastern Europe. In the previous summer, 1980, the strike in the Gdansk shipyard, followed by widespread strikes thoughout Poland, had forced the Communist government to allow independent trade unions. Solidarity – the trade union movement led by Lech Walesa – became a powerful, vocal organisation getting massive international attention. The Polish tennis star, Jozsef Stanski, was an outspoken supporter of Solidarity who criticised the state regime whenever he was interviewed.

The luck of the draw, as they say, had matched Stanski with Voronin, a diehard Soviet Communist, almost certainly a KGB agent. Later, it was alleged that Voronin was a state assassin.

Before all this, the training of the ball boys went on, a totalitarian regime of its own, always efficient, performed to numbers and timed on the stopwatch. There was usually a slogan to sum up whichever phase of ball boy lore we were mastering. "Show before you throw, Richards, show before you throw, lad."

No one dared to defy the Brigadier.

The early weeks were on indoor courts. In April, we got outside. We learned everything a ball boy could possibly need to know, how to hold three balls at once, collect a towel, offer a cold drink and dispose of the cup afterwards, stand in front of a player between games without making eye contact. The training didn't miss a trick.

At the end of the month we 'stood' for a club tournament at Queen's. It went well, I thought, until the Brigadier debriefed us. Debriefed? He tore strips off us for over an hour. We'd learnt nothing, he said. The Championships would be a disaster if we got within a mile of them. We were slow, we fumbled, stumbled and forgot to show before the throw. Worse, he saw a couple of us (Eddie and me, to be honest) exchange some words as we crouched either side of the net.

"If any ball boy under my direction so much as moves his lips ever again in the course of a match, I will come onto the court and seal his revolting mouth with packing tape."

We believed him.

And we persevered. Miraculously the months went by and June arrived, and with it the Championships.

The Brigadier addressed us on the eve of the first day's play and to my amazement, he didn't put the fear of God into me. By his standards, it was a vote of confidence. "You boys and girls have given me problems enough this year, but you're as ready as you ever will be, and I want you to know I have total confidence in you. When this great tournament is over and the best of you line up on the Centre Court to be presented to Her Royal Highness before she meets the Champion, my pulse will beat faster and my heart will swell with pride, as will each of yours. And one of you, of course, will get a special award as best ball boy – or girl. That's the Championship that counts, you know. Never mind Mr Borg and Miss Navratilova. The real winner will be one of you. The decision will be mine, and you all start tomorrow as equals. In the second week I will draw up a short list. The pick of you, my elite squad, will stand in the finals. I will nominate the winner only when the tournament is over."

I suppose it had been the severity of the build-up; to me those words were as thrilling and inspiring as King Henry's before the Battle of Agincourt. I wanted to be on Centre Court on that final day. I wanted to be best ball boy. I could see that all the others felt like me and had the same gleam in their eyes.

I've never felt so nervous as I did at noon that first day, approaching the tall, creeper-covered walls of the All England Club, and passing inside and finding it was already busy with people on the terraces and promenades chatting loudly in accents that would have got you past any security guard in the world. Wimbledon twenty years ago was part of the social season, a blazer and tie occasion, entirely alien to a kid like me from a working-class family.

My first match was on an outside court, thanks be to the Brigadier. Men's singles, between a tall Californian and a wiry Frenchman. I marched on court with the other five ball boys and mysteriously my nerves ended the moment the umpire called "Play". We were so well-drilled that the training took over. My concentration was absolute. I knew precisely what I had to do. I was a small, invisible part of a well-oiled, perfectly tuned machine, the Rolls Royce of tennis tournaments. Six-three, six-three, six-three to the Californian, and we lined up and marched off again.

I stood in two more matches that first day, and they were equally straightforward in spite of some racquet abuse by one unhappy player whose service wouldn't go in. A ball boy is above all that. At home, exhausted, I slept better than I had for a week.

Day Two was Ladies' Day, when most of the women's first round matches were played. At the end of my second match I lined up for an ice-cream and heard a familiar voice, "Got overheated in that last one, Richards?"

I turned to face the Brigadier, expecting a rollicking. I wasn't sure if ball boys in uniform were allowed to consume ice cream.

But the scar twitched into a grin. "I watched you at work. You're doing a decent job, lad. Not invisible yet, but getting there. Keep it up and you might make Centre Court."

I can tell you exactly what happened in the Stanski–Voronin match because I was one of the ball boys and my buddy Eddie Pringle was another, and has recently reminded me of it. Neither player was seeded. Stanski had won a five-setter in the first round against a little-known Englishman, and Voronin had been lucky enough to get a bye.

Court Eleven is hardly one of the show courts, and these two weren't well known players, but we still had plenty of swivelling heads following the action.

I'm sure some of the crowd understood that the players were at opposite extremes politically, but I doubt if anyone foresaw the terrible outcome of this clash. They may have noticed the coolness between the players, but that's one of the conventions of sport, particularly in a Grand Slam tournament. You shake hands at the end, but you psych yourself up to beat hell out of your rival first.

Back to the tennis. The first set went narrowly to Voronin, seven-five. I was so absorbed in my ball boy duties that the score almost passed me by. I retrieved the balls and passed them to the players when they needed them. Between games, I helped them to drinks and waited on them, just as we were programmed to do. I rather liked Stanski. His English wasn't up to much, but he made up for it with the occasional nod and even a hint of a smile.

Stanski won the next two sets, six-four, six-three.

Half the time I was at Voronin's end. Being strictly neutral, I treated him with the same courtesy I gave his opponent, but I can't say he was as appreciative. You can tell a lot about players from the way they grab the towel from you or discard a ball they don't fancy serving. The Russian was a hard man, with vicious thoughts in his head.

He secured the next set in a tie-break and took the match to a fifth. The crowd was growing. People from other courts had heard something special was happening. Several long, exciting rallies drew gasps and shrieks.

Voronin had extraordinary eyes like wet pebbles, the irises as black as the pupils. I was drilled to look at him each time I offered him a ball, and his expression never changed. Once or twice when Stanski had some luck with a ball that bounced on the net, Voronin eyeballed him. Terrifying.

The final set exceeded everyone's expectations. Voronin broke Stanski's service in the first game with some amazing passing shots and then held his own in game two. In the third, Stanski served three double faults and missed a simple volley.

"Game to Voronin. Voronin leads by three games to love. Final set."

When I offered Stanski the water he poured it over his head and covered his face with the towel.

Voronin started game four with an ace. Stanski blocked the next serve and it nicked the cord and just dropped over. He was treated to another eyeballing for that piece of impertinence. Voronin walked slowly back to the line, turned, glared and fired a big serve that was called out. The second was softer and Stanski risked a blinder, a mighty forehand, and succeeded – the first winner he'd made in the set. Fifteen-thirty. Voronin nodded towards my friend Eddie for balls, scowled at one and chucked it aside. Eddie gave him another. He served long. Then foot-faulted. This time the line judge received the eyeballing. Fifteen-forty.

Stanski jigged on his toes. He would never have a better opportunity of breaking back.

The serve from Voronin was cautious. The spin deceived Stanski and the ball flew high. Voronin stood under, waiting to pick it out of the sun and kill it. He connected, but heroically Stanski got the racquet in place at the far end and almost fell into the crowd doing it. The return looked a sitter for the Russian and he steered it cross-court with nonchalance. Somehow Stanski dashed to the right place again. The crowd roared its appreciation.

Voronin chipped the return with a dinky shot that barely cleared the net and brought Stanski sprinting from the back to launch himself into a dive. The ball had bounced and risen through another arc and was inches from the turf when Stanski's racquet slid under it. Miraculously he found enough lift to sneak it over at a near-impossible angle. Voronin netted. Game to Stanski.

Now there was an anxious moment. Stanski's dive had taken him sliding out of court and heavily into the net-post, just a yard from where I was crouching in my set position. He was rubbing his right forearm, green from the skid across the grass, and everyone feared he'd broken a bone. After a delay of a few seconds the umpire asked if he needed medical attention. He shook his head.

Play resumed at three games to one, and it felt as if they'd played a full set already. The fascination of the game of tennis is that a single shot can turn a match. That diving winner of Stanski's was a prime example. He won the next game to love, serving brilliantly, though clearly anxious about his sore arm, which he massaged at every opportunity. Between games the umpire again asked if he needed assistance, but he shook his head.

Voronin was still a break up, and when play resumed after the change of ends he was first on court. He beckoned to me aggressively with his right hand, white with resin. I let him see he wouldn't intimidate me. I was a credit to the Brigadier, showing and throwing with the single bounce, straight to the player.

Stanski marched to the receiving end, twirling his racquet. Voronin hit the first serve too deep. The second spun in, shaved the line and was allowed. Fifteen-love. Stanski took the next two points with fine, looping returns. Then Voronin met a return of serve with a volley that failed to clear the net. Fifteen-forty. The mind-game was being won by Stanski. A feeble serve from the Russian allowed him to close the game.

Three all.

The critical moment was past. Stanski's confidence was high. He wiped his forehead with his wristband, tossed the ball up and served an ace that Bjorn Borg himself would have been incapable of reaching. From that moment, Voronin was doomed. Stanski was nerveless, accurate, domineering. He took the game to love. He dropped only one point in winning the next two. It was over. The crowd was in ecstasy. Voronin walked to the side without shaking hands, slung his racquets into his bag and left the court without waiting for his opponent – which is always regarded as bad form at Wimbledon. Some of the crowd booed him.

Stanski seemed to be taking longer than usual in packing up. He lingered by the net-post looking down, repeatedly dragging his foot across the worn patch of turf and raising dust. Then he bent and picked something up that to me looked liked like one of the needles my mother used on her sewing-machine. After staring at it for some time he showed it to the umpire, who had descended from his chair. At the same time he pointed to a scratch on his forearm. The umpire nodded indulgently and I heard him promise to speak to the groundsman.

I learned next day that Stanski was ill and had withdrawn from the tournament. It was a disappointment to everyone, because he had seemed to be on a roll and might have put out one of the seeds in a later round.

Two days after, the world of tennis was shocked to learn that Jozsef Stanski had died. He'd been admitted to St Thomas's complaining of weakness, vomiting and a high temperature. His pulse-rate was abnormally high and his lymph glands were swollen. There was an area of hardening under the scratch on his right forearm. In the night, his pulse rose to almost two hundred a minute and his temperature fell sharply. He was taken into intensive care and treated for septicaemia. Tests showed an exceptionally high count of white blood cells. Blood was appearing in his vomit and he was having difficulty in passing water, suggesting damage to the kidneys.

The next day an electrocardiogram indicated further critical problems, this time with the heart. Attempts were made to fit a pacemaker, but he died whilst under the anaesthetic. It was announced that a post mortem would be held the following day.

I'm bound to admit that these medical details only came to my attention years later, through my interest in the case. At the time it happened, I was wholly taken up with my duties at Wimbledon, programmed by the Brigadier to let nothing distract me. We were soon into the second week and the crowds grew steadily, with most interest on the show courts.

Eddie and I were picked for the men's semi-finals and I had my first experience of the Centre Court in the greatest match ever played at Wimbledon, between Bjorn Borg, the champion for the previous five years, and Jimmy Connors. Borg came back from two sets down, love-six and four-six, to win with a display of skill and guts that finally wore down the seemingly unstoppable Connors. I will go to my grave proud that I had a minor role in that epic.

I'm proud, also, that I was one of the ball boys in the final, though the match lacked passion and didn't quite live up to its promise. John McEnroe deserved his Championship, but we all felt Borg had fired his best shots in the semi.

Like Borg, I was forced to choke back some disappointment that afternoon. I'd secretly hoped to be named best ball boy, but a kid from another school was picked by the Brigadier. My pal Eddie (who wasn't on court for the final) put an arm around my shoulder when it was over. We told each other that the kid had to be a brown-noser and the Brigadier's nephew as well.

I may have heard something later on radio or television about the post mortem on poor Jozsef Stanski. They concluded he died from blood-poisoning. Samples were sent for further analysis, but the lab couldn't trace the source. At the inquest, a pathologist mentioned the scratch on the arm and said some sharp point had dug quite deeply into the flesh. The match umpire gave evidence and spoke of the needle Stanski had picked up. He described the small eye close to the point. Unfortunately the needle had not been seen since the day of the match. In summing up, the coroner said it would not be helpful to speculate about the needle. The match had been played in full view of a large crowd and there was no evidence of anyone attempting to cause Stanski's death.

Huge controversy surrounded the verdict. The international press made a lot of the incident, pointing out that as recently as 1978 a Bulgarian writer, Georgi Markov, a rebel against his Communist government, had been executed in a London street by a tiny poison pellet forced into his thigh, apparently by the tip of an umbrella. The poison used was ricin, a protein derived from the castor oil seed, deadly and in those days almost undetectable in the human bloodstream. He took four days to die, protesting that he was the victim of political assassination. Nobody except his wife took him seriously until after he died. The presence of the poison was only discovered because the pellet was still embedded in a piece of Markov's flesh sent for analysis. If ricin could be injected in a public street using an umbrella, was it so fanciful to suggest Jozsef Stansky was targeted by the KGB and poisoned at Wimbledon two years later?

In Poland, the first months of 1981 had been extremely tense. A new Prime Minister, General Jaruzelski, had taken over and a permanent committee was set up to liaise with Solidarity. Moscow was incensed by this outbreak of liberalism and summoned Jaruzelski and his team to the Kremlin. The Politburo made its anger known. Repression followed. Many trade union activists were beaten up.

The papers noted that Stanski's opponent Voronin had quit Britain by an Aeroflot plane the same evening he had lost. He was unavailable for comment, in spite of strenuous efforts by reporters. The Soviet crackdown on Solidarity was mentioned. It was widely suspected that the KGB had been monitoring Stanski for over a year. He was believed to be acting as a conduit to the free world for Walesa and his organisation. At the end of the year, martial law was imposed in Poland and the leaders of Solidarity were detained and union activity suspended.

Although nothing was announced officially, the press claimed Scotland Yard investigated the assassination theory and kept the file open.

Since the Cold War ended and the Soviet bloc disintegrated, it is hard to think oneself back into the oppression of those days, harder still to believe orders may have been given for one tennis player to execute another at the world's top tournament.

In the years since, I kept an open mind about the incident, troubled to think murder may have happened so close to me. In my mind's eye I can still see Stanski rubbing his arm and reaching for the water I poured.

Then, last April, I had a phone call from Eddie Pringle. I hadn't seen him in almost twenty years. He was coming my way on a trip and wondered if we might meet for a drink.

To be truthful, I wasn't all that keen. I couldn't imagine we had much in common these days. Eddie seemed to sense my reluctance, because he went on to say, "I wouldn't take up your time if it wasn't important – well, important to me, if not to you. I'm not on the cadge, by the way. I'm asking no favours except for one half-hour of your time."

How could I refuse?

We arranged to meet in the bar of a local hotel. I told him I have a beard these days and what I would wear, just in case we didn't recognise each other.

I certainly wouldn't have known Eddie if he hadn't come up to me and spoken my name. He was gaunt, hairless and on two sticks.

"Sorry," he said. "Chemo. Didn't like to tell you on the phone in case I put you off."

"I'm the one who should be sorry," I said. "Is the treatment doing any good?"

"Not really. I'll be lucky to see the year out. But I'm allowed to drink in moderation. What's yours?"

We found a table. He asked what line of work I'd gone into and I told him I was a journalist.

"Sport?"

"No. Showbiz. I know why you asked," I said. "That stint we did as ball boys would have been a useful grounding. No one ever believes I was on court with McEnroe and Borg, so I rarely mention it."

"I made a big effort to forget," Eddie said. "The treatment we got from that Brigadier fellow was shameful."

"No worse than any military training."

"Yes, but we were young kids barely into our teens. At that age it amounted to brain-washing."

"That's a bit strong, Eddie."

"Think about it," he said. "He had us totally under his control. Destroyed any individuality we had. We thought about nothing else but chasing after tennis balls and handing them over in the approved style. It was the peak of everyone's ambition to be the best ball boy. You were as fixated as I was. Don't deny it."

"True. It became my main ambition."

"Obsession."

"OK. Have it your way. Obsession." I smiled, wanting to lighten the mood a bit.

"You were the hotshot ball boy," he said. "You deserved to win."

"I doubt it. Anyway, I was too absorbed in it all to see how the other kids shaped up."

"Believe me, you were the best. I couldn't match you for speed or stillness. The need to be invisible he was always on about."

"I remember that."

"I believed I was as good as anyone, except you." Eddie took a long sip of beer and was silent for some time.

I waited. It was obvious some boyhood memory was troubling him.

He cleared his throat nervously. "Something has been on my mind all these years. It's a burden I can't take with me when I go. I don't have long, and I want to clear my conscience. You remember the match between the Russian and the Pole?"

"Voronin and, er...?"

"Stanski – the one who died. It should never have happened. You're the one who should have died."

Staring at him, I played the last statement over in my head.

He said, "You've got to remember the mental state we were in, totally committed to being best boy. It was crazy, but nothing else in the world mattered. I could tell you were better than I was, and you told me yourself that the Brigadier spoke to you after one of your matches on Ladies' Day."

"Did I?" I said, amazed he still had such a clear recollection.

"He didn't say anything to me. It was obvious you were booked for the final. While you were on the squad, I stood no chance. It sounds like lunacy now, but I was so fired up I had to stop you."

"How?"

"With poison."

"Now come on, Eddie. You're not serious."

But his tone insisted he was. "If you remember, when we were in the first year, there was a sensational story in the papers about a man, a Bulgarian, who was murdered in London by a pellet the size of a pinhead that contained an almost unknown poison called ricin."

"Georgi Markov."

"Yes. We talked about it in chemistry with Blind Pugh. Remember?"

"Vaguely."

"He said a gram of the stuff was enough to kill thirty-six thousand people and it attacked the red blood cells. It was obtained from the seeds or beans of the castor-oil plant, *ricinus communis*. They had to be ground up in a pestle and mortar because otherwise the hard seed-coat prevented absorption. Just a few seeds would be enough. Old Pugh told us all this in the belief that castor oil plants are tropical, but he was wrong. They've been grown in this country as border plants ever since Tudor times."

"You're saying you got hold of some?"

"From a local seedsman, and no health warning. I'm sorry if all this sounds callous. I felt driven at the time. I plotted how to do it, using this."

Eddie spread his palm and a small piece of metal lay across it. "I picked it out of a litter bin after Stanski threw it away. This is the sewing machine needle he found. My murder weapon."

I said with distaste, "You were responsible for that?"

"It came from my mother's machine. I ground the needle to a really fine point and made a gelatine capsule containing the poison and filled the eye of the needle with it."

"What were you going to do with it – stick it into my arm?"

"No. Remember how we were drilled to return to the same spot just behind the tramlines beside the umpire's chair? If you watch tennis, that place gets as worn as the serving area at the back of the court. The ballboys always return to the same spot. My plan was simple. Stick the needle into the turf with the sharp point upwards and you would kneel on it and inject the ricin into your bloodstream. I'm telling you this because I want the truth to come out before I die. I meant to kill you and it went wrong. Stanski dived at a difficult ball and his arm went straight down on the needle."

"But he went on to win the match."

"The effects take days to kick in, but there's no antidote. Even if I'd confessed at the time, they couldn't have saved him. It was unforgivable. I was obsessed and it's preyed on my mind ever since."

"So all that stuff in the papers about Voronin being an assassin …"

"Was rubbish. It was me. If you want to go to the police," he said, "I don't mind confessing everything I've told you. I just want the truth to be known before I go. I'm told I have six months at most."

I was silent, reflecting on what I'd heard, the conflicting motives that had driven a young boy to kill and a dying man to confess twenty years later.

"Or you could wait until after I've gone. You say you're a journalist. You could write it up and tell it in your own way."

He left me to make up my own mind.

Eddie died in November.

And you are the first after me to get the full story.

THE BOOKBINDER'S APPRENTICE

MARTIN EDWARDS

As Joly closed his book, he was conscious of someone watching him. A feeling he relished, warm as the sun burning high above Campo Santi Apostoli. Leaning back, he stretched his arms, a languorous movement that allowed his eyes to roam behind dark wrap-around Gucci glasses.

A tall, stooped man in a straw hat and white suit was limping towards the row of red benches, tapping a long wooden walking stick against the paving slabs, somehow avoiding a collision with the small, whooping children on scooters and tricycles. Joly sighed. He wasn't unaccustomed to the attentions of older men, but soon they became tedious. Yet the impeccable manners instilled at one of England's minor public schools never deserted him; besides, he was thirsty. A drink would be nice, provided someone else was paying. The benches were crowded with mothers talking while their offspring scrambled and shouted over the covered well and a group of sweaty tourists listening to their guide's machine-gun description of the frescoes within the church. As the man drew near, Joly squeezed up on the bench to make a small place beside him.

"Why, thank you." American accent, a courtly drawl. "It is good to rest one's feet in the middle of the day."

Joly guessed the man had been studying him from the small bridge over the canal, in front of the row of shops. He smiled, didn't speak. In a casual encounter, his rule was not to give anything away too soon.

The man considered the book on Joly's lap. "*Death in Venice.* Fascinating."

"He writes well," Joly allowed.

"I meant the volume itself, not the words within it." The man waved towards the green kiosk in front of them. Jostling in the window with the magazines and panoramic views of the Canal Grande were the gaudy covers of translated Georgette Heyer and Conan the Barbarian. "Though your taste in reading matter is plainly more sophisticated than the common herd's. But it is the book as *objet d'art* that fascinates me these days, I must confess. May I take a closer look?"

Without awaiting a reply, he picked up the novel, weighing it in his hand with the fond assurance of a Manhattan jeweller caressing a heavy diamond. The book was bound in green cloth, with faded gilt lettering on the grubby spine. Someone had spilled ink on the front cover and an insect had nibbled at the early pages.

"Ah, the first English edition by Secker. I cannot help but be impressed by your discernment. Most young fellows wishing to read Thomas Mann would content themselves with a cheap paperback."

"It is a little out of the ordinary. I like unusual things." Joly let the words hang in the air for several seconds. "As for cost, I fear I don't have deep pockets. I picked up the copy from a second hand dealer's stall on the Embankment for rather less than I would have paid in a paperback shop. It's worth rather more than the few pence I spent, but it's hardly valuable, I'm afraid. The condition is poor, as you can see. All the same, I'd rather own a first edition than a modern reprint without a trace of character."

The man proferred a thin, weathered hand. "You are a fellow after my own heart, then! A love of rare books, it represents a bond between us. My name is Sanborn, by the way, Darius Sanborn."

"Joly Maddox."

"Joly? Not short for Jolyon, by any chance?"

"You guessed it. My mother loved *The Forsyte Saga*."

"Ah, so the fondness for good books is inherited. Joly, it is splendid to make your acquaintance."

Joly ventured an apologetic cough and made a show of consulting his fake Rolex as the church bell chimed the hour. "Well, I suppose I'd better be running along."

Sanborn murmured, "Oh, but do you have to go so soon? It is a hot day, would you care to have a drink with me?"

A pantomime of hesitation. "Well, I'm tempted. I'm not due to meet up with my girlfriend till she finishes work in another hour..."

A tactical move, to mention Lucia. Get the message over to Sanborn, just so that was no misunderstanding. The American did not seem in the least put out; his leathery face creased into a broad smile. Joly thought he was like one of the pigeons in the square, swooping the moment it glimpsed the tiniest crumb.

"Then you have time aplenty. Come with me, I know a little spot a few metres away where the wine is as fine as the skin of a priceless first edition."

There was no harm in it. Adjusting his pace to the old man's halting gait, he followed him over the bridge, past the shop with all the cacti outside. Their weird shapes always amused him. Sanborn noticed his sideways glance. He was sharp, Joly thought, he wasn't a fool.

"As you say, the unusual intrigues you."

Joly nodded. He wouldn't have been startled if the old man had suggested going to a hotel instead of for a drink, but thankfully the dilemma of how to respond to a proposition never arose. After half a dozen twists and turns through a maze of alleyways, they reached an ill-lit bar and stepped inside. After the noise and bustle of the *campo*, the place was as quiet as a church in the Ghetto. No-one stood behind the counter and, straining his eyes to adjust from the glare outside, Joly spied only a single customer. In a corner at the back, where no beam from the sun could reach, a small wizened man in a corduroy jacket sat at a table, a half-empty wine glass in front of him. Sanborn limped up to the man and indicated his guest with a wave of the stick.

"Zuichini, meet Joly Maddox. A fellow connoisseur of the unusual. Including rare books."

The man at the table had a hooked nose and small dark cruel eyes. His face resembled a carnival mask, with a plague doctor's beak, long enough to keep disease at bay. He extended his hand. It was more like a claw, Joly thought. And it was trembling, although not from nerves – for his toothless smile conveyed a strange, almost malevolent glee. Zuichini must suffer from some form of palsy, perhaps Parkinson's disease. Joly, young and fit, knew little of sickness.

"You wonder why I make specific mention of books, Joly?" Sanborn asked with a rhetorical flourish. "It is because my good friend here is the finest bookbinder in Italy. Zuichini is not a household name, not even here in Venice, but his mastery of his craft, I assure you, is second to none. As a collector of unique treasures, few appreciate his talents more than I."

A simian waiter shuffled out from a doorway, bearing wine and three large glasses. He did not utter a word, but plainly Sanborn and Zuichini were familiar customers. Sanborn did not spare the man's retreating back a glance as he poured.

"You will taste nothing finer in Italy, I assure you. Liquid silk."

Joly took a sip and savoured the bouquet. Sanborn was right about the wine, but what did he want? Everyone wanted something.

"You are here as a tourist?" the American asked. "Who knows, you might follow my example. I first came to this city for a week. That was nineteen years ago and now I could not tear myself away if my life depended on it."

Joly explained that he'd arrived in Venice a month earlier. He had no money, but he knew how to blag. For a few days he'd dressed himself up as Charlie Chaplin and become a living statue, miming for tourists in the vicinity of San Zaccaria and earning enough from the coins they threw into his tin to keep himself fed and watered. But he hated standing still and after a few hours even his narcissistic pleasure in posing for photographs began to pall. One afternoon, taking a break in a cheap pizzeria, he'd fallen into conversation with Lucia when she served him with a capuccino. She was a stranger in the city as well; she'd left her native Taormina after the death of her parents and drifted around the country ever since. What they had in common was that neither of them could settle to anything. That night she'd taken him to her room in Dorsoduro and he'd stayed with her ever since.

"Excellent!" Sanborn applauded as he refilled his new young friend's glass. "What is your profession?"

Joly said he was still searching for something to which he would care to devote himself, body and soul. His degree was in English, but a career in teaching or the civil service struck him as akin to living death. He liked to think of himself as a free spirit, but he enjoyed working with his hands. For six months he'd amused himself as a puppeteer, performing for children's parties and at municipal fun days. When that became wearisome, he'd headed across the Channel. He'd spent three months in France, twice as long in Spain, soon he planned to try his luck in Rome.

"I wondered about learning a trade as a boat-builder, I spent a day in the *squero* talking to a man who builds gondolas." He risked a cheeky glance at Zuichini's profile. "I even thought about making masks…"

"An over-subscribed profession in this city," Sanborn interrupted. "I understand why you didn't pursue it."

"Well, who knows? One of these days, I may come back here to try my luck."

"You have family?"

"My parents dead, my sister emigrated to Australia where she married some layabout who looked like a surf god. So I have no ties, I can please myself."

"And your girlfriend?" Sanborn asked. "Any chance of wedding bells?"

Joly couldn't help laughing. Not the effect of the wine, heady though it was, but the very idea that he and Lucia might have a future together. She was a pretty *prima donna*, only good for one thing. Although he didn't say it, the contemplative look in

Sanborn's pale grey eyes made it clear that he'd got the message.

"You and she must join us for dinner, be my guests, it would be a pleasure."

"Oh no, really, we couldn't impose…"

Sanborn dismissed the protestations with a flick of his hand. He was old and deliberate and yet Joly recognised this was a man accustomed to getting his own way. "Please. I insist. I know a little seafood restaurant, they serve food so wonderful you will never forget it. Am I right, Zuichini?"

The wizened man cackled and nodded. A gleam lit his small eyes.

"Well, I'm not sure…"

But within a couple of minutes it was agreed and Joly stumbled out into the glare of the sun with the American's good wishes ringing in his ears. Zuichini's small, plague-mask head merely nodded farewell; he'd uttered no more than two dozen words in the space of half an hour. Joly blinked, unaccustomed to wine that hit so hard; but the pleasure was worth the pain.

When he met up with Lucia, she made a fuss about the dinner. It was in her nature to complain, she regarded it as a duty not to agree to anything he suggested without making him struggle.

"With two old men? Why would we wish to do this? After tomorrow we will be apart, perhaps for ever. Are you tired with me already?"

Exaggeration was her stock-in-trade, but he supposed she was right and that they would not see each other again after he left the city. The plan was for him to travel to Rome and for her to join him there in a fortnight, after she'd been paid for the month by the restaurant. He'd arranged it like that so there was an opportunity for their relationship to die a natural death. He hated break-up scenes. It would be so easy for them not to get together again in the Eternal City. If he wanted to return to Venice, he would rather do so free from encumbrances. Plenty more fish in the sea. As for their argument, in truth she too found the prospect of a slap-up meal at a rich man's expense appealing. After twenty minutes she stopped grumbling and started to deliberate about what she might wear.

They went back to her place and made love. By the time she'd dressed up for the evening, she was relishing the prospect of meeting someone new. She would love parading before the old men; admiration turned her on more than anything exotic he tried with her in bed. At first he'd found her delightful. He'd even persuaded himself that she might have hidden depths. But in truth Lucia was as shallow as the meanest canal in the city.

Against his expectations, the dinner was a success, early awkwardness and stilted conversation soon smoothed by a rich, full-blooded and frighteningly expensive red wine. Sanborn, in a fresh white suit, did most of the talking. Zuichini remained content to let his patron speak for him, occupying himself with a lascivious scrutiny of the ample stretches of flesh displayed by Lucia's little black dress. Her ankle tattoo, a small blue heart, had caught the American's eye.

"In honour of young Joly?" he asked, with an ostentatious twinkle.

Lucia tossed her head. "I had it done in Sicily, the day of my sixteenth birthday. The first time I fell in love."

"It is as elegant and charming as the lady whom it adorns." Sanborn had a habit of giving a little bow whenever he paid a compliment. "Take a look, Zuichini, do you not agree?"

The wizened man leaned over to study the tattoo. His beak twitched in approval, the gleam in his dark eyes was positively sly. Even Lucia blushed under his scrutiny.

Sanborn said smoothly, "I have long admired the tattooist's skill. Your heart is a fine example."

Lucia smiled prettily. "Thank you, Mr Sanborn."

"Darius, please. I like to think we are friends."

"Darius, of course."

She basked in the glow of his genial scrutiny. Joly broke off a piece of bread and chewed hard. He was revising his opinion about their host's sexual orientation. Perhaps the old goat fancied trying his luck once Joly had left town. Fair enough. He was welcome to her.

"Do you know, Zuichini, I rather think that young Lucia's heart is as elegant as Sophia's dove. What do you say?"

The bookbinder paused in the act of picking something from his teeth and treated Lucia to a satyr's grin. "Uh-huh, I guess."

He didn't speak much English and his accent was a weird pastiche American. Perhaps he'd picked it up from watching old movies. His idea of a matinee idol was probably Peter Lorre. Why did Sanborn spend so much time with him, if they were not lovers, past or present? Joly asked if Sophia was Sanborn's daughter.

"Good heavens, no. Alas, like you, I have no family. Sophia was a young lady whom Zuichini and I came to know – what? – two or three years ago. She worked behind a bar down the Via Garibaldi. We were both very fond of her. And she had this rather lovely neck tattoo, in the shape of a flying dove with broad, outstretched wings. As with Lucia's lovely heart, I have no doubt that it was carved by a gifted artist."

"You admire well-made creations?" Lucia asked, preening.

Sanborn patted her lightly on the hand. "Indeed I do, my dear. My tastes are not confined to fine books."

Over the meal, he told them a little about his life. He'd inherited money – his grandfather had been president of an oil company – and he'd devoted years to travelling the world and indulging his taste for curios. Although he had never visited Venice until he was fifty years old, as he sailed into the lagoon and drank in the sights from the Bacino di San Marco, he resolved to make the city his home. By the sound of it, he lived in some grand *palazzo* overlooking the Canal Grande, and kept his income topped up with the rent from apartments that he'd been wise enough to buy up as the years passed. For all the talk of flooding, you could make good money on property in the city. Demand would always exceed supply.

"I always had a love of books, though it was not until I met Zuichini here that I started to collect in earnest. Are you a reader, Lucia, my dear?"

She shook her head. "No, I am too young. I tell this to Joly. He is of an age where there should be no time to read. He should live a bit."

"Well, books are not simply a delight for desiccated old rascals like me or Zuichini here You must not be hard on your young man. Seems to me he does pretty well for himself, living the *dolce vita* on a budget while indulging in old books whenever he finds a moment to spare."

Joly caught Zuichini peering down the front of Lucia's dress. Their eyes met briefly and the little man gave his toothless smile. Perhaps even he would find time to break off from binding books if only he could spend a night with Lucia. It wouldn't happen, though, unless Sanborn was in a mood to share. Joly savoured his swordfish. He didn't care. If the American showered her with money and presents, there was little doubt that Lucia would be content to do his bidding until she got bored. She'd confided in Joly that she'd worked in a lap dancing club in Milan and finished up living with the man who owned the joint. He was something high up in the Mafia, but after a few weeks he'd tired of her complaining and she'd managed to escape him without a scratch. Joly reckoned there wasn't much she wasn't willing to do, provided the price was right.

He felt his eyelids drooping before Sanborn snapped knobbly, arthritic fingers and asked the waiter to bring coffee. Before he knew what was happening, Lucia had accepted Sanborn's offer that they dine together again as his guests the following night. He didn't object – it was a free meal, and who cared if Sanborn was a dirty old man with an ulterior motive? Already he had spent enough time in the American's company to know that he was both persuasive and determined. If he wanted to spend his money, if Lucia wanted to sell her favours, who was Joly to stand in their way?

Sanborn insisted on paying a gondolier to take them back to a landing stage not far from Lucia's apartment. On the way home, she prattled about how interesting the American was. Joly knew it was unwise to argue, but in the end he couldn't resist pointing out that she was the one who had been unwilling to waste her evening in the company of two old men. Now she had committed them to a repeat, on his very last night in the city, when he would have preferred them to be alone.

"Could you have matched Darius's hospitality? I do not think so, Joly."

The next day was even hotter. Lucia went out to work early on and was intent on shopping during the afternoon. After lunching on a ham sandwich – no point in spoiling his appetite for the evening's feast – Joly embarked on a last stroll around the gardens of Castello. Finding a seat beneath a leafy tree, he finished *Death in Venice*, then ambled back through the alleyways, absorbing the smells of the fish-sellers' stalls and the chocolate shops, wondering how long it would be before he returned to La Serenissima. He understood what had kept Sanborn here. Once you became intoxicated with the beauties of Venice, the rest of the world must seem drab by comparison. But he was keen to sample Rome and after the previous night, he was more than ever convinced that this was the right time to break with Lucia.

When he arrived back at the flat, Lucia was short-tempered in the way that he now associated with her rare attacks of nervousness. She was bent upon impressing Sanborn, and she'd bought a slinky new red dress with a neckline so daring it bordered on indecent. It must have cost her a month's wages. A carefully targeted investment – assuming she had footed the bill. Joly wondered if she'd met up with Sanborn during the day and managed to charm the cash out of him. He wouldn't put it past either of them. So what? It was none of his business, soon he would be out of here.

The American and his sidekick were waiting for them at the appointed time, sitting at a table inside a restaurant close to Rialto. Sanborn's suit tonight was a shade of pale cream. Zuichini was scruffy by comparison, his face more like a scary carnival mask than ever.

"Lucia, you look dazzling!"

Sanborn kissed her on both cheeks and Zuichini did likewise. Joly had never seen the bookbinder show such animation. The little dark eyes seemed to be measuring Lucia's tanned flesh, no doubt wondering what she might look like when wearing no clothes. His attention pleased her. Perhaps she was hoping the two old men would fight over her. Even the waiter who took their order allowed his gaze to linger on her half-exposed breasts for longer than was seemly. The restaurant specialised in finest beef steak and Sanborn ordered four bottles of Bollinger.

"Tonight we celebrate!" he announced. "Over the past twenty-four hours, we have become firm friends. And although Joly is to move on tomorrow, with the lovely Lucia to follow, it is my firm conviction that all four of us will be reunited before too long."

As their glasses clinked, Lucia's eyes glowed. While they ate, the conversation turned to Joly's plans. He made it clear that they remained fluid. It was his style, he said, to trust to luck. Sanborn challenged this, arguing that even a young man needed roots.

"Learn from my mistake, Joly. Until I discovered the wonders of this marvellous city, my life lacked direction. You need something to anchor your existence. A place, firm friends, perhaps a trade."

Zuichini nodded with unaccustomed animation. "Right. That is right."

"Listen to this good man. He knows the joys of a craft, the unique pleasure that comes with creation. This is where you can steal a march on me, Joly. I am proud of my collection of books, undeniably, but I have never experienced the delight of creating a masterpiece of my own. I cannot paint, or compose, or write to any level of acceptable competence. I lack skills of a practical nature. But you, my young friend, are different. If you were to put your talents to good purpose…"

"I have an idea!" Lucia clapped her hands. Champagne went to her head. After a single glass, already she was raising her voice and her skin was flushed. "Once you have seen Rome, you could come back here and train as Zuichini's apprentice!"

The plague doctor's face split in a horrid smile, while Sanborn exclaimed with delight.

"Perfect! There, Joly, you have your answer. How clever you are, Lucia. That way two birds could be killed with one stone. Joly would learn from a master at the height of his powers, and Zuichini would have a good man to whom he could pass on the tricks of his trade before it is too late." Sanborn lowered his voice. "And there is something else that I have omitted to mention. Zuichini, may I? You see, Joly. This good fellow here, as you may have notice, is afflicted by a dreadful malady. Parkinson's attacks the nervous system and he has been suffering stoically for some time. But it becomes increasingly difficult for him to work. An utter tragedy, sometimes I despair. Not only because Zuichini's disability saddens me, but also from a selfish motive. For who will succeed him in business, who will practise his very special skills, so as to keep me supplied in fine books? In you, perhaps I have found the answer to my prayers."

"I don't think so," Joly said slowly.

"Oh, but you must!" Lucia exclaimed. "Such an opportunity, to learn from a genius!"

Sanborn must have primed her with this idea and asked her to offer support. They'd met during the day, not only so that Sanborn could pay for the new dress. The American was, Joly thought, like the most demanding parent. He wanted to have the young folk beholden to him, at his beck and call and used his control of the purse strings to make sure they did not escape.

"I suppose I can mull it over, when I am in Rome."

He'd expected Sanborn to suggest he abandoned his trip, but the old man surprised him, giving a broad smile and murmuring that he could not say fairer than that. Zuichini went so far as to give him a playful punch on the shoulder.

"Good apprentice, yes?"

While Joly tucked into the succulent beef, Sanborn talked about the art of binding books. He spoke of the pouch binding of Japanese books and the unique technique of *nakatoji*, of Jean Groller's leather-bound tomes covered with intricate geometric paterns, inlaid with coloured enamels and books bound in the flayed skin of murderers and highwaymen. He told them about cheverell, a goatskin parchment transformed into a binding both supple and strong with a bold, grainy pattern, popular in Italy during the fourteenth century, he described methods of fatliquoring leather, he explained...

"Joly, wake up!"

He became aware of Lucia's sharp elbow, digging into his side. Sanborn was beaming at him like a benevolent uncle, surveying a favourite nephew who has overdone the Christmas pudding. Zuichini was savouring his wine, still casting the occasional frank glance at Lucia's ample cleavage.

"Sorry, must have dropped off."

"Please do not apologise, I beg you," Sanborn said. "Put your sleepiness down to a combination of the wine and the weather. Perhaps accompanied by a tinge of *tristesse* – am I right, young man? This is your last night in La Serenissima for a little while and who could fail to experience a *frisson* of regret at departing from here?" He refilled their glasses, taking no notice when Joly shook his head. "So let us drink to our good friend Joly, and express the sincere hope that soon he will be back here for good!"

He reached out and patted Joly's arm. Blearily, Joly tried to focus on how to interpret the old man's behaviour. His hand did not linger. Had it been unfair to impute to him some sexual motive for such generosity? Perhaps in truth Sanborn's generosity did not amount to anything out of the ordinary. For a rich man, the cost of the dinner was small change. Sanborn was probably no more than he seemed, a lonely old millionaire, keen to share the company of the young and beautiful, as well as that of his ailing friend.

Sanborn made some remark and Lucia laughed long and loud, a noise that reminded Joly of a workman drilling in the road. She had a good head for drink, Joly knew that from experience, but even she was beginning to lose control. He remembered her describing her last night with the Mafia boss. She'd plucked up the courage to put a small knife in her bag. If he'd attacked her, she'd steeled herself to fight for her life. Joly did not doubt the strength of her survival instinct. If she thought herself threatened, she would lash out without a moment's hesitation. What would happen if Zuichini made her afraid with the clumsiness of his overtures?

He yawned. His head was spinning and he couldn't keep worrying about what might happen between consenting adults. *Que sera, sera.*

Next thing he knew, someone was tapping him on the arm. Through the fog of a hangover, he heard Sanborn's gentle voice.

"Joly, my boy. Are you all right?"

Even the act of opening his eyes made him want to cry out, it hurt so much. Christ, how much had he drunk? He had no head for champagne, but he'd never felt this bad before. He blinked hard and tried to take in his surroundings. He was lying on a hard bed in a small, musty room. The sun was shining in through a small high window but he had no idea where he might be. Sanborn was standing beside the bed, arms folded, studying him. Suddenly, he felt afraid.

"Where am I?"

"Listen, my friend, you have nothing to fear. You just had rather too much to drink, that's all."

"The drinks were spiked." Nothing else could explain how he had come to black out, this had never happened to him before.

"No, no, no." Sanborn had a first class bedside manner, though Joly was sure he was lying. "You overdid it, simple as that. And you threw up all over Lucia, which frankly wasn't such a good idea."

"Lucia?" He gazed at the peeling wallpaper, the unfamiliar cupboard and door. "Where have you brought me?"

"Listen, it's all right. Lucia was upset, that's all. Zuichini took care of her, no need to worry. As she wouldn't entertain you in her bed last night, I volunteered to bring you here. Now, you need to get up and dressed. I think you said you plan to take the one o'clock coach from Piazzale Roma?"

A wave of panic engulfed him. Effectively, he was the old man's prisoner.

"You haven't told me where you've brought me."

"There's no secret, Joly, keep your hair on, my dear fellow. This is an apartment I bought six months ago. Hardly the lap of luxury, but it's only a stone's throw from the restaurant. It seemed like the best solution, we could hardly leave you to your own devices, the state you were in, and Lucia was in no mood to take you back with her."

Joly coughed. "Then – I'm free to go?"

Sanborn's parchment features conveyed benign bewilderment. "I don't understand. Why should you not be? I was only striving to do you a good turn."

I've been a fool, Joly thought, this isn't a man to fear. The question is – what happened between Lucia and Zuichini? Did he try it on, did she let him get away with it?

"Sorry, Darius. I'm not myself."

"Not to worry, these things happen. There's a bathroom next door. No gold taps, I'm afraid, but you'll find the basic necessities. I'll leave you to it, if I may. Your bag's over by the door, incidentally. I went over to Lucia's this morning to pick it up."

"Thanks," Joly whispered.

"Here's the key to the front door. Would you be kind enough to lock up for me? I have a little business to attend to, but I'll be there at the coach station to see you off, it's the least I can do."

Joly stared at the old man's genial expression. Hoarsely, he said, "Thanks."

"Think nothing of it. That's what friends are for, don't you agree?"

Two hours later, Joly arrived at the Piazzale Roma, bag in hand. Within moments he caught sight of Sanborn by an advertisement hoarding and the American lifted his stick in greeting before limping to greet him. He had a black velvet bag slung over his shoulder.

"You're looking much better. Remarkable what wonders can be worked by a simple wash and brush up."

"I'm very grateful to you," Joly said humbly, handing over the key to the apartment.

"Think nothing of it." Sanborn cleared his throat. "Actually, I talked to Lucia before I made my way over here. There isn't an easy way to put this, Joly, but I don't believe she intends to join you in Rome. I'm sorry."

Joly took a breath. "Maybe things had run their course."

Sanborn bowed his head. "That was rather the impression that I had gained. Well, I don't care for prolonged farewells. I hope you will reflect on our conversation last night and that soon we shall see you again in La Serenissima."

Forcing a smile, Joly said, "Who knows, I might take Zuichini up on his kind offer. There are worse ways of making a living than binding fine books, I guess."

A light flared in Sanborn's old eyes. Voice trembling, he said, "Joly, the moment I first saw you, I knew you were made of the right stuff. In fact, I'll let you into a secret. I'd seen you a couple of times at the Campo Santi Apostoli before I made so bold as to introduce myself."

"Is that so?" Joly didn't know whether to be puzzled or flattered. "So did you see Lucia as well?"

"As a matter of fact, I did. Such a pretty creature, with that gorgeous dark hair and honey skin. Oh well, there are many more lovely girls in Venice. Despite my age, I can guess how sad you must feel. I felt the same about my friend Sophia, after I'd talked to her for the last time. But she and I were not lovers, the physical loss makes it doubly hard for you."

"These things happen."

"Yes, life goes on. And you will never forget Lucia, of that I am sure. But your life will be so much richer if you take up Zuichini's offer. Truly, his craftsmanship is unique. Think of it! You could follow in his footsteps. Make a name for yourself and earn a not inconsiderable fortune."

"Is Zuichini rich?"

"My dear fellow, do not be deceived by appearances. If – no, *when* you return, you will have a chance to visit his splendid home near the Rialto. Even though he and I are close associates, he never fails to drive a hard bargain. But I, and others like me, are willing to pay for the best. For something unique."

They shook hands and Sanborn pulled out of his shoulder bag a parcel wrapped in gift paper. He thrust it at Joly.

"I want you to have this. A token of our friendship. And a reminder of the esoteric pleasures that lie in store, should you accept Zuichini's offer to help you learn his trade."

"Thanks." Joly's cheeks were burning. He'd harboured so many false suspicions and now he couldn't help feeling a mite embarrassed. "I'm not sure that bookbinding is…"

"Think about it. That's all I ask." Sanborn smiled. "I have seen enough of you in a short space of time to be confident that you would relish the chance to become a craftsman in your own right. As you told me, you have a taste for the unusual. And with your love of books…ah well, you must be going. Goodbye, my friend. Or as I should say, *a rivederci.*"

Joly found himself waving at the old man's back as he limped away. At the notice board, just before he moved out of sight, Sanborn raised his stick in salute, but he did not turn his head. The bus was waiting and Joly found himself a seat by the window. As the driver got into gear, Joly tore the wrapping paper from his present. He stared at it for a long time.

The present was a book, carefully protected by bubble wrap and old newspapers and that came as no surprise. The title was *A Short Treatise on the Finer Points of Bookbinding.* But it was not the text that seized Joly's attention, though deep down he knew already that, one day, this would become his Bible.

The front cover was tanned and polished to a smooth golden brown. He'd never come across anything quite like it. To the touch, it had slight bumps, like a soft sandpaper. The spine and back cover felt more like suede. But what entranced him was not the texture of the binding.

At first sight, he thought the cover bore a logo. But with a second glance, he realised his mistake. In the bottom corner was a design in blue-black. A picture of a flying dove, with broad outstretched wings.

He held his breath as he recalled kissing Lucia's toes. Recalled the delicate heart shape traced in ink upon her ankle. Recalled, with a shiver of fear and excitement, Zuichini's admiration of the tattooist's work, the way those dark and deadly little eyes kept being drawn to Lucia's tender, honey-coloured skin.

He settled back on the hard seat. The countryside was passing by outside, but he paid it no heed. Sanborn understood him better than he understood himself. After searching for so long, he'd finally found what he was looking for. Soon he would return to La Serenissima. And there Zuichini would share with him the darkest secrets of the bookbinder's craft. He would teach him how to make the book that Sanborn craved. A book for all three of them to remember Lucia by.

HOMEWORK

PHIL LOVESEY

English Homework
Judy Harris – Year 10

In your opinion, is Hamlet merely faking his madness, or is he really insane?

This term we have been studying *Hamlet*, a play written ages ago by William Shakespeare. It's quite good, though the words are all strange for modern people to really understand. There's lots of stuff that is really, really old that Sir had to try and explain to us before it made any sense, not that most of the class seemed bothered, goofing around as usual.

Most of us thought the film was way better than the book, but that Mel Gibson bloke still used all the old words, so that when there wasn't much going on except him talking, I noticed quite a few of the class were either mucking about or texting. I even told Sir about this after one lesson but all he did was sort of smile at me and say Shakespeare wasn't for everyone, and maybe it was better for me if the class didn't think I was telling tales – which seemed quite harsh, as I was only trying to help him.

The story of *Hamlet* goes like this: There's this prince (Hamlet) who lives in another country a long time ago. His dad dies, and his mum marries Hamlet's uncle, so he doesn't get to become king. He gets real mad about this and reckons his mum's a bit of a whore, especially when the ghost of his dad comes back and tells Hamlet that the pair of them were an item before he died, and that the uncle even dripped poison into his ear and murdered him to get off with Hamlet's mum and become king.

This was quite a spooky bit in the film, the ghost thing, and most of the class were watching except Cheryl Bassington who was texting her boyfriend under the desk. He's an apprentice plumber who lives down our road, and I often see him pick her up on his crappy little motorbike thing. She says they've 'done it' loads of times, which I think is really lame at her age, as I reckon you should save yourself for someone who really loves you.

Hamlet has a woman who loves him. Her name's Ophelia and she sort of hangs around the palace pining for him. It's that Helena Bonham Carter in the film, and all the lads in the class were right crude about her in her nightie. Steve Norris made a sort of 'joke' about boning-Bonham-Carter which even Sir sniggered at, but I just thought was sick. I think Ophelia's really sad because she really does love Hamlet, and when he starts acting a bit mental, she gets really upset. He even tells her that he never loved her, and that she should go away and become a nun. Even Polonius (her own dad) uses Ophelia to test if Hamlet really is mad, which seems well odd – but then he gets stabbed behind a curtain, which serves him right for being such a bad dad in the first place.

My Dad wouldn't ever do such a thing to me, regardless of what the papers said about him at the time of the robbery.

It seems that in *Hamlet* everyone's only after power and are prepared to do anything to get it even if it means killing their family, marrying incestuously, using their kids, or faking madness that really hurts people. I think that's very bad of all them. Ophelia is so cut up about Hamlet being horrible to her that she goes and drowns herself, not that he seems that bothered about it. And neither were the boys in the class, either, who asked for that bit to be shown again, as they reckoned you could see Helena Bonham Carter's tits through her wet nightie. Thank goodness someone tells Hamlet's brother what a schemer he is so that he comes back really angry and tries to kill Hamlet in a duel.

We all thought the ending was right crap because nearly everyone dies. Hamlet, his uncle, his mum, Ophelia's bother; they all end up dead in this big hall, either poisoned or stabbed with poison-tipped swords. Dave Coles reckoned the *Macbeth* we studied in SATS for Year 9 was better because there were real nude women to perv over, and hangings and beheadings and stuff. When I told him I'd hated that film, loads of people laughed at me and I felt right stupid, especially as Sir didn't tell them off for being cruel.

Maybe that was the moment I decided to do what I've done to you, Sir. Perhaps it was the moment it all made a sort of sense. Like I've written, some people just want power and don't really care about other people's feelings. Like you, just two terms into the school and obviously wanting to be the trendy young teacher, joining in with them laughing, not stopping it like other teachers would have done. Perhaps it was simply another all too quickly forgotten moment for you. But believe me, Sir, it went in deep with me. Well deep.

That night I told my mum about what had happened in your class, how you'd let them laugh. She was cooking – well, I say cooking – putting a ready-meal in the microwave for Uncle Tony for his tea, more like. Because she has to have it on the table for him when he gets in, or there's trouble. He rings on his mobile from The Wellington Arms, tells her to have it ready in five minutes, then suddenly she's all action, heaving herself up from the sofa and sending me up to my room as she gets it done.

Once, his meal wasn't ready and I heard the result. Lots of shouting, then a scream. Mum's scream. Then what sounded like moaning. I didn't come down until the door slammed half an hour later. Mum wouldn't look at me, sort of flinched when I tried to put my arm around her. She was trying to stick a torn-up photo of her and dad back together, but her hands were shaking too much, and she was trying not to cry. I asked if I could help. It was nice photo – her and Dad on honeymoon in Greece, both looking right young and happy on the beach in front of all these white hotels. She swore at me and told me to get back upstairs to my room.

Hamlet used to love his dad as well. Then he went away to some college somewhere, and when he came back his dad was dead, and his uncle had married his mum. The problem is that his dad is now a ghost and tells him he was murdered, which makes Hamlet very angry. He also doesn't know if his mind is being tricky with him, so he decides to set a trap to find out if his uncle is really guilty or not. So, Hamlet gets these actors to do a play sort of like his uncle killing his dad, then watches his uncle's reaction. He wants to 'prick his conscience'.

Dave Coles went 'Whay!' when Mel Gibson said the word 'prick' – which everyone but me thought was really funny. I just thought it was a really good plan of Hamlet's. He wasn't saying 'prick' like a penis; he was saying it was like a needle, pricking his uncle's guilt. I think I'm cleverer than most of them in the class because I read more and understand these things, know that words can have more than just the obvious meaning. I think its because I'm not allowed to use the computer at home (Uncle Tony's on it most of the time). Nor do I have a mobile. Just books, really. Sometimes a bit of telly when Mum's finished watching the soaps downstairs. But mostly, I'm just in my room, thinking and reading.

I write to Dad a lot. Tell him about school. Mum says I can't talk about some of the stuff that goes on in the house, as it would only upset him. She says that although Uncle Tony isn't my real uncle, he's doing us a massive favour by staying here when Dad's away. They used to be good mates, Dad and Uncle Tony, working at the warehouse together, going down the pub. But when it all went wrong, and the police came for Dad, they sort of fell out.

What's really great is that Dad's letters are getting longer each time. Just a page in the beginning, now it's often three or four. His spelling's really coming on, too, because of all the classes he's been taking. He's been well behaved, so they've allowed him more time to study. He says he's taking his GCSE's as well! Strange, isn't it, Sir? There I am, in your class, studying *Hamlet*, and my Dad's doing exactly the same thing. At thirty-eight, too. He reckons once he's done his English, Maths and Science, he'll do loads more subjects after that. He says one bloke further down the wing as got nineteen GCSE's! See, Sir? They tell you all this stuff about people in prison being thick and scummy, but there's some of them really trying to improve themselves. Dad's still got another two years left, so I reckon he'll have more qualifications than me when he gets out. How weird will that be?

In his last letter, he mentioned Uncle Tony, saying that even though they weren't best mates anymore, it was good he had agreed to lodge at ours and pay the rent and stuff. He said it was the least Uncle Tony could do, as he owed Dad big time. He also said that the years would fly by, and when he finally gets released, he's got a surprise that will keep me, Mum and him happy for years. But when I showed Mum the letter, she screwed it up and chucked it away, saying he was talking nonsense, then told me never to mention it again. I'm not sure, but I think it was to do with the robbery at the warehouse. Thing is, although the police had CCTV film of Dad loading stuff into a van when he shouldn't have been, the actual stuff was never found. The local newspaper said it was worth over a £100,000 – but you can't believe everything they say, *can you*, Sir?

Dad doesn't like me to visit and see him where he is, so every other Saturday when Mum and Uncle Tony go out, I head for the reference library in town. It's nice there, warm. I don't use the computers, prefer to look through the books and old newspapers they have on this stuff called microfilm. Honestly, Sir, it's amazing. Thousands and thousands of newspapers from all over the place, going back years. All catalogued to make searches easier. People think the internet is the place to find stuff out, but I reckon searching through old newspapers is better. There's loads of interesting stuff, articles people can't be bothered to upload because I guess it would maybe take too long. Can be frustrating, though, and you have to have a little bit of luck and patience.

Yeah. Luck. I guess that's how I managed to find you, Sir. Luck and patience. And, of course, a really good reason. And you made sure you gave me plenty of those, didn't you, Sir? Calling me a sneak, not helping when the others all laughed. I began to wonder just why you did that. Why you wouldn't help me? And then I figured it out. Just one of those chance things that no one else saw, but I did.

It was a Wednesday, the last lesson before lunch, and we all in your classroom as Mel Gibson was waffling on about whether or not to kill himself (*To be, or not to be*; remember, Sir, you made us watch the bloody thing ten times that lesson). True to form, I could see Cheryl Bassington texting away in the darkness on the mobile phone under her desk. Except it wasn't her plumber boyfriend she was texting, was it, Sir? Because when she pressed *Send*, you got your phone out of your pocket and tried to read it as discreetly as possible. I saw you, Sir. Watched it happen. You, Sir. Someone who should be trusted to educate us, getting secret texts from a fifteen-year-old girl. Well naturally, my conscience was 'pricked', as Shakespeare might have said...

I began wondering what Hamlet would do in my situation. You know, needing to find stuff out, but not wanting to be caught doing it? So, I did what he did – pretended to go loony for a bit. That lunchtime, I went and sat right next to Cheryl Bassington and started eating a bit weirdly, mixing my pudding into my pizza and making stupid noises and giggling. Very Hamlet, Sir, you'd have been proud. Anyway, I could see my plan was working, and that Cheryl and her mates couldn't wait to get up and leave. They next bit was so easy – just as they were going and calling me all sorts of names, I suddenly leant over and clung on to Cheryl, slipping a hand into her pocket and grabbing her mobile as she yelped and tried to get me away. Mr Price came over and began shouting at us to behave, but Cheryl and her mates just swore at him and ran off. Next, I went straight to the toilet block, locked myself in and went through the phone.

They're really quite easy to figure out, these mobile things. There's a kind of menu with all sorts of symbols to help you. I found Cheryl's pictures first, and let me tell you, Sir, there's all sorts of rude stuff on there. Not just ones of the plumber, but some of you, as well. And not just shots taken in class when you weren't watching, but others of you smiling right at the camera, in bed, with her. Well, you were there, you know the rest…

I couldn't believe just how bloody stupid you'd been, what a crazy risk you'd been taking. If Cheryl showed any of this stuff to the wrong person – you'd be out of a job, wouldn't you, Sir? They'd probably stick you in prison. And my Dad tells me what they do to people like you inside. Horrible things that even the wardens (he calls them 'screws') turn a blind eye to. Really, really stupid of you, Sir.

Next, I found the texts. Loads of them. From you to her; from her back to you. Some of them went back as far as six weeks, which considering you've only been here two terms, kind of makes you a pretty fast worker, I guess. They have names for people like you, Sir.

Anyway, the most recent series of texts were about meeting up on a Saturday night. At the 'usual place', apparently, wherever that was. You suggested half-eight, and Cheryl had replied with one of those really lame smiley-face things. Sad. And sick.

But seeing as no one else had complained, no rumours had started, I had to assume that no one else knew about you and her. Except me, of course. Which really made me think about things for a while.

Strange life you've led, Sir. Like I say, the reference library comes up with all sorts of stuff. One of the main reasons I went there was to find out more about what had happened to my dad. It even made one or two of the national papers, because I guess it all happened in what those newspaper people refer to as a 'slow news week'. Seems one of the main things was that the police reckoned Dad had to have had someone helping him that night. There were two CCTV cameras covering the warehouse, but only one was trained where it was supposed to be, on the loading yard. The other was pointing across the road (and here I'm going to use a quotation just like you told me to) 'the entrance to a nearby youth club, where a group of underage girls could be seen drinking and cavorting with young lads.'

See what I'm saying, Sir? If someone *had* been helping Dad (and he's never admitted as much, even to me) then the camera wasn't pointing in the right direction to catch them. It was watching young girls, instead. Maybe it was looking for trouble from them, but then again, you know better than that, don't you, Sir? For guess what I found when I researched into our town's CCTV company a little further? That's right, a picture of you, stood with two other operators at the launch five years ago. You – unmistakably. Your name on the caption, everything. A big photo of all three of you smiling in front of loads of television screens, the article telling people how you could remotely direct and move all these little cameras to catch criminals and keep us safer. Sort of like playing Big Brother, wasn't it, Sir? But not the crappy programme on the telly – the book by George Orwell. Like I say, I read a lot, I really do.

And once I found out about your 'preferences' from Cheryl's mobile, things started to drop into place. I began piecing it together in those toilets on that Wednesday lunchtime. Just under a year, you'd been teaching. Eighteen month's my Dad's been inside. According to the papers, at my Dad's trial, the CCTV company admitted they'd received a resignation from one of their operators for 'failing to comply with company policy whilst monitoring the immediate area around the warehouse.' That was *you*, wasn't it, Sir?

I reckoned you left the job, took a quick teacher-training course somewhere, then turned up here. But like I say, it was only a theory. I could have been wildly wrong. So, I decided to do what Hamlet does, and devise a test (another conscience-pricker) to see if I was right. Here's what I did…

Firstly, I texted you back on Cheryl's phone. You remember that one, Sir? The one where she asked to meet you that very night at The Wellington Arms? That was me, not her. But less than a minute later the phone buzzed in my hands with your reply, something about having to be really careful as it was such a public place.

And I was giggling now, as you replied back again, insisting we must meet, that I had something to tell you I might need to see a doctor about. I remember having to stop myself from laughing out loud as I pressed Send.

Next, I deleted the messages and dropped the phone in the toilet cistern. Now, even if Cheryl and her mates did find it, the thing wouldn't work, and you wouldn't be able to contact her before meeting up in The Wellington. You were most likely going to turn up, and she had no idea about any of it. Quite a scheme, eh? I think even Hamlet would have been proud of me, don't you, Sir?

It's a good play, *Hamlet*, and has often been interpreted in many different ways. It seems to me that the central question – does he fake his madness to get revenge on those who've betrayed him? – is almost impossible to answer. Perhaps Shakespeare was trying to say that all revenge is a form of madness, as it can consume our minds if we're not careful.

I think Dad's the sanest man I know. Yes, he did a stupid thing and got caught, and now he's being punished for it. But he's never talked of revenge – even though I reckon he'd probably want to get that CCTV operator who spent too long watching young girls getting drunk, rather than catching the apprentice on the night of the robbery. The police never found any fingerprints or anything, but the fact is that Dad *couldn't* have done it on his own. Someone else must have helped him, been inside the warehouse, handing him boxes to load into the van just out of sight of the camera. But when the police when through the tapes, Dad was the only person on them. Doesn't seem very fair, does it, Sir? My dad in prison, and the other man going free because you didn't do your job properly.

Chances are, Sir, you never made the connection between Dad and me. Judy Harris, I mean it's not an uncommon surname, is it? Sort of invisible to you, aren't I? The swotty kid who complains about the others, tells tales on them; the easy one to ridicule. The plain one, the one that doesn't wear make-up or giggle as you pass by in the corridor. Just invisible old Judy Harris, does her homework, tries her best. Strange how life can turn out, isn't it, Sir?

Back to my conscience pricker. Having arranged for you to be in The Wellington, I decided that Mum and Uncle Tony needed a little more culture in their lives. I went to the shopping precinct on the way home and bought myself a copy of the *Hamlet* DVD, telling them after tea that I thought it would be a really nice idea if we all sat down and watched it together. Well, of course, Uncle Tony – already a little drunk at this point – raised a few objections, saying he didn't mind watching Mel Gibson stuff, *Mad Max* and the like, but he was buggered if he was going to sit down and watch 'a load of Shakespeare shit all night'. (See? Another quotation. Makes two so far. Doing right well, aren't I, Sir?)

Anyway, I made a bit of a fuss, and eventually Mum decided to smooth things over and ask Uncle Tony really nicely if he'd do this one thing. I said it'd make us all feel more like a proper family, and Uncle Tony sort of made a throaty noise, shrugged and gave way, saying he'd give it half an hour, and if it was bollocks, then he'd leave it.

So, Sir, just after half-seven that night, I put *Hamlet* on. Imagine that, a real bit of culture in our grotty house. Amazing, eh? And then I did what Hamlet does, watched my mother and uncle real close as the story unravelled...

It didn't take long, twenty minutes at the most, and that's even with all the old language to cope with. Mum and Uncle Tony soon go the gist of it – the betrayal of Hamlet's father – and sort of began shifting uncomfortably and giving these sideways looks at each other. Honestly, Sir, it worked a treat.

Uncle Tony started coming out with all this stuff about Mel Gibson going 'poofy', and he was much better in *Braveheart* and all the *Lethal Weapon* stuff. I knew he was just begging for an excuse to leave what was becoming more and more embarrassing for him. So, at that point I decided to tell him about you, Sir. Not the Cheryl Bassington stuff, or even the way you were so mean to me; instead, I told him some other stuff.

Yeah, I know. I lied. But just a white one, really. And Hamlet himself does that, doesn't he, when he tells Ophelia that he doesn't really love her anymore? I told Uncle Tony that when I was buying the DVD, a strange bloke had come up to me asking me my name and wanting to know where I lived, and when I told him, he asked if Tony Watts lived with us. When I said he did, the bloke said he'd wanted to speak to him about the 'favour' he'd done Uncle Tony with the security cameras, and as far as he was concerned, he was owed 'big style', and that he would be waiting in The Wellington at eight-thirty to 'sort it all out'.

Well, my Uncle Tony being the sort of bloke he is, you don't have to try too hard to imagine his reaction. He was well angry, and began swearing and cursing, telling me I should have told him much earlier, asking for a description of you, then grabbing his coat and storming off, slamming the front door so loudly the walls shook. Mum looked right ashen, turned the DVD off, then ordered me up to my room saying I caused quite enough trouble for one night. Uncle Tony didn't come home that night.

That was two weeks ago, and you've been off school ever since, haven't you, Sir? At Thursday morning's assembly, the Head told us you'd been attacked the previous night, and you were staying away to recover. Two broken ribs and a fractured jaw, the local paper said, with a couple of witnesses saying you'd been beaten up by a Tony Watts (unemployed) in the car park of The Wellington Arms. Police, apparently, are still trying to find a motive, but I'm sure with a little 'help' they'll have a clearer picture of why he did that cruel thing to you.

Uncle Tony's on remand as we can't afford the bail, so he'll be inside until the court case, which should be really interesting. The police have already interviewed my mum about Uncle Tony, but they haven't got round to me yet. I'm not sure whether to tell them what I know, or to keep quiet about it. I'll write to Dad and ask him what he thinks.

Our substitute teacher isn't very good, but she's told us to finish these assignments so the school can send them to you to mark while you recover. I'm sure that when you read this, Sir, you'll realise why you were attacked that night. Together with how much I now know about you that you'd rather other people didn't.

In conclusion, I say that whether or not Hamlet was faking his madness is irrelevant. How sane are any of us, anyway? And isn't the very idea of faking madness a bit mad in the first place? Maybe you should know, Sir, the amount of faking you've done in the last few years.

I look forward to receiving an A for this essay. After all, I really did my homework on you.

LAPTOP

CATH STAINCLIFFE

I'd been boosting laptops for a couple of years but never with such bloody disastrous consequences. Up until then it'd been easy money. Two or three a week kept body and soul together and was a damn sight more conducive to the good life than temping in some god-awful office with all the crap about diets and botox and endless squabbles over the state of the kitchen. Shorter working week, too. Eight maybe ten hours, the rest of the time my own.

I always dressed well for work – part of the scam, isn't it? People are much less guarded if I'm in a designer suit: something smart, fully lined along with good shoes, hair and make-up. Helps me mingle. Looking like an executive, some high-flying businesswoman, gives me access to the most fertile picking grounds: conference centres, business parks, commuter trains, the best restaurants and coffee bars. And, after all, if someone nicks your laptop who's going spring to mind? Me with my crisp clothes, my detached air, snag-free tights or some lad in a beanie hat and dirty fingernails?

So, that fateful day, as I came to think of it, I was working at Manchester Airport. I do it four or five times a year; the train service is handy and with all the business flights I've plenty of targets to choose from.

As with any type of thieving, opportunity is all. The aim being to get the goods and get away with it. When I started working for Danny, he came out with me but I was quick on the uptake and after a few runs he left me to it. I'm one of his best operators but he reckons I'm lazy. You could make more, he tells me near enough every time I swap the merchandise for cash, a bit of ambition you could be clearing fifty a year, higher tax bracket. The last bit's a joke. No one in the business pays any tax. But I'm not greedy. I enjoy the time I have. Gives me chance to indulge my passion. I paint watercolours. Surprised? So was I when I first drifted into it. Then it became the centre of my life. It was what got me out of bed and kept me up late.

That day when I spotted the mark I dubbed him The Wolf. He had a large head, the coarse brown hair brushed straight back from his face, a long, sharp nose and lips that didn't quite meet; too many teeth for his mouth. Like a kid with those vampire fangs stuffed in their gob. I assumed he was meeting someone as he made no move to check in and we were near the arrivals hall. He had the laptop on the floor, to his right, at the side of his feet. He was in prime position at the end of a row of seats, in the lounge where people have coffee while they wait for the information boards to change or for a disembodied voice to make hard-to-hear announcements.

After walking about a bit, checking my exit routes and getting a feel for the atmosphere that day and the people hanging around (no nutters, drunks or a surfeit of security guards) I settled myself on the end seat of the row adjoining his. He and I were back to back. I put my large bag down beside me at my left. My bag and his laptop were maybe five inches apart. On the seat next to me I put my own laptop and handbag. When I turned to my left I could see us both reflected in the plain glass of the offices that ran along the edge of the concourse. There were coloured screens behind the glass to mask the work areas so no danger of my being seen from in there.

Timing is crucial. I watched his reflection as he glanced down to check his laptop and I moved a few seconds after, just as a large family with raucous kids and two trolley-loads of bags hoved into view, squabbling about where to wait. Keeping my upper body straight, I reached my left arm back and grasped the handle of his laptop, pulled it forward and lifted it up and into my big bag. I grabbed the handles of that, hitched it onto my shoulder, collected my other things, stood and walked steadily away. Belly clamped, mouth dry, senses singing.

Twice I've been rumbled at that very moment, before I'm out of range. Both in the early days. Turning, I look confused. "Sorry?"

"My laptop!" They are incandescent with outrage, ready to thump me. Except I don't run or resist. I gawp at them, look completely befuddled, furrowed brow. Mouth the word 'laptop?' My hand flies to my mouth, I stare in my bag. "Oh, my god." Both hands to my mouth. I blush furiously. Wrestle the shopper from my shoulder. "God, I am so sorry." Withdraw the offending article, hand it back, talking all the time, on the brink of tears. "It's exactly like mine." I hold up my own laptop (case only: I'm not lugging around something that heavy all day – besides someone might nick it). "I was miles away, oh, god, I feel awful. You must think, oh, please I am so, so sorry. I don't know what to say." Deliberately making a scene, drawing attention, flustered woman in a state. Their expressions morph: rage, distrust, exasperation, embarrassment and eventually relief tinged with discomfort. They just want me to shut up and disappear. Which I do. With The Wolf, though, all goes smooth as silk.

Until I get the bastard thing home and open it.

I generally check to see if they're password protected. Danny has a little code that cracks about fifty per cent of them, the rest he passes on to a geek who sorts them out. Danny appreciates it if I let him know which ones need further attention when I hand them over.

So I got home, changed into something more comfortable, had lunch on my little balcony. On a clear day to the east I can see the hills beyond the City of Manchester stadium and the velodrome and to the west the city centre: a jumble of Victorian gothic punctuated by modern glass and steel, wood and funny angles, strong colours. It's a vista I love to paint. But that day was damp, hazy, shrouding the skyline. I polished off a smoked salmon salad, some green tea, then got down to business.

Danny's code didn't work. And I could have left it at that. I should have. But there was a memory stick there: small, black, inoffensive looking. I picked it up and slotted it into the USB port on my own machine. There wasn't much on it, that's what I thought at the time, just one file, called *Accounts*. I opened it expecting credits and debits, loss carried forward or whatever. Perhaps bank details that Danny could milk. Overseas accounts, savings.

Not those sort of accounts.

June 12th 2010

She was very drunk when she left the club. Falling into a taxi, falling out at her place. I let her get inside and waited for a while before I went in the back. She was stumbling about for long enough. When I judged she was asleep I crept upstairs. I had everything ready. She woke. But I'd done it by then. The colour flooded her face and she tried to get up, jerking, but couldn't, then the flush drained away and her eyes glazed over. I closed her eyes. She looked more peaceful that way. It was wonderful. Better than I'd imagined. A pure rush. Cleaner, brighter than drugs or religion or sex. On a different plane. I wish I'd stayed there longer now. I didn't want to leave her but I was being cautious. Everything meticulously done. Precise, tidy. I've waited all my life for this. I wasn't going to ruin it by being clumsy and leaving anything they could trace back to me.

June 18th 2010

Lady Luck must be smiling down on me. No one suspects a thing.

The Wolf obviously fancied himself as a scribe. Some sort of crime thriller. I wondered if he'd got this backed up anywhere else or if he'd just lost his life's work. I read on. I mainly read biographies but it was intriguing. The next entry was a couple of months later.

Aug 23rd 2010

I'm getting restless again. Low after the high? Things are difficult. I can't remember her face anymore. I should have taken a photograph.

Sept 4th 2010

I've found the next one. Not sure how to get in but the good weather might make things easier. An open window, patio doors? She has a beautiful face; very simple, strong mouth, wide eyes. I want to see those eyes change.

A tinge of unease made me pause. I scrolled down the document – it was only four pages long. I scanned it all again. The dates spanned a nine-month period. The latest entry was from February 2011, only two weeks earlier. Four pages, hardly a novel. A short story maybe? Or real?

The thought made my stomach lurch and my throat close. I switched the machine off, my hand trembling a little. Stupid. Just some sad bloke's sick fantasy. But like sand in an oyster shell the notion stuck. It grated on me while I tried to paint, making it impossible to concentrate.

I haven't picked up a brush since.

That evening I sat in front of the television flicking the channels. Nothing held my attention. The memory stick crouched at the edge of my vision, a shiny black carapace, like a malevolent beetle or a cockroach. I decided then there was one way to stop the flights of fancy. I just needed to prove to myself that the accounts were fictional.

Sept 24th 2010

She never locks up when she goes next door for the morning paper. I hid in the spare room all day. The excitement was unbearable, delicious. And then I waited while she cooked herself a meal and bathed and watched television. It was after midnight before she turned out the lights. She'd been drinking whisky, I could smell it on her breath and from the glass beside her. I thought it would make her drowsy but she flinched when I touched her and struggled and almost ruined everything. She made me angry. I had to punish her. After all it could have been perfect. She had robbed me of that. She soon learnt her lesson and then I did it and the spasms started; the life bucking from her. I felt her go cold.

Then we were even. I still laid her out nicely, enjoyed her till the sun rose. Not long enough. With her spoiling it like that I had to cover my tracks. Everyone has candles around these days and some people forget to replace the smoke alarm batteries. Whisky's an accelerant. I want the next one to be perfect even if it takes me longer to find her.

I re-read the entries and made a note of the dates. There were no names or addresses, not even locations but I reckoned I could check those dates – for deaths. I looked online first, found the Office of National Statistics site. But their records only went up to the year 2009 and there were practically half a million deaths a year. That's getting on for ten thousand a week. Without more details there was no way to find out about a specific death on a particular date.

Oct 5th 2010

Every day, going about my business, knowing that what I am sets me apart. I have gone beyond the boundaries and reaped the rewards. If anyone could bottle this and sell it they'd make a killing (hah!).

I tried the Local Records Office next. They had registered deaths for 2010 on microfiche. It took me several trips, booking the viewers for a couple of hours at a time. I started by eliminating all the men and then anyone under fifteen and over forty. Arbitrary I know, but I had to narrow it down somehow. And I focused on

Manchester. After all he'd been to the airport and he mentions the Metrolink when he talks about the third victim.

Dec 11th 2010

She got on at Cornbrook. It was like recognising someone. I followed her home. I can't wait – though I will. The anticipation makes it hard to think straight.

Even then I still had lists with dozens of deaths for each of the two dates in 2010. It was hopeless.

Danny rang the following week. Had I retired? Or was I just being even more lazy than usual? A virus, I told him, couldn't shake it off. So I hadn't got anything for him.

It became harder to sleep. The Wolf stalked my dreams. I thought about pills but that frightened me more. If he did come and I was comatose, I might never wake up. I tried to imagine what he'd done to the women. He was never explicit in what he wrote.

I spent a fortune on increased security. I could have gone to the police then, I had rehearsed a cover story about finding the laptop, but I feared the police would dig deeper. Want to know how I'd paid for my flat when I hadn't had any employment for over two years. They'd only have to check my bank records to see I handled a lot of cash. They were bound to be suspicious. I could end up in court for no good reason. In prison. So I delayed – hoping to find out it was all invented.

Jan 7th 2011

Tomorrow I'll be with her. This has been a long time coming, tricky with her going away so often. But now she's back. She'll soon be mine.

More than once I considered destroying the memory stick but what if it was all true and The Wolf was a killer, then this was proof. In one dream the memory stick was missing, I searched the flat in a frantic panic and woke up, drenched in sweat. The fear forced me from my bed to check that I still had it. I copied it to my own machine for back-up.

I stopped going to bed. The doctor suggested sleeping pills but I lied and said that side of things was fine, I just needed something for my anxiety during the daytime. He prescribed Prozac. It didn't help. But they say it takes a while to have any effect. As it turned out, I didn't have that long.

Jan 8th 2011

I was all ready but she brought a man home and he stayed with her. I'd been looking forward to it so very much. Everything focused, concentrated. I won't let her ruin it. I will not get angry. I won't give up either. She's the next one. No matter how long it takes.

Then I thought about trying the newspapers. Central Library was closed for refurbishment and they'd moved the archive to the records office so I went back there and trawled the newspapers they had on microfiche for the dates of the first two entries. June 12th 2010 had been a Saturday. Tucked away inside the following Monday's *Evening News* there was a paragraph headed *UNTIMELY DEATH*. My pulse raced and my stomach contracted as though I'd been thumped.

The story identified her as Janet Carr, 37, an administrator who was discovered by friends when she failed to turn up for a social engagement and didn't answer her phone. Miss Carr was a chronic asthmatic. There were no suspicious circumstances. The only reason her death was in the paper was the fact that Miss Carr was administrator of a charity involved in raising money for asthma research. It made good copy. Human interest.

I sat there in front of the microfiche reader, staring at the screen, feeling nauseous and the horror of it creeping across my skin like a rash. There was no mention of foul play. I'd imagined The Wolf strangling them but whatever he'd done, he'd done it in a way that avoided detection. Poisoning? Gassing? How else could he have killed and left it looking natural? Something to aggravate Janet Carr's asthma? Had he known she was asthmatic? Were the others? What else could he have used? I'd no idea.

I swapped that microfiche for the September one; the woman he had punished for flinching. It didn't take me long to find her. *Tragic Blaze Kills Nurse.* Fiona Neeson, 24, a nurse at Wythenshawe Hospital. An address in Sale. A spokesman for the Fire Service urged everyone to check their smoke alarms and to be aware of the very real hazards associated with candles in the home. This was a preventable death, he said.

The newspapers for 2011 hadn't been put onto the system yet.

When I came out of the library the bright light made me giddy, my knees buckled and I had to hold onto a lamppost till it passed.

Jan 10th 2011

Each time I reach a higher level. The intensity is impossible to describe. As if I'm able to fly, go anywhere, do anything. I can. I am. What else is there? Nothing else comes anywhere close. She watched me. Her eyes flew open as she felt it but she didn't move. No scream, no begging, just those wide, wild eyes and then her body took over and her eyes rolled back in her head while she started dancing. She was marvellous. And I was even better than before. I never really knew what joy was. Superb, sublime. I stayed until dawn. Those precious hours. Felt like shouting from the rooftops. My dancing queen.

How had he killed them?

At home I tried the internet. I found myself at sites covering topics as diverse as assisted suicide, medical negligence and armed revolution. Surfing in the company of rednecks, criminologists, surgeons and serial killer fans. Anything remotely useful I cut and pasted. I had also made photocopies of the relevant articles from the newspaper microfiche and read and re-read them hoping to find something that helped me make sense of the whole affair.

Jan 11th 2011

All day I relive it. Feel the thrill singing through my veins, every sense heightened, each memory like a snapshot: the terror in her stare, the grating noise of her last breath, the final tremors, the rhythm of her dance of death, long limbs jerking so fiercely. I'm put in mind of surfers, the ones who ride the big one. On top of the world. Invincible.

I was scared. I no longer ate. The textures felt all wrong. I'd take a mouthful and it would turn to dust or slime in my mouth.

Feb 20th 2011

The hunger is growing again, already. But I cannot risk it yet. I close my eyes and see her, the last one and it's the best trip in the world. To hell and back. Myself in her eyes. The last hopeless suck of breath. Body twitching and jolting. I can't stop. How could I ever stop. This is my life now. Rich beyond dreams.

Then I caught a news item, a young woman found dead in her Levenshulme flat had been identified as Kate Cruickshank. Don't ask me how I knew. I switched the television off but I couldn't get rid of the tension, my guts were knotted and I had an awful sense of foreboding.

I fell asleep in my chair. In my dream The Wolf came and I ran and locked myself in the shower room. I leant back against the door to catch my breath and there he was reflected in the mirror. I was trapped. Waking with awful pains in my chest and my heart hammering, I knew I had to go to the police.

My timing was shot at. I planned to go at lunchtime, imagining that people would be taking lunch breaks and coming and going, and I could just leave it all on the doorstep without being noticed. The laptop and the memory stick. Enclose an anonymous note telling them about The Wolf, about Janet Carr and Fiona Neeson and a woman whose name I didn't know who had died around January 10th. Tell them to investigate Kate Cruickshank.

There wasn't any doorstep. I walked past the place a couple of times and realised if I left it outside on the pavement someone could take it and The Wolf would carry on. Killing women. Haunting me.

So, I went in through the glass doors. There was no one at the desk in the small foyer, I placed the laptop on the counter and was turning to go when a policeman came out of the door behind.

"Miss?"

I began to walk away.

"Is this your bag, Miss?"

"No," I moved more quickly. Ahead of me the doors clicked shut and then an alarm began to sound. I wheeled round in time to see the man disappear.

They thought it was a bomb.

Steel shutters began to roll down the glass frontage and I could see people evacuating the building from other exits, racing to cross the street. The alarm was deafening and then voices began shouting at me over the intercom. It was hard to hear above the din.

"It's just a laptop," I yelled. "Lost property." The sirens continued to whoop and screech. I went and grabbed the laptop, looked up at the CCTV camera in the corner. "Look," I yelled, unzipping the case, opening the cover, so they could see, lifting out the anonymous note I'd left.

There was a hissing sound, and smoke and a peculiar smell and it was hard to breathe. My eyes were streaming, I was choking.

I wasn't Miss Popularity.

Once the Bomb Squad had stepped down and the building was re-opened I was taken to a small interview room and waited with a woman officer until a man came to take my details. He was a short, skinny man with chapped lips. There was an order to the paperwork which he stuck to rigidly. Having established my name, address, date of birth, nearest living relative (none) and occupation (unemployed artist), he finally let me talk.

While I explained about 'finding' the computer on the Metro and that it contained accounts of a series of murders, that the dates tallied with actual deaths in Manchester, his expression changed from weary to wary, then hardened. He hated me.

"Read it," I urged.

"It could be a journalist's – research."

That took me aback. I thought for a moment. "No facts or figures, no names or addresses. I'm sure it's a diary. And the deaths have never been seen as murders – so what are they investigating? Just read the memory stick."

"It was destroyed, along with the computer."

"What?" I was appalled.

"Procedure."

But there was still hope, "I made a back-up file, it's at home on my machine. I've copies of newspapers too, they match the accounts."

He still didn't seem to believe a word I said. "How long have you had it?"

"A couple of days," I lied. How could I explain I'd held onto it for nearly a month?

"You found this on Tuesday?"

"Yes, on the tram. The man who lost it, I can describe him, he got off at Mosley Street." I gave him a description of The Wolf.

"And you were going?"

"To the Lowry."

He rose without speaking, hitched his trousers up, left the room.

"Could I have a cup of tea?" I asked the PC.

She shrugged.

I began to cry.

The skinny man came back and grilled me some more, all about where I'd got the laptop. He seemed angry. I stuck to my story.

Looking back, it was all very fractured. Surreal even. Everyone still treating me like the mad bomber. Then they asked me to accompany them to my house. Show them the file and the other information.

I felt sick and light-headed on the way. I couldn't remember when I'd last eaten and the petrol fumes and the smell of fast food grease on the air made me queasy. The traffic was terrible; it took us an hour to get there. The skinny man drove and the woman sat with me in the back.

At my flat it took a while to get in, with all the locks and that. I showed them the photocopies of the newspapers, and the back-up copy of *Accounts* on my laptop. They took me into the kitchen. I was shivering even though it was so close. I could never get warm anymore. The woman poured me a glass of water but it tasted filthy.

There were more voices in the living room and a little hubbub of excitement in the interchange. At last, I thought, they were taking me seriously.

The Wolf came into my kitchen.

I knocked over my water in panic, scrambled to my feet, screaming, "That's him, that's the man, it's his diary."

Someone grabbed my arms and pinned them behind me. Someone else tried to calm me down.

The Wolf raised his eyebrows and lifted his hand. He held a small plastic bag, inside was a syringe.

"Not very well hidden," his voice was soft.

"That's not mine," I yelled. "I am not a junkie." I turned to the woman holding me. "Check my arms. I've never taken anything like that."

"You slipped up, last time," The Wolf said. "Kate Cruickshank. We found the mark." He held up the bag again. Gave a wolfish grin. "Rebecca Colne, I am arresting you for the murder of Kate Cruickshank on …"

I didn't hear the end of the caution. The room spun then dimmed. I passed out.

They gave me four life sentences. They tried me for four murders. The third one, she was Alison Devlin. She was two months pregnant.

The Metrolink had been closed the day I claimed to have seen the man leave the laptop and get off at Mosley Street: a system failure. When I told them the truth about the airport, they raised questions about my delay. Why wait so long? If I honestly thought this was information about a series of murders, why wait at all? I'd stolen the machine, I told them, I was frightened that I'd be prosecuted, I wanted to make sure it was true. None of my excuses made any difference. My change of story made them even more convinced I was responsible. And when I repeatedly claimed that the man who owned the laptop was one of the officers investigating me, they clearly thought me deranged.

They seized my own computer and found all the other files. All the internet junk I'd copied: methods of murder. My defence counsel argued about the dates, demonstrating that I'd downloaded stuff long after the first three murders, but I could see the jury turning against me. Looking at me sideways. I was told not to make accusations about The Wolf, it wouldn't help my case. They linked me to Fiona Neeson. We'd been members at the same gym. It was news to me.

The clincher was the DNA evidence. A hair of mine at the scene of Kate Cruickshank's death. It didn't matter that I'd never been there. Someone had – with a hair of mine, or dropped it into the forensics lab. That coupled with the syringe 'recovered' from my flat.

Juries love forensics, ask anyone. Never mind about logic or witnesses or other evidence – a bit of sexy science has them frothing at the mouth. Clamouring for conviction.

Like quicksand the more I struggled for the truth the deeper I sank. Till I was swallowing mud day after day in the courtroom. The weight of it crushing my lungs.

A stream of acquaintances and people I barely knew were wheeled out to attest to my controlling, cold and dubious character. The prosecution harped on about my lonely and dysfunctional upbringing, my isolation, my prior mental health problems. They held up my severe weight loss, my Prozac use, my insomnia as evidence of a guilty conscience. And my stunt at the police station as a cry for help. They never had a motive. How could they? I was a psychopath, I had a personality disorder – no motive required.

After the conviction, much was made of my lack of remorse and even more of the word murderess. The female of the species and all that.

They've turned down my application for an appeal. No new evidence. And no hope of being considered for parole until I admit my guilt.

Maybe I'm safer in here. The bars, the locks, the cameras. If they let me out he'd be waiting, wouldn't he? Lips slightly parted, hair slicked back, those lupine teeth. Waiting to get me once and for all. The sting of the syringe as he inserts the needle. The dull ache as he presses the plunger, forcing the air into a vein. The seconds left as the bubble speeds around my bloodstream. Zipping along as if in a flume. An embolism. Fizzing through my heart and on into my lung – tangling with my blood vessels. Making me gasp, claw for air. A jig of death. Stopping everything. Blowing me away.

THE MESSAGE

MARGARET MURPHY

Rules of the game:
One, find your spot.
Two, stake your claim.
Three, warn off all comers.
Four, wait.

Vincent Connolly is keeping dixie on the corner of Roscoe Street and Mount Pleasant. Roscoe Street isn't much more than an alley; you'd have a job squeezing a car down – which means he can watch without fear of being disturbed. He's halfway between The Antrim and Aachen hotels, keeping an eye on both at once. They're busy, because of the official opening of the second Mersey tunnel tomorrow; the queen's going to make a speech, thousands are expected to turn out – and the city centre hotels are filling up fast. It's the biggest thing the city has seen since The Beatles' concert at The Empire on their triumphal return from America in 1964. That was seven years ago, when Vincent was only four years old – too young to remember much, except it was November and freezing, and he was wearing short trousers, so his knees felt like two hard lumps of stone. They stood at the traffic lights in Rodney Street, him holding his dad's hand, waiting for the four most famous Liverpudlians to drive past. As the limo slowed to turn the corner, Paul McCartney noticed him and waved. Vincent had got a lot of mileage out of that one little wave. He decided then that he would be rich and famous, like Paul McCartney, and ride in a big limo with his own chauffeur.

Now it's 1971, Vincent is eleven, The Beatles broke up a year ago, T-Rex is the band to watch, and Vincent's new hero is Evil Knievel. For months, he's had his eye on a Raleigh Chopper in the window of Quinn's in Edge Lane. It's bright orange, it does wheelies, and it's the most beautiful thing Vincent has ever seen.

He doesn't mind working for it. He's never had a newspaper round, or a Saturday job, but he is a grafter. October, he can be found outside the pubs in town, collecting a Penny for the Guy. From Bonfire Night to New Year, he'll team up with a couple of mates, going door-to-door, carol singing. Summertime, he'll scour the streets for pop bottles, turning them in for the thrupenny deposit – one-and-a-half pence in new money. Saturdays, in the football season, he'll take himself off to the city's north end to mind cars in the streets around Goodison Park – practically the dark side of the moon, as far as his mates are concerned, but Vincent's entrepreneurial spirit tells him if you want something bad enough, you've got to where the action is.

He lacks the muscle to claim the prime spots – he's got the scars to prove it – so, for now, he's happy enough working the margins.

The Antrim is the bigger of the two hotels, and he angles himself so he's got a good view. A half hour passes, three lots of tourists arrive – all of them, disappointingly, by taxi. He settles to a game of single ollies in the gutter for a bit, practising long shots with his best marble, just to keep his eye in. It's a warm, sunny June evening, so he doesn't really mind.

Another fifteen minutes, and the traffic heading out of town is lighter; Wednesday, some of the shops close half day. By six, Mount Pleasant is mostly quiet. A bus wheezes up the hill, a few cars pass, left and right, but you can count the minutes by them, now. Things won't pick up again until after tea-time, when the pubs start to fill up. By six-thirty, he's thinking of heading back for his own tea, when he sees a car stop outside the Aachen, off to his right.

One man, on his own. He sits with the engine running while he folds up a map. *Tourist.*

"You're on, Vinnie," Vincent whispers softly. He picks up his marbles and stuffs them into his pocket.

He's still wearing his school uniform, so he's presentable, but he's pinned an SFX school badge over his own as a disguise. He licks both hands and smoothes them over his head in an attempt to flatten his double crown, then he rubs the grit off the knees of his trousers. Now he's ready, poised on the balls of his feet, waiting for the driver to get out so he can make his play.

In Vincent's book, you can't beat car-minding. It seems nobler than the rest, somehow, and it couldn't be easier – no special props required – you just walk up, say, "Mind your car, mister?" – and agree your price. Ten new pence is the going rate, but he'll go as low as five, if the owner decides he wants to barter. It's a contract. The unspoken clause – the small print, if you like – is cough up the fee, or you might come back to find your car on bricks.

The man shoves open the door and hoists himself out of the driver's seat. He's not especially tall, it's just that the car he's wedged into is a Morris Minor, a little granny car. Vincent squints into the sun, taking in more details: spots of rust mar the smoke grey paintwork, nibbling at the sills and lower rims of the door. Even the wheel arches are wrecked. He curls his lip in disgust; a heap of tin – hardly even worth crossing the road for.

The man is five-nine or -ten, and spare. Collar length hair – dark brown, maybe – it's hard to tell from twenty-five yards away. He's wearing a leather bomber jacket over an open-necked shirt. He stretches, cricks his neck, left, right, goes round to the car boot, and checks up and down the street, which gets Vincent's spider-sense tingling.

He ducks deeper into the shadow of the alleyway, crouching behind the railings of the corner house. The man lifts out a vinyl suitcase in dirty cream. He sets it down on the road, reaches inside the car boot again, and brings out a small blue carry-all. He looks up and down the hill a second time, opens the driver's door and leans inside. Vincent grips the railing, holding his breath. The man straightens up and – *hey, presto* – the bag is gone.

Still crouched in the shadows, Vincent watches him walk up the steps of the hotel. The front door is open, but he has to ring to gain entry though the vestibule door. Someone answers, the man steps inside, and Vincent sags against the wall. The bricks are cool against his back, but he's sweating. He can't decide if it's fear, or guilt, or excitement, because he's made up his mind to find out what's in that small blue bag.

Taking money off strangers to mind their cars is a bit scally, but breaking into a car is Borstal territory. Not that he hasn't done it before – for sunglasses left on the dashboard, or loose change in the glove compartment – small stuff, in and out in less than a minute.

But this isn't small stuff; the way the man had looked around before he ducked inside the car, it had to be something special in that bag. Money, maybe; a big fat wad of crisp new notes. Or stolen jewels: emeralds as green as mossy caves, rubies that glow like communion wine. Vincent sees himself raking his fingers through a mound of gold coins, scooping out emeralds and sapphires and diamonds, buried like shells in sand.

He is about to break cover when the lobby door opens and the man steps out. For a second, he stands in the hotel doorway and stares straight across the road, into the shadows of the alleyway. Vincent's heart seizes. He flattens himself against the wall and turns his head, hiding his face.

For a long minute, he shuts his eyes tight and wills the man away. When he dares to look, the man is already heading down the hill, into the westering sun. As he reaches the bend of the road, a shaft of sunlight catches his hair and it flares red for an instant, then he is gone.

Vincent can't take his eyes off the car, almost afraid it will vanish into thin air if he so much as blinks. *Less than a minute*, he tells himself. *That's all it'll take*. But his heart is thudding hard in his chest, and he can't make his legs work. Five minutes. Ten. Fifteen. Because what if the man had forgot his wallet in his hurry? What if he comes back? What if someone is watching from the hotel?

"And what if you're a big girl's blouse, Vincent Connolly?"

The sound of his own voice makes him jump, and he's walking before he even knows it – one moment he's squatting in the shadows, gripping the railings like they will save him from falling, the next, he's at the car, his penknife in his hand.

Close to, the rust is even worse. *Moggy Minor,* he thinks, disgustedly – *one doddering step up from an invalid carriage.* Still ... on the plus side, they're easy: the quarter-light catch wears loose with age – and this one's ready for the scrap yard. He pushes gently at the lower corner with the point of the knife blade and it gives. He dips into his pocket for his jemmy. It's made from a cola tin, cut to one inch width, and fashioned into a small hook at one end. The metal is flexible, but strong, and thin enough to fit between the door and the window frame. In an instant, he's flipped the catch, reached in and lifted the door handle.

A Wolseley slows down as he swings the door open. A shaft of fear jolts through him, and he thinks of abandoning the job, but the chance to get his hands on all that money makes him reckless. He turns and waves the driver on with a smile, sees him clock the fake school badge on his blazer and grins even broader. The driver's eyes swivel to the road and he motors on to the traffic lights.

Vincent slides inside the car, closes the door, and keeps his head down. The interior reeks of petrol fumes and cigarettes. The vinyl of the driver's seat is cracked, and greyish stuffing curdles from the seams. He reaches underneath and comes up empty.

Certain that any second he'll be yanked out feet first, he leans across to the passenger side and feels under the seat. Nothing. Zilch. Zero. Just grit and dust and tufts of cotton. But the passenger seat is in good nick: no cracks or splits in the leatherette. So where has the stuffing come from?

Frowning, he reaches under again, but this time he turns his palm up, pats the underside of the seat. His heart begins to thud pleasantly; he's found something solid. He tugs gently and it drops onto his hand.

He's grinning as he barrels up the steps to his house. Vincent lives in a narrow Georgian terrace in Clarence Street, less than a minute's walk from where the car is parked, but he has run past his own street, left and then left again, crossing Clarence Street a second time, on the look-out for anyone following, before cutting south, down Green Lane, covering four sides of a square to end up back at his house.

The door is on the latch. His mum is cooking lamb stew: summer or winter, you can tell the day of the week by what's cooking; Wednesday is Irish stew. He scoops up the *Liverpool Echo* from the doormat and leaves the carry-all at the foot of the stairs, under his blazer, before sauntering to the kitchen.

"Is that you, Vincent?" his mother glances over her shoulder. "I thought you were at rehearsals." His class has been chosen to perform for the queen.

"We were so good, they let us finish early."

He must have sounded less than enthusiastic, because she scolded, "It's a great honour. You'll remember tomorrow for the rest of your life."

Vincent's mum is a patriotic Irish immigrant. And she says *he's* full of contradictions.

"*The Echo's* full of it," he says, slapping the newspaper onto the table.

She balances the spoon on the rim of the pot and turns to him. Her face is flushed from the heat of the pot; or maybe it's excitement. She wipes her hands on her apron and picks up the paper. "Well, go and change out of your school uniform. You can tell Cathy, tea's almost ready. And wash your hands before you come down."

For once, he doesn't complain.

He tiptoes past his sister's bedroom door and sidles into his room like a burglar. He shuts the door, then slides the carry-all under his bed. He untucks the blankets from his mattress and lets them hang. They are grey army surplus, not made for luxury, and the drop finishes a good three inches clear of the floor. He steps back to the door to inspect his handywork. He can just spy one corner of the bag. He casts about the room and his eyes snag on a pile of laundry his mum has been on at him to fetch downstairs. He smiles. Given the choice between picking up his dirty socks and eating worms, Cathy Connolly would reach for a knife and fork. Smiling to himself, he heaps the ripe-smelling jumble of dirty clothing on top of the bag.

He says hardly a word at the dinner table, evading his mother's questions about the rehearsal by shovelling great spoonfuls of stew into his mouth. All the while, his sister looks at him from under her lashes, with that smirk on her face that says she knows something. He tries to ignore her, gulping down his meal so fast it scalds his throat, pleading homework to get out of washing the dishes.

His mother might be gullible, but she's no pushover.

"You've plenty of time to do your homework *after* you've done the dishes," she says.

"But Cathy could—"

"It's not Cathy's turn. And she has more homework than you do, but you don't hear your sister whining about doing her fair share."

Cathy widens her eyes and flutters her eyelashes at him, enjoying her beatification.

He stamps up the stairs twenty minutes later, grumbling to himself under his breath.

"Where were you?"

His heart does a quick skip. Cathy, waiting to pounce on the landing.

"When?"

"Well, I'm not talking about when God was handing out brains, 'cos we both know you were scuffing your shoes at the back of the queue, *that* day."

He scowls at her, but his sister is armour-plated and his scowls bounce harmlessly off her thick skull.

"Mary Thomas said you went home sick at four."

"It's none of your business."

"Is."

He tries to barge past, but she's got long arms and she is fast on her feet. "You're a little liar, Vincent Connolly."

"Am not."

"Are. How would you know if the dress rehearsal went well. How would *you* know dress rehearsal finished early, when you *missed* the dress rehearsal?" She adds spitefully, "It's a shame, really. Miss Taggart says you make a *lovely* little dancer."

He feels the familiar burn of humiliation and outrage at the intrusion. She's *no right* to talk to his class teacher like he's just a little kid. He sees the gleam of triumph in her eyes and hates her for it.

Cathy is fourteen and attends the convent school on Mount Pleasant; she'll be at the big parade, too. But while she gets to keep her dignity, playing the recorder, Vincent is expected to make a tit of himself, prancing about in an animal mask. In an animal mask *in front of the queen.*

"Get lost, Cathy."

Cathy pulls a sad face. "Now Miss Taggart says you won't be able to be in the pageant."

"You can have my mask, if you like," he says. "Be an improvement." Silly moo doesn't know she's just made his day. He makes a break for his room, and she gives way; it doesn't occur to him that she let him pass. He's thinking he'll buy that Chopper bike with the money in the bag, take his mum shopping, buy her a whole new outfit. He'll get his dad a carton of ciggies – the good ones in the gold packs. As for Cathy, she can whistle. *No* – he thinks, shoving open his bedroom door – *I'll get her a paper bag – a big one to fit over her big fat ugly head. No, a tarantula – no, two tarantulas – no, a whole nest of tarantulas. Six of them – a dozen – big enough to eat a bird in one gulp; evil creatures with bone-crushing jaws and fat bodies and great goggly eyes on stalks. He'll make a cosy den for them under her pillow and stay awake until she comes up to bed* – a whole hour later than him, by the way, cos Cathy's a *big* girl—

He loses the thread of his fantasy. His bed has been carefully remade, the blankets tucked in. The dirty linen he'd used to camouflage the bag is folded neatly at the foot of the bed. And the bag has gone. He feels its absence like a hole in the centre of him.

Horrified, he whirls to face the door, but Cathy has slipped quietly away. Her bedroom door is shut. He boots it open.

Cathy is sitting cross-legged on her bed, the bag in front of her.

"You bloody—"

"Thief?" she says, in that pert way that drives him crackers. "Takes one to know one, doesn't it, Vincent?"

"You give it back!"

She puts a finger to her lips and cocks her head. The front door slams. It's Dad. She whispers, "Anybody home?"

Their father's voice booms out, a second after, like an echo in reverse: "Anybody home?"

Her eyes sparkle with malicious good humour. "What would Dad say if he knew you'd been thieving?"

Vincent clenches his fists, tears of impotent rage pricking his eyes. He considers rushing her, but Dad would hear and come to investigate.

"Give me it. It's mine."

"Now, Vincent, we both know that's not true." She plucks at the zip and he wants to fling himself at her, to claw it from her grasp.

She shouts, "Is that you, Dad?" putting on her girly voice just for him.

Their father's footsteps clump up the stairs. "How's my girl?" he says.

"Just getting changed." She raises her eyebrows, and reluctantly, Vincent back-heels the door shut.

Their father passes her door and they hear a heavy sigh as he slumps onto the bed to take off his shoes.

Cathy is smiling as she unzips the bag, and Vincent wants to kill her.

First, she looks blank, then puzzled, then worried.

"You can turn off the big act," he whispers furiously.

Only she doesn't look like she's acting. And when she finally turns her face to him, her expression is one of sick horror.

"Oh, Vincent," she whispers.

His stomach flips. The anticipated wealth – the bundles of cash, the glittering treasures of his imagination – all crumble to dust.

Carefully, reverently, she lifts a bible and a set of rosary beads out of the bag. The beads are dark, solid wood; a serious rosary, a man's rosary. She holds it up so the silver crucifix swings, and he stares at it, almost hypnotised.

She reaches into the carry-all again, and brings out a small package, wrapped in brown paper. Three words are printed in neat block capitals on the front of it: 'FOR FATHER O'BRIEN'.

They stare at it for a long moment.

"Vinnie, you robbed a priest."

"He *isn't*," Vincent whispers, his voice hoarse. He feels sweat break out on his forehead.

Wordlessly, she holds up the rosary, the Jersusalem Bible.

"He *can't* be – he was wearing *normal clothes.*"

"Shh!" She looks past him to the bedroom door, and he realises he had been shouting. They hold their breath, listening for their father. There's no sound, and after a moment she whispers: "He might be on his holidays."

"He was wearing a leather *jacket*, Cath."

She looks into his face, absorbing the information, but her eyes stray again to the parcel, as if pulled by a magnet. "So, maybe it's his brother, or a friend. It doesn't *matter* Vinnie: that parcel is addressed to Father O'Brien. There's no getting away from it – you robbed a priest." She bites her lip. "And that's a mortal sin."

Cathy is in the Legion of Mary, and she's been on two retreats with the sisters of Notre Dame. She always got an A in Religious Education – so if Cathy says it's a mortal sin, he knows for sure that the Devil is already stoking the fires of hell, chucking on extra coals, ready to roast him.

"I'll go to confession, I'll do penance – I'll do a novena," he gabbles, trying to think of something that will appease. "I'll do the Nine First Fridays—"

The shocked look on his sister's face makes him stop. But the Nine First Fridays are the most powerful prayer he knows: a special devotion to the Sacred Heart, getting up at six o'clock on the first Friday each month for nine solid months to attend early mass and receive the Holy Eucharist – surely that will wipe his sin away?

"Vincent," she says, gently, "There's no penance for a mortal sin – and you can't receive Holy Communion with a big black stain on your soul: it would be like inviting Jesus into your home with the devil sitting by the fire in your favourite armchair."

When he was little, Vincent's mum and dad both had to work, and Cathy would take care of him after school, in the holidays – even weekends, if Mum got the chance of overtime. Between the ages of five and eight, Cathy had been his minder, his teacher, his best mate, the maker-up of games and adventures. But he'd got bigger, and by his ninth birthday he wanted his independence. He became rebellious, and she was offended and hurt and that made her superior and sarcastic. Now, feeling the Devil squatting deep inside him, chiselling away at his soot-blackened soul, he feels small again, frightened and lost, and he wishes she would take charge.

"What'm I gonna do, Cath?"

She stares at the neat brown package as if it's radioactive.

"Vinnie …" She frowns, distracted, like she's doing a difficult sum in her head. "There's only one way to get let off a mortal sin." She turns her eyes on him, and they are so filled with fear that Vincent is seized by a terrible dread.

"What d'you mean, 'it's gone'?"

The man in the leather jacket is standing in a phone box, opposite the clock tower of the university's Victoria Building. The quarter chimes have sounded and the clock's gilt hands read six thirty-two; he should be in position by now. He closes his eyes. "Gone, vanished. Stolen."

"You lost it." His unit commander's voice is hard, nasal, contemptuous.

"I thought it would be safe in the car."

"Oh, well, that's all right then – anyone can make a mistake."

"It was well hidden."

"Not that well, eh?"

The man fixes his gaze on the gleaming face of the clock, willing the hands to move, but the silence seems to last an eternity.

"When?"

"Sometime between six last night and five this morning."

"*Twelve hours* you left it?"

"Wouldn't it draw attention if I checked the damn thing every five minutes?"

"Watch your tone."

The man grips the phone receiver hard. The sun has been up since four-thirty and the temperature in the glass box must be eighty degrees, but he daren't ease the door open for air.

"Is it set to go?"

"It's on a twenty-four-hour timer, like you said. It'll trigger automatically at three, this afternoon." He takes a breath to speak again, but the voice on the line interrupts:

"Shut up – I'm thinking."

He waits in obedient silence.

"Whoever took it must've dumped it, otherwise you'd be locked up in a police cell by now."

"That's what I—"

"I'm speaking, here."

He clamps his mouth shut so fast he bites his tongue.

"Even so, you'd better not go back to the hotel. Leave the car, catch a bus to Manchester. I'll have someone pick you up."

"I have a weapon. I could still complete my mission."

"And how close d'you think you'd get?"

"I could mingle with the crowd. They won't even see me."

A snort of derision. "You've whiff of the zealot about you, lad. They'll sniff you out in a heartbeat, so they will – be all over you like flies on shit." The man listened to the metallic harshness of the voice, his eyes closed. "This's what you get when you send a *dalta* to do a soldier's job."

That stings – he's no raw recruit. "Haven't I proved myself a dozen times?"

"Not this time, son – and this is the one that counts."

"It's a setback – I'll make up for it."

"You will. But not in Liverpool; not today."

"Look, I checked it out – the approach roads are closed, but there's a bridge—"

"What d'you think you'll hit with a thirty-eight calibre service revolver from a bloody bridge?"

He wants to say he's been practising – that he can hit a can from thirty yards, but that would sound childish – a tin can isn't a moving target, and it takes more than a steady hand to look another human being in the face and fire a bullet into them. So he says nothing.

"No," his superior says. "No. They'd catch you. And make no mistake – they would shoot you like a dog."

"I don't care."

"Only fools want to be martyrs, son. And if *you* don't care, *I* do. I care that we've spent money on equipment, and you let a scouse scallywag walk away with it. I *care* that security will be stepped up for every official visit after today – even if you walk away right now. Because there's the small matter of a package that will turn up at three p.m." He sighed angrily. "We'll just have to pray to God the thieving bastard left it somewhere useful, like the city centre."

He books his ticket for one o'clock and walks down to the docks to clear his head. They are still adding the finishing touches to the stands when he stops by the tunnel approach on his way back to the coach station. He joins a group of kids gawping through the wire mesh at the chippies hammering the final nails in the platform. He can see the plaque above the tunnel, draped in blue cloth. This is where the queen will make her speech. A team of men are sweeping the road leading to the tunnel entrance and a dozen more are raking smooth the bare soil of the verges.

Attendance is by invitation only, but a man dressed in overalls and looking like he has a job to do might pass unchallenged and find a good spot under the stands. Only what would be the point? Without the device, it would be hopeless: even if he did manage to remain undiscovered, he would have to abandon his hiding place, walk out in front of thousands of people, place himself close enough to aim his pistol and fire.

Police are already clustered in threes and fours along the newly metalled road; there will be sharpshooters along the route – and true enough, they would shoot him like a dog.

Father O'Brien hadn't been anyone important. He didn't have the ear of the bishop and he wasn't destined for Rome; he hadn't a scholarly brain nor a Jesuit's mind to play the kind of politics it would take to elevate him above parish priest.

But he was a good man. He came from the fertile chalklands of Wexford, around Bantry Bay, where they spoke in softer tones, and faces were more given to smile. He liked a drink, and would stand you a pint if he fell into conversation with you at the Crown Bar, but he wouldn't hesitate to tell a man when he'd had enough, and he'd tipped more than one out onto the street before he'd drunk his fill. The man's father and the priest had come to blows over that; he'd taken to drinking after he lost his job on the shipyard. Father O'Brien had kicked his da out of that bar every night for a fortnight, until on the last day, his da got murderous mad. He swung wildly at Father O'Brien, out on the street, but the priest ducked and dodged, light on his feet, deflecting and blocking, until at last, dizzy and exhausted, his da had sunk to the pavement and wept.

"Ten thousand men work at the Belfast shipyard, Father," he'd said, his words sloshing out of his mouth. "And just four hundred Catholics among them. You've a good education: can you tell me what makes a Protestant better at lugging sacks of grain than a Catholic? Is there some calculation that adds up the worth of a man and subtracts a measure of humanity because he was born a Catholic?"

Father O'Brien didn't have an answer, but he sat with the boy's father on the kerb, until he'd raged and wept the anger out of him, and then the priest walked him home. He knew this to be the gods-honest truth, for the man had seen it with his own eyes, as a boy of fourteen.

Father O'Brien didn't preach taking up arms against the oppressor. He wasn't affiliated to the IRA, nor even Sinn Féin. "My only affiliation," he would say, "is to God Almighty; my only obligation is to my flock." Which was how he came to die. Not in a hail of bullets, but in the stupidest, most pointless way imaginable. A macho squaddie – a bad driver trying to impress his oppos – lost control of his vehicle turning a corner. Father O'Brien had been visiting a house in the next street, delivering the last sacraments to an old man dying of the cancer. The armoured vehicle skidded, clipped the opposite kerb, spun one hundred-and-eighty degrees, and smashed into the end of a terrace decorated with a painting of the Irish tricolour. Father O'Brien was pinned against the wall and died instantly.

He had been a gentle man, and a modest one, yet the violence and futility of his death had made a spectacle of him: a thing to point to as evidence of the British army's lack of respect; a dread event for old men to sigh and shake their heads over; a lurid tale for children to whisper in the playground, of the priest who was cut in half by an armoured car. Father O'Brien was no longer remembered for the good he'd done in life – only for the notoriety of his death.

The man had meant to deliver a message: that Father O'Brien's death would not go unpunished, and in failing in his mission he had failed Father O'Brien.

Vincent and Cathy stand in the porch. It's just shy of seven o'clock, and the sun is shining hot through the top light of the front door. Cathy's face is pale.

"You know what you have to do?"

He nods, but he has a lump in his throat as big as a bottle-washer ollie, so he can't speak.

She straightens his tie and combs her fingers through his hair, staring solemnly down at him. He doesn't squirm; in truth, he wouldn't complain if she took him by the hand and walked with him down the street in broad daylight, because he does not want to do this alone.

She seems taller, today. Grown up.

"I'll tell Mum you had to go early to rehearsals."

He frowns, wishing he hadn't skipped rehearsals the day before, thinks that dancing in an animal mask seems small humiliation, compared with what he has to do now.

"I'll tell Miss Taggart you've got a tummy bug, in case it takes a while, so you'll have to make yourself scarce for the rest of the day. All right?"

He nods again.

She hands him the small blue carry-all and blinks tears from her eyes.

He hefts the bag and squares his shoulders, setting off down the street like a soldier off to war.

The car is parked outside the hotel, but he waits an hour, and still the man hasn't come out. Another half hour, and the manager appears on the doorstep.

"What're you up to?" he asks.

"Is the man here – the one that owns the Morris Minor?"

The manager is broad faced, with small eyes. He jams his hands in his trouser pockets and says, "What's it to you?"

He's wearing grey flannel trousers and a matching waistcoat to hide his soft belly; Vincent reckons he could easy out-run him, but his great sin burns his soul like acid, so he stills his itchy feet, and composes his face into an approximation of innocence.

"Got something for him."

The manager lifts his chin. "That it?" He holds a hand out for the bag. "I'll make sure he gets it."

Vincent tightens his grip on the carry-all and takes a step back. "Is he in?"

"Went out early," the man says. "Missed his breakfast."

"I'll wait."

"Not here, you won't – you're making my guests nervous, loitering outside."

"You can't stop me. It's a free country." He feels a pang of guilt: he promised Cathy he'd mind his manners.

"We'll see what the police've got to say about that." The man narrows his eyes. "Anyway, shouldn't you be in school?" His small eyes fasten on Vincent's blazer pocket. He's forgotten to pin the SFX badge over the real one. He clamps his hand over his pocket and the man comes at him, pitching forwards as he comes down the steps. Vincent turns and flees.

He pelts up the hill and cuts right into Rodney Street up, then dodges left into the Scotch Churchyard, and ducks behind one of the gravestones, hugging the bag close to his chest. He can't stop shaking. The gardens of the convent back onto the graveyard; he'll catch his sister in the grounds during break. He checks his watch – playtime won't be for another hour-and-a-half. He sits down behind McKenzie's pyramid to wait.

He would have gone – in fact, he was already on his way. If the bus hadn't been diverted. If the driver hadn't turned down Shaw Street. If the new route hadn't taken them through Everton. If he'd looked out of the window to his left, rather than his right.

If, if, if … He would have stayed on the bus and been picked up in Manchester and made his ignominious way home. But in Everton, Orange Lodge and Catholic sectarianism was as strong as on any street in Belfast. A long stretch of grey wall ran beneath the new high-rise blocks on Netherfield Road. If he had turned away, just for a second, bored by the monotony of grey concrete and dusty pavements … But something had caught his eye; he glanced right and had seen the insult, daubed in orange paint on a grey wall – ill-spelt, angry, hateful: 'THE POPE IS A BASTERD'.

He recoiled like he'd been spat at. All morning, a rage had smouldered, built from the tinder of grief and loss, fuelled by the shock of finding the device gone and, yes, by the mortification he had suffered in telling his commander. Now it sparked and flared, and he blazed with righteous fire.

He lurched from his seat to the front. "Stop the bus," he said.

The driver didn't even take his eyes off the road. "It's not a request service, Paddy, lad."

"Oh, good – 'cos this is not a request."

The driver swivelled his head to look at him. "And who d'you think you are?"

The man took hold of the driver's seatback and leaned in, allowing his leather jacket to fall open just enough to show the revolver tucked in his belt. "I'm the Angel of Death, son."

It's four minutes to three as he heads south west down Birkenhead Road on the other side of the Mersey. He'd crossed the great wide dock of East Float and crossed it again, tracking over every one of the Four Bridges, lost. Forty-five minutes later, he'd fetched up at the Seacombe Ferry terminal, with just a handrail between him and the muddy waters of the Mersey. He could happily have thrown himself in, had a kindly ferryman not asked him if he was off to the parade, and given him clear directions to Wheatland Lane, where he might stand on the bridge and wave to the queen. He barrels along, the little car's engine screaming, past a stretch of blasted landscape. His heart is beating like an Orange Man's Lambeg. It's two minutes before the hour. She'll give her speech on the Liverpool side, then motor through to Wallasey; giving him time to find a spot. He *will* deliver the message for Father O'Brien. He almost misses the sharp turn westward and wrestles the wheel right. The gun slides in his lap, and he catches it, tucking it firmly in his waistband.

He's driving full into the afternoon sun, now; it scorches his face, burning through the windscreen, and he yanks the visor down. A sheet of paper flutters onto the dashboard. His foot hard on the pedal, he picks it up, squints at it as he powers towards the bridge.

It's a note, written on lined paper, in a child's neat handwriting:

'Dear Mister,

I came to see you at the hotel but you weren't there. I wanted to say to your face that I am truly sorry I stole Father O'Brien's present. My sister says it's a Mortal Sin to steal from a Priest. I waited for ages, but the manager told me to push off, and he would of got me arrested if I didn't so I couldn't stay. My sister said it would be O.K. if I wrote you a message instead. So I hope you will forgive me and ask Father to forgive me as well. I never opened it or nothing, so I hope it will be O.K. and that you will forgive me.

Sorry.

PS – I put it back ~~esac~~ exacly like I found it.

His eyes widen. He hits the brakes. The car skids, turning ninety degrees, sliding sideways along the empty road. He reaches for the door, but his fingers seem too big, too clumsy to work the handle, he can't seem to get a grip of the lever. He can't seem to—

The thin, electronic beep of the electronic clock in the bag under his seat sounds a fraction of a second before the flash. Then the windows shatter and the grey bodywork blows apart like a tin can on a bonfire.

FEDORA

JOHN HARVEY

When they had first met, amused by his occupation, Kate had sent him copies of Hammett and Chandler, two neat piles of paperbacks, bubble-wrapped, courier-delivered. A note: *If you're going to do, do it right. Fedora follows.* He hadn't been certain exactly what a fedora was.

Jack Kiley, private investigator. Security work of all kinds undertaken. Ex-Metropolitan Police.

Most of his assignments came from bigger security firms, PR agencies with clients in need of baby sitting, steering clear of trouble; solicitors after witness confirmation, a little dirt. If it didn't make him rich, most months it paid the rent: a second-floor flat above a charity shop in north London, Tufnell Park. He still didn't have a hat.

Till now.

One of the volunteers in the shop had taken it in. 'An admirer, Jack, is that what it is?'

There was a card attached to the outside of the box: *Chris Ruocco of London, Bespoke Tailoring.* It hadn't come far. A quarter mile, at most. Kiley had paused often enough outside the shop, coveting suits in the window he could ill afford.

But this was a broad-brimmed felt hat, not quite black. Midnight blue? He tried it on for size. More or less a perfect fit.

There was a note sticking up from the band: on one side, a quote from Chandler; on the other a message: *Ozone, tomorrow. 11am?* Both in Kate Keenan's hand.

He took the hat back off and placed it on the table alongside his mobile phone. Had half a mind to call her and decline. Thanks, but no thanks. Make some excuse. Drop the fedora back at Ruocco's next time he caught the overground from Kentish Town.

It had been six months now since he and Kate had last met, the premiere of a new Turkish–Albanian film to which she'd been invited, Kiley leaving halfway through and consoling himself with several large whiskies in the cinema bar. When Kate had finally emerged, preoccupied by the piece she was going to write for her column in the *Independent*, something praising the film's mysterious grandeur, its uncompromising pessimism – the phrases already forming inside her head – Kiley's sarcastic 'Got better, did it?' precipitated a row which ended on the street outside with her calling him a hopeless philistine and Kiley suggesting she take whatever pretentious arty crap she was going to write for her bloody newspaper and shove it.

Since then, silence.

Now what was this? A peace offering? Something more?

Kiley shook his head. Was he really going to put himself through all that again? Kate's companion. Cramped evenings in some tiny theatre upstairs, less room for his knees than the North End at Leyton Orient; standing for what seemed like hours, watching others genuflect before the banality of some Turner Prize winner; another mind-numbing lecture at the British Library; brilliant meals at Moro or the River Café on Kate's expense account; great sex.

Well, thought Kiley, nothing was perfect.

Ozone, or to give it its proper title, Ozone Coffee Roasters, was on a side street close by Old Street station. In full view in the basement, industrial-size roasting machines had their way with carefully harvested beans from the best single-estate coffee farms in the world – Kiley had Googled the place before leaving – while upstairs smart young people sat either side of a long counter or at heavy wooden tables, most of them busy at their laptops as their flat whites or espressos grew cold around them. Not that Kiley had anything against a good flat white – twenty-first century man, or so he sometimes liked to think, he could navigate his way round the coffee houses in London with the best of them.

Chalked on a slate at the front of one of the tables was Kate Keenan's name and a time, 11.00, but no Kate to be seen.

Just time to reassess, change his mind.

Kiley slid along the bench seat and gave his order to a waitress who seemed to be wearing mostly tattoos. Five minutes later, Kate arrived.

She was wearing a long, loose crepe coat that swayed around her as she walked; black trousers, a white shirt, soft leather bag slung over one shoulder. Her dark hair was cut short, shorter than he remembered, taking an extra shine from the lighting overhead. As she approached the table her face broke into a smile. She looked Kiley thought, allowing himself the odd ageist indiscretion, lovelier that any forty-four year old woman had the right.

"Jack, you could at least have worn the hat."

"Saving it for a special occasion."

"You mean this isn't one?"

"We'll see."

She kissed him on the mouth.

"I'm famished," she said. "You going to eat?"

"I don't know."

"The food's good. Very good."

There was an omelette on the menu, the cost, Kiley reckoned, of a meal at McDonald's or Subway for a family of five. When it came it was fat and delicious, stuffed with spinach, shallots and red pepper and bright with the taste of fresh chillis. Kate had poached eggs on sourdough toast with portobello mushrooms. She'd scarcely punctured the first egg when she got down to it.

"Jack, a favour."

He paused with his fork half-way to his mouth.

"Graeme Fisher, mean anything to you?"

"Vaguely." He didn't know how or in what connection.

"Photographer, big in the sixties. Bailey, Duffy, Fisher. The big three, according to some. Fashion, that was his thing. Everyone's thing. *Biba. Vogue.* You couldn't open a magazine, look at a hoarding without one of his pictures staring back at you." She took a sip from her espresso. "He disappeared for a while in the eighties – early seventies, eighties. Australia, maybe, I'm not sure. Resurfaced with a show at Victoria Miro, new work, quite a bit different. Cooler, more detached: buildings, interiors, mostly empty. Very few people."

Skip the art history, Kiley thought, this is leading where?

"I did a profile of him for the *Independent on Sunday*," Kate said. "Liked him. Self-deprecating, almost humble. Genuine."

"What's he done?" Kiley asked.

"Nothing."

"But he is in some kind of trouble?"

"Maybe."

"Shenanigans."

"Sorry?"

"Someone else's wife; someone else's son, daughter. What used to be called indiscretions. Now it's something more serious."

Following the high-profile arrests of several prominent media personalities, accused of a variety of sexual offences dating back up to forty years, reports to the police of historic rape and serious sexual abuse had increased four-fold. Men – it was mostly men – who had enjoyed both the spotlight and the supposed sexual liberation of the sixties and later were contacting their lawyers, setting up damage limitation exercises, quaking in their shoes.

"You've still got contacts in the Met, haven't you, Jack?"

"A few."

"I thought if there was anyone you knew – Operation Yewtree, is that what it's called? – I thought you might be able to have a word on the quiet, find out if Fisher was one of the people they were taking an interest in."

"Should they be?"

"No. No."

"Because if they're not, the minute I mention his name, they're going to be all over him like flies."

Kate cut away a small piece of toast, added mushroom, a smidgeon of egg. "Maybe there's another way."

Kiley said nothing.

As if forgetting she'd changed the style, Kate smoothed a hand across her forehead to brush away a strand of hair. "When he was what? Twenty-nine? Thirty? He had this relationship with a girl, a model."

Kiley nodded, sensing where this was going.

"She was young," Kate said. "Fifteen. Fifteen when it started."

"Fifteen," Kiley said quietly.

"It wasn't aggressive, wasn't in any sense against her will, it was … like I say, it was a relationship, a proper relationship. It wasn't even secret. People knew."

"People?"

"In the business. Friends. They were an item."

"And that made it okay? An item?"

"Jack …"

"What?"

"Don't prejudge. And stop repeating everything I say."

Kiley chased a last mouthful of spinach around his plate. The waitress with the tattoos stopped by their table to ask if there was anything else they wanted and Kate sent her on her way.

"He's afraid of her," Kate said. "Afraid she'll go to the police herself."

"Why now?"

"It's in the air, Jack. You read the papers, watch the news. Cleaning out the Augean stables doesn't come into it."

Kiley was tempted to look at his watch: ten minutes without Kate making a reference he failed to understand. Maybe fifteen. "A proper relationship, isn't that what you said?"

"It ended badly. She didn't want to accept things had run their course. Made it difficult. When it became clear he wasn't going to change his mind, she attempted suicide."

"Pills?"

Kate nodded. "It was all hushed up at the time. Back then, that was still possible."

"And now he's terrified it'll all come out …"

"Go and talk to him, Jack. Do that at least. I think you'll like him."

Liking him, Kiley knew, would be neither here nor there, a hindrance at best.

There was a bookshop specialising in fashion and photography on Charing Cross Road. Claire de Rouen. Kiley had walked past there a hundred times without ever going in. Two narrow flights of stairs and then an interior slightly larger than the average bathroom. Books floor to ceiling, wall to wall. There was a catalogue from Fisher's show at Victoria Miro, alongside a fat retrospective, several inches thick. Most of the photographs, the early ones, were in glossy black and white. Beautiful young women slumming in fashionable clothes: standing, arms aloft, in a bomb site, dripping with costume jewellery and furs; laughing outside Tubby Isaac's Jellied Eel Stall at Spitalfields; stretched out along a coster's barrow, legs kicking high in the air. One picture that Kiley kept flicking back to, a thin-hipped, almost waif-like girl standing, marooned, in an empty swimming pool, naked save for a pair of skimpy pants and gold bangles snaking up both arms, a gold necklace hanging down between her breasts. Lisa Arnold. Kate had told him her name. Lisa. He wondered if this were her.

The house was between Ladbroke Grove and Notting Hill, not so far from the Portobello Road. Flat fronted, once grand, paint beginning to flake away round the windows on the upper floors. Slabs of York Stone leading, uneven, to the front door. Three bells. Graeme Fisher lived on the ground floor.

He took his time responding.

White hair fell in wisps around his ears; several days since he'd shaved. Corduroy trousers, collarless shirt, cardigan wrongly buttoned, slippers on his feet.

"You'll be Kate's friend."

Kiley nodded and held out his hand.

The grip was firm enough, though when he walked it was slow, more of a shuffle, with a pronounced tilt to one side.

"Better come through here."

Here was a large room towards the back of the house, now dining room and kitchen combined. A short line of servants' bells, polished brass, was still attached to the wall close by the door.

Fisher sat at the scrubbed oak table and waited for Kiley to do the same.

"Bought this place for a song in sixty-four. All divided up since then, rented out. Investment banker and his lady friend on the top floor – when they're not down at his place in Dorset. Bloke above us, something in the social media." He said it as if it were a particularly nasty disease. "Keeps the bailiffs from the sodding door."

There were photographs, framed, on the far wall. A street scene, deserted, muted colours, late afternoon light. An open-top truck, its sides bright red, driving away up a dusty road, fields to either side. Café tables in bright sunshine, crowded, lively, in the corner of a square; then the same tables, towards evening, empty save for an old man, head down, sleeping. Set a little to one side, two near-abstracts, sharp angles, flat planes.

"Costa Rica," Fisher said, "seventy-two. On assignment. Never bloody used. Too fucking arty by half."

He made tea, brought it to the table in plain white mugs, added two sugars to his own and then, after a moment's thought, a third.

"Tell me about Lisa," Kiley said.

Fisher laughed, no shred of humour. "You don't have the time."

"It ended badly, Kate said."

"It always ends fucking badly." He coughed, a rasp low in the throat, turning his head aside.

"And you think she might be harbouring a grudge?"

"Harbouring? Who knows? Life of her own. Kids. Grandkids by now, most like. Doubt she gives me a second thought, one year's end to the next."

"Then why … ?"

"This woman a couple of days back, right? Lisa's age. There she is on TV, evening news. Some bloke, some third-rate comedian, French-kissed her in the back of a taxi when she was fifteen, copped a feel. Now she's reckoning sexual assault. Poor bastard's picture all over the papers. Paedophile. That's not a fucking paedophile." He shook his head. "I'd sooner bloody die."

Kiley cushioned his mug in both hands. "Why don't you talk to her? Make sure?"

Fisher smiled. "A while back, round the time I met Kate, I was going to have this show, Victoria Miro, first one in ages, and I thought, Lisa, I'll give her a bell. See if she might, you know, come along. Last minute, I couldn't, couldn't do it. I sent her a note instead, invitation to the private view. Never replied, never came."

He wiped a hand across his mouth, finished his tea.

"You'll go see her? Kate said you would. Just help me rest easy." He laughed. "Too much tension, not good for the heart."

Google Maps said the London Borough of Haringey, estate agents called it Muswell Hill. A street of Arts and Crafts houses, nestled together, white louvred shutters at the windows, prettily painted doors. She was tall, taller than Kiley had expected, hair pulled back off her face, little make-up; tunic top, skinny jeans. He could still see the girl who'd stood in the empty pool through the lines that ran from the corners of her mouth and eyes.

"Lisa Arnold?"

"Not for thirty years."

"Jack Kiley." He held out a hand. "An old friend of yours asked me to stop by."

"An old friend?"

"Yes."

"Then he should have told you it's Collins. Lisa Collins." She still didn't take his hand and Kiley let it fall back by his side.

"This old friend, he have a name?" But, of course, she knew. "You better come in," she said. "Just mind the mess in the hall."

Kiley stepped around a miniature pram, various dolls, a wooden puzzle, skittles, soft toys.

"Grandkids," she explained, "two of them, Tuesdays and Thursday mornings, Wednesday afternoons. Run me ragged."

Two small rooms had been knocked through to give a view of the garden: flowering shrubs, a small fruit tree, more toys on the lawn.

Lisa Collins sat in a wing-backed chair, motioning Kiley to the settee. There were paintings on the wall, watercolours; no photographs other than a cluster of family pictures above the fireplace. Two narrow bookcases; rugs on polished boards; dried flowers. It was difficult to believe she was over sixty years old.

"How is Graeme?"

Kiley shrugged. "He seemed okay. Not brilliant, maybe, but okay."

"You're not really a friend, are you?"

"No?"

"Graeme doesn't do friends."

"Maybe he's changed."

She looked beyond Kiley towards the window, distracted by the shadow of someone passing along the street outside.

"You don't smoke, I suppose?"

"Afraid not."

"No. Well, in that case, you'll have to join me in a glass of wine. And don't say no."

"I wasn't about to."

"White okay?"

"White's fine."

She left the room and he heard the fridge door open and close; the glasses were tissue-thin, tinged with green; the wine grassy, cold.

"All this hoo-hah going on," she said. "People digging up the past, I'd been half-expecting someone doorstepping me on the way to Budgens." She gave a little laugh. "Me and my shopping trolley. Some reporter or other. Expecting me to dig up the dirt, spill the beans."

Kiley said nothing.

"That's what he's worried about, isn't it? After all this time, the big exposé, shit hitting the fan."

"Yes."

"That invitation he sent me, the private view. I should have gone."

"Why didn't you?"

"I was afraid."

"What of?"

"Seeing him again. After all this time. Afraid what it would do to all this." She gestured round the room, the two rooms. "Afraid it could blow it all apart."

"It could do that?"

"Oh, yes." She drank some wine and set the glass carefully back down. "People said it was just a phase. Too young, you know, like in the song? Too young to know. You'll snap out of it, they said, the other girls. Get away, move on, get a life of your own. Cradle snatcher, they'd say to Graeme, and laugh."

Shaking her head, she smiled.

"Four years we were together. Four years. Say it like that, it doesn't seem so long." She shook her head again. "A lifetime, that's what it was. When it started I was just a kid and then ..."

She was seeing something Kiley couldn't see; as if, for a moment, he were no longer there.

"I knew – I wasn't stupid – I knew it wasn't going to last forever, I even forced it a bit myself, looking back, but then, when it happened, I don't know, I suppose I sort of fell apart."

She reached for her glass.

"What's that they say? Whatever doesn't kill you, makes you strong. Having your stomach pumped out, that helps, too. Didn't want to do that again in a hurry, I can tell you. And thanks to Graeme, I had contacts, a portfolio, I could work. David Bailey, round knocking at the door. Brian bloody Duffy. *Harper's Bazaar*. I had a life. A good one. Still have."

Still holding the wine glass, she got to her feet.

"You can tell Graeme, I don't regret a thing. Tell him I love him, the old bastard. But now ..." A glance at her watch. "... Mr Collins

– that's that I call him – Mr Collins will be home soon. Golf widow, that's me. Stops him getting under my feet, I suppose."

She walked Kiley to the door.

"There was someone sniffing round. Oh, a good month ago now. More. Some journalist or other. That piece by Kate Moss had just been in the news. How when she was getting started she used to feel awkward, posing, you know, half-naked. Nude. Not feeling able to say no. Wanted to know, the reporter, had I ever felt exploited? Back then. Fifteen, she said, it's very young after all. I told her I'd felt fine. Asked her to leave, hello and goodbye. Might have been the *Telegraph*, I'm not sure."

She shook Kiley's hand.

When he was crossing the street she called after him. "Don't forget, give Graeme my love."

The article appeared a week later, eight pages stripped across the Sunday magazine, accompanied by a hefty news item in the main paper. *Art or Exploitation?* Ballet dancers and fashion models, a few gymnasts and tennis players thrown in for good measure. Unhealthy relationships between fathers and daughters, young girls and their coaches or mentors. The swimming pool shot of Lisa was there, along with several others. Snatched from somewhere, a recent picture of Graeme Fisher, looking old, startled.

"The bastards," Kate said, vehemently. "The bastards."

Your profession, Kiley thought, biting back the words.

They were on their way to Amsterdam, Kate there to cover the reopening of the Stedelijk Museum after nine years of renovations, Kiley invited along as his reward for services rendered. "Three days in Amsterdam, Jack. What's not to like?"

At her insistence, he'd worn the hat.

They were staying at a small but smart hotel on the Prinsengracht Canal, theirs one of the quiet rooms at the back, looking out onto a small square. For old times sake, she insisted on taking him for breakfast, the first morning, to the art deco Café Americain in the Amsterdam American Hotel.

"First time I ever came here, Jack, to Amsterdam, this is where we stayed."

He didn't ask.

The news from England, a bright 12 point on her iPad, erased the smile from her face: as a result of recent revelations in the media, officers from Operation Yewtree yesterday made two arrests; others were expected.

"Fisher?" Kiley asked.

She shook her head. "Not yet." When she tried to reach him on her mobile, there was no reply.

"Maybe he'll be okay," Kiley said.

"Let's hope," Kate said, and pushed back her chair, signalling it was time to go. Whatever was happening back in England, there was nothing they could do.

From the outside, Kiley thought, the new extension to the Stedelijk looked like a giant bathtub on stilts; inside didn't get much better. Kate seemed to be enthralled.

Kiley found the café, pulled out the copy of *The Glass Key* he'd taken the precaution of stuffing into his pocket, and read. Instead of getting better, as the story progressed things went from bad to worse, the hero chasing round in ever-widening circles, only pausing, every now and then, to get punched in the face.

"Fantastic!" Kate said, a good couple of hours later. "Just amazing."

There was a restaurant some friends had suggested they try for dinner, Le Hollandais; Kate wanted to go back to the hotel first, write up her notes, rest a little, change.

In the room, she switched on the TV to catch the news. Over her shoulder, Kiley thought he recognised the street in Ladbroke Grove. Officers from the Metropolitan Police arriving at the residence of former photographer, Graeme Fisher, wishing to question him with regard to allegations of historic sexual abuse, found Fisher hanging from a light flex at the rear of the house. Despite efforts by paramedics and ambulance staff to revive him, he was pronounced dead at the scene.

A sound, somewhere between a gasp and a sob, broke from Kate's throat and when Kiley went across to comfort her, she shrugged him off.

There would be no dinner, Le Hollandais or elsewhere.

When she came out of the bathroom, Kate used her laptop to book the next available flight, ordered a taxi, rang down to reception to explain.

Kiley walked to the window and stood there, looking out across the square. Already the light was starting to change. Two runners loped by in breathless conversation, then an elderly woman walking her dog, then no one. The tables outside the café at right angles to the hotel were empty, save for an old man, head down, sleeping. Behind him, Kate moved, business-like, around the room, readying their departure, her reflection picked out, ghost-like, in the glass. When Kiley looked back towards the tables, the old man had gone.

APOCRYPHA

RICHARD LANGE

If I had money, I'd go to Mexico. Not Tijuana or Ensenada, but farther down, *real* Mexico. Get my ass out of L.A. There was this guy in the army, Marcos, who was from a little town on the coast called Mazunte. He said you could live pretty good there for practically nothing. Tacos were fifty cents, beers a buck.

"How do they feel about black folks?" I asked him.

"They don't care about anything but the color of your money," he said.

I already know how to speak enough Spanish to get by, how to ask for things and order food. *Por favor* and *muchas gracias*. The numbers to a hundred.

The Chinese family across the hall are always cooking in their room. I told Papa-san to cut it out, but he just stood there nodding and smiling with his little boy and little girl wrapped around his legs. The next day I saw Mama-san coming up the stairs with another bag of groceries, and this morning the whole floor smells like deep-fried fish heads again. I'm not an unreasonable man. I ignore that there are four of them living in a room meant for two, and I put up with the kids playing in the hall when I'm trying to sleep, but I'm not going to let them torch the building.

I pull on some pants and head downstairs. The elevator is broken, so it's four flights on foot. The elevator's always broken, or the toilet, or the sink. Roaches like you wouldn't believe too. The hotel was built in 1928, and nobody's done anything to it since. Why should they? There's just a bunch of poor people living here, Chinamen and wetbacks, dope fiends and drunks. Hell, I'm sure the men with the money are on their knees every night praying this heap falls down so they can collect on the insurance and put up something new.

The first person I see when I hit the lobby—the first person who sees *me*—is Alan. I call him Youngblood. He's the boy who sweeps the floors and hoses off the sidewalk.

"Hey, B, morning, B," he says, bouncing off the couch and coming at me. "Gimme a dollar, man. I'm hungry as a motherfucker."

I raise my hand to shut him up, walk right past him. I don't have time for his hustle today.

"They're cooking up there again," I say to the man at the desk, yell at him through the bulletproof glass. He's Chinese too, and every month so are more of the tenants. I know what's going on, don't think I don't.

"Okay, I talk to them," the man says, barely looking up from his phone.

"It's a safety hazard," I say.

"Yeah, yeah, okay," he says.

"Yeah, yeah, okay to you," I say. "Next time I'm calling the fire department."

Youngblood is waiting for me when I finish. He's so skinny he uses one hand to hold up his jeans when he walks. Got lint in his hair, boogers in the corners of his eyes, and he smells like he hasn't bathed in a week. That's what dope'll do to you.

"Come on, B, slide me a dollar, and I'll give you this," he says.

He holds out his hand. There's a little silver disk in his palm, smaller than a dime.

"What is it?" I say.

"It's a battery, for a watch."

"And what am I supposed to do with it?"

"Come on, B, be cool."

Right then the front door opens, and three dudes come gliding in, the light so bright behind them they look like they're stepping out of the sun. I know two of them: J Bone, who stays down the hall from me, and his homeboy Dallas. A couple of grown-up crack babies, crazy as hell. The third one, the tall, good-looking kid in the suit and shiny shoes, is a stranger. He has an air about him like he doesn't belong down here, like he ought to be pulling that suitcase through an airport in Vegas or Miami. He moves and laughs like a high roller, a player, the kind of brother you feel good just standing next to.

He and his boys walk across the lobby, goofing on one another. When they get to the stairs, the player stops and says, "You mean I got to carry my shit up four floors?"

"I'll get it for you," J Bone says. "No problem."

The Chinaman at the desk buzzes them through the gate, and up they go, their boisterousness lingering for a minute like a pretty girl's perfume.

"Who was that?" I say, mostly to myself.

"That's J Bone's cousin," Youngblood says. "Fresh outta County."

No, it's not. It's trouble. Come looking for me again.

The old man asks if I know anything about computers. He's sitting in his office in back, jabbing at the keys of the laptop his son bought him to use for inventory but that the old man mainly plays solitaire on. He picks the thing up and sets it down hard on his desk as if trying to smack some sense into it.

"Everything's stuck," he says.

"Can't help you there, boss," I say. "I was out of school before they started teaching that stuff."

I'm up front in the showroom. I've been the security guard here for six years now, ten to six, Tuesday through Saturday. Just me and the old man, day after day, killing time in the smallest jewelry store in the district, where he's lucky to buzz in ten customers a week. If I was eighty-two years old and had his money, I wouldn't be running out my string here, but his wife's dead, and his friends have moved away, and the world keeps changing so fast that I guess this is all he has left to anchor him, his trade, the last thing he knows by heart.

I get up out of my chair—he doesn't care if I sit when nobody's in the store—and tuck in my uniform. Every so often I like to stretch my legs with a stroll around the showroom. The old man keeps the display cases looking nice, dusts the rings and bracelets and watches every day, wipes down the glass. I test him now and then by leaving a thumbprint somewhere, and it's always gone the next morning.

Another game I play to pass the time, I'll watch the people walking by outside and bet myself whether the next one'll be black or Mexican, a man or a woman, wearing a hat or not, things like that. Or I'll lean my chair back as far as it'll go, see how long I can balance on the rear legs. The old man doesn't like that one, always yells, "Stop fidgeting. You make me nervous." And I've also learned to kind of sleep with my eyes open and my head up, half in this world, half in the other.

I walk over to the door and look outside. It's a hot day, and folks are keeping to the shade where they can. Some are waiting for a bus across the street, in front of the music store that blasts that *oom pah pah oom pah pah* all day long. Next to that's a McDonald's, then a bridal shop, then a big jewelry store with signs in the windows saying *Compramos Oro, We Buy Gold.*

A kid ducks into our doorway to get out of the sun. He's yelling into his phone in Spanish and doesn't see me standing on the other side of the glass, close enough I can count the pimples on his chin.

"*¿Por qué?*" he says. That's "Why?" or sometimes "Because." "*¿Por qué? ¿Por qué?*"

When he feels my eyes on him, he flinches, startled. I chuckle as he moves out to the curb. He glances over his shoulder a couple times like I'm something he's still not sure of.

"Is it too cold in here?" the old man shouts.

He's short already, but hunched over like he is these days, he's practically a midget. Got about ten hairs left on his head, all white, ears as big as a goddamn monkey's, and those kind of thick glasses that make your eyes look like they belong to someone else.

"You want me to dial it down?" I say.

"What about you? Are you cold?" he says.

"Don't worry about me," I say.

Irving Mandelbaum. I call him Mr. M or boss. He's taken to using a cane lately, if he's going any distance, and I had to call 911 a while back when I found him facedown on the office floor. It was just a fainting spell, but I still worry.

"Five degrees, then," he says. "If you don't mind."

I adjust the thermostat and return to my chair. When I'm sure Mr. M is in the office, I rock back and get myself balanced. My world record is three minutes and twenty-seven seconds.

I've been living in the hotel awhile now. Before that it was someplace worse, over on Fifth. Someplace where you had crackheads and hypes puking in the hallways and OD'ing in the bathrooms we shared. Someplace where you had women knocking on your door at all hours, asking could they suck your dick for five dollars. It was barely better than being on the street, which is where I ended up after my release from Lancaster. Hell, it was barely better than Lancaster.

A Mexican died in the room next to mine while I was living there. I was the one who found him, and how I figured it out was the smell. I was doing janitorial work in those days, getting home at dawn and sleeping all morning, or trying to, anyway. At first the odor was just a tickle in my nostrils, but then I started to taste something in the air that made me gag if I breathed too deeply. I didn't think anything of it because it was the middle of summer and there was no air-conditioning and half the time the showers were broken. To put it plainly, everybody stunk in that place. I went out and bought a couple of rose-scented deodorizers and set them next to my bed.

A couple of days later I was walking to my room when something strange on the floor in front of 316 caught my eye. I bent down for a closer look and one second later almost fell over trying to get up again.

What it was was three fat maggots, all swole up like overcooked rice. I got back down on my hands and knees and pressed my cheek to the floor to see under the door, and more maggots wriggled on the carpet inside the room, dancing around the dead man they'd sprung from.

Nobody would tell me how the guy died, but they said it was so hot in the room during the time he lay in there that he exploded. It took a special crew in white coveralls and rebreathers almost a week to clean up the mess, and even then the smell never quite went away. It was one of the happiest days of my life when I moved from there.

J Bone's cousin, the player from the lobby, is laughing at me. I'm not trying to be funny, but the man is high, so everything makes him laugh. His name is Leon.

It's 6:30 in the evening outside. In here, with tinfoil covering the windows, it might as well be midnight. I suspect time isn't the main thing on the minds of Leon and Bone and the two girls passing a blunt on the bed. They've been at it for hours already and seem to be planning on keeping the party going way past what's wise.

The door to Bone's room was wide open when I walked by after work, still wearing my uniform. I heard music playing, saw people sitting around.

"Who that, McGruff the Crime Dog?" Leon called out.

Some places it's okay to keep going when you hear something like that. Not here. Here, if you give a man an inch on you, he'll most definitely take a mile. So I went back.

"What was that?" I said, serious but smiling, not weighting it one way or the other.

"Naw, man, naw," Leon said. "I's just fucking with you. Come on in and have a beer."

All I wanted was to get home and watch *Jeopardy!*, but I couldn't say no now, now that Leon had backed down. I had to have at least one drink. One of the girls handed me a Natural Light, and Leon joked that I better not let anybody see me with it while I was in uniform.

"That's cops, man, not guards," I said, and that's what got him laughing.

"You know what, though," he says. "Most cops be getting high as motherfuckers."

Everybody nods and murmurs, "That's right, that's right."

"I mean, who got the best dope?" he continues. "Cops' girlfriends, right?"

He's wearing the same suit he had on the other day, the shirt unbuttoned and the jacket hanging on the back of his chair. He's got the gift of always looking more relaxed than any man has a right to, and that relaxes other people. And then he strikes.

"So what you guarding?" he asks me.

"A little jewelry store on Hill," I say.

"You got a gun?" he says.

"Don't need one," I say. "It's pretty quiet."

I don't tell him I'm not allowed to carry because of my record. We aren't friends yet. Some of these youngsters, first thing out of their mouths is their crimes and their times. They've got no shame at all.

"What you gonna do if some motherfucker comes in waving a gat, wanting to take the place down?" Leon says.

I sip my beer and shrug. "Ain't my store," I say. "I'll be ducking and covering."

"Listen at him," Leon hoots. "Ducking and covering. My man be ducking and covering."

The smoke hanging in the air is starting to get to me. The music pulses in my fingertips, and my grin turns goofy. I'm looking right at the girls now, not even trying to be sly about it. The little one's titty is about to fall out of her blouse.

Leon's voice comes to me from a long way off. "I like you, man," he says. "You all right."

Satan's a sweet talker. I shake the fog from my head and down the rest of my beer. If you're a weak man, you better at least be smart enough to know when to walk away. I thank them for the drink, then hurry to my room. With the TV up loud, I can't hear the music, and pretty soon it gets back to being just like any other night.

Except that I dream about those girls. Dreams like I haven't dreamed in years. Wild dreams. Teenage dreams. And when I wake up humping nothing but the sheets, the disappointment almost does me in.

The darkness is a dead weight on my chest, and the hot air is like trying to breathe tar. My mind spins itself stupid, names ringing out, faces flying past. The little girl who'd lift her dress for us when we were eight or nine and show us what she got. My junior high and high-school finger bangs and fumble fucks. Monique Carter and Shawnita Weber and that one that didn't wear panties because she didn't like how they looked under her skirt. Sharon, the mother of one of my kids, and Queenie, the mother of the other. All the whores I was with when I was stationed in Germany and all the whores I've been with since.

The right woman can work miracles. I've seen beasts tamed and crooked made straight. But in order for that to happen, you have to be the right man, and I've never been anybody's idea of right.

We close from one to two for lunch, and I walk over and eat a cheeseburger at the same joint every afternoon. Then I go back to the store, the old man buzzes me in, and I flip the sign on the door to Open. Today the showroom smells like Windex when I return. Mr. M's been cleaning. I sit in my chair and close my eyes. It was a slow morning— one Mexican couple, a bucktoothed kid and a pregnant girl, looking at wedding rings— and it's going to be a slow afternoon. The days fly by, but the hours drag on forever.

Around three thirty someone hits the Press for Entry button outside. The chime goes off loud as hell, goosing me to my feet. I peer through the window and see a couple of girls. I don't recognize them until the old man has already buzzed them in. It's the two from the other night, from the party in J Bone's room. They walk right past me, and if they know who I am, they don't show it.

Mr. M asks can he help them. "Let me look at this," they say, "let me look at that," and while the old man is busy inside the case, their eyes roam the store. I realize then they aren't interested in any watches or gold chains. They're scoping out the place, searching for cameras and trying to peek into the back room.

I look out the window again, and there's Leon standing on the curb with J Bone and Dallas. They've got their backs to me, but I know Leon's suit and Bone's restless shuffle. Leon throws a glance over his shoulder at the store, can't resist. There's no way he can see me through the reflections on the glass, but I duck just the same.

I go back and stand next to my chair. I cross my arms over my chest and stare up at the clock on the wall. In prison, there's a way of *being*, of making yourself invisible while still holding down your place. I feel like I'm on the yard again or in line for chow. You walk out that gate, but you're never free. What your time has taught you is a chain that hobbles you for the rest of your days.

The girls put on a show, something about being late to meet somebody. They're easing their way out.

"I could go $375 on this," the old man says, holding up a bracelet.

"We're gonna keep looking," they say.

"$350."

"Not today."

The old man sighs as they head for the door, puts the bracelet back in the case. Every lost sale stings him like it's his first. The girls walk past me, again without a glance or nod, anything that a cop studying a tape might spot. The heat rushes in when the door opens but is quickly gobbled up by the air-conditioning, and the store is even quieter than it was before the girls came in.

I don't look at Mr. M because I'm afraid he'll see how worried I am. I sit in my chair like I normally do, stare at the floor like always. The girls are right now telling Leon what they saw, how easy it would be, and J Bone is saying, *We should do it today, nigga, nobody but the old man and McGruff in there, and him with no gun.*

But Leon is smarter than that. *That ain't how we planned it,* he says. *We're gonna take our time and do it right.*

Him sending those girls in to case the store doesn't bode well for me. There's no way he didn't think I'd remember them, which means he didn't care if I did. He either figures I won't talk afterward or, more likely, that I won't be able to.

There are lots of Leons out there. The first one I ever met was named Malcolm, after Malcolm X. He was twelve, a year younger than me, but acted fifteen or sixteen. He was already into girls, into clothes, into making sure his hair was just right. I'd see him shooting craps with the older boys. I'd see him smoking Kools. The first time he spoke to me, I was like, *What's this slick motherfucker want with a broke-ass fool like me?* I was living in a foster home then, wearing hand-me-down hand-me-downs, and the growling of my empty stomach kept me awake at night.

Malcolm's thing was shoplifting, and he taught me how. We started out taking candy from the Korean store, the two of us together, but after a while he had me in supermarkets, boosting laundry detergent, disposable razors, and baby formula while he waited outside. Then this junkie named Maria would return the stuff to another store, saying she'd lost the receipt. We'd hit a few different places a day and split the money three ways. I never questioned why Maria and I were doing Malcolm's dirty work, I was just happy to have him as a friend. Old men called this kid sir, and the police let him be. It was like I'd lived in the dark before I met him. The problem was, every few years after that, a new Malcolm came along, and pretty soon I'd find myself in the middle of some shit I shouldn't have been in the middle of, trying to impress him. "You know what's wrong with you?" Queenie, the mother of my son, once said. She always claimed to have me figured out. "You think you can follow someone to get somewhere, but don't nobody you know have any idea where the hell they're going either."

She was right about that. In fact, the last flashy bastard who got past my good sense talked me right into prison, two years in Lancaster. I was a thirty-three-year-old man about to get fired from Popeyes Chicken for mouthing off to my twenty-year-old boss. "That's ridiculous," Kelvin said. "You're better than that." He had a friend who ran a chop shop, he said. Dude had a shopping list of cars he'd pay for.

"Yeah, but I'm trying to stay out of trouble," I said.

"This ain't trouble," Kelvin said. "This is easy money."

I ended up going down for the second car I stole. The police lit me up before I'd driven half a block, and I never heard from Kelvin again, not a *Tough luck, bro*, nothing. It took that to teach me my lesson. I can joke about it now and say I was a slow learner, but it still hurts to think I was so stupid for so long.

When the heat breaks late in the day, people crawl out of their sweatboxes and drag themselves down to the street to get some fresh air and let the breeze cool their skin. They sit on the sidewalk with their backs to a wall or stand on busy corners and tell each other jokes while passing a bottle. The dope dealers work the crowd, signaling with winks and whistles, along with the Mexican woman who peddles T-shirts and tube socks out of a shopping cart and a kid trying to sell a phone that he swears up and down is legit.

I usually enjoy walking through the bustle, a man who's done a day of work and earned a night of rest. I like seeing the easy light of the setting sun on everybody's faces and hearing all of them laugh. Brothers call out to me and shake my hand as I pass by, and there's an old man who plays the trumpet like you've never heard anyone play the trumpet for pocket change.

I barrel past it all today, not even pausing to drop a quarter in the old man's case. My mind is knotted around one worry: what I'm gonna say to Leon. I haven't settled on anything by the time I see him and his boys standing in front of the hotel, so it won't be a pretty sermon, just the truth.

The three of them are puffing on cigars, squinting against the smoke as I roll up.

"Evening, fellas," I say.

"What up, Officer," J Bone drawls.

Dallas giggles at his foolishness, but Leon doesn't crack a smile. The boy's already got a stain on his suit, on the lapel of the coat. He blows a smoke ring and looks down his nose at me.

"I saw them girls in the store today," I say to him.

"They was doing some shopping," he says.

"I saw you all too."

"We was waiting on them."

He's been drinking. His eyes are red and yellow, and his breath stinks. I get right to my point.

"Ain't nothing in there worth losing your freedom for," I say.

"What you talking about?" Leon says.

"Come on, man, I been around," I say.

"He been around," Bone says, giggling again.

"You've got an imagination, I'll give you that," Leon says.

"I hope that's all it is," I say.

Leon steps up so he's right in my face. We're not two inches apart, and the electricity coming off him makes the hair on my arms stand up.

"Are you fucking crazy?" he says.

"Maybe so," I mumble, and turn to go. When I'm about to pull open the lobby door, he calls after me.

"How much that old man pay you?"

"He pays me what he pays me," I say.

"I was wondering, 'cause you act like you the owner."

"I'm just looking out for my own ass."

Leon smiles, trying to get back to being charming. With his kind, though, once you've seen them without their masks, it's never the same.

"And you know the best way to do that, right?" he says.

"Huh?" I say.

"Duck and cover," he says.

He's going to shoot me dead. I hear it in his voice. He's already got his mind made up.

Youngblood says he knows someone who can get me a gun, a white boy named Paul, a gambler, a loser, one of them who's always selling something. I tell Youngblood I'll give him twenty to set it up. Youngblood calls the guy, and the guy says he has a little .25 auto he wants a hundred bucks for. That's fine, I say. I have three hundred dollars hidden in my room. It's supposed to be Mexico money, but there isn't gonna be any Mexico if Leon puts a bullet in me.

Paul wants to meet on Sixth and San Pedro at nine p.m. It's a long walk over, and Youngblood talks the whole way there about his usual nothing. He has to stop three times. Once to piss and twice to ask some shaky-looking brothers where's a dude named Breezy. I'm glad I have my money in my sock. I don't like to dawdle after dark. They'll cut you for a quarter down here, for half a can of beer.

We're a few minutes late to the corner, but this Paul acts like it was an hour. "What the fuck?" he keeps saying, "what the fuck?" looking up and down the street like he expects the police to pop out any second. He has a bandage over one eye and is wearing a T-shirt with cartoon racehorses on it, the kind they give away at the track.

"Show me what you got," I say, interrupting his complaining.

"Show you what I got?" he says. "Show me what you got."

I reach into my sock and bring out the roll of five twenties. I hand it to him, and he thumbs quickly through the bills.

"Wait here," he says.

"Hold on, now," I say.

"It's in my car," he says. "You motherfuckers may walk around with guns on you, but I don't."

He hurries off toward a beat-up Nissan parked in a loading zone.

"It's cool," Youngblood says. "Relax."

Paul opens the door of the car and gets in. He starts the engine, revs it, then drives away. I stand there with my mouth open, wondering if I misunderstood him, that he meant he was going somewhere else to get the gun and then bring it back. But that isn't what he said. Thirty years on the street, and I haven't learned a goddamn thing. I hit Youngblood so hard, his eyes roll up in his head. Then I kick him when he falls, leave him whining like a whipped puppy.

I don't sleep that night or the next, and at work I can't sit still, waiting for what's coming. Two days pass, three, four. At the hotel, I see Leon hanging around the lobby and partying in J Bone's room. We don't say anything to each other as I pass by, I don't even look at him, but our souls scrape like ships' hulls, and I shudder from stem to stern.

When Friday rolls around and still nothing has happened, I start to think I'm wrong. Maybe what I said to Leon was enough to back him off. Maybe he was never serious about robbing the store. My load feels a little lighter. For the first time in a week I can twist my head without the bones in my neck popping.

To celebrate, I take myself to Denny's for dinner. Chicken-fried steak and mashed potatoes. A big Mexican family is there celebrating something. Mom and Dad and Grandma and a bunch of kids, everyone all dressed up. I'm forty-two years old, not young anymore, but I'd still like to have something like that someday. Cancer took my daughter when she was ten, and my son's stuck in prison. If I ever make it to Mexico, maybe I'll get a second chance, and this time, this time, it'll mean something.

They show up at 2:15 on Saturday. We've just reopened after lunch, and I haven't even settled into my chair yet when the three of them crowd into the doorway. Dallas is in front, the hood of his sweatshirt pulled low over his face. He's the one who pushes the buzzer, the one Leon's got doing the dirty work.

"Don't let 'em in!" I shout to Mr. M.

The old man toddles in from the back room, confused.

"What?"

"Don't touch the buzzer."

Dallas rings again, then raps on the glass with his knuckles. I've been afraid for my life before—in prison, on the street, in rooms crowded with men not much more than animals—but it's not something you get used to. My legs shake like they have every other time I've been sure death is near, and my heart tries to tear itself loose and run away. I crouch, get up, then crouch again, a chicken with its head cut off.

J Bone tugs a ski mask down over his face and pushes Dallas out of the way. He charges the door, slamming into it shoulder-first, which makes a hell of a noise, but that's about it. He backs up, tries again, then lifts his foot and drives his heel into the thick, bulletproof glass a couple of times. The door doesn't budge.

"I'm calling the police!" the old man shouts at him. "I've already pressed the alarm."

Leon yells at Bone, and Bone yells at Leon, but I can't hear what they're saying. Leon also has his mask on now. He draws a gun from his pocket, and I scramble for cover behind a display case as he fires two rounds into the lock. He doesn't understand the mechanics, the bolts that shoot into steel and concrete above and below when you turn the key.

People on the street are stopping to see what's going on. Dallas runs off, followed by Bone. Leon grabs the door handle and yanks on it, then gives up too. He peels off his mask and starts to walk one way before turning quickly and jogging in the other.

I get up and go to the door to make sure they're gone for real. I should be relieved, but I'm not. I'm already worried about what's going to happen next.

"Those black bastards," Mr. M says. "Those fucking black bastards."

Once they find out about my record, the police get it in their heads that we were all in it together and it's just that I lost my nerve at the last minute.

How did you know not to let them in? they ask me twenty different times in twenty different ways.

"I saw the gun," I say, simple as that.

Mr. M ends up going to the hospital with chest pains, and his son shows up to square everything away. He keeps thanking me for protecting his father.

"You may have saved his life," he says, and I wish I could say that's whose life I was thinking about.

The police don't finish investigating until after six. I hang around the store until then because I'm not ready to go back to the hotel.

When the cops finally pack up, I walk home slowly, expecting Leon to come out of nowhere at any minute like a lightning bolt. There'll be a gun in his hand, or a knife. He knows how it goes: if you're worried about a snitch, take him out before he talks.

I make it back safely, though. Leon's not waiting out front or in the lobby or on the stairs. The door to J Bone's room is open, but no music is playing, and nobody's laughing. I glance in, time sticking a bit, and see that the room is empty except for a bunch of greasy burger bags and half-finished forties with cigarettes sunk in them.

I lock my door when I get inside my room, open the window, turn on the fan. My legs stop working, and I collapse on the bed, exhausted. I dig out a bottle of Ten High that I keep for when the demons come dancing and swear that if I make it through tonight, I'll treat every hour I have left as a gift.

I talk to the Chinaman at the desk the next morning, and he tells me J Bone checked out yesterday, ran off in a hurry. Youngblood is listening in, pretending to watch the lobby TV. We haven't spoken since I lost my temper.

"What do you know about it?" I call to him, not sure if he'll answer.

"Cost you five dollars to find out," he says.

I hand over the money, and he jumps up off the couch, eager to share. He says Leon and Bone had words yesterday afternoon, talking about the police being after them, and "You stupid," "No, you stupid." Next thing they went upstairs, came down with their shit, and split.

"Where do you think they went?" Youngblood asks me.

"Fuck if I know," I say. "Ask your friend Paul."

"He ain't my friend," Youngblood says. "I put the word out on him. I'm gonna get you your money back."

I'm so happy to have Leon gone that I don't even care about the money. I ask Youngblood if he wants to go for breakfast, my treat. He's a good kid. A couple of hours from now, after he takes his first shot, he'll be useless, but right this minute, I can see the little boy he once was in his crooked smile.

He talks about LeBron James— LeBron this, LeBron that— as we walk to McDonald's. We go back and forth from shady patches still cool as night to blocks that even this early are being scorched by the sun. Nobody's getting crazy yet, and it doesn't smell too bad except in the alleys. Almost like morning anywhere. I keep looking over my shoulder, but I can feel myself relaxing already. A couple more days, and I'll be back to normal.

Mr. M's son told me before I left the store that it'd be closed for at least a week but not to worry because they'd pay me like I was still working. The next Thursday he calls and asks me to come down. The old man is still in the hospital, and it doesn't look like he'll be getting out anytime soon, so the son has decided to shut the store up for good. He hands me an envelope with $2,500 inside, calls it severance.

"Thank you again for taking care of my father," he says.

"Tell him I said hello and get well soon," I reply.

The next minute I'm out on the street, unemployed for the first time in years. I have to laugh. I barely gave Leon the time of day, didn't fall for his mess, didn't jump when he said to, and he still managed to fuck up the good thing I had going. That's the way it is. Every time you manage to stack a few bricks, a wave's bound to come along and knock them down.

They run girls out of vans over on Towne. You pay a little more than you would for a street whore, but they're generally younger and cleaner, and doing it in the van is better than doing it behind a dumpster or in an Andy Gump. I shower and shave before I head out, get a hundred bucks from my stash behind the light switch and stick it in my sock.

Mama-san is carrying more groceries up the stairs, both kids hanging on her, as I'm going down.

"No cooking," I say. "No cooking."

She doesn't reply, but the kids look scared. I didn't mean for that to happen.

The freaks come out at night, and the farther east you go, the worse it gets. Sidewalk shitters living in cardboard boxes, ghosts who eat out of garbage cans, a blind man showing his dick on the corner. I keep my gaze forward, my hands balled into fists. Walking hard, we used to call it.

Three vans are parked at the curb tonight. I make a first pass to scope out the setup. The pimps stand together, a trio of cocky little *vatos* with gold chains and shiny shirts. My second time by, they start in hissing through their teeth and whispering, "Big tits, tight pussy."

"You looking for a party?" one of them asks me.

"What if I am?" I say.

The pimp walks me to his van and slides open the side door. I smell weed and something coconut. A chubby Mexican girl wearing a red bra and panties is lying on a mattress back there. She's pretty enough, for a whore, but I'd still like to check out what's in the other vans. I don't want to raise a ruckus though.

"How much," I say to nobody in particular.

The pimp says forty for head, a hundred for half and half. I get him down to eighty. I crawl inside the van, and he closes the door behind me. There's cardboard taped to the windshield and the other windows. The only light is what seeps in around the edges. I'm sweating already, big drops of it racing down my chest inside my shirt.

"How you doing tonight?" I say to the girl.

"Okay," she says.

She uses her hand to get me hard, then slips the rubber on with her mouth. I make her stop after just a few seconds and have her lie back on the mattress. I come as soon as I stick it in. It's been a long time.

"Can I rest here a minute?" I say.

The girl shrugs and cleans herself with a baby wipe. She has nice hair, long and black, and big brown eyes. I ask her where she's from. She says Mexico.

"I'm moving down there someday," I say.

My mouth gets away from me. I tell her I was in Germany once, when I was in the army, and that I came back and had two kids. I tell her about leaving them just like my mom and dad left me, and how you say you're never gonna do certain things, but then you do. I tell her that's why God's turned away from us and Jesus is a joke. When I run out of words, I'm crying some.

"It's okay," the girl says. "It's okay."

Her pimp bangs on the side of the van and opens the door. Time's up.

———

I've seen enough that I could write my own bible. For example, here's the parable of the brother who hung on and the one who fell: Two months later I'm walking home from my new job guarding a Mexican dollar store on Los Angeles. A bum steps out in front of me, shoves his dirty hand in my face, and asks for a buck. I don't like when they're pushy, and I'm about to tell him to step off, but then I realize it's Leon.

He's still wearing his suit, only now it's filthy rags. His eyes are dull and dead-looking, his lips burned black from the pipe. All his charm is gone, all his kiss-my-ass cockiness. Nobody is following this boy anymore but the reaper.

"Leon?" I say. I'm not scared of him. One punch now would turn him back to dust.

"Who you?" he asks, warily.

"You don't remember?"

He opens his eyes wide, then squints. A quiet laugh rattles his bones.

"Old McGruff," he says. "Gimme a dollar, Crime Dog."

I give him two.

"Be good to yourself," I say as I walk away.

"You're a lucky man," he calls after me.

No, I'm not, but I *am* careful. Got a couple bricks stacked, a couple bucks put away, and one eye watching for the next wave. Forever and ever, amen.

ON *THE ANATOMIZATION OF AN UNKNOWN MAN* (1637) BY FRANS MIER

JOHN CONNOLLY

I

The painting titled *The Anatomization of an Unknown Man* is one of the more obscure works by the minor Dutch painter, Frans Mier. It is an unusual piece, although its subject may be said to be typical of our time: the opening up of a body by what is, one initially assumes, a surgeon or anatomist, the light from a suspended lamp falling over the naked body of the anonymous man, his scalp peeled back to reveal his skull, his innards exposed as the anatomist's blade hangs suspended, ready to explore further the intricacies of his workings, the central physical component of the universe's rich complexity.

I was not long ago in England, and witnessed there the hanging of one Elizabeth Evans – Canberry Bess, they called her – a notorious murderer and cutpurse, who was taken with her partner, one Thomas Shearwood. Country Tom was hanged and then gibbeted at Gray's Inn fields, but it was the fate of Elizabeth Evans to be dissected after her death at the Barber-Surgeons' Hall, for the body of a woman is of more interest to the surgeons than that of a man, and harder to come by. She wept and screamed as she was brought to the gallows, and cried out for a Christian burial, for the terror of the Hall was greater to her than that of the noose itself. Eventually, the hangman silenced her with a rag, for she was disturbing the crowd, and an end was put to her.

Something of her fear had communicated itself to the onlookers, though, and a commotion commenced at the base of the gallows. Although the surgeons wore the guise of commoners, yet the crowd knew them for what they were, and a shout arose that the woman had suffered enough under the Law, and should have no further barbarities visited upon her, although I fear their concern was less for the dignity of her repose than the knowledge that the mob was to be deprived of the display of her carcass in chains at St Pancras, and the slow exposure of her bones at King's Cross. Still, the surgeons had their way for, when the noose had done its work, she was cut down and stripped of her apparel, then laid naked in a chest and thrown into a cart. From there, she was carried to the Hall near unto Cripplegate. For a penny, I was permitted, with others, to watch as the surgeons went about their work, and a revelation it was to me.

But I digress. I merely speak of it to stress that Mier's painting cannot be understood in isolation. It is a record of our time, and should be seen in the context of the work of Valverde and Estienne, of Spigelius and Berrettini and Berengarius, those other great illustrators of the inner mysteries of our corporeal form.

Yet look closer and it becomes clear that the subject of Mier's painting is not as it first appears. The unknown man's face is contorted in its final agony, but there is no visible sign of strangulation, and his neck is unmarked. If he is a malefactor taken from the gallows, then by what means was his life ended? Although the light is dim, it is clear that his hands have been tied to the anatomist's table by means of stout rope. Only the right hand is visible, admittedly, but one would hardly secure that and not the other. On his wrist are gashes where he has struggled against his bonds, and blood pours from the table to the floor in great quantities. The dead do not bleed in this way.

And if this is truly a surgeon, then why does he not wear the attire of a learned man? Why does he labor alone in some dank place, and not in a hall or theater? Where are his peers? Why are there no other men of science, no assistants, no curious onlookers enjoying their penny's worth? This, it would appear, is secret work.

Look: there, in the corner, behind the anatomist, face tilted to stare down at the dissected man. Is that not the head and upper body of a woman? Her left hand is raised to her mouth, and her eyes are wide with grief and horror, but here too a rope is visible. She is also restrained, although not so firmly as the anatomist's victim. Yes, perhaps 'victim' is the word, for the only conclusion to be drawn is that the man on the table is suffering under the knife. This is no corpse from the gallows, and this is not a dissection.

This is something much worse.

II

The question of attribution is always difficult in such circumstances. It resembles, one supposes, the investigation into the commission of a crime. There are clues left behind by the murderer, and it is the duty of an astute and careful observer to connect such evidence to the man responsible. The use of a single source of light, shining from right to left, is typical of Mier. So, too, is the elongation of the faces, so that they resemble wraiths more than people, as though their journey into the next life has already begun. The hands, by contrast, are clumsily rendered, those of the anatomist excepted. It may be that they are the work of another, for Mier would not be alone among artists in allowing his students to complete his paintings. But then, it could also be the case that it is Mier's intention to draw our gaze to the anatomist's hands. There is a grace, a subtlety, to the scientist's calling, and Mier is perhaps suggesting that these are skilled fingers holding the blade.

To Mier, this is an artist at work.

III

I admit that I have never seen the painting in question. I have only a vision of it in my mind based upon my knowledge of such matters. But why should that concern us? Is not imagining the first step towards bringing something into being? One must envisage it, and then one can begin to make it a reality. All great art commences with a vision, and perhaps it may be that this vision is closer to God than that which is ultimately created by the artist's brush. There will always be human flaws in the execution. Only in the mind can the artist achieve true perfection.

IV

It is possible that the painting called *The Anatomization of an Unknown Man* may not exist.

V

What is the identity of the woman? Why would someone force her to watch as a man is torn apart, and compel her to listen to his screams as the blade takes him slowly, exquisitely apart? Surgeons and scientists do not torture in this way.

VI

So, if we are not gazing upon a surgeon, then, for want of a better word, perhaps we are looking at a murderer. He is older than the others in the picture, although not so ancient that his beard has turned grey. The woman, meanwhile, is beautiful; let there be no doubt of that. Mier was not a sentimental man, and would not have portrayed her as other than she was. The victim, too, is closer in age to the woman than the man. We can see it in his face, and in the once youthful perfection of his now ruined body.

Yes, it may be that he has the look of a Spaniard about him.

VII

I admit that Frans Mier may not exist.

VIII

With this knowledge, gleaned from close examination of the painting in question, let us now construct a narrative. The man with the knife is not a surgeon, although he might wish to be, but he has a curiosity about the nature of the human form that has led him to observe closely the actions of the anatomists. The woman? Let us say: his wife, lovely yet unfaithful, fickle in her affections, weary of the ageing body that shares her bed and hungry for firmer flesh.

And the man on the table, then, is, or was, her lover. What if we were to suppose that the husband has discovered his wife's infidelity? Perhaps the young man is his apprentice, one whom he has trusted and loved as a substitute for the child that has never blessed his marriage. Realizing the nature of his betrayal, the master lures his apprentice to the cellar, where the table is waiting. No, wait: he drugs him with tainted wine, for the apprentice is younger and stronger than he, and the master is unsure of his ability to overpower him. When the apprentice regains consciousness, woken by the screams of the woman trapped with him, he is powerless to move. He adds his voice to hers, but the walls are thick, and the cellar deep. There is no one to hear.

A figure advances, the lamp catches the sharp blade, and the grim work begins.

IX

So: this is our version of the truth, our answer to the question of attribution. I, Nicolaes Deyman, did kill my apprentice Mantegna. I anatomized him in my cellar, slowly taking him apart as though, like the physicians of old, I might be able to find some as yet unsuspected fifth humour within him, the black and malignant thing responsible for his betrayal. I did force my wife, my beloved Judith, to watch as I removed skin from flesh, and flesh from bone. When her lover was dead, I strangled her with a rope, and I wept as I did so.

I accept the wisdom and justice of the court's verdict: that my name should be struck from all titles and records and never uttered again; that I should be taken from this place and hanged in secret and then, while still breathing, that I should be handed over to the anatomists and carried to their great temple of learning, there to be taken apart while my heart beats so that the slow manner of my dying might contribute to the greater sum of human knowledge, and thereby make some recompense for my crimes.

I ask only this: that an artist, a man of some small talent, might be permitted to observe and record all that transpires so the painting called *The Anatomization of an Unknown Man* might at last come into existence. After all, I have begun the work for him. I have imagined it. I have described it. I have given him his subject, and willed it into being.

For I, too, am an artist, in my way.

THE TRIALS OF MARGARET

L.C. TYLER

Margaret's first thought on waking was that she had had an unusually good night's sleep. It was only as she rolled over in bed and came face to face (as it were) with the back of Lionel's head that she remembered she had murdered her husband the evening before.

She rolled back again thoughtfully and then just stared at the ceiling for a while. There was a crack in the plaster that Lionel had been promising for months that he would fix. He probably wouldn't be doing that now.

There were clearly things that she hadn't thought through as well as she might, including what to do with the body. Still, for the moment she could afford to lie there and listen to the early morning birdsong and watch the first rays of the sun flickering on the oak chest of drawers. Such was the inward peace that she felt that she was only slightly resentful that it was, strictly speaking, Lionel's turn to make tea that morning. Somewhere in the house a clock struck six, then another slightly further off, then another.

Lionel, in his pre-victim days, had always liked his clocks. He spent half an hour every Sunday going round the house winding them all; she thought she probably wouldn't bother with that.

Margaret slowly slipped out of bed, trying not to disturb the duvet over her husband, and tiptoed out of the room – it was unlikely she would wake Lionel, but it seemed more respectful somehow. It wasn't until she got to the kitchen that she allowed herself to start humming something from *South Pacific*.

Sitting at the table, tapping her foot to the tune and sipping her tea, she ran through the events of the night before. There had been the argument – what they had argued about wasn't so important as the fact that Lionel had flatly refused to see it as a problem of any sort. Men didn't see that sort of thing as a problem. Being a man had, frankly, been Lionel's fatal mistake. Afterwards, he had gone off to wind clocks or something and she had sat there regretting the fact that they did not keep cyanide handy under the kitchen sink. Then she had remembered that she did have a lot of sleeping pills that might be ground up very finely and put into something.

"Would you like an omelette for supper, Lionel?"

"That would be nice, dear," he had replied, doubtless reflecting that she had got over whatever-it-was quite quickly this time. She opened a bottle of Chablis to go with the food. He had appreciated that and attributed his later drowsiness to the wine.

"I'd get an early night, dear, if I were you. I'll follow you up later."

Oh yes, and when serving the two omelettes – the pill-laden one and her own – she had for a moment lost track of which was which, but then thought she could detect just a trace of white powder in the one in her left hand. It must have been the excitement of the moment, because she was always quite good at remembering, for example, which cup of tea had sugar in it and which did not. She had presumably got it right, because Lionel was dead and she wasn't.

She drained the last of her tea, then realisation finally hit her that she would have to Do Something fairly soon. The initial plan had not gone much beyond poisoning her husband. After that she had assumed there might be a certain amount of awkwardness. Now she thought it through, that awkwardness might include having to spend the rest of her life in prison – in pleasanter company than Lionel's of course, but still …

Lionel's body was too heavy for her to carry to the car unaided and, even then, it would be difficult dumping it in a river (or whatever you were supposed to do) without somebody noticing. She could bury it in the vegetable patch of course, but Lionel had always been the gardener in the family. And again, she was sure that her neighbour would find it odd that she was digging such a deep hole in the early hours of the morning.

The issue of the near-miss with the fatal omelette started an interesting second line of thought however. What if she were to claim that Lionel, not she, had cooked the omelettes (some husbands did such things apparently). What if he had done it with the intention of poisoning *her* and had then mixed up the plates, as she almost had, and eaten the deadlier supper of the two. In that case she would have woken up, gone down to make two cups of tea and then on her return to the marital bed discovered her husband already cold and stiff. She would initially have had no idea what had caused his death, because (being *totally* innocent) how could she possibly guess that he would have ever contemplated such a thing? So, she would have phoned for an ambulance or something and then looked on with innocent incredulity as events unfolded …

It needed working on a bit, but that seemed the general direction to go in.

"So, you had no idea," said the policeman, "what had caused his death?"

Margaret wiped a tear from her eye and shook her head. "He went to bed early," she said. "I didn't try to wake him when I came to bed myself. It wasn't until I brought him a nice cup of tea the following morning that I found I was unable to … unable to …"

"Would you like a tissue?" asked the policeman.

"No, I'm fine. Really."

"So you made tea and took it up. And then?" asked the policeman.

"I dialled 999," said Margaret. "An ambulance came at once, but it was too late. Too late! A heart attack, they thought. At first, anyway. Until the autopsy report."

"So you now know the cause of death?"

"Sleeping pills …" Margaret fingered the top button of her blouse and bit her lip.

"Do you know where he might have got them?"

"I checked the bedside table and mine were all gone. Lionel must have found them and taken them."

"He must have taken a large number of them. Is it possible that he was trying to commit suicide? Had he ever expressed any suicidal thoughts?"

Margaret considered this. A simple 'yes' was tempting. On the other hand a brief discussion with any of Lionel's friends would contradict that. Lionel's joviality had been one of the more irritating of his characteristics. To lie quite so blatantly at this stage might attract suspicion. And the idea that he might have died trying to kill her was so much more appropriate.

"No. That's the odd thing. He didn't. I wondered, though … You see, that last evening he made omelettes for the two of us. And I did notice sort of little white specks in one of them. I mean – what if he'd crumbled my pills into one of the omelettes intending to kill me, then mixed them up … ?"

The policeman looked at her oddly. "Why would he do that?"

"Well, we had had a bit of an argument …"

"What about?"

She told him. The policeman shook his head. "Hardly enough to justify murder," he said.

"On the contrary," she said indignantly.

The policeman flicked through his notebook. "Your neighbour reported overhearing an argument that evening," he said. "But we thought—"

"He was an irritating troublemaker?"

"That had occurred to us."

"Well, yes, he is. But he can be trusted on that. There was an argument."

"Your neighbour's evidence was that you had threatened to kill your husband."

"Really? I doubt he heard that distinctly."

"He says he did."

"He's a bit deaf."

"He told us he happened to have his ear pressed up against the wall, for some reason he can no longer remember. He heard every single word. It's just that it seemed a bit improbable, until now …"

"Look," said Margaret, "we had an argument, then Lionel tried to poison my omelette. Any idiot should be able to see that."

"You're sure it wasn't the other way round?"

"Of course not," said Margaret.

"Would you like to phone your lawyer now or later?" asked the policeman.

"It would," said the barrister, "be ridiculous to suppose that the argument that you had would cause you to poison your husband."

"It wasn't exactly what we argued about that was so important," said Margaret, "so much as the fact that Lionel refused to see that it was actually a problem of any sort. Typical man."

The barrister was pensive for a moment. "Well," he said, "for my part, I can't imagine that any sensible jury would see it as a motive for murder."

"But it may conversely have been enough to make *him* try to murder *me*," said Margaret. "You see, I have this theory …"

"I know you do," said the barrister. He had a patronising manner not entirely unlike Lionel's. "That's why we're where we are. Please leave this to me. I think we should stick to the facts, which are that there is no evidence that it wasn't suicide. That was what the police thought. That is what they would still think if you hadn't talked so much about omelettes."

Fine. Suicide then, if that's what he reckoned.

"Which of course it *was*," said Margaret.

"Precisely," said the barrister.

The barrister was scarcely much older than her son, Margaret thought. "Anyway," she said, "if any reasonable jury – I mean a jury of women – knew what Lionel had done and what he said, they would never convict me. Can we fix it so that I get a jury made up entirely of women?"

"No," said the barrister.

"That seems very unreasonable."

"The law sometimes is."

"But I might just get an all-woman jury by pure chance?"

"The odds are two to the power of eleven against."

"Sounds good enough to me," said Margaret.

Margaret counted the jurors as they were sworn in. Nine women and three men. Hopefully the women would keep the three men under control.

The prosecution barrister outlined the case for the Crown. Margaret could see his heart wasn't really in it. Being a man too, he couldn't really see that what Lionel had done was worth killing anyone for. A lot of his questioning was perfunctory.

Margaret's neighbour gave evidence (after which he could forget any chance she'd ever take in a parcel for him again or warn him when the parking wardens were on the prowl). Yes, he'd heard the argument. They often argued. On this occasion she'd definitely threatened to kill him. It wasn't the first time he heard her say that. At this point, one or two of the female jurors glanced at Margaret sympathetically. She smiled back when she hoped the judge wasn't looking.

During the lunch break on the second day she got a text message from somebody claiming to be a member of the jury. *Hang in there, sister,* it read. She deleted it at once, but it gave her a comfortable glow all afternoon. When her turn came to be cross-examined she watched the jury carefully and noticed several women nodding in agreement with her answers. The male jurors looked less certain but, she was pleased to notice, they already had a beaten expression. They had been spoken to. Firmly.

"I think that went well," said her barrister, removing his wig and easing his collar. "Other than your raising that idea that he might have been trying to poison you. Could you *please* not do that?"

"It was worth a try."

"No, it wasn't. You will kindly allow me to decide what is and isn't worth a try."

"You are arguing the case very cogently."

The barrister nodded. "Yes," he said. "I am."

That night she had another text message – goodness knows how they had found her phone number, but everything is out there on the internet if you look. It read: *Lionel was completely in the wrong. You have the full sympathy of nine out of twelve of the jury.*

Margaret deleted it. You couldn't be too careful. It would be a shame if they had to go for a retrial just because she had been chatting harmlessly to the jury.

On the third day she listened to the evidence of various expert witnesses with varying degrees of indifference. Let them pontificate on the effects of barbiturates. Let them quote statistics on suicides. Let them talk about the unlikelihood of blah, blah, blahdy, blah. This jury was never going to convict her. It would have been pleasant to show that professor of toxicology the texts she had received and to see his face when he realised how futile his words were.

She scanned the jury to see if she could guess who had sent her the messages. A young-ish woman in a batik dress, no make-up and hair tied in a bun looked both sympathetic and capable of locating her on the internet.

Margaret spent much of the afternoon working out what Lionel's clocks were worth and what she could do with the money once the trial was over. She'd always wanted to go to Bhutan.

That evening the text read: *Your barrister doesn't have a clue, does he? Still, we understand, though we did have to explain it to the men on the jury. We're with you all the way.*

On the fourth day both barristers summed up their cases to the jury. The barrister for the prosecution took the minimum time that he decently could to outline what he clearly saw as a very weak argument. He was undoubtedly expecting an acquittal. Her own barrister, however, proceeded slowly and methodically. The argument that had been overheard by the neighbour was, he said, utterly trivial. No reasonable man could believe it would be the motive for a murder. It could be true that somebody had put sleeping tablets into the omelette but, if so, could the jury really be certain who had done it? He rather thought not. People did commit suicide unexpectedly. And if the manner of this suicide was odd, surely the decision to end one's own life was in itself perverse? Logic – and at this point he looked at the male members of the jury – dictated that they could not possibly convict. He had strutted back to his seat, head held high.

Margaret watched her almost-all-women jury return to their room to deliberate.

"So how long until I get acquitted?" asked Margaret. "I need to get to the travel agents. I want to book a flight to Bhutan."

"We can't be certain …" said her barrister.

"Nine out of twelve of them are completely on my side," said Margaret . "I know that much."

"You haven't had any contact with the jurors?" asked the barrister, frowning. "That would mean that the jury would have to be dismissed, and you and they would be in contempt of court—"

"Chill," said Margaret. It was what her children said to her. It sounded cool. "Chill the beans, barrister."

"Just so long as you haven't …"

Margaret looked at him with amused contempt.

"Of course not," she said.

"Well," said the barrister, "if they reach a verdict in the first half hour or so it almost certainly means you have been found not guilty. The longer they take, the more doubters there must be and the less certain we are."

It took the jury ten minutes.

"Guilty," said the foreman of the jury.

The two barristers exchanged puzzled glances.

"But …" said Margaret. She didn't quite hear what the judge said thereafter. She was expecting the foreman to suddenly smile and shake her head and say: "Oh, sorry, did I say *guilty*? What *am* I like? I meant of course …" But she didn't. One or two of the jurors smiled apologetically. The judge finished speaking. The jury filed out. Margaret was taken back to the cells.

As she walked along a dingy corridor a jolly ringtone announced a text message. She took out her phone and read it.

You have the sympathy of the whole jury, it said. *We'd have murdered the bastard for that too.*

NEMO ME IMPUNE LACESSIT

DENISE MINA

G od, they were tired. Long-term tired. Give-up tired. Jake's loud
singing was drawing the eyes of everyone in the street to them.
"The cas-TLE! Cas-TLE! Casss-TLE!"

Audrey wasn't enforcing his rigid behavioural program properly
anymore. It wasn't changing anything. She had even stopped forcing
his medication into him. She was so tired.

Jake was eleven and didn't sleep. He skulked around the house
at night. He stood at the end of their bed for hours, staring at them.
They had installed CCTV in their room and saw him do it. One
morning they found a hammer at the end of the bed. When they
watched the recording back they saw him practice-swing it at
Audrey's head and laugh to himself. They installed pressure alarms
on Jake's bed after that to wake them when he got up. Audrey knew
it was coming to a head. She could feel it. They all could.

At the top of the hill a man in full Braveheart costume crossed
in front of them, looking down at Jake's loud singing. He had a
blue Saltire flag painted on his face. Jake saw it and changed his

shriek to "Blue-LOO-LOO-LOO." He sang in soprano. As they approached the Royal Mile his voice was increasingly amplified by the high tenements.

Trailing behind Jake were six-year-old Simon and seven-year-old Hannah. His little brother and sister kept their hands deep into their pockets, their heads down. Audrey and Pete followed up the rear, both shamefaced and thinking the same thing: they should have kept Jake on his medication. The pills made him fat and tearful, he wet the bed more than usual and that made it hard for them to go away anywhere. Audrey had to corner him and pinch his nose to make him open his mouth. She had to force him to take them. She didn't know if she could manage his behavioural problems anymore.

Years ago, when Jake tried to drown Simon in a paddling pool and laughed when they told him off, Audrey's mum said: "He hasn't got behavioural problems, he's just a vicious little arsehole."

Audrey had sobbed at that. Her mum cuddled her and cried with her and said no, sweetheart, look, he'll grow out of it. If someone doesn't kill him first. Ha ha. Have you considered exorcism?

Audrey stayed away from her mum now. Jake didn't need any more negativity around him. He got enough of that at school. He'd killed the class gerbil, he hurt other children if he was left alone with them. Play dates and parties always ended unceremoniously. Only Audrey saw how isolated Jake was, how vulnerable. He was desperate for friends. He didn't care what age they were. He was always wandering off when they were shopping, following children or adults. He seemed terribly alone and it would only get worse. She knew that.

At the end of the road Jake saw the castle, threw his head back and ululated, "CASTLULULULULULUL!"

Their last faint hope was that Jake would grow out of it. He had been on different types of medication, seen psychologists, psychiatrists, ministers, been on behavioural boot camps. When he beat the neighbour's dog to death with a brick two years ago, social work moved him to a different school. They wanted him to go to a residential facility. Pete was keen but Audrey couldn't send him away. Their last and only hope was that he would grow out of it.

"CASTLULULULUUUUUU!" Jake's eyes were protruding. He was shaking. He was going to blow.

It was a busy street. Everyone was looking at Jake. His body was rigid, his blue hoodie was drawn tight around his intensely red face. Tourists were watching him, not judging, just interested in the mad singing boy. They had no idea how bad things were about to get.

Little Hannah put her arm out to stop her little brother from walking into Jake's clawing radius. She grabbed Simon's green hood, pulled him back down the hill to a safe zone. She looked imploringly back to her parents.

Audrey hurried over and knelt down in front of Jake. He looked feral, eleven but small. His eyes were wide and blank. He couldn't see her. She leaned in, filling his field of vision with her face, and held him firmly by the shoulders.

"Jake, I need you to calm down."

"CALM! CALMLULULULUL!" He ululated in her face. Spit flecked her eyelids.

"I need you to take a deep breath and caaaalm yourself down."

Audrey moved her hands to his upper arms and held him tight, ready for a secure hold if he went for her. "Breathe in and out, in and out. Do it with me." She breathed deeply, setting an example.

315

Sudden as a cat spotting a mouse, Jake focused on her face. "I fucking hate you, Mummy."

"That's it, breathe in."

"I hate you."

"And out."

"I'll bite you again." He looked at the scar he had gnawed on her chin.

Audrey was very, very angry but she blinked it back. Jake was being provocative to get a strong reaction. She would only have to act calm for a short while because it was Pete's turn to drag him back to the hotel and guard him while he had a tantrum in a stimulation-free environment.

"You're too excited." She spoke in a flat voice. "You've let yourself get too excited."

He glanced at the castle again and suddenly realized what 'too excited' meant. He was going to be removed, denied the castle and the cake and the baked potato lunch. She steeled herself as Jake's body tensed, he bared his teeth and bent his knees, ready to spring.

The shadow of Pete fell over them, hands out, in position to apply the hold they had been taught to use on him. Jake's eyes flicked to his father and he flinched, knew his physical attack on his mother was foiled.

"When you're asleep…" Jake growled. He saw the spark of alarm in her eyes and smiled.

This morning in the hotel Audrey had swung her feet over the side of the bed, stepping onto a jagged glass ashtray discarded on the floor. She hadn't told Pete. It was terrifying. It was an escalation.

"I'll do it," he snarled.

Something snapped inside of her, a cold wash over her heart. Eleven years of soul grinding humiliation, of shame and blame, of confrontations about Jake's behavior. And tiredness. Everyone thought it was her fault. Maybe it was her fault. She had done her best. Her best was enough for Hannah and Simon but it wasn't nearly enough for Jake. She couldn't do this anymore.

"Right," she said, "We're going home."

Jake glanced desperately up to the castle. "To the hotel?"

"No. To Surrey. Remember Helen, the social worker? She'll meet us there."

"Why Helen, Mummy?"

He was too old to call her that. It sounded facetious and strengthened her resolve.

"You need help." She squeezed his upper arms hard. "And I've tried but I can't seem to help you. I'm finished."

Never confront him, Pete had said, nursing a bloody cut on his forehead. Audrey didn't care anymore. She shut her eyes, expecting him to start clawing at her, at her eyes, at her lips.

But Jake didn't. He looked at her, expressionless, unblinking, and spoke in an unfamiliar voice, "I'm finished too."

It was a normal voice, not strangled or grating. Not the voice that made strangers in the street want to slap him. "I'm finished too, Mum."

"You've finished what?" she whispered.

"This behaviour. It's finished." He looked at the castle battlements then back at her. He held her eye.

Pete hadn't heard this. When he spoke his voice sounded high and frightened, "We popping back to the hotel for a time out, Jakey?"

Audrey released her grip slowly but Jake didn't move. Hannah and Simon backed away. But Jake didn't go for anyone. Uncertain, Audrey stepped away.

Jake smiled up at her, a warm smile, and his eyebrows tented in a question. He looked up the winding lane to the castle and back at her for permission.

Reckless with exhaustion, Audrey raised an arm to the castle. He trotted away along the pavement.

Hannah and Simon watched their brother run off by himself. Hannah chewed her cuff. She did that when she was scared. Little Simon was baffled by the lack of drama and looked anxiously to his father for reassurance. Pete ruffled Simon's hair and watched Jake walk calmly away. He looked at Audrey. She shrugged that she didn't know what was going on either.

"He said he was finished with his 'behaviour'."

"What, the ululating?" asked Pete.

They watched him walk away, dazed by the change in his mood.

"I don't know what he meant."

Jake glanced back, saw they weren't twenty feet behind – he had been warned about staying a safe distance to the group – and stopped. He waited. Audrey couldn't believe it.

"Okay," said Pete, tentative but hopeful. "It's a castle. There probably isn't that much he can break." He swung Simon onto his shoulders., "Come on then. Let's just see how it goes."

Audrey was cautious but she was desperate enough to hope.

It was an extraordinary hour.

They took in the views of the hills from the wide esplanade leading up to the castle. They queued for cartons of juice from a van. They had to wait because a man in front of them had ordered an elaborate coffee but Jake didn't go crazy. He didn't get frustrated with the lady serving or throw all the food out of the baskets at the front of the van.

They walked together. Jake didn't run or shout. He didn't walk ahead of the group or pester his siblings. He didn't demand Simon's place on his dad's shoulders. He was calm, even cheerful sometimes. He kept trying to get Simon to pull his green hoodie up like him and pull it tight around his face. Eventually Simon did and they laughed together because they both looked bonkers. Usually any concession to a demand by Jake just prompted him to make more and more and more demands but he didn't do that this time. He just touched his little brother fondly on the hood and let him alone.

It was exposed on the castle forecourt. A bitter wind picked up and the sky darkened as they approached the entrance. A little wooden bridge over a twenty-foot sheer drop led to the Portcullis Gate. They were standing near one of the official guides to the castle, an older man wearing the red anorak uniform, with a walkie-talkie clipped to his shoulder. Pete asked him who the statues were on either side of Portcullis Gate. The Guide explained that they were William Wallace and someone else. Audrey wasn't listening. She was watching Jake. He was listening to the man, reacting appropriately, nodding to show he understood. It was remarkable. Apparently he could behave when he wanted to. She was delighted and furious in equal parts.

Pete snapped pictures on his phone and the Guide offered to take a family photo. They gathered dutifully and he took it and gave the phone back to Pete. He showed it to Audrey. They all looked surprised, except Jake. He was in front of the rest of them, smiling straight to the camera.

Pushing their luck, Pete asked what the Latin inscription over the Portcullis Gate meant. *"Nemo me impune lacessit,"* said the Guide, "means 'Cross me and Suffer'." He giggled, a high pitched and contagious laugh, "Oh! It's not very friendly, is it?" He laughed again.

Simon caught Jake's eye and they laughed together. Audrey couldn't remember that happening, not since Simon was a baby. He knew better than to catch Jake's eye now.

Pete was happy and excited. "Okay gang, let's go and see this castle!"

Audrey watched him lead the boys up a steep cobbled lane. Hannah hung back with her mother. She was unsure of New Jake, less willing to trust. She chewed her cuff, keeping her watchful eyes on Jake.

Audrey took Hannah's free hand, "Okay, honey?"

Hannah smiled up at her mum but her eyes were scared.

"What it is, sweetie?"

"What's—" She glanced at Jake and stopped. Hannah didn't talk much. The school had highlighted her 'virtual selective muteness' as a cause for concern. Audrey filled in for her, a habit the school had warned her against. "What is happening with Jake?"

"Hmmm."

"I think he's trying to be good."

Hannah gave her mother a skeptical look. Audrey nodded, "I know, but look how happy Daddy is. We'll see. Let's try to have fun while we can, okay?"

Hannah nodded, keeping her reservations to herself. She had been through so much, suffered because of Jake's behaviour. She was so brave about it. Audrey said, "You're lovely, Hannah, d'you know that?"

Delighted, Hannah blushed at her shoes and squeezed her mum's hand.

Before Jake got really bad, a family counsellor told Audrey and Pete that they simply weren't giving Jake enough positive reinforcement for good behaviour. She was wrong, they did it all the time. They complimented him for anything that wasn't spiteful or vile. He never responded to compliments the way Hannah and Simon did. He didn't really seem to care what they thought.

Wind buffeted them in the steep walled lane. They stepped out of the blustery current, into an exposed yard and a battlement wall where a cannon overlooked the city. It fired at one o'clock every day. Simon and Jake ran over to it.

Magnificent views looked out over the north of the city across to a glittering strip of sea.

A different Guide in the familiar red anorak was giving the history of the western defenses to a Chinese tour group. Pete and Audrey and the three kids loitered nearby, listening in.

The castle was being besieged by Jacobites, announced the Guide. Some of the soldiers inside were sympathetic to the rebel cause and conspired to let in the besieging army. But they were caught. They were hung from these very walls by their own coats, left to rot there as a warning to others.

The tour group took turns looking over the wall, cooing, gasping, giggling with fright. Simon and Jake and Pete looked over the edge. Simon screamed. Jake laughed at him and Simon took it in good part. Audrey looked over and felt her stomach jolt at the sixty foot vertiginous drop to jagged black cliffs below.

Hannah stayed well back, giggled into her cuff and shook her head when Audrey pretended she would make her look.

When they were safely twenty feet away Simon did a little leap sideways towards the wall, pretending he was jumping over, showing off to Jake. Jake threw his head back and laughed. Simon was delighted at his brother's approval. He loved Jake so much but it had never been safe to show it before.

They walked on, Simon pretending to jump over every wall they came to. He wore the joke out, he was only little, but Jake was kind about it and grinned when prompted.

They stopped for a cake and the boys sat together. Jake pretended his ginger cake was jumping off the battlements. Simon was thrilled that Jake was copying him. He was so happy he actually glowed. With their hoodies over their heads, one blue, one green, they looked like mismatched twins. Only Hannah held back.

When they had finished their cakes, Jake asked to see some dungeons. They walked up to an exhibition about prisoners of war. Napoleonic prisoners had been held in these very vaults, the sign said. They were held here for years. Hammocks were strung up high on the walls and plaster models of prison loaves were nailed to wooden plates. The kids wandered around, touching things and looking and Pete and Audrey finally got a minute to speak.

"What is he doing?" she whispered.

"I don't know," beamed Pete.

They watched the kids clamber onto a high bench. Simon and Jake pretended to eat the plaster loaf. It was chipped and worn but they were miming eating it as if it was delicious. Hannah sat apart from them, still watchful, but softening.

"Maybe he *has* just grown out of it?" said Pete.

The boys were getting down and Jake put his arms around little Simon's chest and swung him easily to the floor. He tried to help

Hannah too but she yanked her arm away and wouldn't let him touch her.

Audrey hummed noncommittally. Something felt wrong. Growing out of behavioural problems was gradual, she knew that. It would be fitful, would come and go, if it happened. She should tell Pete about the ashtray by the bed this morning but it would spoil his day. She'd tell him later.

Crown Square was the highest point in the castle, a small courtyard with buildings on each side. It was busy, the clock was creeping towards lunchtime. Tourists thronged in groups, talking loudly in many languages, queuing impatiently for the tea room and the toilets.

They had promised the kids a baked potato for lunch, their favourite, but they had just had a cake so they needed to wait for an hour or so. The least busy door led to the National War Memorial.

Pete led them up the circular steps to the open entrance.

It was a beautiful building. It had been a hospital, then a store, but its insides had been scooped out and it was refurbished as a secular chapel. Across from the entrance was an apse with a steel shrine containing an honour roll of all those who had died in conflicts since 1914. High windows of fine stained glass gave the place a sombre, whispery atmosphere. The kids liked it because there was lots to see. They all walked down to the left, to the western transept and found the memorial to noncombatants. The kids were guessing at Latin translations to the regimental insignia. They were all calm and whispering appropriately. It was how Audrey had always hoped it could be.

She nodded to the Latin motto the kids were struggling with.

"What does it really say?" She whispered to Pete, who had a little Latin.

"Hmmm. 'If.. you like.. pina colada….'." He smothered a smile.

"Interesting." Audrey cupped her chin, playing the part of the interviewer, "And this second line here, what does that say?"

"Ah, something about enjoyment and rain. Just let me conjugate the verb 'to capture',"

They giggled, muffling their laughter, leaning into one another, snorting. Their foreheads touched, just briefly, but it felt like a kiss. They hadn't laughed together for such a long time. Audrey and Pete looked at each other, here in this unexpected pocket of calm. He mouthed "You're gorgeous, Audie" and she smiled and slapped his arm playfully. She looked up for the cause of all their worries.

Jake was gone.

Simon and Hannah were together, she chewing her cuff, he with his green hoodie pulled up and tight around his face, tracing names carved into marble with his finger. The War Memorial was crammed with people.

"Jake!" Audrey's voice reverberated around the silent stone room. Every face turned to look at her, none of them Jake.

Pete grabbed Hannah and Simon by the shoulders and ploughed his way through the crowd to the door. Audrey followed in his wake.

From the top of the stairs they could see the entire courtyard, see the alleys and doors. Even at a gallop he couldn't have gone far.

"STAY HERE!," she shouted at Pete and the kids.

She ran diagonally across the courtyard, past David's Tower and up to a wide battlement with a low wall.

No Jake.

A pack of French school children milled around her chatting, checking phones, waiting for someone. She ran over the wall and scanned back towards the Portcullis Gate.

No man, no Jake.

Getting her bearings, she realized that there were lots of places to hide over at the other side of the castle. Loos and cafes and doorways. She bolted downhill, running over the lawn at the back of the War Memorial, scanning the thinning crowds for Jake's blue hooded head. Nothing.

Down through a narrow lane, she elbowed her way through a tight group of Korean women. She could hear them calling indignant reproaches after her as she ran, back to the cafe where they had eaten their cakes. She kept thinking *I am going to find him. I am going to find him.* She ran the phrases over and over in her head like a mantra, as if she could will it true.

Down by the cannon where the Jacobite soldiers were hung. No sign.

In the cafe, no sign.

She sprinted down into another courtyard. No sign.

She checked all the toilets she passed, holding open the doors of the gents and shouting "Jake?" but nothing. Then she saw a Guide with his walkie-talkie crackling on his shoulder. She ran over to him.

"Help me!" She was out of breath, sounded rude, "Sorry, I've lost my son."

He nodded calmly, as if this happened all the time, and held his walkie-talkie up to his mouth. "What's he wearing?"

"Blue hoodie top. Cotton, pale blue. Hood up, pulled tight around his face. He's eleven. He's lost."

The Guide put out a call to all of his colleagues, giving them her description of Jake and the last place he was seen.

Audrey caught her breath and looked around. Walking towards her, trotting down through the narrow lane, was Pete. He was alone.

"THE KIDS?!"

"I saw Jake! On the corner! I left the kids with a Guide and ran but he disappeared. He's still here!"

"Was he alone?"

"I don't know. I caught a glimpse of his hood and turned to tell the Guide to watch the kids. I ran to the corner where he was but he was gone."

The Guide who had put out the call for Jake reassured her that no one could leave the castle without passing two gates. If any child came that way they would stop them. They had CCTV everywhere as well. It would be all right.

He sounded so confident that Audrey covered her face and cried with relief. Peter held her shoulders. "Come on. We'll find him."

Audrey was out of breath. She put her head between her knees and caught up with herself. A lady from the cafe brought her a glass of water. She thanked her and drank it. Her throat was terribly dry.

Finally she said, "Let's go back. He might appear again." She wanted to see Hannah and Simon. She wanted to hold them.

Pete kept his arm around her shoulders as they walked back up the steep path. They were in the narrow, crowded alleyway when they heard the scream. Bare and animal, it was a cry of visceral panic. They ran back down.

The crowd in front of the cannon were arranged around a blonde woman. She was standing back from the wall, hands wide at her sides, her mouth open in shock. The Guide reached her and the woman screamed again, quieter this time, and pointed a shaking finger to the wall. The Guide went over and looked down. He staggered back. He stood still for a moment.

Moving very slowly, he lifted his hand across his chest and reached up to his walkie-talkie. He muttered something and then his head dropped to his chest.

Audrey broke away from Pete and ran to the edge, shoving through the startled crowd to look.

Jake. Broken on the cliffs below. She couldn't scream. She couldn't breathe. She couldn't move. Finished. He was finished.

Pete was there. He looked and saw it too. Far down on a cliff ledge lay a tiny body. It was face down, the blue hood turning red, redness creeping through the blue was the only movement. Legs bent in wrong ways. Inaccessible from above and below.

Audrey staggered backwards and curled over her knees. She vomited acid chunks of cake.

The Guide had moved everyone back from the wall when a sudden flurry of movement heralded the arrival of more red anoraks and other men in black fleeces. The air crackled with radio messages, to and fro, fast voices. Pete was sitting on the ground, head dropped, hands resting on his knees. He looked drunk.

"I'll get Han and Si…" Audrey backed away on rubber legs.

She turned and walked blind. *No*, she thought now, a new mantra. *No. No. Nonononononono. No.*

The tourists in Crown Square were oblivious to the tragedy unfolding below them. They moved in audio guide trances, slow, lazy, diffident. Audrey barged straight through them. She turned the corner to the National War Memorial and climbed the steps. When she saw the Guide's face she knew he had heard. He was shocked. He stood to attention when he saw her.

He touched her shoulder, tilted his head, search her face for eye contact. Audrey shook her head at the ground. "Can't," she hissed. "I can't."

He understood. She couldn't feel this now. He stood straight, shoulders back and spoke very clearly. "What can I do for you?"

"My other children. Boy and girl. Here. Who are they with?"

He searched her face again. "With me. Their brother came and got them."

He had misunderstood.

She took a breath and said it again: "My daughter and son were left with a Guide while we looked for the boy in the blue hoodie."

He nodded. "They were left with me, ma'am. The wee laddie in the blue top with the hood all tied up tight, that wee fella's came up and said they were to go with him. Ten minutes ago."

She couldn't process that but the man was certain, "He was just himself, I made sure of that. The call just came that you couldn't find him and a minute later his Dad spotted him and ran after him. Then he came back and said his Daddy said to bring the wee ones. They all went down that way." He pointed to David's Tower, "I'm a father myself. I thought you'd be over the moon. He was bringing them to you—"

Audrey ran as fast as she could down to Pete, to the crowd, to the shocked guides and the men in black who were lowering a thick black rope over the wall.

A stretcher and paramedic in a harness were preparing to go over. An ambulance was rumbling up the hill towards them.

"He came back," she said quietly. Pete looked up from the ground. "After you ran. He came back and said you'd sent him for Hannah and Simon. They left with him…"

NEMO ME IMPUNE LACESSIT

The police sealed the castle. No one was allowed to leave. The ambulance parked on the forecourt of the cafe, the doors propped open.

At first the other tourists were sympathetic. They thought it was a terrorist attack. They became angry when they realized it was about careless parenting and lost children. Tour organizers approached the cops and made their cases angrily: they had a flight to catch, a restaurant booking, tickets for other attractions. But no one was allowed to leave.

The Guides were kind. Chairs from the cafe appeared for Pete and Audrey. There was still no sign of Simon and Hannah. They asked them what sort of kids they were? Sensible? Nervous? Naughty? A complete search of the castle grounds was organized. The police were led by the Guides to all the sneaky corners and hidden places.

Audrey and Pete sat side by side on chairs, upright, watching the black rope snaking over the wall. They couldn't tell the police or the guides what might have happened. What could have happened. Who they were dealing with.

Men formed a tight circle around the rope and a pulley was fitted. They watched the rope tug and tighten. Jake was coming up.

Audrey stood up, legs so stiff with terror that she nearly fell over. Pete had to catch her.

They stood, watching the men crank the pulley, lifting the basket stretcher up to the battlement walls. The stretcher was for an adult. The slack little body barely half filled it. He was strapped in tight with neon yellow belts, turning pink from all the blood. He had a tiny neck brace on, his face covered in a bloody cotton wool with a hole in the middle for the oxygen mask. His chest wasn't moving.

Audrey could tell from thirty feet away.

So could Pete.

The blue hoodie was too long.

Her knees buckled. It wasn't Jake in the stretcher. It was Simon with Jake's top on. Pete didn't catch her this time. She slipped slowly down to the ground as the red plastic stretcher was placed into the ambulance. A shocked quiet fell over the crowd, as if they were all praying in their many languages, to their many gods.

Suddenly the police walkie-talkies crackled to life in a chorus: *a girl matching Hannah's description had been found deep in the bowels of David's Tower. She had been strangled with her own coat. Don't tell the parents yet.*

Too late. They could see Audrey and Pete had already heard.

Pete sank down next to Audrey on the ground. Crowds shrank away from the couple as if their sorrows were a stain, as if they were contagious.

In the silence Audrey could hear the wind, the rumble of the ambulance engine, Pete breathing, short despairing puffs.

A voice behind her, familiar, loud, pleased.

"I'm finished, Mummy."

THE DUMMIES' GUIDE TO SERIAL KILLING

DANUTA REAH

The girl jogged up the path, her legs gleaming below the cut-off shorts. In the moonlight, her shadow danced between her feet as she ran through the gate and onto the road.

He'd watched her before. Within the hour, she would be back.

And tonight was the night.

The moon was shining through his bedroom window, cold and remote. He held the knife up so the pale light caught the blade. It was flat, it could almost be dull, but the edge glinted. The tip curved slightly upwards. The bolster – he'd been studying knives, so he knew what each part was called – fitted seamlessly into the handle which was wrapped with a leather thong to give the best grip.

It was a thing of beauty.

He lifted it in his hand – *hefted* it, that's what you did with a knife – trying to test the balance, but he wasn't sure what he was looking for. It didn't matter. It was a good knife. The balance would be right.

He slipped it into the inside pocket of his jacket. His late mother's cat watched him from its place on the window-sill. It was thin and bedraggled. His mother used to spoil it, but he was teaching it a few hard lessons.

His breath quickened with excitement but he needed to be cool. He needed to keep his head.

The Dummies' Guide to Serial Killing says:

What is a serial killer? A true serial killer:
- has at least three victims
- has a distinctive signature
- takes a 'cooling off' period which spaces out his killings.

Even if you are tempted to try and find short cuts, multiple victims are not the way to go. A disaffected school student, or an employee with a grudge and a gun have not earned the title 'serial killer'. The true serial killer is an artist, and the true artist is passionate but painstaking. He cares. Remember: the soubriquet 'Zodiac' was not earned overnight!

The Dummies' Guide to Serial Killing says that successful serial killers are intelligent and well-informed, so he always looked up the words he didn't know like 'soubriquet', 'disaffected', and 'painstaking'. He was a bit disappointed with the definition of painstaking. It had sounded more interesting than it actually was, but he mustn't let himself get bogged down in minor issues. He had to remain focused on the task.

And the task was now. Tonight. He had an hour to complete his preparations. He began his checklist.

The weapon.

The Dummies' Guide to Serial Killing said:

Your weapon is your true friend. You must know it and understand it, so when the time comes, it will do your bidding.

He took the knife out of his pocket and stood upright in front of the mirror, holding the blade over the palm of his left hand. That's what you did when you were going to make an oath. He'd seen it on TV. You drew the blade across your palm and then shared the blood. His blood would be on the knife when he – did all the things he planned to do. He would share his blood.

With her.

He admired himself in the mirror for a moment longer. The serial killer. Then he took a deep breath and drew the knife across the exposed flesh.

There was a clatter as the knife hit the floor. He doubled over, tucking his hand between his legs, his face screwed up. Shit. *Shit*! He hadn't expected it to hurt so much, he hadn't expected *his* knife, to hurt *him*. And despite the pain there wasn't much to see. The cut wasn't deep. It was a red line with a few beads of blood welling up.

He squeezed it, and the beads became a trickle that stopped as soon as he stopped squeezing. Still, blood was blood. He picked up the knife and returned it to his pocket.

Back to the checklist.

Weapon.

Tick.

Practice.

The Dummies' Guide said a lot about the importance of practising, of familiarising yourself with the rituals of killing.

Successful serial killers never flinch at the crucial point.

He was a bit upset at the accusation he might flinch, but in fact, the book – The Book – was right. The first cat – he'd done his first cat before he read The Book, and he had flinched. A bit. After a few more, he didn't flinch at all. His gaze moved to his mother's cat hunched on the window-sill. He'd been saving it up for the real thing.

Tonight.

For years, he'd been a dreamer, a pathetic wannabe who read about the heroes and tried to pretend he was one of them – one who hadn't actually started yet. But who would. Who had he thought he was kidding?

And then he found the book. He'd found it online, through one of his forums.

He spent a lot of time on forums. There was the one about his heroes, the greatest serial killers. That was good. And the one about The Manson Family – they weren't true serial killers, he realised that now. But they were cool, everyone agreed they were cool.

And then he'd found the Meet-Up space, *Dying for a Chat.*

That was pretty hardcore – or so he'd thought. At first. You had to be invited, and there was security and passwords and different levels. After he found it and got accepted, he'd spent night after night on the site, talking and sharing, stories and images – oh, the images – until the small hours. He'd really believed, then, that they were people like him, people who understood. He'd called himself Killer, and they had names like Candyman and Hunter.

But after a while, it wasn't enough anymore. Everyone talked a lot, everyone had stories, but no one really did anything. One of them, who called himself Cannibal, actually said how he'd eaten someone's liver with what he called *favour* beans and *a nice Chianti*, and another had an icon that made the *fefefefe* noise. Cannibal probably thought that fava beans was just another name for Heinz. And that Chianti was a kind of lager.

He'd looked up fava beans – and Chianti – later that night.

He was learning. *He* was improving himself.

Gradually he'd come to understand that none of these people were the real deal, but he'd hung around anyway. There was nothing else. Until the day he posted about the cat. His first cat. Some of them had actually criticised him. Criticised. Him. *That's not cool, Killer*, Candyman said. Cannibal actually blocked him.

Pathetic.

He almost gave up on the forum then, but the cat post was the one that did it. Shortly after, he saw the private message box flashing at the bottom right of his screen. That was interesting in itself because he hadn't turned messaging on. But there it was.

It was from someone called Karma. Karma used an icon like two tombstones, which was cool, and the message was short and to the point: *Killer. Your name is tragic. Check out this link.*

At first, it made him angry. His name was *tragic*, was it? What kind of stupid name was *Karma*? Some kind of sex book, wasn't it? A bit of politeness wouldn't have hurt. It didn't cost anything.

But real serial killers weren't polite. And somehow Karma had bypassed all the site security to make contact.

That was cool. So he clicked on the link.

At first, it looked like a bust. Karma, whoever he was with his pathetic name, was making fun of him. It was a site selling honey, of all things. Expensive jars of honey.

But later the same day, Karma got in touch again. *Before you sign up, read the Terms and Conditions carefully. Very carefully.* So he did, pages of them until he found the secret link. And that …

That *was* the real thing.

There were pictures. Videos. Sound files.

He spent a long time with those, especially the videos.

And that was where he found the link to The Book. *The Dummies' Guide to Serial Killing.* At first, he was angry. It was like the writer was making fun of him. *Dummies' Guide.* But that was just camouflage. The Book explained it. Serial killers need to wear camouflage – not really, he understood once he'd read a bit more. Serial killers had to hide in the crowd, make themselves the same as the crowd. That was what camouflage meant. It was a pity because the clothes were cool and had been quite expensive, but he trusted The Book now.

The Book told him who he was and what he had to do.

And now it was almost time …

He needed to finish his checklist. Practice.

A few stray cats, his oath – he knew he wasn't going to flinch.

Practice. *Tick.*

Choosing the right name.

The Dummies' Guide to Serial Killing was very clear about the importance of a good name:

A successful serial killer will select a name with the same care he works out his modus operandi. (Modus operandi means the way you work. He'd looked it up.)

The name must be memorable. If you don't get this right, the reporters might name you themselves (and remember: all successful serial killers get on the news) or even worse, they may not name you at all.

Tip: you can make a name memorable by choosing certain features. A name can:

Rhyme: everyone remembers Hannibal the Cannibal.

Alliterate: Darkly Dreaming Dexter and Buffalo Bill are hard to forget.

Inform: The Collector, Jack the Ripper. These names make it clear exactly what this serial killer does.

Describe: Bluebeard. These names describe a physical attribute of the killer and create fear.

Without a name, a serial killer is just another murderer.

He'd never heard of Bluebeard. It sounded a bit sad to him, but when he looked it up, he saw that Bluebeard was one of the best. Ever. Still, these days you couldn't go round with your beard dyed blue. He didn't even have a beard, for that matter.

He liked The Collector, but his *modus operandi* couldn't involve collecting. His flat was too small. A physical attribute? He looked at himself in the mirror. He didn't really have any, or not any good ones. Maybe he should have got a tattoo – a discrete one of course. Only a stupid serial killer would get tattooed on the face, though he kind of liked the thought.

She would look at him, and he'd draw his scarf back and she'd see the tattoo and know who he was. She'd scream then, but of course, it would be too late ...

What about The Slayer …

Or The Gutter …

Great. He had almost named himself after a bit of roof. He hit the table with his fist in frustration. If he wasn't careful, he'd end up making a fool of himself. Tonight was the night and he didn't have a name. He'd got the weapon, he'd done the practice but he still didn't know what he was going to call himself!

Choosing a name … He couldn't tick that box yet.

OK. Moving on.

Choosing your first victim.

The Dummies' Guide to Serial Killing said:

Great care must be taken over victim selection, especially your first victim. You will make most of your mistakes with her.

Tip: don't choose someone you know well. Remember that's how they caught Buffalo Bill!

He was right on top of this. Or – he wished he'd get a chance to say this out loud, or at least say it on the right forum – *she* was right on top of *him*. He'd done his research. It was *serendipity* (another word The Book had taught him). She'd moved into the upstairs flat a couple of weeks ago, but he didn't know her. They'd never spoken.

She went out each morning, presumably to work, and each evening, she came running down the stairs in those tiny shorts that showed off all her legs, and her … things … joggling about under her T-shirt.

Dumb cow.

And when she came home from her run, about an hour later – he knew because he spent a lot of time watching her – she didn't come back through the front gate where the road was and all the people going past. No, she came through the back gate that led into the small yard and went into the flats through the basement entrance.

The basement entrance was dark and hidden. No one else used it.

In the basement, there was just a storage cupboard for each flat and steps that ran up into the main building. If the door at the top of the steps was locked, then anyone who went into the basement was trapped.

Like a fly, in the web *he* had created.

Choosing your first victim. *Tick*.

He looked at his watch. Twenty minutes to go. It was time for the cat. First the cat, and then the dumb cow. That was his way. The cat was still watching him from the windowsill. He picked up his knife and reached over the pile of comics on top of the shelf to grab it by the scruff.

The cat arched and spat. Its paw moved fast and a sharp pain stabbed into the back of his hand. The knife dropped to the floor with a clatter. There was a hiss, and the cat was on top of the wardrobe.

He sucked the blood off his hand, angry now. The cat was going to learn a hard lesson. It had hurt him, and you didn't get away with that. You didn't hurt–

Of course. *The Cat*. That was it. That was his name. That was his signature – the dumb cow and the cat, together. His check list was complete.

Choosing a name. *Tick*.

Oh, he was going to have fun now. He pulled the chair across the room and stood on it, reaching towards the animal who backed away, still hissing, almost like it knew. He grabbed at it again but it twisted away, bit him and leapt over his shoulder onto the floor. The chair teetered and he jumped off, making the room shake. The bedroom door sprung open and the cat fled. He swore, sucking the blood from his hand where the cat had bitten him.

The cat was going to spoil it all.

But then he realised it didn't matter. It couldn't escape from the flat. It would be hiding, but he'd find it. He could do it later.

Afterwards.

Now it was time to get ready. He shook out the dark blue coverall and pulled it on, standing in front of the mirror to check the effect. In his pocket he had his knife and what The Book called the serial killer's best friend, a roll of duct tape.

Modus operandi.

He knew exactly what he was going to do. She'd come through the back gate, go to the basement entrance. The basement light would be on – she wouldn't go in if there was no light – but it would be dim because he'd changed the bulb. She wouldn't see him standing in the shadows by the door. She'd go up the steps leading into the flats, turn the handle of the door at the top.

Which would be locked.

Should he come up the stairs behind her? Even say, 'Good evening'? Or should he be waiting for her at the bottom?

The Dummies' Guide to Serial Killing said: *plan well but be flexible. Always be prepared for the unexpected and adapt your plans accordingly. Tip: measure twice, cut once!*

And then – he could take his time. Thanks to the duct tape, he could take all the time he wanted.

He stared out of the window, thinking about it, then he shook himself back into the here and now. Don't waste time dreaming. It's going to happen. It's going to be real.

Soon, he told himself.

Soon.

And afterwards he would leave her there. They'd find her quickly enough. He'd go back to his flat and grab the cat – he'd have to do it fast, but it wouldn't matter, not after what he'd just done.

Should he go back into the basement so he could leave the cat beside her? No, that was too much of a risk. He'd leave the cat in the bushes outside. It wasn't perfect, but he was being flexible, like The Book said. *Measure twice, cut once.* Then he'd clean the knife and put it away. Until the next time. The coverall would go into a big padded envelope.

And tomorrow – this was genius – he was going to take the envelope down to the post office and send it to a made-up address in Glasgow. He'd have to get it weighed, have to talk to the woman behind the counter who always looked at him as if he smelt or something, but that didn't matter. By the time they found it – *if* they found it – she would have forgotten. Or it would be too late.

He knew quite a lot about her. She lived on her own. With her cat. Modus operandi. *Tick.*

Tick.

Tick.

And now he's waiting in the shadows by the door that leads into the basement. He feels as though he's been waiting a long time, but it's only been five minutes when he checks his watch.

He can hear her. She's approaching the basement, breathing hard, stumbling slightly as if she's more tired than she expected to be. She opens the door, and he can see her silhouetted against the moonlight. She doesn't see him in his cave of shadows.

Then she's past him, heading towards the steps up out of the basement, towards the locked door.

She's trapped. He's got her.

Moving silently, he follows her. Then something brushes past him and he freezes, his heart hammering.

Not now! Not when he's so ready.

But it's only the cat, running up the stairs behind her. It must have got out of the flat when he opened the door.

It doesn't matter. In fact, it's even better. If she heard anything – and she didn't he's sure of that – but if she did, she'll think it's the cat. And now he'll have the cat in here with him. Just like he planned. No one can stop him now.

The dumb cow. Dead.

The cat. Dead.

She's almost at the door. He hangs back, wanting to hear what she does when she finds it's locked. Will she be scared? Will she realise?

He jumps as he hears her speak. He's never heard her voice before. "Hello, puss. What are you doing down here? You hungry again? He doesn't look after you, does he?"

Oh, she'll pay for that. And he'll let her see how well he can look after a cat in a few minutes. Once the duct tape is in place he can take all the time in the world.

But she's not talking to the cat any more. She says something under her breath, sounding annoyed, a bit irritated, and she rattles the door. He can't let her do that. His heart is beating fast. It's now. Now! Quietly, quickly, he flies up the steps.

She hears him, and half turns, the cat in her arms, but he's right in front of her holding the knife towards her face.

"Shut up. I won't hurt you."

She lets the cat fall from her hands and it flees.

Too late, cat. Too late.

But she ducks and slides, and suddenly she's under his arm and past him, running down the steps ahead of him.

Running towards the outer door.

He leaps down the steps behind her, momentum carrying him forward, and she's there, in front of him, kneeling, just the way it was supposed to be, only not, only not …

In his dreams, she wasn't the one holding the knife.

Karma watched the final twitches with clinical interest. This bit was always an anti-climax, frankly. Still, she was done here. It had been trickier than she'd expected. She thought he would attack as she came into the basement. She hadn't credited him with the intelligence to lock the door at the top of the steps. Oh well. You live, and you learn.

So much for planning.

The cat wound round her legs, purring. She picked it up. It was going to need a home. Well, she could do that. It was time to take a break after all, take – she smiled – her 'cool down' period. Then she could go back to her site and wait for another one to walk into her honey trap.

The Dummies' Guide to Serial Killing, by Karma.

First find your dummy.

That's it.

#METOO

LAUREN HENDERSON

Mary Poppins. That's what he called me. Book my car, Mary Poppins. Get me the penthouse suite, Mary Poppins, and stay there with me pretending to make notes until I want to be alone with the latest actress wannabe and give you the nod to leave. Get my Viagra out of the fridge. Pour me a shot of tequila. Suck my cock, Mary Poppins.

He must have told me to suck his cock a thousand times. But it was reflexive; he spewed out that command to everyone, men as well as women.

No, that's not true, now I think about it. He never said it to women over thirty-five.

The first time he told me to do it, on my starting day as his latest PA, I raised my eyebrows and said: "I'm sure you're joking, Mr Van Stratten, but I don't find that very amusing," and he roared with laughter and said: "Jesus, they hired me Mary Poppins! Where's your umbrella!"

Thank God, by then I'd been in New York long enough to learn

345

how much Americans love a posh British accent. Now that I've smoothed out the rolling Cambridgeshire accent that had people at university asking where I came from, my own is bog-standard middle class. I wanted to be neutral, not to stand out; that's always been my preference. I'm an observer, not a participant. It's what made me such a good PA. I always said that in interviews, and it always got me the job, because people could see it was true.

But in New York, it was harder to be neutral. Everyone was something; everyone was pigeonholed and classified. Being English in itself was laden with meaning. They thought you were more intelligent, more sophisticated, more educated than they were. And if you could manage an upper-class, Downton Abbey above-stairs accent, that put ten grand right away on your yearly salary.

I could never pass for posh back home, never. There are a million little things that give you away. We're so attuned to accents in the UK, so aware of the tiniest inflexion, turn of phrase, inability to spell *hors d'oeuvres* or *per se* correctly. I don't even think I could pass for upper-middle. You need to know about opera and ballet and classical music for that. Posh people don't do culture, necessarily, but upper-middle ones do.

I said I was an observer.

But in New York, I watched other Brit expats and poshed up my accent, and it gave me power and money. Not only that: for Jared Van Stratten, I was Mary Poppins, and no one wants to have sex with Mary Poppins. As Jared once said, she could kill your boner just by looking at it.

Which suited me fine. It was protection. He had such a choice of starlets available to him that we office workers were far, far down any list of women he'd want to have sex with.

But Jared was an animal. I never believed in sex addiction until I started working for him; I thought it was an excuse that men use to cheat on their wives. I had never seen anything like his behaviour before, and I still can't quite believe it. Trust me, if you'd been sitting just outside his office, and regularly gone in there after one of his sessions to clear up, you wouldn't have believed it either. And yes, if you're wondering, he got a big kick out of strolling out of that office once the starlet had left, adjusting his trousers, watching Mary Poppins snapping on a pair of latex gloves, picking up a box of disinfectant wipes and heading into a room that smelt of semen and poppers and fear sweat and sometimes, slightly, of urine, to clean bodily fluids off his leather sofas.

America had introduced me to the near-miracle that was Scotchgard. With the job I did, its ridiculously long hours, its frequent travel, the possibility that Jared might call me any time demanding something as ridiculous as the hours, when I was at home I mostly ate comfort food takeaway on my sofa in front of Bravo. I still love reality tv. Scripted stuff is a busman's holiday for me; reality, fake though it may be, soothes my nerves. The shows I like the most feature people screaming at each other, because they're trapped inside the screen, under control.

They couldn't, for instance, reach through the glass and yell at me to fill the script for their dick shots, an immortal line that Jared uttered to me on the first day I worked for him. I had no idea what he meant, and I stared at him, baffled, aware my mouth was hanging slightly open. It sounded as if he wanted an update on a porn movie they were shooting; but Parador, as far as I knew, specialised in popular, feel-good art films, the kind that won Oscars because they made the viewer feel intellectual and sophisticated.

'Script', it turned out, was American for 'prescription'. And 'dick shots' was American for 'penis injection'. I'm fairly sure that even if I'd understood what he was saying, I'd have goggled at him in exactly the same way.

It's amazing what you can get used to, given time and, more importantly, everyone around you taking outrageousness for granted and expecting you to do the same.

Anyway, Scotchgard. All the catered food at Parador was really health: protein-rich kale salads, sushi rolls made with brown rice, superfoods and quinoa coming out of your ears. Jared was a health nut. So at home I tucked into messy, sloppy, delicious fatty food: enchiladas, pad thai, General Tso's chicken, food that I could never get in London. After I got my first bonus, I went to West Elm and spent it all on a top-notch velvet corner sofa that practically fills my small living room. And I ticked the Scotchgard option. Best money I ever spent; spilled takeaway wiped right off the velvet.

Pad thai, however, isn't a biohazard. I used disinfectant wipes every single time on those sofas, and they were replaced very regularly.

Every year, my bonus went up by a considerable amount. Not only did I scare HR rigid with my euphemisms, Jared loved my work. (My actual work, not my sideline as a sofa cleaner and needle disposal technician.) I didn't mind the sideline that much: I waitressed through university to help pay my tuition fees. University towns don't have the best behaved clientele: I cleaned a lot of toilets. Once I had my degree, if my job required me to wipe up other people's bodily fluids, it had better come with a great salary, yearly bonuses and the best health and dental care plan available to humanity. Which it did.

Besides, the office manager told me the real reason we had a personal copy of the *New York Times* delivered every morning, when Jared never even glanced at it. It was a thick stack of paper with several supplements every day, more than enough to wrap up the used syringes for safe disposal. I did suggest a sharps bin in the toilets, but the manager gave me to understand that this would make the situation too blatant. I had a whole system for making sure the needle was driven through layers and layers of paper, completely covered, so that the cleaners would never get hurt.

"Mary Poppins!" he yelled, striding into my office, the antechamber to his, with a couple of elegant, beautiful twenty-something women forming a phalanx behind him, arrow formation. As always with the particular type of assistants Jared called his wing women, their hair was long, their heels high and their smiles bright.

"Present and correct," I said in my Mary voice. The more formally I talked, the better he liked it.

"Get me the latest version of the nun script!" he shouted.

This was his normal pitch, so I didn't even blink.

"Absolutely, sir," I said, extracting it from the stack of scripts on my desk and carrying it through to his office.

There was a pile of head shots waiting for him there already, which I had printed out earlier. Everything was done electronically nowadays, but Jared insisted on having them on paper. It wasn't because he was old-fashioned; no, he had a ritual he always performed with the latest batch of young female possibilities. Standing in front of his big glass table, he reached out one hand, placed his palm on top of the pile and smeared it over the surface with a sweeping gesture until every face was visible. He didn't care if he covered the text, their names, their accent and dialect skills, their performance skills, whether they could ride sidesaddle, dance the Argentine tango, shoot a bow and arrow; all he cared about were the faces.

Then he stared down at them and touched the tip of his tongue to his bottom lip, entirely unselfconscious, a glutton contemplating an all-you-can-eat buffet.

The wing women were sitting side by side on the leather desk chairs. No one went near that sofa unless they had to. They were scrolling through their phones, I presumed surveying casting agencies' offering of the latest propositions for a demanding gourmet: fresh meat between eighteen and twenty-five, thin and white and coercible. They knew his tastes perfectly. Jared would have gone younger, of course, but he was self-protective enough to limit himself to legal flesh.

Having picked out several options, they would present Jared with the list. Calls would be placed, appointments made, reservations made at the hotels in London and New York and LA that Jared favoured; young women who might be nervous of meeting a famous film producer in his hotel suite would be reassured by the presence of another attractive young woman, taking notes, clearly there in a professional capacity.

Until she got an urgent phone call and had to excuse herself, a couple of drinks later…

"What do you think, Mary P?" Jared asked, and I looked down at the latest crop of sacrificial victims, still holding the script, careful not to look anywhere near his crotch area.

Colour photos, luminous skin, as natural looking as possible, any retouching minimal. No overt grooming, hair shown off, if it was luxuriant, or pulled back if it wasn't. Only the slightest of smiles, nothing provocative or enticing. These weren't modelling shots.

They were neutral canvases onto which producers and directors could project their fantasies and desires.

I hadn't looked at them before, apart from checking that they had all printed clearly. There were so many. There were always so many. But as I stared at the latest offerings, young women to be considered for the lead in the nun film, one face stared right back at me, and I could not take my eyes from hers.

She was strong-featured, sculptural, her brows straight dark lines, her cheekbones slanting upwards towards them, a perfect triangle which echoed her wide forehead and pointed chin. Her wide-set eyes gazed directly at the camera, very distinctive: they were pale blue, but the irises were rimmed by a circle of darker blue, extraordinarily striking. If she photographed this well, she would pop on screen.

I knew straight away that he would want her. It was obvious in the set of her chin, the way her lips were pressed lightly together, that she had both character and personality. He liked ones he could break; he loved a challenge.

His hand was at his crotch now, and the three of us women were pretending that it wasn't.

"Script," he said to me, holding out the other hand.

I gave it to him and left the room, closing the door behind me: I knew I'd be needing the gloves and the wipes in about half an hour. At least he wasn't requiring me to give him the injection, the way the nurse had shown me, into the side of the penis, avoiding the head and underside and any visible veins. One of the wing women would take care of that.

I sat down and stared at the screen in front of me, on which a complex spreadsheet ranked a long, long list of women's names in order of current preference. The ones at the top were those who would snag the coveted parts they had been through hell to achieve. At the bottom was the blacklist: women who had turned him down, fought him off, got to the door of the suite before he could, possessed some God-given instinct which had kept them from ever being alone with him in the first place.

Many of the names would make people's foreheads pucker, wondering what had happened to them. They had burnt bright, been talented and charming and charismatic, made the cover of *Vanity Fair*, seemed on track for stellar careers. The answer, of course, was Jared. Jared had happened to them.

If a male director or producer was a predator, he just had to tell him that the women wouldn't bend over the casting couch. If the guy had some scruples, he spread the word that the women who had rejected him were unreliable, emotional, *difficult*, that word which attaches so stickily to a female that it's almost impossible to peel it from your skin. There were so many easy women to choose from; why pick difficult when you didn't need to?

No one ever made it off the blacklist.

But I wasn't looking at the screen. I was seeing her, Siobhan Black, the name that had been at the top of the headshot. Irish, with a whole list of accents. She could ride a horse, drive a carriage, play the violin, cycle and rollerblade, had basic screen combat training.

Well, she wouldn't need any of those for the nun script. The part mostly required the nun to lie on her back, crying and screaming while she was being gang raped. It was one of the hottest scripts of the year: young women were lining up to compete for it.

It was called 'Ave Maria', and it was written by an older English director, who was well known for his defiantly eccentric films, often involving a great deal of nudity, featuring malleable up-and-coming actresses who would be unlikely to push back against unscripted additions or 'improvisations' he might make once shooting started. He had been struggling for a while, falling out of fashion, making films that seemed almost wilfully obscure.

Realising that, he had cleverly come up with this pitch. Jared loved it. All his male cohorts loved it. Ostensibly, it made a strong feminist statement: a young nun was raped to death by monks in the Middle Ages as punishment for defying their authority and trying to save a witch they were persecuting. The witch was forced to watch the rapes before being burned to death; she and the nun then proceeded to haunt the monastery, their ghosts increasingly vengeful, inflicting a series of nightmares and hallucinations on the monks, turning them against each other with grisly results.

It was a horror art film, by far the director's most commercial idea to date. But, of course, it wasn't merely the potential returns that so powerfully attracted Jared. He was licking his lips at the prospect of the auditions. One thin young vulnerable white woman after another, lying on the floor of a rehearsal room, feigning being raped, sobbing, pleading, struggling; stripping down in front of Jared, the director, the casting director, Jared's buddies at Parador, a couple of money men, so they could 'see if she looked physically right for the role'; and then, if Jared liked them, trooping into his office, his suite at the Plaza or the Ritz Carlton, nervous but reassured by the presence of one of his wing women. Until she had to take that urgent phone call.

Or me. I must be honest. I had been summoned to those suites several times when the wing women weren't available. I knew what was expected of me, and I did it. It was part of my job.

But this time...

I don't know why Siobhan Black affected me so much. She was part of a long, long line of young women just like her. No, not like her.

Who knows why one face in particular calls out to you? After the myriad faces I'd seen spread out on Jared's desk, a smorgasbord of availability, who knows why hers and hers alone affected me so much? I never had a type. Never felt especially drawn to strong straight eyebrows or white skin or light blue eyes limned in darker blue. It wasn't her looks, though of course I was drawn to beauty; who isn't? It was something in her gaze.

Maybe she reminded me of my first-ever crush, but who was that? How can I possibly remember? Some little girl at kindergarten, sitting opposite me on the bus, playing with me at the sandpit at the local park? Features that imprinted on me, formed some image of my ideal woman before I was even able to remember, some alchemical combination of elegance and strength, straight eyebrows, pointed chin? A babysitter, a friend of my parents, a next door neighbour?

Perhaps there was never a template. Perhaps it was just her, Siobhan herself. Something in the way she looked at the camera, something that made me fall in love with her without knowing anything about her. If so, she would be a wondrous success as an actress. I couldn't be the only one in whom she stirred these feelings, this need, this desperate compulsion to protect her from a predator who had stared at her photograph and licked his lips and stroked himself through his trousers, picturing her naked on his leather sofa.

There was a commotion just outside my office, and I braced myself, recognising the particular quality of bustle and noise. A few seconds later in swept Mrs Van Stratten, over six foot tall and looking, as always, like a finalist for Miss World in the Trophy Wife dress category, hair over fur over silk over skinny jeans over heels barely thicker than a darning needle, on which she moved as easily as if she were barefoot.

Gold and diamonds dripped from her ears, her throat, and her wrists, and flashed from the designer sunglasses holding back her thick blonde-streaked tresses. Behind her trailed the Van Stratten twins, a matched pair of five year-old boys which were biologically hers but had been carried by another woman, as Natalia Van Stratten's IBS had prevented her from being able to do so.

I know. Me neither.

They were adorable children, if you liked that kind of thing, which I didn't. Each was shadowed by his own nanny, silent Filipinas whose eyes never left their respective charges.

"His door's closed, Mrs Van Stratten," I said, but she had already come to a halt in the middle of the room.

Natalia Van Stratten knew the situation perfectly well, had served her time, I had been told, as an aspirant actress on a previous incarnation of that sofa. Now she was happily ensconced in Jared's twenty-two million dollar penthouse in one of the Richard Meier-designed towers on the edge of the West Village, the twins and nannies sequestered on the lower floor of the duplex. She gave him respectability, accompanied him to red carpet events and premieres, trotted out the children when he needed family friendly publicity, wore the latest designers and smiled a lot in public.

In private, she compensated for the smiling.

"Ugh!" she complained, frowning as much as her Botox permitted. "I need to talk to him right away! The doctor rang me and he's skipped his appointment *again*!"

I knew that, of course. I had texted his driver to confirm, and reminded Jared first thing that morning and an hour before the car was due. Then I had given him a ten minute prompt, at which point he told me to fuck off because he wasn't fucking going.

"You should have made him go!" she ranted, and I nodded in agreement with her, because what alternative did I have?

"I'm so sorry," I said humbly, and as I did, I noticed one of the nannies shoot the other a glance that said: *Look, they yell at the white women just like they do with us for completely unreasonable things we can't do anything about. It's not personal.*

"It's important!" Natalia said, stamping her foot. "This crazy new diet's putting such a strain on his kidneys the doctor says he needs to stop it immediately! It could be dangerous!"

Honestly, I thought, *what do you care if he drops dead tomorrow?*

And I was pretty sure, from their blank stares at the floor, that the nannies were thinking exactly the same thing.

Jared was always trying new diets, as if there were some miracle fix to be accessed, when he knew perfectly well, from working with actors, that there was no substitute for lean protein and a hardcore personal trainer. His weight fluctuated wildly; he could come back from a weeklong business trip a stone heavier, fly to Canyon Ranch for a few days and starve himself back down again, then pile two stone back on when he got back to New York.

To me, it didn't seem that big a deal. But I had very swiftly learned that rich Americans could be obsessive about their health. Sometimes I thought that they secretly believed they could live forever if they ate and took the right supplements and exercised compulsively. Besides, if Jared's doctor fussed about the yo-yo dieting, kept calling him in for check-ups and tests, it spiked the bill; so wasn't it in the doctor's interest to take the strain on his kidneys more seriously than it warranted?

However, if the doctor's concern turned out to be warranted, enough to worry Natalia van Stratten like this, I was guessing that her pre-nup wouldn't fully pay out if she couldn't keep her husband alive for another few years, and that the will might not be in her favour. New York had been quite the learning curve for me. Trophy wives regularly signed agreements that gave them bonuses per every five years of marriage, for instance; maybe Natalia came into a major lump sum at the end of her first decade with Jared.

The office door swung open, and the wing women emerged, sleek as always, quite as if nothing had been going on in there that shouldn't have been. They acknowledged Natalia with deferential nods, gliding past her, their heads bowed like subservient swans. She ignored them completely in magnificent style.

"Jared!" she yelled, and one of the twins ran over to his nanny and drove his head against her waist in a primitive need for comfort. "You need to go to the doctor, now!"

"Fuck you!" her husband yelled back, appearing into view. "If I wanted some bitch who nagged me, I wouldn't have married a Russian, would I? I'd have picked a Jew, or a Chinese, or an Italian!"

Natalia set her hands on her waist and threw her head back, ready for combat. The other twin took refuge with his nanny, who started stroking his curls. And as my employer and his wife continued screeching at each other, I did a Google search for branches of the New York Public Library in Harlem.

I lived in Brooklyn.

It took a fortnight. Michael, the British film director, flew to NYC so that he and Jared could started initial auditions with an enthusiasm that was marked even by their standards. Video clips of young women sobbing and pleading not to be raped by invisible monks accumulated in my in-box, self-taped by prospects who were unable to present themselves in person because they were working on another job. Appointments racked up for the young women available to sob and plead in person. One of them was Siobhan, who had been flown over by Parador from the UK, together with several other prospects, every one of whose agents knew exactly what her client was in for.

As did the female casting director. The only extenuating circumstance for her acquiescing to this was that, as I had learnt from office canteen chat, women blocked by the boys' club from the opportunity to be editors, producers, directors, became agents or took casting jobs instead. Roles which were traditionally perceived as female, and which, not uncoincidentally, paid considerably less. And if they didn't throw under women under the bus that was Jared, Michael and their ilk, they would have no jobs at all.

This afternoon, Siobhan was booked into the casting suite. We had our own, a large meeting room with cameras and lighting permanently set up; other production companies used rented space, but Jared loved auditions – technically called 'meetings', I had learned when I came to Parador – and he wanted to be on the spot for as many as possible. It was my job to meet the actors in reception, to calm their nerves, bring them up to the suite, reassure them with my lovely manners and my Mary Poppins voice. After all, what could be more calming than being escorted by Mary Poppins?

Jared was highly predictable. If an actress piqued his interest in the casting suite, he would bring them back to his office straight afterwards. And as soon as I saw her in person, I knew that was what would happen. She was even more beautiful in real life, which isn't always the case. Her Irish colouring was very strong, the black hair, the light blue eyes, the milk-white skin so pale it almost had a bluish tinge, a delicate Milky Way of freckles across the bridge of her long straight nose.

She was dressed in the usual way for actors coming to meetings, like models for go-sees. Casual, functional, showing she was there to work. Faded jeans, a black roll-neck sweater, form-fitting enough to reassure everyone that she was as slim as leading actresses needed to be. A black leather jacket was slung over her shoulders, and her hair was pulled back from her face in an artfully messy twist.

"Oh, you're English!" she said, smiling at me, holding out her hand. "Nice to hear a familiar accent over here."

Mine shook as I took hers, but hopefully not enough for her to realise. It was cool and dry, a little too much so; she needed to moisturise more.

"Nice to have an Irish person be happy to meet an English one," I said in response, and she grinned like an urchin.

"Hey," she said, "I'll take what I can get so far from home."

"Is your hotel okay?" I asked, the standard question I asked everyone, as I turned to lead her through security. The big glass gate swung open for us.

"Oh yeah, thanks," she said a little too casually.

They had put her up in the latest hip place on the Bowery, I knew. I had checked the travel department's reservation for her. It had the usual complement of try-hard décor and gimmicks: single shots of gin, made in the hotel's on-site distillery, served from a machine in the check-in area; an entirely gluten-free menu; a dedicated ballet barre studio in the gym. All charges to Parador's card. Siobhan couldn't fail to be impressed, but she was doing her best to act cool, for which I couldn't blame her.

"I haven't been there yet," I said at random, trying not to babble. "Is it nice? How's your room?"

Was that creepy? No, I decided. It sounded like small talk, not as if I were asking her for a photo of her bed so I could imagine her on it.

I didn't need it. I already saw it on her Instagram a couple of hours ago.

"Small but perfectly formed," she said with a lilt of amusement. "And some things I've never even heard of in the minibar."

"They'll be very healthy and taste a bit like seaweed," I said, pressing the button for the lift. "Just don't look at the ingredients."

This was small talk at its finest, words intended merely to spackle and plaster over any awkward silences, pure filler. And yet it felt to me as if every word that dropped from her lips was a diamond, or a pearl, like a fairy tale I remembered, where the heroine was given that blessing in return for her sweet nature.

I led her into the casting suite, and I saw Jared and Michael's expressions as they took her in, that particular toxic flicker in their eyes, the burning darkness inside them crawling out for a moment, a flash of feral red. And she thanked me for bringing her to them as sweetly as the girl in the fairy tale would have done.

I couldn't access the video recording system from my computer to watch it live, not until the recording was finished and it streamed automatically to my database. I sat in my office in a pool of sweat for half an hour. It was the longest thirty minutes of my life. I took handfuls of antiseptic wipes and dabbed myself down under my blouse. They stung: I welcomed the sensation. I had seen some of the other auditions for *Ave Maria*. I knew what kinds of things she was having to do, the questions she was being asked.

Finally the door opened and Jared walked in, Siobhan following directly behind him. On her face was the identical expression I had seen on so many starlets accompanying him into his office; dazed, disbelieving, afraid to hope their dream was coming true, struggling to keep their spiking optimism under control. And just a little apprehensive.

Jared didn't look at me as he passed. He didn't need to tell me not to disturb him or to hold his calls. I was very well-trained, and I knew exactly what to do.

The door closed behind them. His office was practically sound-proof. I had barely ever heard anything through the thick wenge wood walls, the door with rubber flanges that enabled it to close with only the faintest sigh and click.

I went through two more handfuls of disinfectant wipes.

Then the door flew open with such force that my heart slammed just as powerfully into my ribcage. Siobhan stood there, wearing only a small lace bralette on the upper half of her body. The top button of her jeans was unfastened. Her eyes were wild, the pupils hugely enlarged.

"He – he –" she stammered.

I was on my feet, running towards her in stockinged feet: Jared made his female employees wear high heels, but I had kicked them off as soon as I sat down. I caught her and pushed her back into his office, guiding her to one of the chairs in front of his huge desk. She was shaking like a birch tree in high winds.

Jared was collapsed across one arm of the sofa, face down, trousers and boxers down. The kidney-straining diet had been effective, I noticed; his bare buttocks were slim and toned. From the floor, I grabbed her sweater, the thin t-shirt she had been wearing underneath it, and shoved them at her, telling her to put them on and button her jeans. As she obeyed, clumsily fumbling to pull the clothes over her head, I dived for the used syringe on his desk. All I had to do was to substitute it; I had kept the one he'd used a couple of days ago, hidden at the back of a drawer, his fingerprints on it, and now I pulled that out, switching them over.

I was very fast. Siobhan wouldn't have seen me; her head was buried in her black sweater, her arms struggling to find the sleeves. I dashed into my office and buried the syringe Jared had just used in the usual crumple of newspapers in my desk bin, which the cleaners were briefed to empty carefully.

I was back in his office as her head emerged from the neck of the sweater. She was in shock, I thought, her pupils still dilated, so pale that her freckles were even more visible than they had been an hour ago.

"Sit still," I said to her, going round the desk, taking up his cellphone, dialling the direct line to our head of security, Caspar Petersen, the man who knew the precise location of every single Parador corpse. "It'll be okay. I promise you, it'll be okay. Everything's going to work out fine."

Petersen was there in five minutes. By that time I was sitting in the other desk chair, having drawn it next to Siobhan. I was holding her hands, murmuring quiet words of reassurance.

I had felt for Jared's pulse. There wasn't one.

Then a whole crowd of Parador employees whirled in like a

tornado which picked us up and whisked us into the outer office, the head of HR cooing over us, asking us how we were. Siobhan was clinging to me, and I put my arm around her narrow waist. If I shook when I touched her now, like this, no one would know why.

Petersen was making phone calls to the Mayor, the state governor and Jared's guy in the NYPD, a deputy chief. I heard the fridge open and close: one of Petersen's henchmen emerged from the office, carrying a stack of boxes of loaded syringes, other medications, popper vials, and something on top wrapped in hand tissue. The used needle.

He was moving very gingerly, and I couldn't blame him. A wave of relief hit me: I would never have to touch those things again. It was extraordinary that I hadn't developed a phobia of injections myself. Through the open door, I saw two more of Petersen's men wrestling Jared's corpse off the sofa, dragging up his trousers: returning him to respectability, a film magnate tragically struck by an unexpected heart attack.

They brought us water. We drank it. A doctor summoned by Petersen examined Siobhan briefly and offered her some pills that she refused. Petersen and the head of PR told us we would be taken care of and not to worry. One of the henchmen guided us out of the building, and, with considerable irony, into Jared's waiting limo and thence to his suite at the Plaza. There we were ensconced in unbelievable luxury high above the city as the storm broke a few blocks below us. We watched it on New York 1, the local channel, Jared's body carried out of the Parador building, journalists shouting questions, the ambulance lights flashing bright, Jared's partner delivering a brief, grim-faced statement about what a terrible loss Jared would be to the industry.

They said it was a heart attack, and they were quite right, though no autopsy was conducted, as nobody wanted there to be a record of what precisely had been in Jared's body. I had seen them cover up plenty of scandals. I knew I was safe there. More precisely, he died of hyperkalemia, which, according to the New York Public Library computer in a particularly obscure Harlem branch, occurs when you already have weak kidneys and you inject yourself with a huge dose of potassium chloride, thinking that it's your erection drug.

To be fair, the New York Public Library didn't quite put it that way. But it did also tell me that potassium chloride is a generic drug and you can buy it in liquid form at any health shop, after I Googled 'weak kidney die' and it gave me the answer to my unspoken question.

I didn't need to be told to wear a baseball cap and a faceful of makeup in the library and then at the Vitamin Shoppe, plus layers of clothes that made me look a lot bigger than I am. I had no intention of being spotted on CCTV. Nor did I need to be advised to pay in cash, not use my loyalty card, and remove all traces of potassium chloride and the packaging from my apartment after I filled that syringe and took it back to the office. I read a lot of mystery novels.

With Jared's death, Parador was in a positive scramble to sanitise his memory, literally and metaphorically. Natalia sobbed on cue for the benefit of the paparazzi, her arms wrapped around the adorable twins. Everyone on the long list of employees and actresses who had signed non-disclosure agreements with Parador for lucrative settlements was contacted by lawyers and gently reminded that those agreements were just as valid whether Jared was alive or dead.

Siobhan and I, visited in our suite by the NYPD deputy chief, recounted how Jared had suddenly collapsed while talking to Siobhan about the part. Through the open doorway, I said, noticing his approving nod at this, I had heard her cry out, seen him clasp his chest and fall to the sofa.

She was superb at improvising. That was her RADA training, I suppose. I followed along, careful to add nothing to her story, simply agree. We had been heavily coached, of course, by the head of publicity and a media handler who were both present during the entirety of the pro-forma interview. The deputy chief left, expressing his sympathy to both of us and assuring us we would not be bothered again. The head of publicity told us to charge anything we wanted to the room, and not to leave it until they told us it was okay, and the media handler told us not to answer any call that wasn't from Parador.

Jared's partner rang Siobhan and told her that she could have her pick of roles on Parador's upcoming roster of films.

The head of HR rang me and said I was being given a fifty grand hardship bonus for my loyalty and the exemplary way I had handled matters. Would I like to transfer to the LA office, all expenses paid? The precise nature of my role was still to be confirmed, but was I at all interested in producing?

I booked an Ayurvedic aromatherapy in-room massage for two. We ordered tuna poke and sweet potato fries. We got into the master bed, drank Tattinger and watched a Bravo series with attractive young people working on a luxury yacht, bickering and getting drunk and serving exotic cocktails to entitled guests. Eventually, we made love.

Siobhan had a boyfriend back in London. Some young actresses were coming out now, as lesbian or bisexual, but only women who had already had major Hollywood blockbuster success and now wanted to work in art films. One of them took the part of the nun in *Ave Maria*; she said in interviews that, like Jodie Foster in *The Betrayed*, it was much easier for her, as a gay woman, to play the victim of a male gang rape, than it would have been for a straight one.

Siobhan asked for and got the coveted part of a sexy assassin in a well-received thriller which led to a role in a Marvel franchise. I moved to LA and got into production. It had been a nominal job title, given to me under the assumption that everyone wanted to produce, but to my surprise, I turned out to be very skilled at it. I have a sense of how to sell a story, what people will believe, what they won't... And there's quite the lesbian network in Los Angeles. They're all big fans of Julie Andrews and Mary Poppins.

I was Siobhan's maid of honour at her wedding to her understanding long-term boyfriend. We're still very close, though I'm married now myself, to a writer/director who was nominated for an Oscar last year. The boys' club has realised it needs to let in more than a token couple of women, and we're shoving hard at the floodgates.

Siobhan and I don't talk about that afternoon in Jared's office; we spent four days holed up at the Plaza, talking, crying, sleeping, working through it, and then we were done. She didn't realise then that I was the one who filled his prescriptions, stocked his fridge with them, cleaned up the used needles, provided the starlets' contact details for the lawyers to move in smoothly with their NDAs and settlement offers. It may have occurred to her since, but she's never brought it up to me; why would an actress unnecessarily antagonise a producer?

Sometimes I think I see a little flicker of speculation in her eye as we hang out on the terrace of my house high in the Hollywood Hills, the lights of downtown glittering below, Katrine grilling a paleo-suitable slab of meat over our fire pit, Siobhan and I sipping dry, low-sugar red wine, the fountain playing down the living wall of our vertical garden. But that could so easily be a glimmer reflected from the leaping flames, the glint of light on moving water.

It's very unlikely that she's wondering if I emptied out that syringe of erectile dysfunction disorder medication and replaced its contents with heavily condensed potassium chloride, boiled down on my kitchen stove. That she's remembering my passion for her in that huge bed at the Plaza, and asking herself whether, after all the starlets I'd seen come and go, I finally killed him to protect her, putting that syringe in his fridge, the last one in the box, after I took her to the casting suite.

Because then it would dawn on her that, if my only motive had been to protect her, I hadn't done the best of jobs. I had subjected her to his aggression, his insistence that she show him her tits, unbutton her jeans, as he sat at his desk chair, pulled the last syringe out from the packet, unzipped his trousers, discarded the plastic needle cover and stuck the needle into the side of his penis – avoiding, of course, the head and underside and any visible veins.

I had forced her to watch him stand up, lurch towards her, tears forming in her beautiful eyes as he told her that good girls get leading roles, and to strip down, get on her knees and show him what a good girl she could be. To stand there, paralysed, terrified, conflicted, before he gasped and grabbed his left arm, his own knees buckling, his torso bending forward, hitting the wide leather arm of the sofa, his head crashing down like a heavy weight, pulling his body with it. To watch him die.

If I had truly done it out of pure love for her, I wouldn't have put her through that. I would have loaded that syringe for another actress's 'meeting' with him in his office and spared her the entire experience.

But then, she wouldn't have owed me. I wouldn't have been the one who rushed to her side, comforting her, telling her everything would be all right, and was as good as her word. I wouldn't have been holed up with her in the Plaza for four beautiful, miraculous, heaven-sent days. Wouldn't have been perfectly positioned to take advantage of her in a state of extreme shock and vulnerability.

In my defence, however, she had sex with me entirely willingly. On that score, at least, I'm morally superior to Jared.

COPYRIGHT

ACKNOWLEDGMENTS

Apocrypha by Richard Lange; © 2015; first appeared in *Sweet Nothing*; reprinted by permission of Hachette Book Group, USA and Hodder & Stoughton.

On The Anatomization of an Unknown Man (1637) by Frans Mier by John Connolly; © 2016; first appeared in the UK in *Night Music, Nocturnes 2*; reprinted by permission of the author.

The Trials of Margaret by L.C. Tyler; © 2017; first appeared in *Motives for Murder*, edited by Martin Edwards; reprinted by permission of the author.

Nemo Me Impune Lacessit by Denise Mina; © 2018; first appeared in *Bloody Scotland*; reprinted by permission of the author.

The Dummies' Guide to Serial Killing by Danuta Kot writing as Danuta Reah; © 2019; first appeared in *The Dummies' Guide to Serial Killing*; reprinted by permission of the author.

#Me Too by Lauren Henderson; © 2020; first appeared in *Invisible Blood* edited by Maxim Jakubowski; reprinted by permission of the author.

ABOUT THE EDITOR

Maxim Jakubowski is a noted anthology editor based in London, just a mile or so away from where he was born. With over 70 volumes to his credit, including *Invisible Blood,* the 13 annual volumes of *The Mammoth Book of Best British Mysteries,* and titles on Professor Moriarty, Jack the Ripper, Future Crime and Vintage whodunits. A publisher for over 20 years, he was also the co-owner of London's Murder One bookstore and the crime columnist for *Time Out* and then *The Guardian* for 22 years. Stories from his anthologies have won most of the awards in the field on numerous occasions. He is currently the Chair of the Crime Writers' Association and a *Sunday Times* bestselling novelist in another genre.

For more fantastic fiction, author events, exclusive
excerpts, competitions, limited editions and more

VISIT OUR WEBSITE
titanbooks.com

LIKE US ON FACEBOOK
facebook.com/titanbooks

FOLLOW US ON TWITTER
@TitanBooks

EMAIL US
readerfeedback@titanemail.com